THE GHOST

A NOVEL

Books by the Author

AUTHORED BOOKS
The Psychoanalysis of Symptoms
Dictionary of Psychopathology
Group Psychotherapy and Personality: Intersecting Structures
(Reissued with the subtitle: A Theoretical Model, 2015)
Sleep Disorders: Insomnia and Narcolepsy
The 4 Steps to Peace of Mind: The Simple Effective Way to Cure Our Emotional Symptoms.
(Romanian edition, 2008; Japanese edition, 2011)
Love Is Not Enough: What It Takes to Make It Work
Greedy, Cowardly, and Weak: Hollywood's Jewish Stereotypes
Hollywood Movies on the Couch: A Psychoanalyst Examines 15 Famous Films
Haggadah: A Passover Seder for the Rest of Us
Personality: How it Forms (Korean edition, 2016)
The Discovery of God: A Psycho/Evolutionary Perspective
A Consilience of Natural and Social Sciences: A Memoir of Original Contributions
Anatomy of Delusion
Psychoanalysis of Evil: Perspectives on Destructive Behavior
There's No Handle on My Door: Stories of Patients in Mental Hospitals
On the Nature of Nature
Psychotherapeutic Traction: Uncovering the Patient's Power-Theme and Basic Wish

THE GHOST TRILOGY
The Making of Ghosts: A Novel
Ghosts of Dreams: A Novel
The Ghost: A Novel

CO-AUTHORED BOOKS   (with Anthony Burry, Ph.D.)
Psychopathology and Differential Diagnosis: A Primer
Volume 1: History of Psychopathology
Volume 2: Diagnostic Primer
Handbook of Psychodiagnostic Testing: Analysis of Personality in the Psychological Report
(1st edition, 1981; 2nd edition, 1991; 3rd edition, 1997; 4th edition, 2007; Japanese
edition, 2011)

EDITED BOOKS
Group Cohesion: Theoretical and Clinical Perspectives
The Nightmare: Psychological and Biological Foundations

CO-EDITED BOOKS   (with Robert Plutchik, Ph.D.)
Emotion: Theory, Research, and Experience.
Volume 1: Theories of Emotion
Volume 2: Emotions in Early Development
Volume 3: Biological Foundations of Emotion
Volume 4: The Measurement of Emotion.
Volume 5: Emotion, Psychopathology, and Psychotherapy
The Emotions Profile Index: Test and Manual. 1976.

THE GHOST

A NOVEL

HENRY KELLERMAN

Published by Barricade Books Inc.
Fort Lee, N.J. 07024
www.barricadebooks.com

Library of Congress Cataloging-in-Publication Data

Names: Kellerman, Henry, author.
Title: The Ghost : A Novel / Henry Kellerman.
Description: Fort Lee, N.J. : Barricade Books Inc., [2018]
Identifiers: LCCN 2017046912 | ISBN 9781569808221
    (hardcover : acid-free paper)
Subjects: LCSH: War criminals--Fiction. | Assassins--Fiction. |
    Nazis--Fiction. | GSAFD: Suspense fiction. | Historical fiction.
Classification: LCC PS3611.E435 G47 2018 | DDC 813/.6--dc23
LC record available at *https://lccn.loc.gov/2017046912*

10 9 8 7 6 5 4 3 2 1

Manufactured in the United States of America

To
The memory of
Mordecai Anielevitch
Leader of the Warsaw Ghetto uprising

CONTENTS

PART 1

THE BRONX

· 1 ·

FRANKIE

"It was very dark. Deep into the night. I heard him shouting: 'Frankie, Frankie, help, help.'"

"So what time would you say it was?"

"I dunno. Maybe two in the morning. Sumthin' like that?"

"How do you know it was about two?"

"They kicked me outta the bar at one, but I was so looped I couldn't walk. I couldn't walk a straight line. I was smashed. I swear I did about three or four shots of vodkas and then another four or five ponies. So, I did what I always do. I don't cross the street because I'm afraid I'll fall and just sleep even in the middle of the street. So instead I lean up against the building where the bar is and just slide down onto the pavement and sleep sitting up against the wall of the building. I'm so gone I don't even hear the sound of the trains. The next thing I usually know is that it's morning. No one has ever come near me to wake me. At least not that I can remember. But this time I opened my eyes. It's because I heard Willy.

"I didn't hear the trains but I heard Willy. I must've heard him because my eyes popped open when I was sure it was Willy's voice. That I can swear to. He was shouting my name and I swear he could see me sitting up against the building the way I could see him standing there. It was above the El on Third Avenue.

"Like I said, I could see him from where I was sitting against the wall.

He was standing outside the window on the ledge. It's the third floor so it's higher than the El, and from where I was sitting, the El didn't block my view. It's not high enough to kill the view of the third floor of our building."

"Easy. Easy does it. Relax."

He was carefully quizzing me, and at this point he was trying to calm me down. I'm lucky they weren't suspicious of me, as if in my drunken state I would've been the one to have caused it all. But here, by this time, it was the next night at the precinct—and that's where we were—at the precinct.

They had me going over exactly where I was and what I saw and they had me repeat it a few times. Apparently, they'd been at the hospital all day and took some eye witness reports from the bartender, Leo, along with my drinking buddy Tommy, who also witnessed it all. Now it was my turn.

"Like I said, I saw him standing on the ledge right outside of our third-floor apartment window, plastered up against the outside of the window exactly across from where I was sitting on the pavement against the building. Like I said, when my eyes popped open I just looked up at him. The first thing I noticed was that we were both motionless; him against the wall, like I said, outside of our third-floor window plastered up against the outside of the window on the ledge, and me just sitting there, coming out of my drunken world and feeling plastered and smashed up sitting against that wall.

"I could barely see him, but the light from the bar was just enough for me to make out his face and his, well, like how his body looked up against the window. I could tell the window was open. That scared me right there. It scared the hell out of me because even though it's the third floor, it's still a long drop. I kinda was sure he was going down. Yup, I knew he was going down. He kept screaming my name. The strange thing is, I also remember that the flower pot was missing from the side of the ledge. But I just knew he was going down.

"It was at that point that Leo, the bartender, and Tommy, my drinking buddy came outta the bar and into the street because Willy was screaming so loud that they heard it too, from inside the bar. Then I noticed other windows opening at the building and people looking out. They couldn't not hear Willy's screams, just like Leo and Tommy. Everyone heard it.

Tommy's in there on weekends like me—all the time. We're drinking buddies. Plain and simple, I'm a weekend drunk—so is he. Plain and simple. Willy's on me always to quit but I don't drink during the week—not a drop. Weekends are another story.

"Whenever Willy can, he comes to get me. Just drags me home. Imagine that?—a twelve-year-old kid dragging his forty-two year old drunk uncle home. When I think of it, it makes me sick. But do I stop? Nah.

Believe it or not, I'm a draftsman. You know, architecture? That's how I'm always noticing little things like spatial things like the flower pot that I saw right away that was missing on the ledge. You know?"

Both detectives were listening to me intently. They weren't taking notes.

"He's right, Mac. We found the flower pot shattered all over and right adjacent to the building. It definitely fell off the ledge. But the kid wasn't near the pieces of the terracotta strewn all over. The kid was pushed. No doubt. We measured where he landed. He was exactly seventeen-feet four-inches away from the building. Oh yeah, he was pushed. No doubt about it. Lucky kid. He was under the dead zone."

When this other detective said, 'dead zone,' I felt cold and I panicked. But I thought quickly—oh yeah, I thought very quickly: 'If Willy was dead they would have told me immediately, so I instantly knew that even though Willy might be in bad shape, for sure he wasn't dead, and besides, he said 'lucky kid.'

I quickly recovered from my ruminations. "What's the dead zone?"

Neither of them answered the question. They were just staring at me.

"By the way, Frankie, this is Detective Davis, Lyle Davis. I'm Detective Loris McIver. They call me Mac. No one calls me Loris. And this is the 48th precinct, off Tremont Avenue, Bronx, New York."

"Are you kidding? I know exactly where this is. I know the whole neighborhood. Besides, I've been here twice before when I was wrecked. I know the nighttime Desk Sgt. downstairs—Sgt. Silverstein. Right?"

"Right. Okay, the fact we now all know is that Willy's in the hospital and he's not dead."

Again, hearing it said definitely that Willy was alive just about completely relaxed me—more like relieved me. It's like I needed to hear it more. I thought that come hell or high water, whatever injuries he would have, I would see to it that he gets better—totally recovers. I know I can get like that, like with some big wish that keeps the other possible reality away. Like maybe he won't get better. I can't let myself think that. He's my nephew but to me he's more like my son. But because of my drinking and how he drags me home, it's more like he takes care of me. So, in certain ways he's not more like my son, he's more like my father, like my guardian.

"But he's alive. Thank God. That's the important thing. I gotta see him. Can't wait till tomorrow. What did you mean Det. Davis, about the dead zone? You're not telling me about this dead zone."

"Mac here will fill you in. I gotta go downstairs first and do some paper work, then get something to eat."

"Lyle, hold it," Mac said. "Since we'll be here for the duration, and now it's almost midnight. When you get back — two burgers and black coffee for me, and Frankie, how about you?"

"Yeah, thanks, that sounds good. I'll take one burger and a beer. Thanks."

"No beer at the precinct."

"Okay, Coke."

As Detective Davis started to leave, I turned to Det. McIver, the one known as Mac. He was getting ready to type on an old Underwood sitting directly center on his desk and he was about to fill out his forms — demographics and stuff, but I interrupted him.

"C'mon, what's the dead zone?"

"Okay. Willy fell or was pushed from the third floor where you live. That's below what we consider the dead zone. The dead zone is four stories or higher above the street. Over forty, maybe fifty but definitely sixty feet up — those heights will do it. If someone falls from there, it's about a ninety-eight percent chance of no survival. Dead is dead! Keep in mind that when a person falls from a high place the deceleration generates a force that's one-hundred-fifty times the weight of the person. In Willy's case, he weighed about one-hundred pounds so that when he hit the ground it would be like he weighed about fifteen-thousand pounds. That's fifteen-thousand! Get it? So even if he survived, which he did, Willy might now be in something like a coma. Actually, according to the admitting doc he's almost in a coma but not quite, so that he still has some consciousness. But the doctors can't really measure the amount of consciousness, and here's the tough one: someone in this kind of condition sometimes can't communicate at all. So, Willy, right now, and as I understand it, can't tell us a thing. But, he was below the dead zone. Like I said, it's lucky you guys live on the third floor. It's the fourth floor or above. That's the dead zone.

"Okay Frankie, let's get down to it. I gottta type this. Last name first then age, and then relation to Willy."

"Carbone, Francis Antonio Carbone. I'm forty-two. I'm Willy's uncle."

"Okay. What else should I know instead of me spending time digging it out. Know what I mean?"

"Wait a minute, he didn't just fall. You're right. I remember that the way he went down from the ledge was like he was pushed from behind. Yeah, that's right. I remember thinking that I kinda saw the uh, what is it, kind of like a, uh the word, maybe like a dark outline—the word might be like 'opaque' or 'fuliginous'—sorry, I like interesting words. It's almost like you can't quite see the background of a kinda big man, yeah, a big guy—yeah, the look of it, of a big guy, definitely a man, not a boy, inside behind the wide open window standing right behind Willy. And I saw Willy going down. But it wasn't down. His hands were stretched out in front of him like almost he was diving into a pool. Oh God, I saw it. My heart was in my mouth.

"Like I said, that's the third avenue elevated train there where we live. So, then a train was passing and at that point I couldn't hear if he was screaming or not. But as the last car was about to pass, I thought I saw under the wheels of the last car of the train a glimpse of Willy falling. Then, even though that last car of the train blocked my view, the next thing I saw was Willy hitting the ground. He was almost into the gutter—right on the street, right at the curb. I tried getting up and running over to him but I fell back down. I was still out of it; hung over like I was dying myself.

"But here's the thing of it. It wasn't straight down like it was that he slipped and fell or even did a suicide jump which I guess would also be more or less straight down. No. And besides, Willy was in no way ever thinking suicide. That's outta the question. Willy was pushed. I remember feeling almost like I myself was being pushed by someone like from the back. I had that reaction when I, in a split-second saw Willy going down away from the building the way he had his hands stretched out—palms out. I felt it like he must've been feeling it, like if someone much bigger and stronger than me pushed me like that and then you go flying.

"But that's not the worst of it because—it's very hard for me to say this—even though I did see Willy hit the ground, the worst of it was that I heard it. I actually heard it. When something like that happens, I now know that you automatically know by the sound of it that it's a body that hit the ground. Like the sound is different than you would imagine—like if it was a heavy object that dropped, like a frigidaire or something like a sewing-machine. Know what I mean?—a heavy object. Something not human. It's just a different sound.

"So, I could tell. I knew right away the moment I heard it that it was the sound of a body, of a human being. And it was Willy's body. I actually heard the sound that Willy's body made when it hit the ground coming outta our window on the third floor. It's like I automatically know what you mean when you say a person who weighs a hundred pounds will hit the ground like he weighs over a thousand pounds. I know you said fifteen thousand pounds."

"You're right. We know that. Police know that. A body makes a different sound then that of some non-human heavy object. In addition, like Detective Davis said, the distance from the face of the building to where Willy landed was measured to be more than seventeen feet. And that's the result of quite a push—along with the effort Willy must have made to kinda we might say, elongate the way down; like he was pushing himself horizontally away from the downward trajectory. Know what I mean?

"He also got smashed up but only on the front of his body so that it gives us more evidence that he was pushed. No one suiciding dives off a building. They just jump and either go straight down, or pinwheel down, or if they change their minds in the middle of the fall, they try to grab the side of the building or anything else they can grab onto so that when we find them, for sure their hands are all scraped up and badly damaged—all broken up, fingers and all. But usually they also have back of the head injuries and injuries all over their bodies, not just on the front. In Willy's case, his hands were also damaged with broken bones but no real scraping and there were no injuries to speak of on his back.

"Okay, now, tell me briefly about Willy's life. I mean a quick look at it from the time he was born, parents, place of birth, and so forth. We'll do more of it after we visit Willy tomorrow at the hospital. We've gotta see if he can communicate. If he can't, then we gotta figure out how maybe *we* can communicate with *him*. Lyle, Det. Davis, spoke to the admitting orthopedic surgeon and he said he can't tell if Willy will be able to tell us anything at all. Okay, g'head—Willy's life."

* * *

"It's like this," Frankie said. "Willy's mother was my sister Olga. And here's the big secret in the family. It doesn't matter now because it's not then, in 1946 when we first got here. Now we're all U.S. citizens. This is 1958. We got here, my sister and me, when she was already twenty-five and I was thirty. That was 1946, a year after the war. So now it would be twelve years ago. She got pregnant, and gave birth to Willy toward the end of 1946. She had been married to the Chief Aide of the Italian Ambassador to Lisbon. It was during Mussolini's time. His name was Ustacio Travali. Ustacio, my sister said, was part of the Ambassador to Lisbon's tight inner circle.

"And that was the big secret we kept in the family because my sister thought that somehow we might have been suspected—even accused of being part of some spy ring because of the Ustacio/Italian/Mussolini connection. My sister knew that Ustacio had a Greek/Croation father and an Italian mother. So that's where the Ustacio name came from. I eventually looked it up. It's from the Greek. Ustacio means healthy and strong. Something like that. The scuttlebutt was that she met Ustacio when him and five or six hundred prisoners were released by the Italian prison commandant who had no use for the Nazis. When the commandant was informed that a Nazi unit was approaching the camp, he released them all. I don't have any information of what happened to the commandant but I'll bet he took off too. This was in Fontanellato near Parma. She told me the prisoners were like an assortment of allied soldiers including some Greeks."

"So, where's the big secret?"

"Okay. Here it is. The crazy thing is that Ustacio was a plant in the prison camp. He was actually some kind of big shot in Mussolini's counter-spy operation. But when the commandant of the camp released everyone, Ustacio never had to run and hide. He just rejoined Mussolini's spy group called OVRA. In Italian, it was called: *Ogganizzazione per la Vigilanza e la Repressione dell' Antifascismo.* It roughly translates into something like: *Organization for Vigilance and Repression of Anti-Fascism.* It was really the

Fascist or Mussolini's secret police. Kind of like equivalent to the *Gestapo* in Germany or something like that.

"My sister Olga met Ustacio at a dance. At first, she didn't know anything about what he did. But he fell for her and she liked him too, so that was that.

"Here's where it gets really interesting. Believe it or not, Ustacio was in charge of some secret papers of the Wannsee Conference that was held outside of Berlin in 1942, in the place called Wannsee. It was where that ultimate cocksucker, Reinhard Heydrich who was Hitler's Chief of the Security Service convened the Wannsee meeting. Its purpose was to knock off the Jews. And by the way, sometime thereafter in 1942, after the conference, Heydrich was assassinated; knocked off by Czech partisans in Prague. But at the conference, Adolph Eichmann presented the plan of how to do it—how to round up the Jews and others, and kill them. That's part of the conference that was made public. But there was another secret part that was never made public.

"Since Ustacio was that Italian Ambassador to Lisbon's trusted Chief Aide, the Ambassador had Ustacio guard the papers. Olga told me that the Ambassador instructed Ustacio to consider guarding the papers to be his main job. Ustacio said the Ambassador told him that Hitler insisted that Mussolini should have the only other copy of the conference papers and that's how the package of papers of the conference got to Italy. Ustacio said Hitler wanted Mussolini in on it so he sent the copy through Lisbon which the Ambassador to Lisbon was to hand over personally to Mussolini when the Ambassador returned to Italy. Ustacio said that Hitler wanted Mussolini to know that Mussolini's name and the assurance that he would be kept alive were part of the secret papers.

"But here's where the story took a turn. The Ambassador died suddenly. My sister said Ustacio told her it was a heart attack. I always thought: 'Who knows what it was? Maybe Ustacio killed him? Who's to say?' I say that because Ustacio decided to keep the package. Olga said that Ustacio had secretly read the part of the Wannsee Conference—the part that was always kept secret—secret, by the way, even to this day, as we're talking now. But this was 1942 or '43, before the end of the war. Even then, Ustacio felt the war was lost. Then Ustacio had the microfilm made.

"Olga always said that Ustacio was very smart about politics. He told Olga that the papers were extremely important and that he was sure the war would be lost and that he decided to finally get out. Olga insisted he take me too. Somehow, he arranged it that along with me and Olga, we were able to just about completely disappear. Olga told me that a widespread search for us was an ongoing thing and that Hitler was out of his mind with rage about why we weren't caught. He really wanted those secret papers.

"The truth is we were working on a farm outside of Parma. It was a place where Ustacio's parents would go on vacation when he was a child. Then in the middle of 1944 Ustacio saw the way to get out completely and he took us out. It's a long story—a helluva story—but Ustacio, my sister Olga, and I, managed to get from Parma to Switzerland, then to Cuba, then to Canada and from there we slipped into the U.S. through the woods and into Plattsburgh, New York, and then made it right to New York City winding up in the Bronx, and as you know, still living on Third Avenue, listening to those elevated trains.

"We travelled by boat, by car, by train, and even for part of the way by wagon. You might say that the whole thing was a back-road deal. But it was a nightmare. We were scared all the way. On the farm where we were stashed, near Parma, we kinda calmed down because we felt safe there. But to get where we got, that was a nightmare.

"And wouldn't you know it, just like that, when we were already in The Bronx, Ustacio disappeared. Vanished in thin air, and we never ever saw him again. I always thought either he was killed or that he headed back to Europe—maybe to arrange to sell the microfilm. Who knows. We just never heard from him again. Now, especially with what just happened to Willy, I'm thinking: Could there be a connection?

"Anyway, before my sister died—she had pancreatic cancer and died within a month of the diagnosis—she gave the microfilm to Willy for him to hide in a place where it wouldn't be found. Willy told me she said that the package could be sold for a lot of money and to guard the package. But Willy also told me that the package must've been folded and wrapped tightly because the package was in a funny shape. He drew the shape for me and it was more like oblong.

"I'm sorry to say that this happened on a weekend and as usual on the weekend, I was plastered, bombed out! So, she said I was a lost cause and trusted the whole thing to Willy. I always thought Willy hid the package in the house but I've looked for it all over the house and it's nowhere. It's not in the house. That I'm sure of. I needed to have Willy tell me what he did with the package but whenever I asked him about it he said he couldn't trust me because I was so drunk on the weekends that he thought I might even show it to someone. He said he never opened the package to see what it was all about but I'm not sure I ever believed him. It could be that he said that so that I wouldn't try to get out of him what the secrets were all about.

"Anyway, now if Willy can't tell us anything, who can ever find the package? But I don't care about that. Fuck the package. I just want my nephew to get better and be normal. The package means nothing to me.

"So now you know something almost no one else does. I'm sick of all these Goddamn secrets anyway. Let the world know about those crazy Nazi mother-fuckers. The truth of it is that when I first heard that my sister said we could get a lot of money for it, I got excited about it. But after all this time I realized I wouldn't know who to sell it to anyway."

"Okay, Frankie," Mac interrupted, "I told you to keep it brief but I admit this was interesting. But I'll bet what they did to Willy—are you ready for this?—was a message to you. From what you told me about the package it *is* what they're after. And it could even implicate Ustacio. But I can't believe that Ustacio would push Willy like that. If Ustacio's alive and implicated he would probably guess that Willy was his kid, I mean his own flesh and blood. So, my guess is that Ustacio is gone—really gone—and that whoever got to Willy may have originally gotten to Ustacio a long time ago. Who knows? This is how detectives think, you know?

"Information in those papers could probably implicate a lot of people—or maybe even some big shot who's still breathing. Know what I mean? That means that you, Frank Carbone need to be closely guarded, because if they get their hands on you, you'll be in a lot of trouble. Your life's in danger, my friend. There's no other way to say it."

"I'm not a potted plant, Detective. In a fight for my life, all I want to do is hit the guy with all my might right smack center in the jaw with a vicious uppercut that drives his jaw bone right into his brain. I'm not kidding. That's the only thing I'd be interested in. He could get to me all he wants because all I want is that one shot to his jaw. Just one shot."

"Okay Frank, so you're a tough guy. Everybody's tough except when there's an American Eagle Colt .45 staring you right in the face. Again, know what I mean? So, let's not be a Hollywood tough guy. I'm putting you under police protection as of right now. I'll get to the other stuff about Willy's condition tomorrow, after we visit the hospital. We'll all be there at ten in the morning seeing Willy and getting the low-down from the doctors. We have two guys there on duty twenty-four hours so, at the moment even if Willy's not aware of it, he's safe. Then we'll reconvene—meaning get together again at the precinct. But first, immediately after the hospital we'll be going to your apartment. No one's allowed in yet, because we have it cordoned off and cops are guarding it. That means you sleep here tonight. We've got a room with cots. I'm sleeping here too. When Lyle gets back—if he gets back—we'll have a lot to eat—that's if we're still awake. If not, then we'll be hungrier in the morning."

"I hope I can sleep," Frank answered. "My motor's going fast and I'm not at all tired. The truth is that I got focused on what you were saying regarding how I might be in danger. I also noticed I was thinking about being in a fist-fight with whoever that bad guy was and hitting him a world-class right uppercut with everything I had right smack dab at his chin bone and driving it. Yup, really driving it!"

I shook out of the thought and fixed on Willy. I thought: 'Willy's alive. That's the important thing.' But then I had another thought. I asked Mac if I could make a phone call.

· 2 ·

WILLY

"Frankie, Frankie, get up."

"I'm up. Been up all night—constantly checking my watch, all night. You didn't have to wake me. I didn't catch a wink."

"Oh yeah? Do you usually snore like that while you're awake?"

"C'mon, Mac, I was snoring?"

"Absolutely."

"The last thing I remember it was 4:20 am. I must've dozed off. What time is it?"

"It's seven. We need to be at the hospital at ten. Get into the bathroom, do your things, put your pants on, and let's get some breakfast. We'll talk over breakfast. Lyle's waiting for us downstairs. He was sleeping most of the night except, like you, he says he was on guard most of the night."

Even at seven in the morning the precinct was already busy. Det. Lyle Davis was waiting and the three of us decided to head directly to the hospital and have breakfast in the hospital cafeteria. Tremont Avenue is not too far from Mosholu Parkway and Montefiore Hospital and it took only about fifteen minutes to get there. That early in the morning traffic was light and we flew. We didn't talk in the car because we were all thinking the same thing. It was obvious.

It was like when the pitcher is pitching a no-hitter and no one in dugout will say anything about it; even some radio announcers will hesitate.

In other words, no one wants to jinx it. In the Bronx, that's how every-one thinks. We were no different. No one wanted to mess with any kind of hex.

Got to the hospital, parked the car, rushed into the lobby, headed straight for the information desk and asked about the condition of Willy Travali. The information guy was right on it. He dialed the phone, asked about Willy, listened to what the person at the other end was saying, and as he was hanging up the receiver he was smiling.

"He's resting comfortably, and the doctor will be visiting him within the hour."

We all looked at one another with relief but still with a sense of urgency. Mac broke the mood. He said: "Food, guys. Let's go."

Then Mac started to say something and began with: "Guys," and I real-ized he considered me to be one of the guys—one of the good guys, which as far as I was concerned, I was—especially when it concerned Willy.

We proceeded to attack the hospital cafeteria. Even at that hour many tables were already taken with various hospital personnel eating and talk-ing. It was like everyone was talking at once. Lots of noise. Both Mac and Lyle were big breakfast eaters. So was I. We ate and talked and were excited about the prospect of getting Willy to communicate but we were also worried about what the doctors would tell us. We were talking excit-edly, but when the subject turned to what the doctors might tell us about Willy we got real quiet, actually, no one said a word.

We were also more or less silent going up in the elevator. We reached the third floor—wouldn't you know it, it had to be the third floor! There we were met by two officers. One of them was walking out of Willy's room while the other one was sitting on one of the chairs outside of the room. Mac and Lyle knew the officers and both cops reported no unusual activity since they first arrived. They were now waiting for their relief team due at eight—at this point in about half an hour. Obviously, we were early.

The three of us and one of the officers all entered Willy's room. Willy was sleeping or unconscious—whatever. We couldn't tell because to me he looked like he was sleeping because he *was* unconscious. He was all hooked up and there were tubes coming out of everywhere. He was also bandaged in a lot of places.

At that point, we were all sitting around waiting for the doctor, when the nurse entered to tell us that the doctor, Dr. Fishman, was held up and would probably be there in about an hour. So, we waited for him in what seemed like too long a time. When he finally arrived, he introduced himself.

"As Detective Davis here knows, I'm Dr. Arnold Fishman. I'm an orthopedic surgeon."

"Good to meet you doctor. I'm Loris McIver, Detective Davis's partner."

Lyle then jumped in: "Doc, call him Mac. Forget the Loris. This gentleman here is the kid's uncle, Frank Carbone."

Then Lyle turned to us and said that Dr. Fishman was the orthopedist who set his arm when he broke it in taking down a guy in a fight. Lyle quickly added: "In the line of duty." The doctor interrupted Lyle.

"Okay gentlemen, this is what we know. Willy has several broken bones. We've detected ten broken bones on the front of his body but nothing on his back. His knee is in bad shape but I can assure you that one is entirely repairable. His left ankle is broken, several bones in his hands are also broken, and he'll need surgery on his chin. He lost three teeth, and he's got a bad, very bad bruise on his forehead where we think he could have hit the ground after bouncing up from the first impact, taking a toll on his chin and mouth.

"There are other breaks here and there including two toes and of course, his ribs. We're taking X-rays on his pelvis which we're fairly certain is also broken—similar to his knee and chin, and perhaps in more than one place. Oh yes, I should mention we also think he's probably going to feel severe pain in the lower portion of his back but nothing is broken there. His spine is okay. So, all of this is in the positive column as far as cure, or shall I say perhaps reasonable cure, can be expected.

"The main concern is that the forehead injury may indicate frontal brain trauma which isn't yet measureable. What this means, with respect to what we feel we already know is that we're pretty sure we may need to accurately diagnose whether Willy may be *locked-in*. Let me explain that. Locked-in means that Willy would be suffering from what we call a disorder of consciousness. Locked-in is frequently bad news. But in Willy's case, we feel we may be more likely dealing with what we also consider to be an MCS—meaning *Minimally Conscious State*. At this point we can't be sure. His heart rate is normal, and his blood pressure, believe it or not is also normal. He's a strong kid.

"Nevertheless, if this is a disorder of consciousness it means that his consciousness is inhibited. Usually this minimal conscious state would be separate from the locked-in condition but in Willy's case, at least at this point, it may be that both or even perhaps neither are indicated; that is, the locked-in and MCS rather than reflecting two distinct conditions, could be only a single fused problem. My hunch is that Willy is not suffering from either. Also, at this point we don't think Willy is in what's known as a vegetative state. That sort of thing, a vegetative state, is diagnostically a guarded condition, meaning a poor prognosis. In other words, if it were the vegetative state, it most often would mean not good, like the worst news. You all should rest easy here because the hallelujah is — that's not the case here.

"At this point, what we need to see is whether Willy can communicate in any way at all — even as little as moving a finger or a toe or of course, a blink, or even communicate while sitting up and talking a little. If he can do the blink and/or the talking then of course we'd be able to communicate with him and he could eventually go home in one piece. You know, things such as whether he can at least smile or even cry, or make some kind of gesture or even talk a bit is what we call *purposeful* behavior, and all of that would be good news."

"Excuse me doctor," Mac interrupted, "that's what we need to have. We need what you call purposeful behavior. We need to question him in any way possible and we could break down the questions into short few-word sentences requiring short few-word answers. Even answers of yes or no. In other words, we need specific information because this was not a suicide attempt. Willy was deliberately pushed off a third-floor ledge of a four story apartment building. We know he was pushed. We don't know why or who did it. We're fairly certain it was a man who pushed him. It would be extremely helpful if God was with us, and Willy could tell us who the man was and why he pushed him."

"It could be, if you don't mind me saying so," said Dr. Fishman, "that even with God checking in here, it all will depend on if Willy is locked-in, which again, my hunch tells me — no. In these kinds of minimally conscious states, if even a little step by step improvement can be measured, then the prognosis is actually good. In other words, in a vegetative state, there is no improvement. But when it is measurable improvement, the improvement is sometimes measured in ten to twelve month intervals."

"Ten to twelve months?!" I practically shouted. "Willy might be like this for a year?"

"I hope not," Dr. Fishman replied. "but if it's severe head trauma as in a locked-in or MCS condition, in some cases, yes that's what we're looking at. But as I've said, it might not be any of that. I'll spare you an advanced lecture on brain anatomy. We have Dr. Sitaram Mehta, a brain specialist also on the case and if you want, which I doubt, he'll be easily able to give you an explanation of this brain trauma stuff that would include phenomena—well just giving you a sample, an earful of what's involved here could have you spinning especially if you're not educated medically. In other words, this stuff is not for the uninitiated. For example, Willy's injuries can involve the medial parietal cortex, the posterior cingulated cortex and some corticocortical connectivity between the auditory cortex and prefrontal cortices. There would also need to be cerebral spinal fluid analyses, and so forth.

"As you can see, we take this quite seriously because as an outside chance, we could be dealing with something more serious than we now know. However, again I say, I don't think so. Of course, we're dealing with managing a great deal of physical and clinical data, and also managing treatment. Keep in mind, if you want to break it down, Willy was essentially and seriously concussed, so if in a locked-in kind of state the patient is aware but there's no movement and like I'm trying to say, practically no communication. To put it as simply as I can, all voluntary movement of the body, except for his eyes would at this point be paralyzed. But that paralysis could be temporary. We're talking also about muscles here. But I'll add—this is not yet the final actual picture. Willy may have none of it. He may be lying unconscious simply because he got knocked out in addition to pain medication that was already administered. As I've said, his spine seems to be in-tact and it could very well be that all those broken bones—including his chin and perhaps his pelvis, along with other things—may, after a complete assessment—only need me and not Dr. Mehta.

"As Detective Lyle knows, I'm an orthopedic surgeon and Willy may only need me for treatment with respect to bones. In any event, Dr. Mehta who is a brain specialist will explain it more in basic terms and you'll be able to consult with him tomorrow when he's here to make his rounds."

Again, I jumped in ahead of Mac or Lyle. "Doctor, from what you say it could be that: a) he's possibly aware, and b) that therefore he might be able to communicate with his eyes or else there may be some other even possible ingenious way of getting him to respond; through his heart rate or blood pressure or whatever. I know I'm grasping at straws but I'm thinking that if we could figure out how to reach him and how he could reach us it would improve his emotional state; he possibly could feel actually hopeful. And best of all, we'd most likely get the information we need."

"Keep in mind," the doctor answered, "if all is well, you may even be able to talk to him. Of course, you're right and it's a good point. As an example, some patients who have brain trauma can in rare cases move facial muscles and not just eye movements. And more good news could be that there's a chance if Willy, in fact, had trauma to the lower brain and brainstem there may be no trauma or even any damage to the upper brain at all. And yes, sometimes it's been reported that a full spontaneous recovery has been seen. That might or might not be the case here depending on finding out what's at the bottom of it all. At this point we just don't know.

"However, everything I've said about brain trauma and what might be involved here is speculation and also keep in mind the very important possibility that Willy may have none of that kind of injury, and would ultimately only be dealing with the healing of surgery on broken bones."

We discussed the entire issue some more and periodically I noticed we all, including both detectives would glance over at Willy and take a quick but optimistic look at him. It reminded me of one of my best buddies, a guy named Alex Kaye. Al would probably say that in order to send waves of healing into Willy, one or two people should sit outside of the hospital and stare at the window of Willy's room with good thoughts directed at the window. Al believed, for example that those kinds of psychic waves could penetrate into the patient and actually have the power to cure.

So, even though I never believed in any such hocus-pocus, at this moment, again, I was hoping Al was right and I was wrong. And despite Al's so-called hocus-pocus healing-wave theory, he's been a private detective for ten years and the word on the street is that he has an uncanny ability to uncover whatever or whoever he's looking for.

"Al once announced to me that 'details need to be specific,' and he said that most people would think of that little home-spun adage as a redundancy but that he knew it was nothing of the sort. He said the detail should not contain the slightest generality. Then he got that supernatural stuff going again and said the detail is the location of the Devil, as in: *The Devil is in the detail.* He said he's always looking for the person as the detail but never attributing the detail to an inanimate object like table or a chair.

* * *

So now here I was, part of a trio along with two detectives, with not one of us really knowing how to get into the mystery of it all, where to look, and what to look for! And what do I think of at such a moment? Actually, it's not a 'what.' It's a 'who.' And of course, I think of Al. I think of Alex Kaye, private detective par excellence. And as God is my witness, as I'm thinking about Al, sure enough, in he walks. He sees me, nods, and then looks knowingly at Lyle.

"Al Kaye, whatya know?" Lyle says. "Mac this is the Alex Kaye who fingered the guy responsible for the kidnapping of Rodriguez's wife, the precinct captain at the 53rd on Webster."

Mac nods as Lyle says: "The guy who kidnapped Rodriguez's wife was furious at the cops for something they did that he thought was unfair. Rod illegally kept him locked up till they were sure he was not the guy they were after. And on top of it, he was roughed up. So, what did this roughed-up guy do? He took the wife. Plucked her right off the street. Then he sent a note saying he wasn't asking for ransom but what he really wanted was for Rodriguez to suffer. Believe that? That's what he said. As far as he was concerned, Rodriquez was to suffer.

"Al here got interested, especially when Rodriguez asked him to look for her—for his wife—to do it on his own, and to feel free to do whatever he needed to do even if it meant getting around any rules that were in effect. Rodriguez swore he would fix any illegal stuff that Al might possibly get into in his search for Rod's wife and for the guy who took her. Rodriguez wanted the guy almost as much as he wanted his wife. And believe me, he *really* wanted his wife!

"So, what does Al here do? The first thing was to go searching in the most recent complaint files."

Looking at Al, Lyle says: "Right, Al?" Al nods and then not skipping a beat, Lyle continues: "Rodriguez gave Al here all access. In record time checking in the files, Al then comes up with a few names that he thought reflected real disgruntled guys who might have had the level of anger that justified doing something drastic. He followed the leads and in short order got the guy. No one knows the details of how he did it, but he did it. Al's tough, right Al? I say that because when Al here roughed him up, the guy gave up the chick.

But that's not the end of the story because then Rodriguez had the guy—I remember the guy's name—Josephs. Raymond Josephs. Rody got him in the back room at the precinct and practically beat him to death. He kicked the shit out of him.

"The key to this story," Lyle continued, "is that we need to find the guy or guys who did Willy. And like I said, Al can find guys. No doubt about it."

At that point, I noticed Mac was chomping at the bit so I introduced them. "Mac," I said, "meet my buddy, Alex Kaye."

Mac nodded to Al but then turned to me and asked how Al knew to arrive at the hospital at this precise time. "Quite a coincidence," Mac said, looking at me.

"Not a coincidence, Mac. It was that phone call I made last night before we turned the lights out. I called Al and told him to meet us here at about 10:30."

Mac turned to Al and asked him what led him to look at the complaint file for the Josephs character? Of course, Al's a stand-up guy and immediately referenced the Mad Bomber Case of New York City and how people suspected that the bomber had something to do with a grievance at Con Ed. Al's not the type to be self-congratulatory so he would never talk about it.

"Al," Lyle says, "tell it. C'mon, tell it."

"Never mind that," Al immediately responded. "I got something here already about Willy that could be important. I went over to P.S. 42—Willy's school, early this morning. It's a block from Third Avenue near where Frankie here and Willy live. Got there 8:30 sharp. The Principal greeted me. I made some inquiries and he answered every one of my questions. And he was quick in answering them.

"From the moment I began questioning him to the end of our contact, it took all of about maybe ten or so minutes. He explained that in addition to being in charge of the school, he also put himself in charge of the street by the school so that he is, as he said himself, 'the self-appointed cop of the street.' No loitering by anyone is allowed. He feels it's his duty to protect the kids coming to, and going home from school.

"Then he hits me with this: he starts describing two guys he chased off the block about a week ago. He said one was burly guy and the other taller and slimmer. You believe that? He felt they were hanging around too much and he got a bad feeling about it and about them. He told them to get off the block and they did—without an argument. They said something but just turned and walked away. Then he gave me descriptions—for each of them.

"Now that's the same description Frankie gave me on the phone last night with the exact words, 'big, burly,' Al said. I also got that certain feeling I get sometimes when a fact just falls into place, especially when you least expect it. And this was one of those times. Then it wasn't hard to see that it could be a connection to those guys and Willy's situation. Because, you know when Frankie called me last night, he filled me in at the speed of light. I could tell he was upset, actually furious. He wanted to get even. You know we've been tight for a long time and I know Frankie."

I interrupted Al and looking at Mac and Lyle I repeated what Al said—that in the phone call I described the whole thing about what happened to Willy and pointed out that I was pretty sure I could make out the figure of a kind of big burly guy I thought I saw behind the window where Willy was standing on the ledge. I never mentioned any other guy.

"Did those guys at the school talk at all?" Lyle asked Al.

"The Principal said the big guy had some kind of European accent—sounded definitely to be German or close, like maybe Austrian or Swiss, and that the other guy, the taller, slimmer one definitely had like a Spanish accent but was light-skinned, more like a guy from some South American country, and speaking with the accent that's different than the kind of Puerto Rican Spanish you can hear in the Bronx now. It was after the Principal told those guys to leave that they first said a few things to one another but then turned and crossed the street. But they said enough for him to catch the accents.

"So," Al continued, "whatya think? Where do we go from here?"

The 'we' sounded to me like a gong went off because it meant that Al had insinuated himself into this investigation of Willy's trauma, really, by writing his own invitation. Of course, I knew why Al was so interested. We'd been friends for about ten years now—soon after I got to this country—and Al had helped me out with all sorts of things. He got me kind of street-smart faster than if I had to learn it or do it all myself. So, Al knew Willy and Olga almost since Willy was born. And further, Willy always looked up to him and Al liked Willy a lot.

The other thing is that Al is Jewish. I'm always impressed with that because like I said, when we got here, we didn't know a thing about what to do and where to go and so forth. Al's mother and father were still alive then. They were also immigrants who had already been here for many years. Anyway, they helped us tremendously and Al and I became best buddies; me, an Italian Catholic with family from Italy and Al, a first generation American Jewish guy whose parents were from a little Jewish ghetto—what's known as a shtetl—from Ukraine. So ever since then, whenever I hear somebody knocking Jews, then they gotta deal with me.

I now felt that with Al in the picture we had the real possibility of catching those guys. And we had something of a lead: two guys—one, possibly German, and the other, possibly, South American. That meant we'd probably made a discovery; that is, that there may have been two men in the apartment when Willy went down, not just one.

Mac put an exclamation point on it all. "Again, Al," Mac said, "we should all remember that Frank is pretty sure Willy was pushed by a big, burly guy and I for one will never believe that it's just a coincidence that the Principal of the school also noted the big guy and to boot, called him 'burly.' But we also need to consider something very important; that the catastrophic thing that happened to Willy was, in all probability, really a message to Frank. It could be that what these guys were after was the package that Olga had hidden. It's got something to do with the war. She brought it with her all the way from Parma."

"I've known about that package for years," Al responded. "Frank told me about it one night when he was a bit, uh, let's call it under the weather. Know what I mean?"

Looking at Frank, Al said: "Frank, you never found it. Right?"

"Right. Never."

"It's possible," Al continued, "that the package contained information that could incriminate certain individuals or maybe even more so, a single person. As far as I'm concerned, it's all pointing to maybe war criminals or maybe even one major criminal. Someone high up in either Mussolini or Hitler's so-called inner circle of nut-jobs. You know

Ustacio was with Mussolini. Even though he so-to-speak defected and wound up here, nevertheless, he took that package with him. That's for sure. And he knew that Hitler wanted Mussolini to have the only copy of those secret papers.

"I sometimes get these intuitions, Al continued, "and I can imagine that Hitler wanted Mussolini to have those papers because something in them would assure Mussolini that Hitler made some kind of arrangement to make sure Mussolini would be protected—like you know, just in case. Of course, at the moment, if I'm right, it could be that there's a mystery guy who could be at the bottom of this thing and maybe it was this mystery guy that arranged for the two guys, or at least the big burly one that pushed Willy, to get the package—and at any cost. And I'll go further. It could be that he's a possible major war criminal himself and that at least one of the secrets in the papers could, if revealed, give him a death sentence.

"So, my way-out assumption is that the mystery guy is probably behind it all. You know, when a big deal is in the works, the boss doesn't do the dirty work to fix it. He sends big, burly guys to fix it. So that's why I'm thinking it's a mystery guy calling the shots, and for us, at the moment, he's an abstraction—like a vague presence—like a ghost.

· 3 ·

The Two Guys

We all agreed. The two guys we were looking for were in the employ or doing the bidding of someone who at the moment, we couldn't see. The fact is, that no one could see it, or them, or him. In view of what they did to Willy, it was clear that they weren't going to stop there. They were determined to get the package. No life mattered. Al said it and Mac and Lyle agreed. So did I — for sure. Then looking at Mac, Lyle came up with a plan.

"First, I think we need to do two things. We need to put a bigger team around the hospital and second, we need to figure a way of using Frank as bait. Sorry, Frank, they're are after you and it's you that's going to pull them in."

"No problem, guys. I'm with it all the way. I especially wanna get my hands on that big guy."

"No, he's mine. Let me handle it," Al said with an obvious look of let's call it — relish-retribution."

"C'mon, Al, you're here as a self-invited guest," Mac answered. "So cool it. We all know what you did to Josephs even before Rodriguez got to him. We can't do anything even remotely like that. It might get these guys off — a claim of police brutality. Right?"

Al immediately nodded and we all sat down on the floor in the hospital corridor. It was like we were having a séance and the topic was how to use me as bait. That was the common thought. But Al couldn't quite shake the feeling that he'd need to at least hit the big guy during the take-down. So, he added to Mac's mature comment by saying: "I know you're right, of course, Mac, but you know, when we get this motha and if he gives us any trouble then we can really do it. See?"

"If we get to that point, then we'll see what happens," Mac said. "But we're not going to jeopardize anything. That's the rule! And it doesn't matter how much of an impulse any of us get to kill that cocksucker. Did I just say something that wasn't clear?"

Mac continued: "Okay, here's what we know for sure. At all costs, they don't want to kill you, Frank. Their main objective is to get you, not kill you. With you gone and Willy unable to communicate, they would have no chance. Therefore, getting you but not killing you is the issue. Once they got you then you'd be in trouble because then they'd torture the shit out of you and believe me they won't believe that you don't know where the package is. But again, you won't be killed. You'll be kept on the edge—on that disgust-line between life and death where you'd be begging to die. Whoever sent these motha-fuckas sent guys who would know not to kill the goose with the golden egg but rather to keep him right on that line."

"Mac, Lyle, I've got an idea," Al piped in. "We gotta move Willy to another hospital on the QT, and of course keep him safe there with the same cops that are guarding him here. Then we announce it in the papers that Willy's at the morgue and that services will be held for him on such and such a date and at such and such a cemetery. It'll be the talk of the town—for sure of the neighborhood—and it'll be read about. Whoever needs that information will realize that either Frank here will be at the morgue identifying Willy, or at the cemetery—where they'd be itching to grab Frank there. They don't know that Frank saw the big guy. So I think the cemetery is where we'll get them."

"It's good, Al," Mac said. "It's good. But a lotta people are going to be devastated with that obituary. But it still might be worth it especially if we get them—either at the morgue or the cemetery. Remember though, no rough stuff unless we need to physically bring them down. Then we bring them down tough! I'm for it that way. And Frank, you'll need a vest even though you would never be a target of any shooting, but there could be incidental fire in your direction. No one would dare endanger your life deliberately. You need to be captured, not killed. So, don't worry. Furthermore, we'll be forgiven for that obit if it all works out. No doubt."

Al agreed. He told Frank that Gloria would visit Willy and then announced he had to take care of a few things and would catch up with us later. Simultaneously, upon Al's departure, the overall plan went into effect as soon as Mac and Lyle called it in. Then before you knew it, Mac had a sit-down with the doctor on duty at Willy's ward and in short order this doctor went right along with Mac's plan to move Willy. They both agreed however, that it was a police responsibility for that to happen so that the doctor's position in the hospital was not at all jeopardized. Of course, the doctor was worried about the possibility of being dismissed for lack of professional judgment resulting in the certain accusation of the endangerment of a patient.

The transfer happened in a blink. Willy was, with stealth, and thus practically with invisibility, transferred in an ambulance to Bronx Hospital on the Grand Concourse—probably the most affluent thoroughfare in The Bronx. He was set up in a private room off a private corridor. Wouldn't you know it, on the third floor, rear. The third floor, for crying out loud! The whole transfer was so good that we were told it was, for all intents and purposes, undetectable. Further, Willy Travali's name was placed on the 'deceased' docket where all such cases are registered. That took care of phase one.

Mac and Lyle both almost simultaneously noted that it had to be a Catholic cemetery and if so it had to be Saint Raymond's Roman Catholic cemetery at Lafayette Avenue, also in The Bronx. It was the famous Saint Raymond's that even gained international notoriety because of the Lindbergh case involving the drop of ransom money for Lindbergh's son's kidnapper. Even though the Lindbergh thing was more than twenty years before, it was perfect because it increased the possibility that the guys we were after just about couldn't miss the notice in the papers.

The very next day, the Daily News, the New York Post, The Daily Mirror, the New York Herald Tribune, the New York World Telegram, the New York Journal American, and the New York Times, all had obit notices on Willy. The obit lamented the end of life of a child who was a great kid, good in school and very interested in his friends and family.

That took care of phase two.

So far, we had what we wanted. Willy was being cared for and guarded from inside Bronx Hospital as well as from the outside with cops in unmarked cars stationed across the street at both entrances/exits. Second, the morgue cops had descriptions—big and burly, tall and slim, and of course, accents of German and Spanish. Then on phase three, I had another idea. Given my concern for my own safety I was also thinking ahead. I began considering other factors about the guy who pushed Willy.

"One of the things we haven't counted on," I proclaimed, "is that those two guys could have arranged for others to replace them at the cemetery while they continue to be holed-up who knows where just waiting for these replacements to bring me in."

"It doesn't matter, Frank," Mac answered. "Lyle and I have also been considering that. There are four exits from the cemetery. Every car leaving the cemetery will be carefully monitored by pistol-packing cops. People in the cars will be ordered to identify themselves. All police have been instructed that we need the suspects alive—at least one of them—hopefully the big burly one. But if he's holed-up somewhere and we get their replacements—if there are any—they would still need to identify themselves.

"The point is that no one gets to Willy inside the hospital and no one gets to you in or outside the morgue or cemetery. In the meantime," Mac continued, "I'm curious to see what Al's up to. He said he needed to do something but he didn't say what. But he did say he'd be in touch later.

*   *   *

When we saw Al later, he told us how he was able to see where we all needed to go from here and what we needed to do. Al lived on Brook Avenue, a block or two from Willy's school and a few blocks from where Willy and I lived on Third Avenue. It was a poor area mostly populated by European families—mainly Italian, Irish, and Puerto Rican. All their kids were first-generation American and all their parents spoke with a variety of foreign accents. Immediately further south started the Negro area.

Al lived one flight up with Gloria –Gloria Messer. Gloria is very smart and very pretty. She's a kindergarten teacher at P.S. 42, where Willy went. P.S. 42 had what they called a pre-junior high-school annex for kids who were ahead of their grade-level and that's where Willy was placed. Al is forty-two, same age as I am. Gloria, who Al's been living with for the past couple of years is thirty-five. Their apartment house was one notch up from a tenement building. I knew that Al and Gloria were both happy. Al repeated to me many times that they always had hot water and that in the winter, they always had heat. That kind of thing was important to him. You know, basic needs and basic conveniences. Al's income was sometimes there and at other times not. Gloria made a steady teacher's salary so that together they lived somewhat frugally, but pretty well; that is, they felt financially more or less secure.

Al was about five foot ten and a muscular hundred and seventy-five pounds. And he was very handsome. He was a black-belt Krav Maga fighter. Gloria was a full figured five six, about a hundred twenty-five pounds—beautiful. Al always made a point to tell me that whenever he walked into the apartment and saw Gloria, he always kissed her. I was imagining that when he walked in this time she was cooking their dinner. I had a feeling he got home in time for dinner—wherever in the world he had been earlier. When Al confirmed it, and told me they sat down to eat during which time he explained the entire Willy story, I told him I knew it and that I imagined it would have gone down with Gloria more or less how he described it.

Before Al could begin telling Gloria all about Willy and what happened, she said she already knew about it and told him that she had spoken to Mac when he went to the school to talk to the principal. Then after talking to her, Mac drove her in his police car to see Willy at his new digs at the Grand Concourse's Bronx Hospital. Apparently, with the doctor's permission, she sat in Willy's room for a few hours. She also told him that in all that time at the hospital Willy was breathing fine but didn't move at all. He just lay there like he was unconscious. Since it was the start of the weekend, she said she was planning to go back there in the morning.

Willy was an orphan; his father, Ustacio, had disappeared, vanished, and his mother Olga, died. So, in his everyday life, I, although his uncle, was functioning as his father, and he already knew Gloria since she and Al were a couple. At that time Willy was about nine or ten—about a year or two ago. Gloria loved Willy. You could see how she mothered him and was very sensitive to his needs. I was thinking that if Willy could choose anyone to be with him, it would be Gloria first and me, second. And that was okay with me. Willy treated Al as an uncle and as a close personal friend as well. As far as Willy was concerned, he was part of a four-person group: him, me, Gloria and Al.

As long as Gloria was watching over Willy, I felt relieved. I was also always interested in how Al described what I thought of as his 'detective-thinking.' In this case, his detective-habit showed up. For example, he would usually ask someone unrelated to his search for whatever — know what I mean — like what guess they would make about this or that with respect to whatever he was explaining or looking for. In this case he couldn't quite figure out what his next lead would be in order to get those guys, or where he should look, or how to uncover even something, anything; that is, if the morgue or cemetery things didn't work out. So in order to expand this rather limited repertoire he decided to ask Gloria for her opinion. He told me that in his offhanded way he said to her:

"Hon, lemme ask you something. Okay, we're looking for these two guys and we're pretty sure that they're looking for Frank. They obviously wouldn't be living around here. Assuming they're looking to grab Frankie, where would you say they're located? Where would you say is their place of operation? How would you say I go about figuring it?"

Gloria thought for a few moments and then blurted out:

"They're living in their car. It's the only way. They're living in their car all the time, eating in the car, even maybe sleeping in the car unless others take over after whatever number of hours they take searching. I get an image of them constantly driving the neighborhood looking and hoping they'll see Frankie in the street. Because what else can they do? I'll bet they're driving all around the neighborhood. All they know is that this is where Frankie lives. And they need to spell each other in the driving.

"I would say the perimeter of their land mass would encapsulate Fulton Avenue on the east and from south to north, 171st street to 173st Street, and the same for Webster and Claremont from 171st north to 173rd. Then to complete the square, they would drive all the east-west and north-south blocks: Claremont, Bathgate, Washington, Brook, Park, Third, Fulton, over and over again, just cruising and watching — looking for Frankie."

When Al caught up to us that evening he told us what we were dying to know; that is, what to do and where to do it?

"So that's it guys. The morgue and the cemetery are good. But this is better. We'll do the morgue and the cemetery, of course. But what that tells me is that they almost for sure had photos of both Willy and you,

Frankie. How else would they know who to get? Whoever planned the whole thing—let's say this guy, this ghost—had the means to do it; had technical people and money to finance the whole thing. Of *course.* They're driving the neighborhood. What else could they be doing except for the morgue and cemetery? And that's if they even read the papers! Otherwise, their only target is Frankie. So how are they gonna get you, Frank? How? Gloria clocked it. They'll be looking for you in the square few blocks that Gloria named. The cemetery is good, the morgue, not bad. Scope and stake them out. Of course, but I feel it. Gloria's idea is better.

"You know, Gloria thinks she's a bit psychic but I think she's totally smart and just figured it out logically. So, what we need is a total stakeout at various points of the neighborhood. And by the way, another genius thing is she also said we shouldn't be driving around looking for them but that we should be in cars parked at the curb and sit tight and watch all cars passing. We're bound to see them. I can feel it. One of us will see them. They'd need to pass us in just about each and every stakeout spot. We'll all have our intercoms on the ready so as soon as they're spotted everyone gets alerted and we surround them."

"Al," Lyle popped in. "Does Gloria have a sister?"

We all laughed but we all naturally caught ourselves. We all felt that given the situation with Willy, laughing might've been inappropriate.' So in view of the Willy thing we killed the laughter. Even the way I said that to myself about using the word "killed," I automatically felt the 'uh oh' that I shouldn't have even thought it. It was my superstition about what a person thinks could influence what actually happens. I know it's stupid, but because I'm always playing ball, I know that that kind of superstition is a very serious thing with ball players. But this time Lyle saved me and without knowing it steered me away from these ruminations.

"Okay, I'll set it up. Mac," Lyle jumped in saying. "How many cars do we need."

"Well, it's about an eighteen block perimeter," Mac answered. "I say five stakeout cars. Two guys in each car. Frank, you place the cars. Where do you think?"

"I would say offhand, one on Washington and Claremont, one on Webster and Claremont, one on Webster and 171st, that's three. I think one on Fulton and 173rd Street, that's four, and the last one on Brook and Claremont so that because Claremont is the only two-way street, then in this way traffic on Claremont will be completely covered. If they're cruising the perimeter, we'll definitely get them.

* * *

It was all set. The five cars were stationed as planned all over the neighborhood. Mac and I were in one car on Claremont and Washington, and Al and Lyle in another on Brook and Claremont, right around where Al lived. The others were stationed at specified points we had figured out.

Al told me later that Lyle was interested in how I had no Italian accent but couldn't figure out how that could be since when I got to the U.S. I was already an adult. The essence of it was that I had this savant ability for hearing language spoken in its perfect dialect. To me language was loaded with accoutrements—intonation, enunciation almost as though it were music. In addition, I had a hunger for words so that my vocabulary and what's known as 'command of language' was always pretty good. It wasn't something I was striving for. It was just something that came naturally. And all of that, is what Al told Lyle as they were continually scanning all passing cars looking for the big guy and maybe someone else with him.

It was funny because here we were, looking for guys who could be killers, and here we were talking about the art and science of language. Oh yes, that reminds me. I almost forgot to tell Mac and Lyle that Al, Alex Kaye is a trained Krav Maga expert—a black belt Maga. It's the most serious and dangerous of the martial arts. It was developed by a Jewish guy by the name of Imi Lichtenfeld, and became required for training Jewish street fighters in Israel more or less at the time Israel became a country. So much for Jews not being able to fight!

But this all started in the late forties. Al, like me, was born in 1916. He in The Bronx and me in Ukraine. In about 1938 when Al was in his early 20's, Lichtenfeld made a clandestine trip to New York City to raise money for the eventual organization of the Jewish army. I'm not sure how he met Al but they did meet and Al told me that's when he began Krav Maga lessons from Lichtenfeld.

A couple of years later, in about 1940 or 1941, Al travelled to the Middle East, first by boat to England which was dangerous because of Nazi U-boats, and from there through practically half of Europe before he got to Turkey and then I think he said to Syria and Jordan and only then to the Palestine Mandate which wasn't that area of the Middle East called Israel yet. And here's the interesting part. Al was baby sitting two cannibalized aircraft with their parts separately packed in crates, destined to be the start of the new Jewish Air Force. Therefore, this air-force, an eventual Israeli Air-Force would consist of exactly two planes—those two. They were entrusted to Al, sent originally by a family of Jewish brothers who owned a machine shop in The Bronx. They were the Tishner brothers—Sammy, Earl, and two others.

When Al finally arrived with the crates in tow, he told me Lichtenfeld met him and it was Lichtenfeld who then had all the crates taken and loaded onto trucks by a waiting squad of men. For his efforts, Lichtenfeld gave Al about five or six more weeks of Krav Maga lessons. Al kept on practicing it on his own for a year with a Krav expert in New York City, in Manhattan, until he became equivalent to a Black Belt. I think Al said Krav Maga translates into 'combat-contact.' According to Al, like I said, it's reputed to be the most dangerous and more to the point, even the deadliest martial art.

Al said that when he arrived at Lichtenfeld's little workout spot, Lichtenfeld was already in Krav sessions with a British guy named Jimmy McKay and an American named Max Palace. Apparently, Lichtenfeld had a rule that if you wanted lessons from him in Krav Maga, he wanted to know why. In other words, you needed to have a pretty damn good reason for wanting to become a killing machine. Imi said Al told him why, this way:

"I live in a tough neighborhood in the southeast Bronx. Sometimes there are gangs that take things into their own hands. Know what I mean? Recently, house break-ins started happening. A house break-in means just that. A few guys break open your door and just like that take over your apartment. I have a girlfriend who's a teacher in a public school. We live together. She's in her thirties and gorgeous. Now as you can see I'm a pretty strong guy and I assure you, I'm not afraid of contact. But if there are three or four guys, that's another story. Whether you're home or not, anything of value is taken, and if any females are there such as a wife, or even a daughter, or even a mother, such girls or women would possibly not be safe from, you guessed it.

"So, if I'm a Krav Maga fighter, and then if anyone should break into my apartment, it would be too bad for them because after they break in, I don't want anyone to leave!"

Imi said he accepted Al immediately and that after Al gave that speech, Jimmy, Imi himself, and Max, laughed out loud. Apparently through their personal four-man Krav Maga in-group, they all became tight — like brothers.

*　*　*

The big burly guy, Ewald, announced in his thick German accent: "Look at hist picture again. He ist tall und erecting. He valking like in straight vay. He hast browna hor. Dis ist vhat day saying. When vee spotting him, even in dis daylight, I stopping car, vee jumping out, I knock him, und vee qvuickly carrying him into dis back seat. You sitting next to him. No ending his life. No shooting. No killing! Remembering, important ting — vee needing package. Vee driving right avay. It no mattering who day seeing because vee going like I saying — mit qvuick."

"But Ewald," answered Eduardo in his Spanish accent, "maybe he could fight good?"

"No, no! No one could fighting good after I hitting."

Eduardo listened and said: "But, Ewald, I still don't think you should have pushed the boy. I hear his screams after you push. I still hear it."

"You crazy, stupid?! Forgetting deese screams. He vould be vitness. He hearing code namen. I having not choice. It vas you. He hearing you saying dis code namen! You know never vee should say dis namen. So even den vee taking him mit uns vee vould sure later getting rid of him. I had to pushing him und you know dis — it vould look like suicide because no vone seeing dis. It vas nighttime, dark. So it looking like dis suicide. Vee never beating him. No mark. Only dis injury from suicide.

"Vee also knowing vhen uncle seeing dis, he knowing, und den giving dis package. Who else having dis package? Only boy's uncle — Ustacio wife broder. Dat ist vhat they told — dat it must be uncle. Sister, she Ustacio wife und Ustacio he having dis package. Vhen they killing him — und day torture good — Ustacio confessing dis package ist mit sister. So after sister die und so who you tink having package? Of course not sister's boy! He no have them. Uncle Travali. Frank Travali. Broder that who hast.

"Now vee concentrating of people — of people valking. Vhen vee see him, next minute vee having him, den next minute driving mit you sit in back nearing to him und he vill be out — knocked out — in back seat mit you. Now I driving. Vatch for police. Ist gun loaded? Making sure gun ist loaded."

*   *   *

In our car on the two-way street of Claremont and Washington, Mac had his eyes peeled on cars going east toward Fulton, and I was keeping close tabs on those going west toward Webster. We were all on duty now for about three and a half hours when suddenly when I was not at all expecting it, Mac grabbed my arm. Instead of keeping his eyes peeled on his side, he glanced for a moment to where I was looking on my side with cars heading west, first toward Brook, then Webster, and he gasped. "Frank, look, there they are. I'll bet."

I couldn't really see what he saw because that suspect car had already passed ours and I couldn't even get a glimpse of what the two men sitting in that car looked like. I could only see the back of their heads. But Mac quickly got Lyle on the intercom.

"Lyle, I think it's them. The car is a black Ford. It's going to reach Brook and you'll be able to see them right now in about three or four seconds. Two guys. The big one driving has a hair cut that I'll swear is not American. The sides are shaved like Europeans do — maybe like Germans do. I caught a glimpse only of the sides of his head because he's wearing a hat."

"Got it, Mac, got it. I see them. I think it could be but maybe not. The guy driving is a burly looking one and the other sitting next to him is taller. They're wearing hats. I'm now following them about two cars behind. I'm going to need Harry and Jack to take over because depending on which way they turn on Webster I'll turn off and go the other way. I'm calling Harry and Jack. They're on Webster and 172nd. If they turn toward them then Harry and Jack take over. We'll all keep tabs on it and take them down in a circle. If they turn toward 171st then we'll take them. Otherwise it's Harry and Jack on 172nd."

"Okay, everyone in all cars," Mac said into his intercom with urgency. "We'll know in a few seconds. I still see them. They're waiting for the light to change on Webster. There it is. Harry, Jack, they're on track toward you. You should pick them up in a few seconds. I'm betting they'll make a right on 172nd and head up to Washington. Let's take a chance. Calling all cars, converge at 172nd and Washington now. Right now! Block off anything going from Washington to Claremont."

Suddenly, we all became unified in a moment of intense alertness and without a doubt we were all feeling a common adrenaline rush. Later, Lyle later told us that Al calmly said: 'Man, oh man, is Gloria something?' Out of nowhere she sees it and now it looks like we got the guys. Now we'll see what's what!"

· 4 ·

JUST DESSERTS

Sure enough, four of the five police cars converged at 172nd Street and Washington Avenue encircling the car they had targeted. The fifth car came careening around the block practically crashing into Jack and Harry. All the cops were now in the street, guns drawn and demanding the two guys get out of the car, hands in the air—which they did—obediently on the orders to do so. They were immediately disarmed. Both were carrying guns.

They were separated and placed in two different cars. Lyle and Al took the taller slimmer one and sat him in the back of their car with two other cops who joined them, leaving their car right where it was—parked away from the sidewalk and into the street.

It was the same with the other burly guy who was put in the car with Mac and me sitting in front and with Jack and Harry who jumped into the back seat flanking our main man. Then two cops from the other cars each drove one of the abandoned police cars away.

Mac instantly said to me and to Jack and Harry: "Don't lay a finger on him. Not a finger!" He meant it. He knew what I was thinking. I was still jazzed-up by my adrenaline-rush. I could barely sit in my seat. Yet, at the same time, in contrast to our excitement in the car I noticed that within seconds of leaving the hectic scene of the capture, everything in the street was suddenly still. I mean that after the dust had cleared, everything at that intersection was again quiet with people left standing there who were staring at the mad scene, that was almost immediately abandoned. I imagined that probably no one could believe it actually happened.

The neighborhood, composed of nothing but four story typical Bronx apartment buildings seemed to be no worse for the wear—as though the buildings themselves weren't concerned—especially since, again, the event happened so fast that it may be that everyone simply wondered about it, thinking it was just another momentary but passing Bronx police extravaganza.

Not so in the cars with each of the suspects. None of us wondered about whether this was happening or whether it was a figment of some collective imagination. No one on our team considered these scumbags as suspects. We knew what we were carrying. It was the real McCoy. And the real McCoy was in my car, the one with Mac and me in the front and with Harry and Jack flanking him in the back—that mother-fucker who I knew pushed Willy.

Lyle and Al had the other one and two cops were flanking him in the back of their car. We had them. Oh man, did we have them! The truth is we were all tightly wound—especially me. He tried to kill Willy and was now after me. But now we had them! Especially, we had *him*!

The truth is that it really felt like I had them. But really the ultimate truth is that here and now, in one of these great American moments, we had this mother-fuckn' Nazi cocksuckn' scumbag—which of course is what they all are! And I kept thinking: he's the one who forced a kid out of a window and onto a third-floor ledge or maybe he scared the kid half to death so that Willy himself tried to escape out of the window, whatever. Either way, it was the big one who pushed Willy off the ledge. I saw it. And I wish someone could read my thoughts because believe me, we'll be getting information from him or the other one. Yes, we will. One way or another! And despite our instruction about not brutalizing them, the truth was I was sure we were all hoping our questioning would lead to the other. Man, oh man, did I wish that!

With this in mind, I knew that none of us could wait to get to the precinct, which was about seven or eight blocks away. Mac called Sgt. Silverstein at the desk and told him we were on our way and he wanted all newspaper men ushered into the back room usually set aside for appearances by the Chief of the precinct for announcements that would be of interest to crime reporters. These are the crime reporters who just hang around the precinct all day drinking coffee, eating sandwiches, and doughnuts and waiting for a story. And then Mac, almost as an afterthought said to Silverstein:

"We've got two. We're not going to book 'em. Not yet."

Silverstein answered: "ten/four." For me that meant that Silverstein understood it so that it was obvious that this non-booking situation had been done before.

* * *

Lyle's car and ours pulled in at about the same time. We marched both guys right in the front door of the precinct. Mac called two other cops to come with us down the stairs, to a room at the end of the long corridor. We all went in — Mac and me, the big guy, Harry and Jack who were flanking him in the car, two other cops who followed us, Lyle and Al, and the two cops flanking the taller guy in Lyle's car.

Once all eleven of us were in, Mac slammed the door shut and bolted it. He slammed it hard, and bolted it hard. It was a very loud angry statement. That's for sure. And I knew it was not lost on our two new friends.

The question was, was the big guy going to feel heroic enough to take us all on? It didn't take a genius to see that there were nine of us and only two of them — and the room was large. There wasn't a glimmer of a chance for any confusion about who was who and who needed to be taken down — hard! That was "A." "B," was that both of them, I was sure, knew that we were itching for them to get frisky — itching for it.

So, both guys just sat where they were told and behaved like perfect gentlemen. Good little Nazis who, without guns are nothing. Then Al started it all by challenging Mac. Al didn't care who heard it. And it was loud.

"Mac, just me and the big one. Let it happen."

Looking at the big burly one, Mac answered: "No, the guy's too big."

At that point I interrupted, walked over to Mac, pulled him aside and whispered: "Mac, I should've told you but I forgot. Al's a black belt Krav Maga guy — you know, that Jewish combat thing? I wouldn't worry about the size difference if I were you. Just-desserts, Mac. Just-desserts."

Then without whispering, Mac answers out loud: "That's not 'just-desserts, Frank. Just-deserts means like one thing is the same thing as another—like one thing equals another; like an eye for an eye. No that's not it. Just-desserts looks and sounds like the same thing but it's not the same thing. In order for this 'just-desserts' to be like equal for Willy, we'd need to knock off a hundred of these motha-fuckas—a thousand, a million. Get it? If we did that, then we'd be talking 'just' desserts'!"

Mac says this all while he's looking directly at the German. Two things to keep in mind: Of course, all of this was said inside that back room in the basement of the precinct and both the big guy and his taller partner were hearing it. Second, the truth was that I knew I personally couldn't take the big one. He had me by at least forty pounds and four inches. But with Al, the forty and four meant nothing. Al could take him apart. And if he wanted to, which I know he did, he would take him apart—slowly.

"Al, cool it," Mac answered. "I know what you have in mind. Not yet. Let's see how it all goes down?"

Then pointing to the big burly one, Mac started:

"You, what's your name?!"

"Ikh bin Evald. Mine nomen ist Evald Krauss. Ikh bin German."

I was a bit startled to hear him say that because I never expected this guy to be a talker, no less a cooperative one. Then I thought that I understood him. I felt he must be scared because he knows he's targeted for something bad especially if he suspects that we might think Willy was pushed and that he was the one who did it. But rather than beating around the bush, Mac went right to it. Looking directly down at the big guy who of course was sitting, Mac stated:

"We know you did it, so don't deny it. We know! Now, the first question is not: Did you do it? No. The first question is: Who sent you? The second question is: Why did they send you? and, are you ready for this third one? Why did *he* send you? And the last question is: Why did you push the kid? We know you did it. It was no suicide. We know."

The German looked like a deer in the headlights. He couldn't figure how anyone could know. Of course, it was easy to figure. I saw him. I saw him push Willy. He never saw me. The German was faltering. He was at a loss for words, not knowing what to say. The taller guy used the pause. He stepped in and short circuited whatever plan Mac had in mind. No doubt both of these guys—the only ones sitting on chairs while the nine of us were standing there looking down at them—sensed they either were in store for permanent jail here in New York City, maybe even in this jail in

The Bronx, or maybe worse. They had no doubt not that they *could*, but that they *would* for sure be beaten to death.

So, the taller guy started: "Excuse me. My name is Eduardo. I am Eduardo Velaro. I am South American. From Argentina. Yes, you are right. Someone sent us. And it was as you say, yes, it was someone. But we do not know who this is. We never got name and we never meet him. They give money to get package from family of Mister Ustacio Travali. We know Ustacio Travali not killed by this person because he has other men to do it. I think the one you are after, but we never see him, we never meet him. Only his men. Two men who give us money. One to me and one to Senor Ewald here. But they never tell who it is—who is the one you need.

"I will tell you everything. I am with family. Two children and wife, Isabella. I am in service of President Juan Peron of Argentina. I am in secret service now for three years. President Peron sent for me because I stop someone want to kill him. He tell me he will make me rich. Yes, he said that to me, that I will be rich. He told I would be contact by some-one and I would get this instruction from him and also money. He said I and other man would be coming to place in America to look for package President Peron want me to bring to him. Then Ewald come to me they and tell Ewald and me what we do and where we go.

"Package not belong to Mr. Ustacio family. It stole by them. People who give the money give instruction when to come with package so we have more of money. I tell you how much it is. First, they give Senor Ewald and me, ten thousand dollars—each. One to me and one to Ewald. Prom-ise when come with package get same again. That is why here we come. You see, I will tell everything."

Meanwhile, while Eduardo was talking, the big guy, Ewald was listen-ing intently but I could see he was looking around carefully checking the positions of everyone in the room as though the most important thing to him was to gain some advantage. Of course, I felt that whatever this big guy said or did was not to be trusted. It seemed to me that the taller guy, Eduardo Velaro, would be ready to make any deal—President Peron or no President Peron!

I also figured that the only advantage the German could have was if he somehow was able to get hold of someone's gun. As far as I could tell, the only people in the room with guns were Mac, Lyle, and the other cops. I wasn't sure about Al. He might have had a firearm. I wouldn't have put it past him. But, if it came to that it made it—two against nine.

I gave myself the job of making sure I could prevent any lunge toward either Mac or Lyle by this Ewald Germ. That's a good one—Germ for German. If that melee happened I would make a grab for his leg, floor him, and break it. That's the only quick leverage I could have—break his leg. That would stop it on the spot no matter how big and strong he was. After that either Al, Mac, or Lyle, or some combination of the cops would make sure everything became copacetic.

I was also certain that as much as the Argentine wanted to escape, he was too smart to try it. He would be the one to make the deal and tell us whatever we wanted. He surely must have realized, that his cooperation, already in evidence, was more valuable than any other cute thing he might try. He wasn't going to jump into any melee. This was not the kind of attempted jail break that he would ever buy into. It was obvious; he knew his best bet was to be a good boy—a very good cooperative one.

'Keep glued to Ewald' was my only focus.

"That's good," Mac answered the Argentinean. "Keep talking."

"I vould telling you dis same ting," Ewald interrupted. "I vould telling you dis same ting."

"Okay, then tell me something you think I might be interested in," Mac insisted.

"I also secret service, Berlin. I RHSA main security office. In German, dis secret service namen ist: 'Reichssicherheitshauptamt.' Herrr Velaro und me, vee just vanting package und den vee going Buenos Aires. Dis ist all. Und den like Herr Velaro saying, vee getting more ten tousand dollar—vone fur him, und vone fur me."

"You guys are stalling," Mac announced. "You haven't given us any hard information. Everything is general. What's in the package? What's so important there? I think you know, you're saying everything but telling us no details. The details need to be specific. Get it? Specific! Now you, Ewald, what's in the package?"

"Okay, I am knowing only vone ting. Dis package halfn informatzie auf namens und platzes in dis vorld on dis list. Dat ist all I knowing."

"I said be specific. What names and what places?"

"I also don't know names—but many names are in papers," the Argentinean blurted out. "But I hear names of places. I hear President Peron say:

'Buenos Aires,' and also 'Sao Paulo'. Sao Paulo, of course, this is Brazil. He say this when he talk about package with papers. He say papers they come from Germany, his job to keep papers safe in Palace in Buenos Aires — in Palace. In Palace is place to be guarded. Two guards to guard room with papers. All guards in Argentina secret service. These guards, I know all them. President Peron say when I come back with package then I will be head of guards of this package."

"Okay," Mac continued. "We all know that Peron was always with Hitler and Mussolini? You also know this, right?"

"Yes, bueno," Eduardo answered. "Peron was a Fascisti. Even when war and even when finished, many Nazis make trip to Buenos Aires. President Peron with wife, Evita, meet them. She too, loved Nazi. These people keep to come more to Buenos Aires before war finished. Start to come Buenos Aires 1943, 1944, 1945, 1946, even to now, 1958. In secret service, we always looking after them. Job is to make comfortable. This is what I can tell you."

At that point, this talkative Argentinean stopped and turned his gaze on Mac.

"Okay, that's good on specifics and details," Mac said. Al piped in. He obviously couldn't hold himself back.

"Sorry, Mac. I gotta get to Willy."

"Hold it Al. I can feel it. Your getting itchy. Just hold it. I'll do the talking."

After Mac said that, then Al calmed down, stopped talking, as Mac continued.

"Okay Herr Ewald Krauss, why did you push the kid."

"No, I never push boy. He jumping."

"First major mother-fuckn' lie," I shouted. Like Al, I couldn't keep it in.

"That's a lie because I saw you do it, mother-fucker. That's right. I saw it."

"Nein, it vas dark. No vone could seeing! Boy jumping out on dis outside of building und he saying to jumping. He vould jumping. He saying to jumping."

"You lyin' mother-fuckn' rat-bastard. Yeah, he was on the outside of the building because either you put him there or he jumped out onto the ledge to get away from you. And he was too far away from the fire-escape so that I knew you were in the living room with him and not in the bedroom.

I live there too. I know which window is for which room. That's why he couldn't get to the fire escape. So, he had no choice. Either he'd be badly beaten by you, you scumbag fuck, or the only other choice he had was to get out of the room. That's when you pushed him. When he was standing on the ledge. I saw it from across the street. And you'd better tell us something important that you haven't said yet or you might die a bad death right here and now and I mean it. I'll say it in German: Toten!"

When I said that last word none of us standing there even flinched. And even if not one of us understood German, we all knew that when I said "toten," it was the German word for 'dead.' All nine of us were glaring at him. We could all see that as far as he was concerned, he was hearing the threat ringing in his ears. That was a moment of truth for him because I instantly had the thought that no matter how he believed his loyalty and fidelity to the Nazi cause was unshakable, at this moment, right now, he realized just how shakable it really was.

It's the old wisdom that nothing focuses the mind as much as an impending hanging, and there was no doubt that with Mac, Al, and especially me standing there—not even counting the rest of the guys—he would probably, at the moment, be quite focused.

The Argentinean stepped in again. It was clear to me and likely everyone else, that whenever the Argentinean stepped in, things seemed to calm down.

"Okay, okay. I think I tell you something more. You see, President Peron tell Evita, his wife and dos friends he trust that living in Vatican is Bishop. Bishop very important man to Nazis. This in Vatican, Rome. Yes, it is Bishop is important man. Bishop I hear President Peron say exact, setecientos pasaportes para setecientos Nazis en Germany who need safe place from Europa. This is meaning seven hundred para seven hundred. This is people need safe place in away to live for all years. This if the war they lose.

"President Peron say more come later this setecientos pasaportes para to running no to be executed for thesa war crime. President Peron say many places for to be safe for these men. I remember Peron word exact. He told places: Argentina, Brazil, also Uruguay, Paraguay, Chile. For sure he say this countries. Ah, yes, y Syria, y Egypt. This I know. I hear. Also, I hear President Peron say el Bishop name by code—only people by code calling him 'H.A.' This man who people say is 'Ghost of Rome,' he is in Vatican.

Si, he is called by name H.A. This Ghost, H.A., he control mission here, we come for it, Ewald and me. Like I say it, this Ghost has passports, pasaportes. He is knowing to have people to travel to the safe places.

"I know when President Peron say this thing, papers in package for sure are their names y place now you want to know. Ewald and me we should bring package to Argentina to Palace of President Peron y names y places of these things would ever not to be discover. Para this they give ten thousand dollars to me and same to senor Krauss."

After that declaration, we all stared at him for a few moments. It was obvious we were all thinking the same thing. We were all convinced that whatever he said was true. We now felt we had the motive for it all and on top of that we had this twist of a ghost thing with the initials H.A. The whole thing was starting to look like a much bigger deal than we originally thought. In other words, they were coming to get the package even if it meant killing a few people—including a kid.

Who the hell was this guy, this so-called Ghost, H.A.? Was he still operating this shipping department from Germany to South America and the Middle East? How many, if any of the seven hundred has he already placed? Of those he got out, assuming any did, who are they and where are they even now about a dozen years after the war?

But before we could even begin a new phase of investigation, Mac told Lyle to call off the cemetery stakeout and to kill it in the morgue as well. When he said "kill it in the morgue as well," Al looked at me with eyebrows lifted. Then Al said it:

"We've gotta get that package, and we've gotta talk to someone I have in mind, who could be just the right person to understand more about all of this."

"Like who, Al?" I asked.

"To a guy who's always interested in this business of escaped Nazi war criminals. His name's Simon Wiesenthal."

Looking at Al, Mac kind of impatiently said: "Simon Wiesenthal? Do you know him? How do you know him? I mean is he a diplomat or a journalist, or maybe a cop? Or have you just heard about him? Better yet, if you know him or not, it doesn't matter. The only thing that matters is if you know how to contact him? Right?

"Okay, Al, can we get him? Who's Simon Wiesenthal?"

"He's a guy who went through the concentration camps during the war and lost family members. He, himself, escaped getting shot or gassed by a hair, and probably on more than one occasion. He's now known as a Nazi hunter. I'm going to call a friend of mine in London. He's actually M-16. He'll know how to contact Wiesenthal.

$\cdot 5 \cdot$

LICHTENFELD TO WIESENTHAL

In the forward basement area of the Precinct where we interrogated both guys were three isolation cells. Mac and Lyle decided to put Ewald Krauss, 'the pusher,' into one of them. But first, he was finally booked. He would be guarded twenty-four/seven. The other one, the Argentinean who gave us that last piece of invaluable information was brought upstairs, booked, and placed in a cell on the second floor of the Precinct. He too, would be guarded twenty-four/seven. Under Mac's orders, they were not to be touched.

Nothing had been decided about how we were going to deal with 'the pusher.' Mac wouldn't say it when Al or I was present, but I kind of knew that his intent was of course to follow what he had to follow; 'the pusher' was going on trial.

Mac was tough but every cop should be like him—a stand-up guy.

But I had other ideas—especially about 'the pusher.' What I didn't say out loud to Mac was that 'the pusher' might go to trial only if he was still breathing. I didn't need to share that thought with Al because, in all likelihood, he probably had that same sentiment.

The issue now was to get to this Wiesenthal guy. For that, Al needed to get in touch with our Krav Maga magician, Imi Lichtenfeld. In telling me about his experience with Lichtenfeld, Al mentioned that immediately after the war, Lichtenfeld, in addition to training Jews in the Krav Maga killing methods which Lichtenfeld, of course, called self-defense, he was especially interested in finding Nazis who were hiding from allied investigators or instead, were secluded and protected by governments. That's plural. It's plural because the governments of Germany, Austria, Argentina, Syria, and even the United States, plus some others, were keeping these individuals who were guilty of war crimes, safe. Various motives were in play. Some governments were keeping them safe because of: a) similar Nazi sentiments of the government; b) financial payoffs; c) for their scientific usefulness; or, d) simply not interested in devoting any money, time, or effort to return to that miserable time.

Of course, these motives were not what was motivating Al or me, and certainly wouldn't interest Lichtenfeld. And further, Al, assured us that such stuff would never interest or persuade Wiesenthal.

I later got the story that in his pursuits, Lichtenfeld was introduced to Mr. Wiesenthal. Apparently, Wiesenthal had quickly developed a reputation for keeping diaries and records of Nazis who were responsible for horrible crimes against humanity—especially against Jews.

Now, it was 1958 and Wiesenthal was already about fifty. He had survived about seven or eight concentration and extermination camps and made it his mission get them—each and every one of them. He wouldn't rest until he did—if he could. One didn't need to read Wiesenthal's mind or try to imagine what his thoughts and fantasies were to see what he was up to; that is, apparently, it was known that Weisenthal would hold forth about wanting to get them all. But that's still too general. To be specific, he wanted them all either dangling from ropes or burning in crematoria. However, practically speaking, he was realistically going to try and locate as many as he could, and in the end, put them all on trial.

Al said that Wiesenthal shared this inspirational vendetta with Lichtenfeld. In turn, Lichtenfeld was a highly interested listener. Therefore, since Al knew Lichtenfeld personally, then the way to get to Wiesenthal was for Al to first contact Lichtenfeld. Ultimately, and not surprisingly, as it turned out, Wiesenthal was a big fan of Lichtenfeld's.

So now, Al was planning the contact with Lichtenfeld. Licthtenfeld was a few years older than Al; Al in his early forties, Lichtenfeld in his late forties. Lichtenfeld's given name was Emrich from which came his shortened or nickname, Imi. Among other similarities between both men was one that underpinned the physical contact interest they both shared. For example, Al was a terrific boxer and Imi had the same interest in boxing and somewhere in Europe he even won some titles—Al says, as a middleweight.

Importantly, they both hated the Nazis; Lichtenfeld escaped them in Europe and made his way to what was then the Palestine Mandate. Al escaped the Nazis because of the best possible reason: He was born in America! It was for many reasons, therefore, that Al and Imi became great friends. Simply stated, they were like-minded.

Al had to get Imi to listen to this story regarding someone in the Vatican, maybe a Bishop whose code name was, H.A., and who is probably in charge of creating a pathway for Nazi war criminals to escape legal judgment and consequent punishment for crimes against humanity. Yet, when I say 'Nazi war criminals,' I begin to get the sense that I'm being redundant. I mean if you're a Nazi, aren't you a criminal?

In any event, Mac, Lyle, and I, had a meeting with Al. I asked Al the first question.

"Al, would it be possible that Wiesenthal himself might have heard about some ghost-guy with the initials H.A.? And the same for Lichtenfeld. Could they already know about all this stuff. So, what now?"

Mac then said what already was in the air:

"Now we've gotta get a budget from the department, then deputize Al here to travel to wherever Lichtenfeld lives—probably somewhere in Israel—and try to get some traction investigating this mess. You ready to travel, Al?"

"Budget or not, absolutely I'm going to find Lichtenfeld."

"Me too," I piped in. "Me too, even if I have to pay for it outta my own pocket."

"Listen Frankie, no good. You've gotta stay here. For Willy," Al immediately answered.

"No—Gloria for Willy," I answered. "Right, Al? Gloria for Willy."

"Okay, good idea. It's good. She'll even insist on it," Al said. "Frankie, but you too. You've gotta be with Willy. Don't argue."

"Before the budget gets approved," Mac interrupted, "and before arrangements are made to travel, we've gotta get back to the hospital and speak to Dr. Mehta. Also, we need to figure a way to talk to Willy."

"Could very well be the doctor has suggestions," I piped in again. It was my fervent hope and maybe my optimism doing the talking—hoping the doctor will tell us that Willy'll be okay.

Mac then called the hospital and was informed that Dr. Mehta was having rounds later at the hospital. Of course, on Mac's orders Willy was transferred back to Montefiore as soon as we caught those loose canons. He was still in the same condition and was comfortable and breathing normally although remaining unconscious.

While Mac was beginning to make arrangements for money to fund Al's trip and also to officially endow him with New York City official police ID, Al was beginning to figure how to locate Lichtenfeld.

But all this was in the thinking phase. At the moment, our first and very immediate focus was the hospital and the meeting with Dr. Mehta, the brain specialist.

* * *

Al was the only one on the team absent. He was busy with doing who knows what, in order to plan his trip to meet with Imi Lichtenfeld. Now the team included Al's representative—his Gloria. And she was good. Along with Gloria in the waiting room at Montefiore Hospital, we were eager to hear what Dr. Mehta had to say. And before we knew it, in he stepped.

"Hello. I know who you all are. It's for Willy Travali. I'm Dr. Sitaram Mehta. First, Willy's okay. I want to tell you that first. Willy will, in my opinion recover. Let's not waste time with introductions. I see you all as one strong unit and that tells me that Willy's reference group makes him also strong.

"Originally we thought he may have suffered what is known as Locked-In Syndrome. That kind of disorder is serious and involves a problem in the brainstem. There's no need for me to explain the ins and outs of Locked-In. We're sure he does not have it, and the same goes for MCA, meaning Minimal Conscious State. As an aside, Locked-In Syndrome was first described in the novel *The Count of Monte Cristo* by Alexandre Dumas, where the victim suffered a stroke and learned to communicate by blinking his eyes. So, thankfully, that's now out of the question.

"Along with the series of broken bones and other problems that Dr. Fishman detailed to you, you should know that Willy is also suffering with a right pneumothorax which simply means he has a right lung collapse. That too, will heal itself and the lung will gradually reflate. He has fractures of the long bones of the arm and leg as well as a pelvic fracture—a single fracture, only one. These will also heal.

"If you hear anything about a vegetative state, please disregard it. It does not apply at all to Willy. Further, there is no fracture of the skull. However, he is badly bruised all over the front of his body and he's in some pain. Again, this will abate. Willy is now on pain medication which also accounts for his deep, relieving sleep.

"The only other diagnosis that occurred to me to investigate would have been what's known as akinetic mutism. I thought of it originally when I saw him because he couldn't talk and couldn't move. This is usually caused by a frontal lobe injury that Willy does not exhibit. Therefore, I am ruling out akinetic mutism.

"So that leaves us with a young boy who is badly beaten up with broken bones, a collapsed lung and a number of other things that will require surgery, but not neurosurgery. Having said all that, I must say with all that has happened to him, Willy is a lucky boy. He'll will become quite familiar with Dr. Fishman for surgery on his knee and chin and he's going to be seeing the hospital dental service to replace a few teeth. The Chief of Service of the pulmonary department will monitor the lung reflation process.

"I believe it will be another day or two before Willy fully comes around so please do not worry if he's not immediately responding. All in all, Willy will be the champion patient of the hospital and I can assure you all the nurses will adore him. But he will be here for a while. I think about at least two months. By the way, I have also heard about Miss Messer here."

For the first time, Dr. Mehta stopped his soliloquy and, bowing slightly to Gloria said:

"How do you do. From what I've been told of your presence here, should you decide to become either a nurse or a doctor, please see me for the stellar reference I plan writing on your behalf."

At that, the mood lightened. We all laughed and hugged.

Dr. Mehta asked if we had any questions? We all shook our heads 'no,' and after saying it was good to meet us and that we could consult with him at any time, he then bid us a gentle farewell and walked out past the officers who were on duty at the door of Willy's room.

We were all relieved but choked up at the same time. Gloria and I had tears running shamelessly down our cheeks. We were laughing as we were crying. Gloria said she would visit Willy every day after her school day was over and would keep the police and Willy company. The two cops stationed there smiled as they shook hands with me, Mac, and Lyle, and kissed Gloria.

Mac then said it: "Willy's gonna be fine and guess what? He's gonna tell us where he deep sixed the package!"

*   *   *

Now we were eager to see what Al was up to. We knew that whatever it was, it would be about his impending trip overseas. There's not a chance in the world of Al not being able to arrange that kind of thing. Something told me he was probably already in touch with Imi Lichtenfeld or very close to it. The objective, of course, was to have Imi link up with Wiesenthal. Al was pretty sure that Imi could and would make that connection.

With that, Al walked into the room. Everyone started speaking at once, as we were all glad to see him. Gloria put her arms around him and he raised his hands signaling everyone should quiet down.

"I can feel it. Willy's gonna be alright. Right?"

"Absolutely right," Gloria answered. "Absolutely right."

Then I launched into telling Al in shorthand what Dr. Mehta had told us. Al was looking at me solemnly, but you could see he was very relieved and of course, very happy.

"Okay," he began. "Let's go to the cafeteria downstairs where we can talk."

Before we left, we all looked at Willy — still unconscious — and wished him a peaceful night. Both cops remained as we walked out and took the elevator down to the hospital cafeteria. The cafeteria manager saw us, and made it easy by taking our orders at the table instead of us needing to get on line. Everyone ordered coffee and the manager sent doughnuts and Danishes to the table. He'd heard about Willy, plus he knew who we were and was exceedingly courteous and accommodating.

As we got settled, Al started.

"I've decided to head for London. Made a transatlantic phone call to that agent I know pretty well who, like I said, is with British Secret Service — M-16, the military security agency of the government. It's Jimmy McKay, Frank. He's the guy I told you I trained with when Lichtenfeld worked with us teaching Krav Maga. We became really close friends. I realized he's the guy who'd know how to reach Imi. He told me that at the moment he's on a case but at first didn't describe it to me. He asked for a hint about why I needed to see him so I said: 'hidden package with never released information about something from the 1942 Wannsee Conference, and something about a guy we're calling a ghost who sent some assassins here to get the package.' After I said that he started laughing. I asked him what was so funny and he said: 'I'll bet you'll never guess what I'm about to say. Here it is: 'Me too! I'm looking for the same thing.'

"You see, Frankie, M-16, like I said is British Secret Service but it's under the umbrella of what they call *Ultra*. Ultra controls the projects of various cells of the whole British Secret Service. And Ultra seems to know everything—especially focused on Europe. Our *CIA* is the equivalent, more or less to their *Ultra*. At around 1947 a lotta guys from our *OSS—Office of Strategic Services*—transferred into the *CIA* that was then formed.

"So, when Jimmy said that, Frank, I almost flipped. We've tapped into something that's on the same wave-length. I think Jimmy is looking for whatever is in that package.

"Unreal," I said. Unreal!"

"I'm leaving tomorrow afternoon—TWA Flight 71 from Idlewild." Al continued. "I also told Jim that we got the assassins and one of them, an Argentinean, implicated Juan Peron for doing something with hundreds of passports."

Jimmy almost choked and said: "Al, not hundreds, thousands. I'll give you the info when you arrive."

"So, Jimmy's picking me up at Heathrow Airport," Al again continued, "and from there I have no idea where we're going. And here's the kicker. Jim's arranging it so that the pilot of the plane will grease it all for me so no waiting anywhere. Jimmy knows him well."

"Al, I'm already worried. I don't want you to go," Gloria said, concerned.

"I know hon. I know. But I also know you know. Okay?!"

That ended the discussion but Al looked at Mac and Lyle. "Guys, I'll keep you continually posted. In the meantime, the minute Willy wakes and after you orient him about what his condition is, then get the location of the package. When you do, and after you find it, call me transatlantic and give me a blow by blow about whatever the hell the secrets are in the package. Jimmy's hungry for it too."

As Al was talking, I knew he had taken the bull by the horns and it was foolish for me to think I would be going with him. He knew I needed to be with Willy and so off he went doing the Al thing. And poor Gloria. It's tough being attached to someone doing police work. That's for sure. But Al's not really a cop; just a private detective. Gloria's not his wife, and besides, Al's very tough. Gloria knows this. They're so close that she might as well be his wife—which I think very soon she will be. Therefore, she knows Al inside out and knows that Al would never shy away from physical contact. So, again, she worries. And that's why I think: 'poor Gloria.' Al's off to London and who knows what then?'

PART 2

LONDON TO ROME

·6·

JIMMY McKAY

Al walked off the plane at Heathrow and stepped right into a black British limo parked fifty feet away from where the plane landed. Jimmy McKay was in the back seat. The driver waited patiently behind the wheel. Al and Jim locked on with broad smiles, and shook hands. Jimmy was as usual his usual strong, self-confident self. Could have been an action-figure—tall, trim, dark, and yes, handsome. Very.

Later, Al told me the whole story.

Jimmy got right to it.

"So, what is it you have?"

Then Al laid it on.

"Like I said on the phone, Jim, we're on to something both important and no doubt, dangerous. These two guys, one a German, the other an Argentinean are after the package. They threw a twelve-year old kid off a third story ledge of his apartment house. I think they did it as bait for the package. I'll spell it out for you later. I know the kid and the family. I'm close with them—like you and me. The kid's gonna survive and there's no brain damage but he's banged up pretty bad. He's unconscious and only he knows where the package is. That's the essence of the whole thing. We also got the guys to tell us about passports that Peron from Argentina had supplied to someone. The Argentinean said there are seven hundred passports."

"Like I said on the phone, Al, it's not seven hundred. It's more like five thousand passports. They're actually visas. Yes, you heard it right. Five thousand. What we know is that there's someone at The Vatican—we could easily call him a ghost. Whoever he is, he's running the show. We know that this ghost and his crew have been trying to protect about five thousand Nazi criminals—war-crime types. Imagine, five thousand? I'm guessing that the seven hundred you heard about may have been the beginning of it all. They started with seven hundred but it's now five thousand. That's right, maybe even more. We don't know how many it really is! You believe that? It's thirteen years after the war and they're still at it. We know that this ghost and his crew are still shuttling these bastards all over the place. Some are settled and of course, undercover. We can't find them but others we almost get and before you know it, they're gone. This *ghost* must be getting information from the inside or from somewhere, but we can't figure it."

"So, who's the ghost? Do you have any idea?"

"No, not yet. How about you? Did these guys you caught, say anything?"

"Yeah, they mentioned something about a Bishop, so that we're thinking it's a Bishop at the Vatican. They also said something about a code. The code is: H.A. Ring a bell?"

"No, it doesn't. I doubt it could be someone's initials. Too simple."

"Right. But first things first. We need to get to Imi. He must know something. Then we need to get to Wiesenthal, Simon Wiesenthal."

"Al, I know about Wiesenthal. But I'm guessing that for what you're going to need, Wiesenthal might not be the right person. First of all, he doesn't get involved with action. He's strictly an information guy. He's definitely a Nazi hunter but not in the way you may be thinking about what needs to be done, and then what actually will be done. Let's face it. This is going to lead to assassinations—and who knows how many?"

"So," Al slowly asked, "if not Wiesenthal, then who?"

"You're going to need some contingent of *NAKAM*," Jimmy answered. "Let me explain it. You see NAKAM was formed right after the war in April 1946. It was known as *Dam Yuhudi Nakam*, meaning '*Jewish Blood Will Be Avenged.*' Eventually it was referred to as *Abba Kovner's Avengers*, or the *Hanakam Group* which translated into *Vengeance 11*. And these guys made a name for themselves. We studied it specifically at M-16, Section 6. I know some of the main names of the Kovner group. Eventually there were a bit more than fifty guys in the group. At first, they would go around shooting known SS guards and accomplished a lot of assassinations.

"But even though this Avner Kovner was jailed, his idea was so persuasive among these other Jewish liberated prisoners from the concentration camps that, as you know, groups like the *United Partison Organization* known as *Fareynikte* Partizaner Organizatsye, and *Nakmim*, the *Jewish Brigade in British Palestine*, also in 1945, quickly formed. *NAKAM*, 'Revenge' is the acronym: *Jewish Blood will be avenged.*

"First, police found known high-ranking Nazis shot in the head, the professional assassination way. Then NAKAM also left them strangled to death. Then they became known as *DIN* meaning *Judgment*. So, as you can tell, these guys weren't fooling around. Each and every one of them lost family and they were after blood. It became worse when the news finally broke that the count of Jews listed in the extermination camps and firing squads reached six million dead or even more. The tabulation was from lists the Nazis kept but they knew that the lists weren't complete, especially because of the mass shootings pre-gas chambers. They figured it must be more than the six million; more like maybe even close to seven million.

"Then they decided that assassinations one by one was inefficient—even ridiculous. They looked for a way to knock off maybe hundreds, maybe thousands with one or two shots. So, some of Kovner's men took jobs at the *Langwasser Internment Camp* near Nuremberg as cooks. Believe it or not, this camp held fifteen-thousand high ranking SS men, Gestapo and Secret Service Nazi prisoners. Some were formerly guards at concentration camps ferrying Jews into the gas chambers and wantonly killing Jewish women and children as well. The aim of Kovner's guys was to poison the loaves of bread with arsenic. And we're here talking about more than three-thousand loaves of bread.

"They went through with it and managed to sicken hundreds but only three-hundred or so actually died. Then the cooks disappeared. But Kovner thought up another biggie. This one was a dilly. But that's when Kovner was jailed, because he was caught with forged papers.

"Al, you still with me?" Jimmy asked.

"What are you kidding? Of course. Keep goin'."

"Okay. Kovner would not be outdone by anyone. His plan was to kill six million Germans by poisoning the water supply in Berlin, Weimar, Nuremburg, Munich, and Hamburg. According to Kovner it would be six-million for six-million. But I believe it was after Kovner was jailed that one of his men, a Shmuel Kishnov came up with what he thought was a better idea which was quickly adopted by the entire Kovner group—as well as by Kovner himself who voted for it from jail.

"At that point one of the men, Yitzhak Avidav took over the leadership of this little in-group composed of guys like: Bezalel Michaeli, Israel Carmi, Robert Grossman, Dov Goren, Rozka Korezak, and Vika Kempner. I'll admit to you, Al, I admire these guys. Guts! That's what they had. Guts! But then came the ace in the hole. Even though that guy, Shmuel Kishnov, was in the background of the group, the insiders knew was 'the thinker'. I have it on good information—meaning on stated debriefings that *Ultra* has in its files—that this Kishnov made extensive proclamations about the entire situation.

"He said something that each one of Kovner's men unanimously agreed with. Concerning the idea of six-million for six-million that Kovner thought was equitable, Kishnov had a second thought that I personally, when I think about it, sounds right—especially when I think about what those V-2 rockets did to London. So, when I heard about it I must confess, it excited me. This guy Kishnov's idea was mathematical. Why kill just six-million Germans when the six-million Jews killed were one-third of all Jews in the world? He argued that if fair is fair, wouldn't that perhaps mean one-third of the German population also had to go. And one-third of sixty-million equals twenty-million. He thought that would be more like it. And he further proclaimed that with this calculus in his mind *and* in his heart, he knew that that would be true justice; a judicious and mathematical analogous eye-for-an-eye.

"But even that didn't end his thinking or satisfy him. Apparently, he felt, when he first heard about Kovner's plan, that just as Dresden, within the German state of Saxony was flattened by American and British bombers, that in addition to twenty-million Germans dead by his calculation, how about flattening every major German city, just for good measure? And that's what he meant by more than one eye for one eye. Obviously, this guy, Shmuel Kishnov was great in mathematics but also very angry. Wouldn't you say?

"But then he went even further. He discussed what the idea of 'critical-mass' meant. He said that when a population reaches a low point of its critical-mass, it may no longer be a viable population and perhaps no longer multiply into a growing population. In that case he reasoned, Hitler put the future of the Jewish people at risk with only twelve-million remaining, and in that case, we should similarly put the German population at risk as well, with another forty-million or so killed. For them, having only ten or twenty-million left would probably amount to such a critical-mass.

"Al, I believe that Kishnov had these ideas because the plan to poison the water supply of these states never came off. And further, he was predicting that the Nazi anti-Jewish agenda would be passed on from one generation to another just as religion is passed on from one generation to another. He felt it couldn't be stopped. Even if the German government might turn out be a democratic one with respect to voting and individual rights of its citizens, in the hearts and minds of individual Germans, the anti-Jewish poison had already soaked into their bones and into every fiber of their bodies. Therefore, he felt that Germany should be cannibalized, fractured into parts and distributed here and there to the allies. And yes, never be permitted to become industrial.

"And here comes the big one, Al. Kishnov came to the conclusion, after Truman dropped those atomic bombs on Japan, it might have been the wrong country to target. Kishnov said Truman missed his chance! Know what I mean? And I personally find that kind of hypothetical truly interesting."

At that point Jimmy almost ended but not quite. "You see," Jimmy continued, "to simplify it, Kishnov was not fooling around. He meant every word and he was entirely obsessed with his mission. "So, Kishnov added: 'We—all of us in this quest—are living in the Kovner tradition.'

"So, Al, whatya think?"

* * *

"Yeah," Al answered. "I know a lotta Jewish men feel like that. The women are different. They don't feel it that way. Women stay with the hurt feelings about what happened and suffer with it. But it stops there. Men, on the other hand, especially if they're part of the group that's been made to feel helpless and then eviscerated, can take it to where Shmuel

Kishnov took it. These kinds of men want revenge—want blood. Some take it down to six for six, others take in further to one-third for one-third, and still others like Kishnov take it to the critical mass of forty-million. Basically, what I think is that it's good to contemplate Kishnov's thinking about the whole thing.

"But, at the moment, Jim, and in the minimalist example of the Kovner tradition, we're starting to take care of business so far *only* with the guys we caught. That means two guys, not the multiples Kovner was considering. And these two are talking. In fact, the Argentinean also said he heard that countries are listed in the package. Something big's happening Jimmy. Huge. Sounds to me that this ghost and his group—I agree, it's gotta be a group—are replacing people or planning to place them in these countries. But how do you place five thousand? Right?"

"Right," Jimmy responded. "I think the first thing we've got to do is contact this guy of the Roman Curia—inside the Vatican. He's an Irish Catholic priest—senior member of the Roman Curia. He knows me. We've spoken a few times. He did me a favor once, I did him one. It's Hugh O'Flaherty.

"During the war O'Flaherty single handedly managed to help both Jews and allied soldiers escape. I'm talking British and American prisoners but mostly those that were stranded—not yet captured. He got a lot of Jews out too. Like I said, he's an Irish guy. And I don't mean one or two that he helped escape. We're talking literally, hundreds, maybe even more. That's right. It was called *The O'Flaherty Rome-Escape-Line.* You believe that? One guy. And he did it all. And he had to deal with Kappler—that's Herbert Kappler, the Gestapo head of Rome. O'Flaherty did it right under Kappler's nose. And Kappler was no joke. Evil, man—evil! Everyone was afraid of him. O'Flaherty then got help from others—actually, other priests. One was from New Zealand, a Father Snedden. The other, I think his name was Father Flanagan. Yes, John Flanagan.

"O'Flaherty had these escapees holed up all over the place and all over Rome. Safe houses. It's a long story, but after the war when Kappler was already in prison, wait till you hear this: O'Flaherty actually converted him to Catholicism. Would even visit him in prison.

"Then, I also needed to visit Kappler in prison because he had information about a case I was working. He accepted my visit and he

told me that he cried when O'Flaherty offered him forgiveness even
though Kappler posted notices during the war that the apprehension of
O'Flaherty would be rewarded. It made me believe that this conversion
stuff is strong. Of course, at that time during the war, O'Flaherty was
doing it all from some invisible place. No one could find him. Was he
hidden within the Vatican or not? No one knew and the bet was on that
Kappler was going to get him. But Kappler never did. No one ever ratted
O'Flaherty out. No one!

"To top it off, O'Flaherty's nemesis within the Vatican was the notorious
Bishop Hudal. Alois Hudal. Hudal was a real Nazi lover. But O'Flaherty
is himself a treasure-trove of information. So, Al, O'Flaherty—he's the
one we've got to see first. He's not in hiding anymore. Ha. Right? It's 1958
not 1943. Let's go get him. I happen to know he has a good relationship
with Imi, and after the war they had a lot of contact."

"Jim, whatya mean, 'let's go get him.' You mean go to Rome?"

"Right. We've got to visit him where he lives—at the Vatican. And
believe me, it's a bee hive over there. The Vatican is pervaded with what
O'Flaherty identified as Group 1—priests, cardinals, bishops, and others—who are still arch conservatives in the sense of retaining their fascist
ideological commitment. And Hudal is number one of number one. See
what I mean? But also, and in contrast, there are the O'Flaherty's—actually many—who were called Group 2, and they're in a constant struggle
with this Group 1. The struggle is for dominance and an always striving goal for a more compelling influence at the Vatican is the constant
refrain."

Before Al knew it, the call to O'Flaherty was made and after the quick
flight to Rome they were pulling up to where O'Flaherty lived; a small but
beautiful townhouse/hotel outside the walls of Vatican City. O'Flaherty
welcomed them gracefully.

Now in 1958, O'Flaherty ws sixty years old. But he looked more like a
man of fifty or even younger. He was physically fit. He walked in an erect
manner. Al said it reminded him of our Irish friends of our Bronx neighborhood like the four Masterson brothers.

Before Al had a chance to say much, O'Flaherty launched into a story
about Mussolini's downfall where, thereafter thousands of allied prisoners were released. The problem was that the Nazis were still in control
of Rome and therefore, these prisoners needed to find places to hide. It

reminded Al of how Ustacio was released from the work camp with hundreds of other allied prisoners when the Italian commandant freed them upon hearing about the imminent Nazi takeover of Rome.

Now, with all these allied soldiers trying to find safe places, enter Hugh O'Flaherty of the Vatican. Hugh saw what he had to do and quickly convened a group of unlikely allies; unlikely because apparently these included priests he trusted like Snedden and Flanagan and the same for certain nuns. There were others he trusted who were nationals from Sweden, France, Switzerland, and other countries. These resistance fighters as Hugh called them, were those in O'Flaherty's Group 2.

That was the war inside the war; Group 1 versus Group 2. The problem was that even though Hugh managed to rescue all those Jews and allied soldiers, as Al and Jimmy already surmised, Group 1 had thousands of passports all ready to go. Both groups felt they were doing rescue. For Group 1 the rescue was to make sure individuals who could be on trial for war crimes could escape, while for Group 2, the rescue was to save innocent lives of those who very likely could or would be summarily killed.

And, here they were, looking at and listening directly to Father Hugh O'Flaherty. O'Flaherty ushered them in to his little apartment. He offered refreshments as Jimmy was already introducing Al. After the three of them ended their introduction phase, Jimmy asked Al to bring O'Flaherty up to date starting with the Ustacio thing, followed by Olga's death, and then all the way to Willy getting shoved off the ledge.

When Al finished, Hugh O'Flaherty was not at all surprised.

"You see," he said, "it's typical, not caring for human life. That's what they do. They kill without the slightest remorse, human reason, or even that thing we call pity."

"So," Al picked it up and addressed O'Flaherty:

"We need to get to Simon Wiesenthal. But first, we're sure that Emerich Lichtenfeld will have something important to tell us, and he'll get us to Wiesenthal. By the way, Jimmy mentioned that you know Imi and that you also know about Wiesenthal. May I ask, what do you know about Wiesenthal?"

"Well, he's turned into a bona fide Nazi hunter. He started slowly right after the war but now he's flying. I understand he's already provided Mossad with information on Mengele, Eichmann, Stangl, Priebke, and others. Apparently, he knows where they are and where they'll go if they're discovered and on the run. When I last spoke to Imi he told me Wiesenthal does not have a copy of the secret undisclosed Wannsee Conference papers—apparently these your kid-off-the-ledge has hidden. Wiesenthal got his information the hard way and I'm not really sure what he needed to do, to get it. But there's no doubt that Wiesenthal knows that the Wannsee papers contain these undisclosed plans that, in my opinion, detail escape plans—that could even be for Hitler himself.

"You know, Wiesenthal was in so many work and death camps that he's seen it all and practically seen *them* all. He can identify many of these criminals by sight. He's actually seen them and he wants every one of them. You might be interested that he's also given information to your State Department, but he stopped doing it. Imi says it's because your State Department actually took in some of those bastards and gave them safe harbor. So, Wiesenthal no longer trusts the U.S. At this point he trusts no one but Mossad. And even there, Imi says he still has information he hasn't passed along.

"You might be interested in this little vignette. I heard that at the beginning of this year, movie people in Hollywood were thinking of making a movie about Wernher von Braun, the German/Nazi scientist who developed the V-2 rocket that partly destroyed London. Von Braun ran to the U.S. after the war because in the U.S.A. he knew he could have a good life especially if the U.S. government exploited his talents. In contrast, if the Soviets got him, he knew they'd also exploit his scientific ability for their own purposes but they wouldn't treat him well and he'd be despised. You know, considering what the Germans did to the Russian people.

"Anyway, the joke that started in Hollywood and reached way over to here and practically all over Europe was that people were sarcastically commenting on the proposed title of the Wernher von Braun movie—*I Aim at the Stars*. They were saying: 'I aim at the stars, but occasionally hit London.'"

"Oh, that's a good one," Jimmy instantly said, and Al laughed out loud. "But," Jimmy said, "let's get back to Wiesenthal."

"Before we contact Imi," O'Flahrety interrupted, "let me just say that the opinion about Wiesenthal by those around him and by some of the historians is that he's always suspicious. Maybe not paranoid, but always suspicious. I think it's because he knows he's a target. He knows these Nazis are thinking: 'Let's get him before he gets us.'

"Jimmy, I know you agree with Hugh," Al said. "What we need is to get to get to Simon Wiesenthal as soon as possible." And even more, I need to catch that motha-fuckn' ghost—sorry, Hugh—and throw him off a third-floor ledge. I mean it! Truth-telling time, Jimmy. Did I say something that wasn't clear? That's what my friend Mac the Bronx detective usually says."

"No, Al, you were perfectly clear," answered Jim."

"Yes, you were very clear," chuckled Hugh.

"Okay then," Jim continued. "Now is the time to introduce Kishnov. Don't you think?"

"Right," Al answered on a reflex.

"Okay," Jim continued. "This is it, Hugh. Al and I have talked it over and we believe that Wiesenthal is not the one we need for this mission. Rather, we should invite to our table, a guy named Shmuel Kishnov. He was a shadow member of the Kovner gang that wanted to decimate five German towns by poisoning their water supply. As I said to Al, Wiesenthal is an information guy. He's not going to be involved in assassinations and that sort of thing. So, at this point the plan is to get in touch with Kishnov. He's not easy to reach but I know people who will be able to reach him. At the moment, I'd like you to forget that I mentioned assassinations.

* * *

O'Flaherty paused and then surprisingly said: "Kishnov's here in Rome! That's right. He's now here."

"Jesus," Al practically shouted. "Sorry Father, sorry. But this means you probably know how to contact him. Am I right?"

"Yes, you're right. Imi's here because rather than Wiesenthal himself, we've invited Shmuel Kishnov to be the action-hero and ferret this ghost who Simon has identified as the one that haunts the Vatican. Wiesenthal wants to get him and he has ultimate faith that it's Imi who is the one to do it. Of course, we've taken out insurance in the form of this Shmuel Kishnov who I'll tell you about."

"How do you know this, Hugh." Jimmy asked.

"I know it because the day before you arrived, Imi was sitting in the chair you're in right now. You see, there is, we might say, an archipelago of informants who are like-minded and keep information flowing between the islands. Imi's in this chain of islands, as am I, and as is Simon Wiesenthal. None of the things can possibly be successful without this information flow between us all. As it turns out, Simon is the information man while Shmuel Kishnov is the one who'll lead the team into physical action if and when it's called for.

"I'll arrange for us and Imi to meet tomorrow. In the meantime, you should stay here. I've made arrangements for you to share apartment # 3 down one flight. Breakfast will be served by one of the cooks at this little townhouse/hotel where I've had this apartment for some time now. The four of us will meet for a late breakfast, let's say about nine at the apartment where you are staying?"

With that, Hugh O'Flaherty escorted Al and Jimmy to their newly rented apartment for the night—a floor below, and then left Jimmy and Al to discuss it all further. He bade his guests a good night.

*   *   *

Al and Jimmy were awakened at 8 am. They waited for Hugh and Imi on the breakfast porch of their apartment # 3 while the cook was preparing it all in the kitchen. And then there he was. Imi rang the bell and walked in wearing a broad smile.

"Alex, Alex, Alex," Imi shouted. "Alex, so good to see you. It's been a while. I think of you often. Jimmy, my Jimmy. You, too. Hello, hello."

They all embraced warmly and then all sat at the breakfast table feeling at home and with the best of friends.

"So, you're after the ghost, Imi started. Everyone, on their own, without even knowing what he's called, automatically calls him that— *The Ghost*. We know he has influence, endless money whenever he needs it, conduits that are so many that we would never be able to track them all, and a very large population of similar rats. You probably know that his underground railroad is known as *The Ratline* although some people refer to it as *Odessa*. Simon knows more about it than anyone. He knows where many of these rats live and he's given a great deal of information to your M-16, Jimmy, and Al, to your CIA—and of course to the Israeli Mossad.

"But it's one thing to know where they are and another to take them down. Please understand, Israel wants the top ones taken alive and transported to Israel—of course to stand trial publicly. The problem is first to get them, and then the hard part—to get them to Israel. But where they all live is protected by the various governments. We're talking about the fascist governments in Argentina, Paraguay, Chile, Spain, Egypt, Syria, and some others.

"These are places inhospitable to Jews even though some of these countries have large Jewish populations—especially, Argentina. And that smiling, quisling-like poor excuse for a diplomat, Juan Peron, is the worst of the worst. He's happy taking in as many Nazis as possible. We don't know for sure, but we're guessing that he's becoming extraordinarily wealthy getting paid off—big time!

"And listen to this one," Imi intoned: "In Chile, in a place called, *Colonia Dignidad*. I guess it's 'Dignidad' for 'dignity.' You know, it's what the Nazis think they're all about. It's also known as *Villa Baviera,* for *Bavarian Village.* We know it's a relatively recently developed community but word has reached us that they torture and rape children—and that Mengele himself spent time there. However, we already know where Mengele is now located and it's no longer in *Colonia Dignidad.* He's already done his dirty work there.

"Now Mengele's safe. I'll tell you where—still South America. We know exactly where and we're planning to get him. And by the way, another two at this Bavarian Village interest us. The first is the leader, Paul Schafer, a Nazi of the first order. The second is this other Nazi pig that we'd love to get—name of Hartmutt Wilheim Hopp. This Hopp is a sadist and it's no wonder that he was head of the hospital in this *Villa Baviera* populated by who else but German nationals all of whom have successfully escaped justice.

"Hopp wound up in this horror-village because just as Mengele tortured children at Auschwitz, Hopp did the same at Dignidad. Its become known that sexual molestation of children is the main activity at their hospital. Simon would love to get hold of Hopp, no need to mention, he'd love to get his hands on Mengele.

The problem is that this German village located on the north bank of the Perquilauquen River of Chile is completely surrounded by barbed wire. Armed guards are also posted all around, night and day. In addition, we know a watchtower exists that's manned by armed lookouts and searchlights are on the ready all night and every night. Of course, without a trace of a doubt they have weapons stored — just in case. That we know for sure."

"Imi, hold it," Al interrupted. "I know you've got a lot to say and you'd love to get a contingent of Israeli commando Krav Maga guys in there. You'd love to wipe it out. But we're not here for that. Right? We're here because of that package with the Wannsee papers — those that have not been revealed — the secret part. This 'village' you're talking about is extremely interesting and yes, important, and we know a few bombs from a low flying plane wouldn't hurt. But other than that, at the moment, it's the package that the kid has. That's the main attraction."

"Alex, my friend," Imi said, "the only reason I'm here with you is that those papers are exactly what Simon is insisting on getting. It's not that I don't want to see you, or you, Jimmy. It's that I'm on assignment and this is taking me away. At the moment, we're after Priebke and he's on the run. He was an SS Captain convicted of war crimes in Italy. He ordered the massacre of more than three hundred citizens in retaliation for the killing of German soldiers. The retaliation was a massacre at the Ardeatine Caves in Rome. That's where Priebke arranged for it to take place. Close to a hundred who were shot were Italian Jews. We know that somehow these murderers keep getting tipped off and we still haven't found the source. We thought maybe our phones were tappped but that wasn't the case.

"We know for sure that Priebke was shuttled to Buenos Aires by a Bishop in Rome and he got there on a Vatican passport. So, there you have it. The Bishop at the Vatican. The ghost. Therefore," Imi continued, "I need to know how you can help *me*. It's not that I can help *you*. It's that you can help *me*. And Hugh here says that you know about this little boy who has the key to it all but that we need to keep an eye on his recovery.

"So, my friends, how is this kid? Have you been in contact with your people back home? How is he?

· 7 ·

THE PACKAGE

The call to me was primarily a great relief to Al but not at all surprisingly, also a great relief to Jimmy. When I told Al the good news he said that Jimmy heard it too and was giving him the A-okay sign. In a rushed manner, the first thing I said was that Willy still was not talking but that otherwise he was not in any danger—either from brain damage or from any outside threat. Cops were still on duty as ordered; three shifts, eight hours each.

The problem I described was that in addition to everything both doctors Fishman and Mehta had told us, Willy had apparently bitten his tongue and the inside of his mouth and the injury accounted for much of the blood on his clothes and on the pavement where he landed. "He's now missing four teeth, not three," I added. "So, we're talking to him and questioning him while he blinks 'yes' and 'no.'"

I was spitting out all this information to Al like I was spitting teeth myself. I told him we were giving Willy possible hiding places in the apartment and in the building and that Willy kept blinking, 'no.' Then I described how Willy was all bound up in medical equipment. I said again that the doctors ruled out any brain damage but that they were concerned about his recent memory. When Al heard that the doctors questioned Willy's memory for recent events, he quickly asked for more.

"Well, it was Gloria who scared us because she thought maybe Willy might not remember where he actually hid the package. It might be," she said, "that he's waiting for us to mention a place so that he would recognize it and then his full memory of it would click in. That one scared me too," I added, "but we still don't know if he remembers it or not. When Gloria asked him, he didn't blink 'yes' or 'no.' That's when Gloria got suspicious. She talked it over with the doctors and that's when they considered that it might take Willy some time to retrieve recent memories but that they seemed sure these memories would in fact return. They called it a possible anterograde amnesia—eight syllables. Got it? an-ter-o-grade-am-nes-i-a?"

"Yeah, I got it," Al answered. "Eight syllables. Frankie, go ahead. Forget the English/biology test."

"Okay, the good news is that Willy's awake and it's a good sign so forget the anterograde amnesia. And by the way, without a doubt, Gloria's a Godsend. Man, oh man, you hit the jackpot there. As far as our interaction with Willy is concerned though, he's under pain-relief medication so he gets drowsy and sleeps a lot. Then we need to wait till he wakes up. And by the way, it's a sight seeing Willy in these casts; you know, ankle, shoulder, elbow, knee. The good news is that they're all still attached to his body—meaning he's in one piece. Otherwise he's had all his fractured and broken bones taken care of.

"Al, the main point is that he still can't say where he hid the package. Where are you, by the way? Where are you?"

"First in London, now in Rome. Too much to describe at the moment but so far, very, very interesting. We're actually with Imi, and we have someone else with us—an interesting like-minded priest who will be escorting us to meet a main man. Get it?"

"Understood. We're on it here, too, Al. Don't worry, and keep calling me since I can't reach you. Seems like you're on the move a lot—London, Rome. Where next?"

"Beats me. I think we'll be seeing another important guy next. It'll probably be a guy named something different than S.W. It's someone who will take charge of whatever needs to be done. S.W. is not a warrior chief. This other guy who's kind of an experienced action-hero will now be the one to handle the action. Also, we've been visiting with Imi quite a lot. By the way has Mac or Lyle interrogated that Ewald Germ and the Argentinean guy, Eduardo?"

"Yeah, they've been on it. The Argentinean guy, Eduardo, keeps spilling. The latest is that he says Peron's girlfriend who he married, Eva or Evita, was a real bitch and she was totally with him and supported him about receiving all these Nazis. He says that Peron's whole inner circle was in cahoots and that payoffs were huge and were happening all over the place.

"Eduardo has a real hard-on for lady Peron. He hates her. He couldn't stop talking about her. He's a virtual treasure trove of information. He said that it was common knowledge in the Argentine Capital that in 1947 when she took her European tour, she visited all the leaders who were fascists and Nazi sympathizers, including Salazar in Portugal, Franco in Spain, and he even mentioned Pope Pius XII with all the implications that might be assumed from her visit to the Pope. Get it? Then he said that Eva bounced around till she got to Switzerland. He used the word 'rebotaba' in Spanish when he wanted to express how Eva bounced around Europe.

"Then he told us the underpinning to it all, which was that she was transferring millions of dollars to Swiss bank accounts all in the name of the Perons via numbered accounts. All of the money, of course, ill gotten. He swore to it. He also swore that in 1945 right at the end of the war, Peron himself arranged for thousands of passports to be issued in the names of those Nazis on the move in order for them to escape. That's right, thousands! First stop—easy guess—Buenos Aires. Some, he said needed to go somewhere else where there were safe houses ready for them in various cities in South America. And it wasn't just safe houses he was talking about. They were also provided jobs. He laughed when he said that many complained that the jobs were menial and were next to nothing compared to the powerful positions they held during the war."

"Okay, Frankie, gotta go. I just got a finger across the throat from Jimmy so I gotta sign off. I'll be in touch at least once a day. Be good."

* * *

Now Al was sure that the next stop for Jimmy, him, and Imi, would be to see Simon Wiesenthal. And how right they were. Hugh O'Flahrety set it up. Next flight was Tel Aviv—for all four of them. What Al wanted to know was what was Wiesenthal doing in Israel? The answer, apparently, was that even though a dozen years or so had elapsed after the war and now it was 1958, Wiesenthal was a known power in Israeli inner circles.

He first gained notoriety in 1947 as a smuggler. What he did was smuggle Jewish people, displaced people, people who lost everything they had into the British Mandate of Palestine. These were people who lost the most precious of all things — their family members as well as their hope.

By this time now in 1958, it became public knowledge that Wiesenthal, in an ingenious way, and right under the nose of the British authority, was doing all this smuggling of human cargo. And he was doing it in the service of the Jewish organization known as *Berihah*, a Hebrew word that translates into the English, as *Flight*, which given the function of that outfit, seems perfectly suitable.

Wiesenthal was not doing it as an independent operator. He had forgers, arms dealers, drivers of automobiles and a variety of other resources, such as trucks at his disposal. In other words, Wiesenthal had his own small army working for him even though he had started alone. For example, in mid 1945, soon after the *Mauthausen concentration camp* was liberated and he was rescued, Wiesenthal had already begun preparing volumes of lists of Nazis responsible for reprehensible, unforgivable and the most repugnant atrocities. He was apparently obsessed with these lists, and soon became a compelling figure surrounded by many others who were streaming information to him about these hidden Nazis.

Now he was back in Israel because Mossad informed him they had some information about this Vatican ghost. They told him they had abducted an important individual whom they referred to as a person of interest.

When Imi, O'Flaherty, Al, and Jimmy, landed at Ben Gurion International Airport they were immediately led by O'Flahrety to a limousine. O'Flahrety ushered Imi, Al and Jimmy into the back and O'Flaherty took the front companion seat. Imi and Al flanked the man in the back sitting there. Of course, it was Wiesenthal himself who then pulled the jumper seat down so that Jimmy would sit opposite to them. Then Wiesenthal told the driver to just drive so that they could take their time and talk while sitting in the car.

"Gentlemen, welcome. I am Simon Wiesenthal and I am exceedingly pleased to meet with you. Hugh has been regaling me with your exploits and with your very valuable situation. And of course, by 'valuable' I mean possession of the erstwhile package. You will be interested to see that I already know that we have the package and so, conversely, I already also know that perhaps we *don't* have the package. However, I've been reassured by Hugh that it will all work out for us—especially now that Shmuel Kishnov is joining us.

"So," Weisenthal continued, "there are two things on the agenda. One is the package and when we get it, how to transport it—and also *who* should transport it. The second item is this 'ghost' business. You should know I personally and several of my staff have been searching for him starting almost immediately after the war. In 1945, '46, and '47, we knew that a ton of passports to South America were provided by some organization and that hundreds of Nazis were using them successfully. This was also true for destinations to Egypt and Syria. We knew it but we couldn't penetrate the system that was accomplishing it. Passports were flying all over and we were stumped; except for one major clue that led directly to the Vatican and then, poof, stopped there.

"Thus, we know for sure that this 'ghost' is stationed at the Vatican. I referred to it as an organization. Of course, the organization is very large and has its tentacles into a vast array of places. But, this organization is most certainly led by a sole person—a person, and assuredly not a ghost. That person is this 'ghost' to whom we are referring. I'm not shy to say that suspicions of who that might be run the course from the lowliest ranking person at the Vatican all the way to the Pope himself."

"Mr. Wiesenthal," Al responded. "We've discovered that the ghost, yes, this person, is probably operating from the Vatican, that he uses a code for all communications, and he probably is a Bishop but not the Pope. He uses two letters of the alphabet as his identification. These letters are: H.A. We've apprehended two men and they are incarcerated in New York City, in a precinct in the Bronx. One is German and the other an Argentinean. They're both Secret Service in their respective countries—the German in Berlin and the Argentine in Buenos Aires. They claim not to know who the ghost is but it actually was the Argentinean who revealed the initials of the ghost and implicated this ghost in the nefarious acts that we are targeting. Again, they both deny knowing this ghost's identity.

"I don't mean to overstep Mr. Wiesenthal but," Al continued," I need to know what we're doing in Israel meeting with you here? I mean we definitely needed to meet with you, but why in Israel?"

"Okay, that's a fair question," Weisenthal replied. "The good Father here, my trusted comrade Hugh O'Flahrety, and my close and trusted comrade, Imi, have assured me that you both are entirely trustworthy. I believe that. I can see it. You see, after all of my experience, I believe I can tell whom to trust. When you've been in as many treacherous places as I've experienced, you begin to develop a diagnostic skill as to who is who and what is what.

"I have recently been in touch with Mossad and they have a dossier on someone they refer to as 'anonymous' who acted as Bishop Alois Hudal's secretary or assistant. Hudal is the German Bishop at the Vatican. Mossad agents interpreted material they had that implicated 'Mr. Anonymous' in the issuance of *International Red Cross* travel documents found in the possession of several captured Nazis who were running from being put on trial and knew they faced certain and final punishment. Final punishment to them obviously meant a death sentence.

"It's been said although never confirmed that in 1946, Mossad abducted someone who remains to this day listed in their files as 'anonymous,' but I personally suspect of being none other than Hudal's chief aide, Joseph Prader's assistant. Prader's assistant is Anton Weber. It's also interesting to me that no one mentions Weber's name. Apparently, it is forbidden to do so. But no one knows for sure that, in fact, it is Weber.

"This anonymous abductee, presumed to be Weber, was in terror of his life because at Mossad Headquarters, whoever it was—Weber or perhaps Prader himself, he was now in the hands of Jews, yes, in the hands of Jews with guns. Weber—if that's who it is—understood vividly that such people who had been so stripped of their humanity wouldn't hesitate to kill him. In exchange for his life—whoever *he* was—he quickly gave up a lot of crucial information.

"The story goes that Mossad captured him based on their tracking expertise. Apparently, they had been tracking him since it was noticed that something was not kosher at the German college/church in Rome. Agents of Mossad then targeted this place. They observed that the number of people who worked there and who entered in the mornings was fewer than those leaving in the evening. Far fewer! At other times, it was noticed that fewer were leaving in the evening than had entered in the morning. It became obvious that something surreptitious was happening there. And of course, they reasoned it was a place of refuge as well as transit for Nazi escapees perhaps in groups of twenty or thirty or even more who were being sheltered there.

"So, they infiltrated. A German Jewish lady named Tatiana Gerhardt, who was an undercover Mossad agent was able to land a job as translator at that place called the *Collegio Tecetonico di Santa Maria dell' Anima,* a college place that could be called the German church of Rome. Her native tongue was German. She was also fluent in French and Italian. She had an iron-clad back story that Mossad was certain the Nazis would check. Mossad was further certain that she would gain employment there based upon her blemish-free non-political background that was set up by Mossad in the first place designed to display her mastery in language translations.

"And now comes the most interesting part," Wiesenthal continued. "I've been told but have never confirmed that she was the one who connected, even ostensibly identified Weber as the person at the church who was in touch with everyone in power there. She indicated that Weber was the one who delivered papers from one office to the other. She also named Bishop Hudal as perhaps Weber's direct contact person and as the assistant to Joseph Prader, leader of this college/church.

"This woman was only guessing that given Weber's handling of all papers and memos going from office to office, and all people coming and going as well, that it was a good bet that he, Weber, was the one to be abducted. It was her best guess, although, made with some tangible evidence that Weber would be a person to offer a wealth of information. After a year or so she resigned, married, and travelled to Belgium to live with her husband, a college professor of engineering. She became a professor of Latin languages at the same college in Belgium.

"The story continues that while interrogating 'anonymous,' who I hypothesize was Weber himself, Mossad agents made it clear that if he didn't provide the necessary information, his life, whoever he was, would need to be forfeited. At that point 'anonymous' then flooded them with information. He told them that the *Anima,* which is what those on the other side called *the place,* actually had a secret passageway that led to the church's crypt. And in the capacious crypt room was where scores of Nazis on the run were hidden. Of course, these were Nazi fugitives who at all costs needed to escape — to change their lives, never again to return to Germany or wherever."

"Of course, the symbolism of 'crypt' didn't escape you," Al commented.

"Yes, of course, you are correct," Wiesenthal answered. "You see, it occurred to me that it was fitting for these lowest forms of life to be secluded in a chamber beneath a church designated as a burial site because I, as well as like-minded others, were going to see to it that they actually ended up in such a place. In addition, this 'anonymous' character, perhaps Weber, apparently confirmed that many were SS men transferred to Munich and then shuttled to Innsbruck, to Bern, to Rome, and from Rome the final destination was either to land in Beirut or Damascus. Some went to Spain but the main transfer-center was from Italy—from Rome. At one point the transfer route was called *The Monastary Route*—the route between Austria and Italy.

"It almost appeared that monastaries along the way were connected as are islands of an archipelago which these war criminals were using as bridges to some other world. We began referring to this so-called underground railroad as *The Rat Line*. Others called the entire transfer operation—*Odessa*.

"From that time on, it became obvious that Hudal was our man. He was the Pope's favorite cleric and he was the one we considered to be *the ghost*—the one chiefly responsible for enlisting Franciscan priests to funnel these Nazis to their destinations. You see, we then had it confirmed that our original suspicion that the so-called transfer agents who delivered these Nazis to their predetermined destinations were actually these fanatical Franciscan priests."

"Hey, wait a minute," Al, suddenly shouted. "Hudal's initials are A.H. The code used by these people was H.A. Hudal just reversed the initials. He's *the ghost*. He's *the ghost!*"

"Yes, I now can say that we've suspected this," Wiesenthal said. "However, still we hold the suspicion that there may be another—even more powerful than Hudal. But this remains only at the level of speculation. And the horrible thought," Wiesenthal continued, "is that along with all the other horrors, it was Pope Pius XII who appointed Hudal to be a Bishop. When he appointed Hudal, Bishop, the Pope was only a Cardinal. And the Cardinal became Pope Pius XII and Hudal remained this Pope's favorite.

"What does that tell you? Yet, it was Montini, Monsignor Montini whose full name was Giovanni Battista Enrico Antonio Maria Montini, who appeared to have the greatest influence on Hudal's decisions and who was also unduly influential with the majority of cardinals.

"We know that Hudal also created what was known as the *Austrian*

Liberation Committee which was another center-point in Hudal's railroad operation. And that reminds me that Eichmann was also a beneficiary of Hudal's machinations. Immediately after the war in 1945, Hudal got him to Austria. He was then transferred to Argentina about five years later, in 1950. That we know as a certainty.

"Be sure of one thing gentlemen. We know where Eichmann is and we know where Mengele was—past tense. Now he's gone. We know that Mengele is already in a predetermined secondary place but we don't yet know where that is. But, we believe that the information in the package will tell us where the secondary hiding places are located.

"Also, we believe the package does not contain papers. We're supposing that the information in the package will be on microfilm. As I've said, we know that Mengele is already in this secondary place but we don't yet know where that is. We do believe that this presumed microfilm will definitely reveal it all. If it is microfilm, the information on it will give us the blueprints for hundreds, maybe thousands—yes, maybe thousands—of those in deep cover living in a number of countries.

"Please do not think I am given to exaggeration. Some think I am. I'm not. Here's what I mean. I want them all. Every one of them. All of those thousands that have gotten away with that evil. If necessary, we will march until the end of time, but we will not rest until we have each and every one of them. The world must learn that there is no statute of limitations on evil! That's why that package the boy can give us, is, I believe, one of the most important documents of this or perhaps of any century.

"I'll give you an example of how important such information really is. We always knew that Franz Stangl was first sent to Syria in the Middle East. We also discovered that the second hiding place awaiting him in the event he needed it was in Brazil. We are reasonably certain that information on this microfilm will contain precise locations of each secondary hiding place for each of the thousands of Nazis who successfully escaped and then disappeared. And, again, I say it: I want them all. Every single one of them!

"And know this," Wiesenthal continued. "I am plagued with some philosophical obsessions. These involve capital punishment, as in governments putting people to death—along with personal vendetta, as in justifiable homicide. And here is where philosophy enters. First, I may state a general principle; that is, to the extent one stands for fairness and against oppression of any people, to that extent one's integrity remains in-tact and I usually define this also metaphorically as that such a person remains non-ghostly. Conversely, to the extent that one operates with unfairness and supports oppression—especially to the extent of genocide—to that extent one becomes ghostly, meaning losing integrity, losing humanity, losing oneself.

"Then I ask myself the question: Is morality absolute or relative? Or, *should* morality be absolute or relative? My answer is I believe in absolute morality. Yet, look at what the Nazis did to us. So even though I feel that way about absolute morality, about killing innocent people, nevertheless, I still want to get every one of them. And for the third or so time, I repeat: every one! So therefore, my truth is that I want them killed—one way or the other; either through trials like those at Nuremburg, or with what Mossad does—assassinations! And therefore, the answer is that morality for me ultimately is relative.

"Therefore, to put it all together, evil does not have a statute of limitations, morality is relative, and one must stand for justice, fairness, and against oppression of any people.

"So, my friends, do you stand with me on these three points—that one must stand for fairness and against oppression, that morality is relative, and that with evil there is no statute of limitations?"

"Mr. Wiesenthal," Al answered, "please know that we here and those also at home agree one hundred percent about the importance of what's in that package. That's number one. Second, I personally agree with every-thing you just said and I believe that all of us here are on the same page. And third, I'd like to know what Mossad did with 'anonymous? Is it all right that I ask that question?"

"Perfectly alright. But let me say that I'm pleased that you all agree with what could be called my philosophical pronouncements. And regarding 'anonymous,' it's an interesting and I believe ongoing story. They let him go. That's what the rumor is. Mossad let him go with the promise that his name would never appear in their files and that he would be referred to as *the anonymous one.* One of the Mossad agents wanted the agency to refer to him as *Our Ghost,* but that was instantly rejected. It remains to this day, I've been told, that if all of this is fact, that whoever he is, *anonymous* would forever be his name. As you can probably surmise, no one from Mossad ever puts out facts so it is possible that we shall never know the truth. And even in Mossad, only less than a handful of agents perhaps—only *perhaps*—know his real name.

"Personally, I believe, but don't know for sure, that if all of it is true, that Weber, if he's 'anonymous,' still, to this day, would be offering Mossad information, and that Hudal wouldn't know a thing about it. Of course, if Hudal did have any kind of even an inkling about it, he would have had, I am sure, 'anonymous' killed—and without a moment's regret; friend or no friend. That's Hudal. But despite all of it, if it was true, 'anonymous' or Weber, would probably still be in league with Hudal, and at the same time, I'm thinking, would probably be receiving from Mossad something in the way of shall we say, remuneration, and then in exchange be giving information to Mossad as well. If that's the case, Hudal certainly would have no knowledge of it. All in all, these are educated guesses.

"So, gentlemen, that's it for me and this meeting. I hope our get-together has been useful to you and that it was not a wasted trip. It was certainly not wasted for me. I feel reassured that the package is, and will be, in good hands, and that I will eventually receive it."

"No, no, it wasn't wasted. Not at all," Al said.

"Mr. Wiesenthal, I believe all of us feel the way Al does. It was wonderful meeting you," Jimmy added. "I assure you we will do everything possible to get the package to you—and only to you."

With that, Wiesenthal enthusiastically thanked Imi and O'Flaherty, and they in turn offered him a very warm and friendly farewell. The driver, as they were saying their farewells, pulled the car to the side of the road. The four of them, with the exception of Wiesenthal, exited, and O'Flaherty escorted Al, Jimmy, and Imi, to another car already waiting some feet away. Al, Jimmy, and Imi in the back of this other car and O'Flaherty in the companion seat in the front was the arrangement.

The car drove away.

· 8 ·

Alois Hudal

Argentina's president, Juan Peron, was not just issuing passports by the thousands, he had also organized a wide network of agents whose task it was to insert themselves into those enclaves in Europe that were infected with hosts of Nazis on the run. They weren't on the run because they believed themselves innocent. Some of the embarkation and disembarkation points included Italy, Austria, and of course, Germany as well as a number of countries in South America and the Middle East. These were the countries where Peron's agents plied their trade.

When he returned from his foray with Wiesenthal, Al reported to me that Hudal, who was perhaps *the ghost*, had set up what became known as the *Nazi Bolt-Hole*. This was established with the help of the Archbishop of Genoa, Cardinal, Giuseppe Siri, and additionally asisted by another energized Nazi sympathizer from Croatia with the unlikely name of Krunoslav Stjepan Dragonovic.

This Bolt-Hole was essentially an escape hatch in the jungle, close to Paraguay, considered by these escape artists to be a 'just-in-case' backdoor. The occupants were fanatical Nazis on the run and their houses were adorned with Nazi symbols and other such artifacts. The Bolt-Hole community had the distinct aura of a Cononia Dignidad in Chile—another Nazi village that Al told me was referred to as Via Baviera or Bavarian Village.

Wiesenthal added that this escape route was aptly named. This 'Hole' was also akin to the tunnel-like escape in South Tyrol leading through the port of Genoa. These Nazi facilitators like Hudal, Siri, and Dragonovic, along with others including Cardinal Caggiano, Bishop Augustin Barrere, Pierre Day, Charles Leska, and Monsignor Montini also created what they identified as the *National Committee for Emigration to Argentina*. It was simply an organization, the function of which was solely to brazenly usher Nazi war criminals who were on the run to successfully reach safe havens. And Hudal was at the pinnacle of success in his ability to accomplish it all.

Wiesenthal spoke for more than an hour telling what he knew personally or had been told about 'anonymous's' description of Hudal's secret meeting with this particular 'Central Committee.'

"It was obvious," Al said, "that Wiesenthal was attributing the source of all this information to 'anonymous'. And apparently 'anonymous' never equivocated. He knew that lying would mean death and that equivocating might mean death or perhaps, worse! 'Anonymous' therefore, needed to make sure that he and his captors were securely aligned—tight as a drum. Achieving this alignment meant survival for him and even some wealth. Nothing more, nothing less."

Al told them that when Wiesenthal was describing things, he and Jimmy glanced a knowing look at one another as though to say: 'Was he there?' In other words, was Wiesenthal in the room when 'anonymous' was questioned?' Because according to Wiesenthal, 'anonymous' directed his entire narrative to describing what his captors asked of him; namely, wanting to know everything surrounding Hudal's conclave with his ad hoc Central Committee composed of Siri, Dragonovic, Caggiano, Barrere, Day, Leska, and several others. It was obvious that there were others because according to Wiesenthal 'anonymous' also referred to at least four others with the monikers of Cardinal so and so, and Bishop so and so. In addition, 'anonymous' also included in this group two men who were never introduced to the others and never referred to by Hudal. These two Scarlet Pimpernals who just sat and listened were no doubt joined at the hip with Hudal in the most insidious propagation of evil—the wanton rescue of evil-dripping genocidal Nazis.

Thus, Wiesenthal seemed to have blow by blow knowledge of how it all went down. Later when Wiesenthal and Al and the others said their goodbyes, Al and Jimmy talked it over and decided that since Wiesenthal probably would not personally sanction specific assassinations or kidnappings, still, he must have been in on at least the aftermath of the 'anonymous' kidnapping. It's just that what he knew was so detailed that it could have only come from an eye-witness. According to Al, Wiesenthal seemed all knowing when he began to describe it down to the smallest details.

"You see," Wiesenthal had related, "the sober looking Mossad agents were never satisfied with generalities. They wanted details—specific details: names, dates, plans, places." There was no good cop, bad cop. It was all bad cop. 'Anonymous' could feel it. So, naturally, he gave it up the best way he possibly could. When 'anonymous' was captured, Wiesenthal said his confession ran for three hours. In those three hours 'anonymous' described the plans that Hudal was making with the upper echelon of his proposed *Odessa,* organized in order to ignite movement on the Rat-Line. Thus, *Odessa* was specifically formed as an organization to solely supervise and accomplish the goal of ushering Nazis on the run onto an underground railroad leading to an escape route primarily either to South America or to the Middle East.

Al said that when Wiesenthal referred to 'anonymous's' capture, he used the word "we" when describing those who kidnapped 'anonymous.' Al guessed that Wiesenthal either was there during the act or referred to the "we" as an expression of solidarity with those who actually did the kidnapping. But Al didn't mention this implication to Wiesenthal. He was more interested in primarily hearing from Wiesenthal what 'anonymous' had to say. Apparently, according to Wiesenthal 'anonymous' recalled that Hudal instructed him "to welcome them as they arrive." It was during the interrogation that 'anonymous' named the arrivals. Al also said thatWiesenthal continued and with uncharacteristic aggression said:

"It was a perfect place to drop the bomb even though it would have been at them in the Vatican. That bomb would have killed them all. We need to remember," Wiesenthal said," "the conclave that Hudal convened was a cauldron, a cauldron of evil-dripping Nazi-Devils. Nothing more, nothing less."

Al then added that during their conversation in the car, Wiesenthal enumerated that 'anonymous' had stated that the first to arrive at that Devil's conclave was Franz Ruffinengo of *DAIE* meaning *The Delegation of Argentine Immigration in Europe.* This was a Peronist organization located in Italy. The second to arrive was Monsignor Montini, the very powerful *Undersecretary in the Vatican Secretary of State office.* Following that, three arrived together—Dragonovic, Cardinal Tisserant, and Cardinal Caggiano. Others arrived in small groups. These included Cardinal Siri, Father Filiberto who was the one to provide supplies, Dr. Willy Nix, Monsignor Heinemann, Monsignor Karl Bayer, and Ernst Kaltenbrunner of the *Security Office SS.*

"Altogether," 'anonymous related, "there were about fifteen or twenty in the room. Wiesenthal then told Al and the others that 'anonymous' was instructed to describe what was discussed at that conclave and to then relate it to the fundamental reason of the meeting. Weisenthal detailed 'anonymous' recounting:

"They had more than three hundred waiting for instructions as to destinations and, hopefully, for travel papers. All of those were the major Nazis who were sought for trial or already had been tried in absentia and found guilty of war crimes. Naturally, all of the more than three hundred were desperate to escape. We're talking about Adolph Eichmann, the so-called architect of the *final solution,* Dr. Josef Mengele, *the angel of death* at Auschwitz, Erich Priebke, the *massacre master* at the Ardeatine Caves, Franz Stangl, Commandant of the *Treblinka extermination camp*—also known as *the slaughterer,* SS Captain, and Walter Kutschmann, the acknowledged *killer* of about twenty thousand Polish Jews. Others counted by 'anonymous included Edward Roschmann called the *Butcher of Riga* who was also the killer of thousands of Jews in Latvia, and *the Nazi spy,* SS officer Fridolin Guth, *the killer* in France."

"Yes," Wiesenthal said, "these catholic priests were the worst of the supporters of all of the Nazis that escaped to South America and to the Middle East. By worst I mean the ones most successful in their objective." Wiesenthal then recited the following:

"Hudal, was indeed, the worst. But Siri and Dragonovic were equally culpable. The anti-Jewish poison had successfully infected all of Europe as well as South America—as seen in the Christian countries, the catholic and protestant countries. On the one hand you had those like Hudal sending, and on the other you had those like Juan Peron, receiving. Even in the U.S.A. the vicious anti-Jewish American bishop Aloisius Muench was doing his best to facilitate amnesty appeals for all Nazi escapees including those who managed to never be put before a judge because of their success in enjoying all the escape plans that were constantly percolating in these countries. We are convinced the directions came from the top—from Hudal!"

Al then repeated what Wiesenthal expressed about what most Jews who had survived the Holocaust felt. "It was," he said, "that the only hope for survival for Jews in the Diaspora was the creation of the state of Israel." He also added that even Jews like those in America feel the same, and feel it strongly. "And," Wiesenthal regretfully but with resentment added, "Pope Pius XII apparently had much sympathy for these so-called aid-organizations such as the *National Committee for Emigration to Argentina*—nothing but a Nazi escape-facilitation organization.

"And make no mistake about it," he continued, "I could name at least another half dozen of such organizations whose sole purpose was to keep Nazi war criminals, safe. It was happening all over Europe. Frequently these organizations were framed as 'charities' of one sort or another. Also, this Monsignor Montini, the *undersecretary of the Vatican's Secretary of State*, was, another of these helpers—an invaluable member of Hudal's snake pit and an example of multitudes of these vipers. And it should be noted again and again—Montini was another ghost-like figure. He apparently had a lot of power—even in concert with, and perhaps even over Hudal.

"I could name others. We have a rather complete dossier of such people and their organizations. I assure you, they have unlimited funds. But we have unlimited motivation to get them all. Despite what I say about getting them all, I know this is quite impossible. It is my anger talking. You see, ten percent of the entire German population were Nazi Party members and another large percentage were fellow travelers. Then there were portions of the population that supported the Nazi movement with their sentiments but were not at all active politically. That equals about eight million or more people supporting Hitler and Nazi ideology, and a great deal of the rest of the country, also supportive in sentiment. Of those, about ten percent were high ranking miscreants. That means that close to one million or more were out and out murderers and I want them all, even though I know I won't be able to do it because the numbers are so overwhelming—but still, I want them all."

Then, Wiesenthal dropped another kind of bomb. Al said that Wiesenthal and his staff were able to count those escaping through the 'bolt-hole.' "Yes, my friends," Wiesenthal recounted, "one hundred a day." He repeated it. "Yes, I said one hundred of these Nazi's—on the average of one hundred per day were travelling both with letters of recommendation as well as passports provided by Hudal, whose base of operations where he secretly housed this armada of Nazi villains preparing to escape, was at the *Anima*—this so-called college. The highest ranking among them of course were Mengele, Eichmann, Stangl, Priebke, Klaus Barbie, and others like them. Hudal saved them all with his usual mastery of providing money, safe houses, secondary locations in case of discovery, and, of course, travel documents and plans directly to pre-determined primary locations.

"Again, according to the rumor, It may have been Anton Weber, aide to Prader, this so-called 'anonymous' one, who described various conversations Hudal had with him as well as with others." Of course, even though by strong implication that Wiesenthal may have been present during the interrogation of 'anonymous,' he never actually confirmed that it was Weber who was the one kidnapped.

Wiesenthal had also said sardonically: "Here's more fascinating material. 'Anonymous' reported that among other things, this group discussed passports that were needed and that these were to be issued by the *International Red Cross* while letters of recommendations were to be provided by the *Pope* himself, and a transportation permit-process was to be organized by the travel association, *Vianord*.

"That essentially was the purpose of the meeting," Wiesenthal continued,—"to set it all up in a more efficient and specifically organized way. The point is that this meeting called by Hudal, was convened after the war. Hudal's experience before this was that things were happening more haphazardly but that now with the torrential cascading of the outflow of their people, he felt they needed a more centralized authority with the ability to ask for and receive reciprocity in favors from all of their supporters.

"In contrast, we know," Wiesenthal continued, "that immediately after the war before this conclave ever took place, Hudal feted several hundred Nazi fugitives. According to 'anonymous,' he said it almost drove Hudal crazy trying to get them all out. He boasted that he actually did the impossible. He got them all out with the necessary travel documents and so forth. That's why he later organized the conclave which took him about another year to accomplish. Wiesenthal added, "after the meeting concluded, all three hundred waiting to leave were dressed—as priests—and most were then welcomed in Buenos Aires while still others disembarked elsewhere in South America."

"For example, at first, Kutschmann was given shelter and protection by the *Carmelite Fathers* in Madrid. After that he appeared in Buenos Aires; Roschmann also landed in Buenos Aires leaving from Genoa, of course, with a *Red Cross* passport; Priebke was given a *Vatican ID card* from none other than what was called, *the Pontifical Commission of Assistance in Rome.* He too, had a *Red Cross* passport as well as a *letter of recommendation* from Hudal himself. The entire operation consisted of a network of people and institutions all cooperating to save these murderers. So, yes, the *Odessa Rat-Line* became a well-oiled underground railroad.

"Even the particular Nazi Bolt-hole from South Tyrol to the port of Genoa," Wiesenthal obsessively continued, "began operating twenty-four hours a day, seven days a week. It required a unified objective and a self-assigned priority to accomplish it all for these poor examples of what being a true Christian means. These Nazis masquerading as Christians, were some of the top crust of the church: Bishop Hudal, Cardinal Siri, *the Archbishop of Genoa*, the *Croation priest,* Krunoslav Stjepan Dragonovic, and especially perhaps Monsignor Montini of the *Vatican's Secretary of State office.* This was what could be considered the upper tier of this evil organization. And yet, the main problem at the beginning of this nefarious enterprise was that most of these Nazi fugitives didn't know that Genoa could be a drop-off embarkation point so that instead they all figured they would need to get to Rome. In fact, it was common knowledge in their circles that at the Vatican they could get help. So instead of looking anywhere else, Rome became their target destination. In addition, the whole operation was also strongly supported by the entire industrial complex of Germany"

And then in an incisive summary, Wiesenthal said: "At first, at the Vatican, the collection of documents could probably be easily arranged. This meant ID cards, recommendation letters, Red Cross passports, and special travel needs such as new ID name, new profession listed, reason for the trip, and name of contact job at the destination city. Only later by 1949 or 1950 was Genoa also outfitted with these necessary preparatory items."

In addition to all of this uncovered information, Wiesenthal also noted that by 1950 his entourage calculated the amount of financial support it took at the Vatican to underwrite the entire Odessa project. Apparently, they figured that the Vatican needed about three hundred million dollars starting in early 1943 and onward for payment to a vast array of supporting organizations both at embarkation and disembarkation points. Apparently, the further disgusting side-deal Hudal was making with these escapees was that each one was extorted for a large amount of money in order to pay for the escape. Yes, Hudal was making money out of it—a mountain of money.

Al said that while sitting in back of that car, that Wiesenthal laughed because he further and at length said: "My friend here, Father O'Flaherty had to scrimp pennies to help Jews and allied soldiers who had escaped, and this Hudal had unlimited funds. Good friend O'Flaherty here knew without a doubt that to request such aid from authorities at the Vatican was equivalent to signing his death warrant or exile or banishment.

"So, it was the church and the Nazis in an evil love affair intertwined in each others arms and lasting for decades. Decades? How about lasting for centuries. Even in so-called modern times, when Pope Pius XI wanted to produce an Encyclical against anti-Semitism, the committee writing it couldn't prevent their Jew-hatred from bleeding in, so this unfinished Encyclical was buried for more than fifty years, and of course, never completed.

"And there are antecedents to it all," Wiesenthal continued." For example, earlier, Pope Pius IX, head of the 1st Vatican Council in 1869 preached that Jews should be kept in confined areas—Ghettos. In addition, Martin Luther the reformer of the Protestant reformation wrote his own Encyclical calling for the torture of Jews and of confiscation of all of their property. And of course, we know that even a church sect is named for him: *The Lutheran Church*!—named for this vituperative atavistic narcissist—this psychotic theologian, Martin Luther, who today is venerated. Are people just stupid or ignorant is my question? And I'm not even mentioning the Inquisition. And of course, now we have the big one. Millions killed.

"No, my friends," Wiesenthal again concluded, "the Vatican, the church, has lost its right in the eyes of God, in the eyes of justice—even to exist." Then he turned to our own favorite friend Father Hugh O'Flaherty and said: "But not you Hugh. Not you. Of course, Hudal is another story. He is the Devil's church-representative at the Vatican which has without a doubt become the Devil's location. And yes, that is the way I feel. True

Christianity has been usurped by Devils! "Yes," Wiesenthal said, "these catholic priests were the worst of the supporters of all of the Nazis that escaped to South America as well as to the Middle East. In this case, by worst I mean the ones most successful in their objective. You know," Wiesenthal stridently said: "Look at Stangl. They got him to Sao Paulo and a job in a Volkswagon factory no less!"

Al then told me that if Wiesenthal knew, if Wiesenthal was there as part of the kidnapping event and the questioning of 'anonymous,' he never said it outright, he never admitted it. 'Anonymous' therefore, for all intents and purposes, remained anonymous.

*　*　*

Later, when Al repeated to me what it was that Wiesenthal felt regarding the church's violation, he added:

"Frankie, Wiesenthal's right. He's right. Shut it down. Shut the mothafucka down." Now, Al's heritage is Jewish. But he's a stone-cold Jewish atheist and identifies himself as a cultural/historical Jew, like secular, meaning non-religious. But he knew he could talk to me that way because although I'm Italian Catholic, like him I'm really culturally Italian and not at all religious. But I responded reasonably and said: "Al, keep in mind that in America nowadays the church helps a lot of people and it's growing and getting better—especially in the cities."

Al wouldn't have any of it and answered: "But Frankie, this is 1958 and Hudal is still operating and all those Nazis got away with it. They got away with it and they're still getting away with it. Hudal's still operating! I don't know why Mossad doesn't just take him out. I can't figure it out. Just take the motha' fucka' out! I think we need to bring back *Murder Incorporated*. Re-incarnate these guys. Bring in Lansky, Bugsy, Lepke, Kid Twist—even Luciano and the boys! Then we'll see what happens."

This brief concoction of a conversation happened when Al called me from across the ocean. Of course, he urgently wanted to hear about Willy. It was I who goaded him into our brief interlude regarding the Wiesenthal stuff. But he prefaced all the Willy questions he had by ending his tirade against the Vatican, the church, and Hudal by also calling the church: "the most successful cult in existence, and the inner machinations of the church, pure evil."

But then he went right to Willy and wouldn't let me distract him again. I began telling him the latest.

"It's Saturday here, Al. I arrived at the hospital kind of early at 9:15am. Gloria was already there. She had me beat by about ten or fifteen minutes. She met me at the elevator with a cup of coffee in her hands, leaned toward me while holding the coffee steady and kissed me on the cheek. Don't get jealous, Al. It's you she really loves."

"Frankie, c'mon, get to it."

"Okay. The precinct kept Morgan on the night-shift inside Willy's room while Tommy was on duty in the hall outside the room. Morgan told us that Willy woke up at exactly 2:10 am and started making sounds. He said Willy seemed eager to talk, like specifically wanting to say something to someone. Morgan told Willy that everything was okay and that Gloria and I would be arriving early in the morning and that Willy should try to sleep until then.

"So now here we were waiting for any sign of Willy at least beginning to stir. Then we were grateful that his eyes suddenly opened. He saw us and ever so slightly nodded along with making some kind of weird facial expression that we could see was his attempt at a smile.

"Hi, Willy," I said.

I spoke softly because there was some new news that I was sure would surprise him—even shock him although it had nothing to do with his condition. Well, here it is. Willy's okay and getting better. But that's not the new news. He woke up this morning and he was alert for the first time. He smiled at Gloria and at me and then at the nurse who walked in to check on him. He also waved to Morgan. No doubt he's healing. Then it happened. He said a few separate words—not part of a single sentence. Just a few separate words and then started blinking once or twice to every question Gloria was asking. One blink meant yes, two meant no."

"Where's the package, Willy?" Where is it?"

After the questioning, Gloria told me that her quizzing of Willy about the package was a ruse. Apparently, she needed to hear from Willy the entire story of how he may have hidden the package and who he might have given it to, up to the time that she herself found it. But she didn't want anyone to know that she found it until you got back. She only wanted to tell you that she had it. She had the utmost confidence that you would know how to take it from there.

"In answer to Gloria's question about where the package was, Willy actually mouthed what looked like the word 'spell.'

"Gloria repeated it to him: 'Spell, you want to spell it out?'

"One blink."

"Then Willy kind of verbally dragged out his answer: 'S-t-e-v-i-e.'"

"You gave the package to Stevie? Stevie from your class? Your girlfriend?"

"One blink. Gloria then told us she knows Stevie and that everyone knows that Willy and Stevie have always liked one another and confide in each other. Then Gloria asked him 'why?'"

"He actually mouthed it answering: 'H-i-d-e.'"

"Gloria repeated herself: 'Stevie has it and is hiding it for you?'"

"One blink."

"Willy, you mean Stevie Wharton? Sheila?"

"One blink."

"What about her, Willy? What about her?"

"'H-a-s,' then he waited. Al, Willy was actually speaking. He seemed all normal. Like his mind was good. Then a new word. It was 'p-a-c-k.'"

"At that, Gloria jumped on it. 'Willy, you mean Stevie has the package?'"

"Willy blinked once."

"F-a-m-i-l-y . . . o-n . . . t-r-i-p."

"Willy, you mean Stevie and her family are on some trip, maybe a vacation and she's holding the package for you?"

"Willy almost smiled and blinked once.

"Gloria then told me that the girl's name is Sheila Wharton and that the humorous story that almost everyone knows because Sheila's always explaining it. It's is when her little toddler brother couldn't say 'Sheila,' and pronounced it something like 'Seemie.' Then that funny sounding name eventually turned into 'Stevie' so that everyone in the family began calling her Stevie, and apparently, she liked it and that's it.

"She's a very cute and intelligent girl, exactly Willy's age and they've been in the same class since Kindergarten. Everyone knows it. They're inseparable. Their friends all think they'll marry some day"

Willy suddenly began to spell."

"P-a-c-k . . . t-r-i-p. . . ."

"What," Gloria astoundingly asked? "Willy, you mean you think the package went along on the trip with Stevie and her family?"

"One blink."

Morgan, Gloria, and me—we started to make guesses. Like, where did the family go if it was a vacation? The first thing Morgan blurted out even without really thinking was "Europe. They're in Europe." Gloria and I looked at each other and instantly felt Morgan hit it. If it was a vacation, probably Europe was it. Of course, it could be a trip to the West Coast or anywhere in the USA, or maybe the Caribbean But somehow Europe sounded right. But the question then was if it was Europe, which country—where?

I guess I wasn't as affected with anxiety or tension about Willy the same as all of us had been, and therefore was more clear-headed. And I wanted to make a good guess about where the Whartons might be but Morgan again blurted out: 'London or Paris!' And again, Gloria and I instantly turned to each other and knew that Morgan was right. It was either London or Paris, or maybe even both.

Even at that, Gloria wouldn't reveal to anyone, including Morgan or me that her motive to find the Wharton's had nothing to do with the package. *She* had the package. Her motive therefore concerned an eerie feeling she had that the Whartons might be a target but that they probably wouldn't know why unless somehow the location of the package was forced out of Stevie.

Nevertheless, despite all the commotion, things started happening fast; we had people at the precinct scouring all the travel agencies located in the Bronx and Manhattan trying to identify any of them that may have booked a trip for the Wharton family. If so, it could be we'll be getting their itinerary—air transport and hotel.

Al's idea was that Jimmy should start calling hotels in London and Paris. So, while we would be doing the travel agencies here, Jimmy and his guys would be doing hotels there. The idea was to intercept the Whartons. Maybe. Hopefully.

But Gloria seemed anxious. She kept referring to not having enough patience waiting for Al. She kind of knew that Jimmy would get Al involved in their pursuit of the Wharton itinerary as it related to hotel reservations for incoming guests and such, so it would be a while till she would see him again. However, she was determined not to reveal to anyone that it was she who had possession of the authentic microfilm.

· 9 ·

THE STEVIE TRAIL

Yes, Gloria was right. Al and Jimmy got right to it. Hotels. It was going to be easy they thought. Father Hugh O'Flaherty offered them free rein; use of telephones, directories, whatever they needed. They thanked him for the offer and for his obvious understanding of what they were after, but the apartment was too cramped. They decided to rent a two-bedroom apartment in another hotel nearby because apartment # 3 in O'Flaherty's building was no longer available.

The crazy thing was that Al and Jimmy felt weird because Hugh's little townhouse/ apartment-hotel was directly outside the walls of the Vatican near to the Vatican Museum. Therefore, it was also near one of the several entrances to the Vatican. Alex Kaye, a private detective from the Bronx, and Jimmy McKay of British Secret Service, stationed in London, figured that a plan might easily be conceived and very definitely implemented that first, could get them into the Vatican, and next, into Hudal's lair. After all, they were there—in this tiny perimeter of Rome named *The Vatican*. They both knew that either could pull the trigger without blinking. Just knowing that Hudal would be within a stone's throw and that all sorts of archival information, including the specific data they wanted was right there. It gave them the feeling that such data could, without a shadow of a doubt, be captured and at the same time, Hudal would be history.

Alas, and of course, they wouldn't do it. It was not a matter of couldn't.

It was only a matter of wouldn't. More pressing they were there to gain access to the trail that would lead them directly to Stevie/Sheila, and then hopefully, to retrieve the package. That was priority number one. But they couldn't neglect talking about any plan to penetrate the Vatican, and with luck on their side, get to Hudal. Of course, the strange parallel issue was that they kept obsessing about the package when in reality Gloria already had it in her possession.

"If that were the case," Al said to O'Flaherty, "Even if we could get to Hudal, we would need to know where to look. Whatdya say?"

"I say," O'Flaherty answered, "that it would have been stored in the Vatican's *Secretary of State* office, and if so the file would be included in the *State Archive* responsible for correspondence and things related to commissions of one sort or another. What comes to mind is any file that might have the title of: *The Pontifical Commission of Assistance in Rome.*

"My associates and I have always felt that this sort of ambiguous title was a cover for the *Odessa Monastery Route*, and for the *Nazi bolt-hole* as an example of escape hatches like the one from South Tyrol to the port of Genoa here in Italy. However, with Monsignor Giovanni Battista Montini's influence, it could be that all such materials were transferred to the *Department of Grants and Appointments* which I believe was perhaps surreptitiously supervised by none other than Bishop Alois Hudal. It was that Montini had been a favorite of the conservatives and was rumored to have ambition to become Pope. Therefore, for many years he had an aura of power.

"I have never seen the office that houses this *Department of Grants and Appointments* but by the process of elimination, I believe it may be housed somewhere in the Vatican Museum, almost right outside of my door here. Probably somewhere in the basement where there is a maze of rooms looking like a labrynthian blueprint."

"It's good to know, Hugh," Al said. "Except that now our first order of business is to get to this Wharton family. Let's do London first."

With that, they decided to first look into three-star hotels figuring that such hotels are nice enough so that it would be safe for the children and, in addition, also reasonably priced. Al then called Gloria at home in the Bronx in order to get any further update on Willy but more important to ask about the financial condition of the Wharton family.

Gloria was ecstatic to hear from him and told him the Wharton father, William, was a real-estate investor and owned more than a dozen buildings in Queens so he was obviously fairly well off. The only other thing Gloria told Al was that she did have something to tell him but wouldn't talk about it over the phone. She told him that Willy was okay and then made it clear that the rest she had to tell him was equally important.

"Gloria," Al quickly stated, "you've got to tell me now."

"Can't do it now—not over the phone," she quickly answered. It's important, even vital, but still I cannot say it over the phone. Come home as soon as possible. That's all I can say now. But trust me. I know what I'm talking about."

They ended the conversation with Al telling Jimmy what Gloria had just said.

"I guess you've got to skedaddle back home," Jimmy answered. "You've got to trust what she says. We both know she's very smart. But at the moment, I'm still wondering what was Stevie doing in a school with Willy since her father was affluent? She probably could have been a student at a private school in Manhattan. Right?"

The answer was that even though Willy and Stevie went to the same school, because it had a special advanced honors program, in this case located in a public grammar school it turned out that in such a school, both more or less affluent kids would be found comingled. With that sort of information regarding Mr. Wharton's affluence, Al and Jimmy had more confidence to investigate three as well as four-star hotels. Jimmy stepped in and called one of his M-16 agents who then put a squad of several of these secret service men on the job of finding any target hotel that had the Wharton family on the register. Jimmy told his contact to let him know immediately if they located the family and asked them if so, to then quarantine them.

Now it was Paris time. They immediately located five or six hotels and began calling them. They called the *Hotel de Crillon, Hotel du Jeu Paume,* and the *Relais Hotel du Vieux Paris*, and got nothing out of it. They were about to dial the *Hotel du Louvre* when Jimmy almost choked on what he was suddenly thinking and eager to say.

Al saw it. "Jim, what?"

Jim walked over to Hugh and whispered in his ear. He then motioned to Al with his finger over his lips indicating Al shouldn't talk. Al got it immediately. The room might be bugged. Al took a sheet of paper and wrote:

"Hugh, have your rooms been swept for any listening devices—bugs?"

Hugh shook his head, 'no,' and Al wrote: "Let's get some air." Then Al said out loud: "Let's all take a walk." He showed the note to Jimmy.

"Good idea," Jim responded.

In the street they talked it over.

"This is scaring me," Hugh said. "If it's bugged which I'm sure it is, then they know what we're up to and they certainly heard you, Jimmy, asking to quarantine the Wharton family—and no less to M-16. They definitely know what M-16 is. Especially M-16, Section 6! It's a half step for them to see that the Wharton family probably has the package."

"The townhouse doubles as a mini hotel," said Hugh. "As you can see I have a one-bedroom apartment with a little nook for my desk and bookcase, as well as a small kitchen, and one bathroom. Since I'm known as a sworn enemy of Hudal and his gang, you might be right. They may have been kept informed of all of my plans. This may have been ongoing for who knows how long—maybe as long as I've been here. Five years now."

"Come to think of it," Hugh continued, "I must have had some vague feeling about this without my really being conscious of it because I made it a point never to be specific on the phone about the addresses of safe houses I used for Jews and allied soldiers. In fact, I never mentioned the word 'Jews' on the phone. How about that? I must have known all along not to trust the phone."

To say this new awareness was alarming is putting it mildly. Al and Jimmy talked it over later and both agreed that Hugh is a knowledgeable guy but as a true Christian, which is what he was, also a bit naïve about insidious moves.

Hugh's story is that he had never married. When they were all together, that is, together with Imi and Wiesenthal, Hugh shared, or perhaps confessed to Al and Jimmy that he had been very tempted by the very attractive wife of one of the cousins of a Vatican Swiss Guard. Hugh said that, as drawn to her as he was, he did not give in to his feelings which were apparently shared by the woman. His commitment to his mission was very strong and he withstood the temptation. Hugh confessed that the entire flirtation put him in an unending panic.

Al related the story as he heard it. Hugh spoke a King's English—in his case also honest and forthright. Now they were all in a different kind of panic. Hugh's panic was about love but their collective panic was about death. Yes, death. And the frightening prospect was the terror of thinking that there were children to protect—the Wharton children—and that their mission to retrieve the package also could be in serious jeopardy.

They ran looking for a pay phone. They knew they couldn't use the phone in Hugh's apartment. They found a public phone and Jimmy called his contacts at M-16. He told them what was what. His contact then told Jimmy that he was about to call him because the Whartons were located the at the *Rubens at the Palace* and an M-16 contingent was on its way as they spoke.

Looking at Al and Hugh, Jimmy said: "They're at the hotel *Rubens at the Palace.* I know it. It's a classic older style hotel but very nice. People love it. Caters to families. My agents are on their way."

"Jim," Al intoned, "there's no doubt that Hudal can also make one phone call to some people who he'll be sure will do his bidding. Those people, Hudal's group, will then get over to the *Rubens* pronto, meaning fast—meaning at the speed of light. Guys, it's still a nail-biter."

"Hugh, Jim and I are leaving for London immediately. You stay here and keep your eyes and ears open for any strange things that may be happening. I'm particularly thinking of Hudal's gangsters slipping the little Stevie girl into his inner sanctum—the Vatican—right into Hudal's hands.

"Let's keep in mind that these people sent a couple of men all the way to the unlikeliest of places, the Bronx, and for the purpose of their mission they even pushed a twelve-year-old boy off a third-floor ledge. Killing him meant nothing to these people. What chance does some little American girl have with them? No chance whatsoever. Not a chance!"

* * *

The landing at *Heathrow* was uneventful. They were met by an M-16 two-man team who took their bags and they all drove off directly to the *Rubens at the Palace.* Of course, the adage is: 'plan for the worst and hope for the best.' No such luck. The desk concierge stated that the Wharton family met some people that morning at about 9:00 am after breakfast. They all left together.

"Now that I think about it, the concierge said, "it was two men who approached them after they had finished breakfast. I noticed two children with the parents. It was the mother, the father, a little boy and a little girl, and the two men. The little girl was a pre-teenager and the boy was about six or seven-years old. All of them walked out of the hotel lobby together. By that time the lobby was getting busy."

The concierge looked at the registration records and confirmed the family had not checked out. Before M-16 departed they flashed ID's, and the one who was speaking to the concierge gave him his card and asked to be updated with a phone call as soon as he might have any further information.

At that point, the concierge, apparently concerned, asked: "Is anything wrong?"

Then two days later, still there was no further development noted by the concierge. The concierge informed the M-16 agents that the Wharton family had not been seen and there was no answer from any phone-call the desk made to their suite or by personally checking the rooms. Maid-service also confirmed that the rooms had not been slept in. It was a two-room suite and all was clean and neat—no trace of any occupancy—save for the closet and drawers of dressers which in contrast, had an array of cosmetics on the table near the beds. It was indeed proof of occupancy.

*   *   *

The Vatican and museums were already busy, occupancy gaining by the hour. And there was Hudal, in the flesh. It was Bishop Alois Hudal accompanied by three others. He took the stairs. His habit was not to use the elevators. Down he went into the bowels of this hallowed place to the basement, where he was weaving here and there through this labrynthian maze of doors and corridors. He was not wearing his clerical vestments. Rather, he was dressed as a European/Italian business man and had instructed his chief aide, Joseph Prader, as well as two assistants never to use his name.

At this time, within the room, the girl and boy were both crying but the mother and father were not. They were all blindfolded.

"Stevie, I need you to try not to cry," said Mr. Wharton. "If you stop then Nate will too. Okay? We'll get out of this, Stevie, and we'll be home sooner than you think."

Whimpering, Stevie answered through her tears: "Okay, Daddy, okay. I'm trying. I'm scared."

"Whoever you are, sir," Mr. Wharton said calmly, "could you please remove the blindfolds. My children are frightened and if you remove the blindfolds it will help."

There was no response. The hulking guy just sat there watching them. Stevie started crying again and so did Nate. "Daddy," she said, "he's not answering. No one is answering."

"Sir," Mrs. Wharton said," please undo the blindfolds. Please"

Mrs. Wharton's entreaty, along with Stevie's courage even to talk, and Mr. Wharton's straightforward request apparently finally softened the hulk who broke his silence and began talking to them in a deep basso voice. It seemed his heart was touched by the alliance and family togetherness of these abductees.

The hulk's voice depicted him as big, strong and of course, dangerous. Nonetheless, and possibly because he was talking — Stevie stopped crying. When they were released she later revealed to one of the M-16 agents that when the hulk started talking, she suddenly knew he wouldn't hurt them and that made her feel somewhat safer. As a result, her fear just as suddenly decreased.

"All I can tell you," the hulking watchdog said, "is that you will be alright. Don't worry."

In the meantime, Hudal and his assistants entered a room deep into the rear of the basement. They walked through an unlit foyer and entered another corridor that led at the end, to a final door. As he opened the door, he saw four people sitting in chairs guarded by a rather large hulking man. The Whartons were sitting in chairs positioned with their backs to the door of the room, facing the opposite furthest wall. The chairs were positioned this way so that whoever entered the room could not be seen — and would never be able to identify who it was that entered. However, Hudal walked around them, unconcerned about being identified, and looked directly at them.

"Who are you?" exclaimed Mr. Wharton, "And what do you want of us? Is this a kidnapping for ransom? If so, how much are you asking? I have some wealth and I can provide you with a reasonably large sum of money."

"We can forgo the money, sir. We are after something rather valuable to us which we think you have. As a matter of fact, we're sure you have it. So, sir, where is it?"

"I swear, for the life of me, I haven't the vaguest idea what you mean — of what you're talking about," answered Mr. Wharton.

"Mr. Wharton, we are not naïve people. We know you do possess what we are after. Please do not deny it because you and your family members will then come to no good. Do you understand? I'm trying to be a bit obtuse because of the children. Are you of the Hebrew faith? Are you Jewish?"

"What?" answered Mr. Wharton. "We're American. American!"

"Daddy," Stevie piped in. "I know what he means."

"You do?" said Mrs. Wharton.

"Well, Stevie, what *is* it?" Mr. Wharton said with intonation.

"It's got something to do with a package that Willy gave me to keep, or rather to hide for him. He said it was important for me not to tell anyone about it."

"Stevie, what package? Where is this package and what does it contain?"

"Daddy, the package is not here with us in London. I have it somewhere at home."

"The package is not here?" interrupted Hudal. "Not here?"

"No, sir, it's not here. It's in New York City, in the borough of the Bronx, where we live a block from the Grand Concourse. We live on Weeks Avenue."

Stevie was rushing her words and repeated herself. "We live on Weeks Avenue in the middle of the hill. It's a steep hill with apartment buildings and we live in the end building."

"Stevie, you never mentioned a word of this. Why?"

"Because I promised Willy, Daddy. I promised I would never tell anyone."

"Okay, sir," Mr. Wharton said to Hudal. "You see, it cannot be denied that my daughter is telling the truth. It's obvious. So, either accompany all of us to the U.S. or leave me here and take my wife and children with you to America and to the Bronx. There, my daughter will hand you the package. When she does and if you're satisfied, please call your assistants and have me released in order to join my family back home. I hope you will see that as a reasonable request."

"Yes, it is reasonable. However, I would like your daughter to tell us here and now where in the Bronx and in or out of your home she hid the package. In other words, Mr. Wharton, please instruct your daughter to tell us now exactly where it is."

"Sheila, tell him! We don't have time to equivocate or delay."

"The package is hidden in Miss Messer's classroom in a secret place."

"You mean Miss Gloria Messer's classroom at the school?

"Yes, but Miss Messer doesn't know about it. I put it there during her recess class when her kids were with her in the schoolyard and not in the classroom. No one saw me."

"Little girl," Hudal sensitively asked: "Stevie, Sheila, where in the classroom?"

"It's on the lower shelf of Miss Messer's storage closet where she keeps all the things she's not using any more—at least not using because it's a different topic Miss Messer is now teaching. The topic she finished was about nouns and verbs and the materials she stored on the lower shelf were many cards with sentences that she used to teach the nouns and verbs. She also added adjectives. I know all of that from last year. Now can we now please go home?"

"Well, here's what we'll do. We will take you, Mrs. Wharton, and your very bright little daughter Stevie/Sheila with us to the Bronx, and you Mr. Wharton, and your son will remain here. As soon as we have the package, you both will be released and escorted to *Urbe*, the airport near here which will take you to Heathrow. There you will be provided with tickets and put on the plane to New York City's Idlewild International Airport. Please be assured that after we have the package, we will leave you, Mrs. Wharton, along with your daughter, unharmed, so that you will be able to again cohere your family when your husband and son return—also unharmed.

"Would you say, Mr. Wharton, that given the circumstances and needs we all here have, that such an arrangement might be the best we can do?"

Mr. Wharton was cool about it all and calmly answered:

"Agreed. It's not ideal but as you say, given the circumstances, I agree."

With that, Hudal told Mr. and Mrs. Wharton that he would see to it that arrangements would get under way posthaste.

· 10 ·

GLORIA

Hudal issued instructions to each of his men. The hulking guard was told to lead Mr.Wharton and his son to a predetermined place that Hudal had prepared for such an occasion. However, Hudal wondered if there would be any of his associates who would not agree to follow an order related to a child's disappearance. The father was another story. His plea for his son's well-being might be granted, but any clemency for him alone would in all likelihood not be heeded.

In any event the guard led the blindfolded father and son out of the room with the father carrying his six-year-old son in his arms. Both had hoods covering their heads.

"We'll be okay," Mr. Wharton gently whispered to his son who was whimpering as they were led out. Wharton held back his feelings. It took all of his energy not to scream out, 'I'll kill you for this! I will kill you!' But he was, in fact, screaming silently.

Yes, this calm seemingly civil gentleman was at that moment feeling homicidal. He was, in his heart, against any organized killing such as capital punishment. Yet, in this moment he could clearly see that justified homicide was not, in his moral universe out of the question. He knew that if he had a weapon capable of erasing these vermin from the face of the earth, he would use it without any consideration of mercy — whatsoever. He was screaming this in his reverberating echo-chamber of a thumping chest, but, of course, — never dared to speak it. He did not utter a word nor did he show a trace of what he was feeling.

In this citadel of Christ, Mr. Wharton would never forget and never forgive. Never! Actually, he had figured out where they were because, despite being led into the place blindfolded, in the darkness of night, he still accumulated enough hints — cues about the place — so that he could sense that it was connected to the Vatican or possibly actually within the Vatican.

He knew they flew the family out of London headed for Italy. He then surmised that the pilot and crew were instructed not to mention Italy or Rome because they conspicuously talked about everything related to where they were headed except mentioning the targeted destination. Nevertheless, while they were talking to one another Mr. Wharton heard the pilot and copilot inadvertently mention "Urbe." And he knew that Urbe was an airport in Rome. Of course, now, this Meister-planner, Hudal, had confirmed it was their Urbe.

Further, when the family had originally been abducted, they were seated close to the pilot's cabin and the cabin door was kept ajar the entire flight. Mr. Wharton could see that because it was a private aircraft, the pilot's cabin door is at least usually ajar. Therefore, the Whartons and their children were able to hear and see everything that was happening.

When they landed Mr. Wharton's suspicions were confirmed when he heard the announcement over the loudspeaker at the airport that they had landed at the Rome Urbe Airport which he knew was a small civilian airport. But when they were taken at night to the location in which they found themselves, the hints became scarce. The male Whartons were still guarded and held in a separate location within the Museum's basement, as Mrs. Wharton and her daughter, Stevie, were about to board a plane heading for the United States — from the Rome Urbe Airport.

The women wore no blindfolds or hoods. Mrs. Wharton was told by the two men who escorted her and her daughter to board the plane and were cautioned not to make any commotion or to scream out.

"Remember," one of the men whispered to her, "we have your son and your husband." It was instantly evident to her that by mentioning her "son" first she knew that he was emphasizing the danger her son was in and his safety depended on her. Of course, Stevie also heard what was said and so both she and her mother did exactly as they were told.

The two men escorted them to the boarding platform and watched as they entered the plane. On board, they were escorted and guarded by another two men.

Hudal was now unburdened and quite excited. He was going to get that package. He was sure its delivery was imminent and he decided if all went well he would definitely abide by his verbal commitment to release the father and son and also have them escorted to the airport. It made him feel cleansed both by acquiring the package as the first order of business and second by erasing the complication of caring for his so-called guests, or needing to take extreme measures.

None of this mattered anyway; Hudal had been dressed down by Montini—the one with all the influence at the Vatican. Hudal's phone call to Monsignor Montini to keep him abreast of the situation, led to a contentious interaction. Montini's answer to Hudal's various options about the possible fate of Wharton and his son was a definite 'No!' Montini said it in no uncertain terms:

"They are not to be touched. The entire family is not to be touched. You see, Hudal, and remember that Hugh O'Flaherty is also not to be touched. Never! Keep in mind—so long as he can be an operative for his cause so can we do the same for what we do. He has become successful in his way and in numbers. But we have outstripped him and his cohorts by some enormous factor—an exponential factor. In all the years, he has spent rescuing perhaps hundreds of these Jews along with allied soldiers we, in contrast, now in our Lord's year of one-thousand nine-hundred fifty-eight, have rescued as I say, multitudes of thousands! And we have seeded them—seeded them in a dispersed fashion on every continent. Our Third Reich my dear Hudal, may not be over.

"In addition, Hugh knows of the package and probably assumes something about its contents. He knows who the two Americans are who appeared at the *Rubens at the Palace*. So now we have their photos that were taken secretly at the *Rubens*. And, by the way, they've been sent to New York City where our people identified them. One is named Alexander Kaye. He is a private detective based in New York. The other is an M-16 operative, James McKay, who is based in London.

"Hugh also knows about the Wharton family—and most of everything else. Therefore, as soon as you receive the package you will release them. Please tell me you understand! We must not add any variables to the complications we already have. Is that clear? It's important that Hugh is untouched and not too distracted by the death of loved ones or driven to blow the top off what we do. There must not be any harm to those in his charge—like the Wharton family.

"To that extent we are limiting our own endangerment. Keep in mind the Pope's position regarding this matter. Our mission is more important than the possible risk entailed by the endangerment of the lives of a few members of a family. Understood?

"However, because his cause can be characterized as a Libertarian one, ours can be characterized as anti-Communist. Therefore, the accusation of the Vatican as a Nazi-loving escape-instrument is nullified. So, any appearance of our connection to the fascist Nazi sympathizer-regimes like those of Peron, Salazar, Franco or Stroessner of Paraguay, and others are similarly nullified.

"You understand? Hugh O'Flaherty is our cover and therefore must at all costs be protected."

"I do understand," Hudal responded. "Please be assured. No harm will come to Hugh or to the Whartons. Once we get the package, we will no longer need to spend energy and time away from, as you say, from what is our anti-communist mission. So, of course, I do agree."

"And listen, Hudal, in any event, it has been more than a month that we need to help Jani Kruger. The Israelis want him very badly. He is the one in the film who beat the old Jewess with a whip. She died. It was horrible. What is the matter with these people filming something like that? What is the matter with them? The world should not be seeing this. Therefore, let us get Kruger out of Germany, immediately. I think it is best to get him to Switzerland and from there I think to Cuba. Batista for sure will take him in because with Batista, it's strictly for the gold. As we know, he loves the gold.

"Am I right? I think I remember that Kruger's first location would be Cuba and then we prepared the second location as the United States. Is that right?"

"Yes, exactly right," answered Hudal. "We had decided that the second location would be the United States where we could get him a job as a mechanic's supervisor in a car repair shop on the West side of Manhattan. I have the name and location."

"Hudal, we also have another problem with Gustav Wagner. Because of his record at Sobibor, many of the concentration camp survivors can identify him as the worst of the worst. We need to transfer him immediately. Where are his locations?"

"I've spoken to Draganovic and Siri," Hudal instantly answered, "and they agree that Wagner goes to Sao Paulo first and then just in case, to Paraguay. We have another machine factory in Asuncion where there will be a managerial position awaiting him, — just in case. When we told him which was first and which, second, he readily agreed. He said that in the event of some catastrophe such as possibly being apprehended, especially imminently apprehended, he had always thought of either going to Sao Paulo or Asuncion but preferred Sao Paulo. That trip is now in contract and should be completed this week. He has provided us with one-hundred- thousand dollars in cash—American dollars. He brought it in one-hundred dollar bills carried by two men in three large suitcases. In addition, in the following two weeks we have a ship all ready to carry seventy others. They will be wearing liturgical garments since we know that such a presentation always works—especially in South American countries like Argentina and Brazil and in the Middle East especially in Egypt and Syria."

They continued talking for another hour discussing travel plans for various highest-ranking Nazis on the run."

Then Montini bade Hudal farewell and said: "Good work Bishop, very good."

*   *   *

Disembarking from Idlewild was uneventful as was the trip itself. Both of Hudal's escorts for Mrs. Wharton and her daughter Stevie were met by a greeter who led them to a limousine that took them straight to the Bronx from Idlewild. Within thirty-five minutes they were at the low end of the Grand Concourse in the Bronx.

They took the Concourse straight to Weeks Avenue where the Whartons lived. After the Whartons freshened up, the escorts insisted they get to the school and Stevie's teacher's classroom. With that, Mrs. Wharton tried to engage the escorts in conversation but they stopped her, with one of the escorts politely but firmly saying:

"Mrs. Wharton, we are trying to be efficient here. We have several instructions. One is to be nice and to treat you with respect. I think we are doing that. But there are other instructions as well. So, I think it's best not to engage us in unnecessary conversation. However, please know that as soon as we obtain the package everything will be back to normal both for you and your daughter and then also for your husband and son."

Without any more conversation or questions from Mrs. Wharton they all found themselves driving to Stevie's school and Miss Messer's classroom heading directly to Claremont Parkway. There they parked at the corner of Claremont Parkway and Washington Avenue, right at the public school number 42 schoolyard. As they were approaching the entrance of the school, Stevie saw two of her friends, young boys playing ball, throwing and catching in the lower schoolyard directly parallel to where the car had parked. One of the boys, Richard Grillo was playing with Henry Namrellek. The boys waved to her and Stevie waved back first to Richie who was closest, and then to Henry who was further away. It was clear that Stevie felt entirely comfortable at the school and apparently had many friends.

At this point it was a late Wednesday late morning and they all entered the school. If they were intercepted by anyone, Stevie was instructed to introduce her mother and the two men as her mother's brothers and to say that her uncles wanted to see one of the classrooms to see what the classrooms in New York looked like.

As luck would have it for the uncles, no one intercepted them, so they climbed the stairs to the second floor. All classes were in session and Miss Messer, Gloria, was standing in front of her desk facing the children and talking. The children were young, and seemed to be third graders. Gloria's door was closed so that Stevie and she couldn't see one another. However, Ms. Messer spotted both uncles looking in through the upper glass portion of the door and she stopped talking and walked to the door. She opened it and immediately saw Stevie, her mother, and these two "uncles." Gloria sensed something just didn't jibe. Of course, Gloria had originally surmised that Willy had given Stevie the package. She was sure of it. In the meantime, she was fully aware that Al was in Europe as were the Whartons, on a vacation. According to Al, the Whartons might have been in danger of some of Hudal's evil doings. That was what Al had told her in the last phone call. The tension of it all for Gloria was that Al still didn't know what she had. Oh boy, Gloria was nervous now, but was a fabulous actor so that apparently, revealed nothing.

"Hi, Stevie. Hi Mrs. Wharton."

Looking at the 'uncles' she said: "Hello."

Then she looked at Stevie. "Stevie, what can I do for you?"

Stevie thought fast. "Oh, your class is almost over. We'll just wait here and I'll talk to you about it when the class is over. Is that okay?"

"Okay. Fine. I won't be long."

The next few minutes for Mrs. Wharton were like a lifetime. The class ended and all the children began leaving the room in bunches. Gloria then exited the room and asked Stevie what she wanted.

"Oh, it's not really anything. It's just that I once needed to keep a package and had nowhere to put it so I came to ask you to keep it for me but the classroom was empty and you weren't here. Well, I just dropped it off on the lower shelf of your closet where I knew it wouldn't be disturbed because that's where you keep all the materials you're no longer using. See? I hope that was alright?"

"Of course, Stevie" she replied reassuringly. "Go ahead and take it."

With that Stevie walked to the closet, kneeled down, rifled through some of the stuff languishing there and found the package. She took the package and walked out into the hall. They all said their goodbyes and Gloria shook hands with Mrs. Wharton and the uncles and embraced Stevie who was quite obviously in a state of distress which Gloria could see.

Mrs. Wharton, Stevie, and the "uncles" left the school and drove away in the limo. One of the uncles held the package, gripping it tightly. Mrs. Wharton and Stevie sat in the back seats and both uncles sat in the back jump-seats facing them. The uncle with the package instructed the limo driver to stop at the nearest public street phone. In a few blocks, the driver pulled the limo to the side of the street and parked adjacent to a public phone booth at the corner of the block. The uncle immediately made a phone call. He was speaking in German and as he was intensely conveying something, Stevie blurted out:

"I want my father and brother let go. You promised."

At that she started crying. Mrs. Wharton jumped in, reassuring Stevie as well as indicating to the escorts that Stevie was right. She said:

"You're right, Stevie, you're right. They promised and they said they would keep their promise. The leader, that man promised."

"The package-carrying uncle, who was on the phone quickly returned to the limo. Stevie was still crying. He held the package, shooshed both

Stevie and Mrs. Wharton, held his hand out with finger pointing as though to say, 'wait a minute,' and then happily announced:

"They're free. Mrs. Wharton, Stevie. Mr. Wharton and the boy are free. They've been released because of what I told my comrades regarding having the package. They're about to be escorted to the airport. There will be no delay. From Rome to London is not that far. They'll be in London soon. They are safe and sound and as soon as we get you home, actually as soon as you step out of the car, you will be free as well."

With that both Mrs. Wharton and Stevie began sobbing.

* * *

As soon as they all left the school, Gloria quickly got on the phone and placed a trans-atlantic call to Hugh in Rome. The phone rang in Hugh's apartment, and sure enough, it was answered.

"Is this Father O'Flaherty?" Gloria asked.

"Yes, it is," was the answer. "Who may I ask is calling?"

"Father O'Flaherty, it's me, Gloria. I know you know who I am. I need to get a message to Al. Tell him that the Wharton mother and daughter were here with two men looking for the package. Stevie, the Wharton daughter who was entrusted by Willy with the package apparently hid the package in my closet at the school.

"Please tell Al that without knowing what Stevie did, a few days ago before I left school at about 4:15 pm in the afternoon, I needed to go to that closet. While searching through my lower shelf for something that I thought I might have mistakenly stored there, I came across a small oblong package. I instantly shuddered because in some way I thought I knew what it was, or might be.

"I opened it right there and unpacked another package that was inside. And there, inside the second package was what looked like microfilm. I've taken the microfilm and hid it elsewhere. Today, Mrs. Wharten and Stevie along with two men with European accents and good manners, seemed nevertheless to be unsavory characters. They visited my classroom and Stevie retrieved the package which I had carefully rewrapped and returned to the place in the closet where I originally found it.

"They then all left with the repacked package. At some point, whoever opens it will see that the package is empty and figure out that probably either Stevie lied to them about where it was, or that I would be the likely person to have discovered Stevie's hiding place and they will probably come after me or try to get Stevie to confess. Do you understand what I've said?"

"Yes, of course. Understood. I will convey everything to Alexander Kaye. Where did you hide the package? I must tell him. He will want to know."

Gloria then froze. A smart girl from the southeast Bronx she probably could detect a con game when she sees or hears it. She later told Al that the way the person at the other end of the phone-call repeated that he would convey it all as he said: "to Alexander Kaye," gave her chills. If that person knew Al why did he say Al's full name. It didn't have the ring of truth and now Gloria was convinced that the bad guys knew everything except of course the exact location of the microfilm. Then she figured that perhaps they, the so-called "unsavory characters" were instructed to deliver the package but to not tamper with it.

"Tell him," Gloria calmly responded, "that Stevie had no idea I had found the package. It was when she was on vacation with her parents that I stumbled upon it."

She then hung up the receiver. She now knew she had no choice but to run home only a few blocks from the school, quickly pack a few things, not to forget her keys, and certainly not to forget the microfilm, and then take off to—yes, she knew where—to the Van Cortlandt Motel, to be exact, at 6393 Broadway, not far from the park that she and Al knew so well. But first she needed to call Mrs. Wharton at home and get her and Stevie to meet her at the hotel, immediately.

"What?" Mrs. Wharton alarmingly asked.

"Yes," Gloria said. "Get out of the house immediately and come to the Van Cortlandt Motel at 6393 Broadway. "Quickly pack some items you may need and meet me there. I'm on my way. Check at the office for my room number. Do you understand? This is not the time to discuss why. It's urgent. Please. Hurry."

As Gloria was leaving and about to lock her door, the phone rang. She rushed back into the apartment and lifted the receiver. When she heard Al's voice she almost choked with relief. She quickly told Al the entire story and told him where she, Mrs. Wharton, and Stevie would be. Al told her she was right on because he figured Hugh's phone was tapped.

Before they said their goodbyes and "take care," and "be careful" and "I love you," Gloria could no longer hold it in and repeated:

"Al, we got it. We got the micro. It'll be with me at the motel."

Al told her to stay put at the motel and that he's on his way home and will meet her there. Al hung up the and made a trans-Atlantic call to the 48th precinct. He asked for Mac or Lyle. He got Mac and told him the story—including that they had the microfilm. They agreed that the only thing to do was to have a squad of cops wait at the gate to TWA flights from Rome to Idlewild. He told Mac it was highly possible that foreign agents were planning to again kidnap Mr. Wharton and son. Al and Mac then agreed that the Wharton father and son should be brought to the motel immediately to a grateful reunion of the entire family. Mac also said that only Lyle and he and their other two buddies at the precinct, Detectives Jack Lehrman and Harry Harrison would know where the Whartons and Gloria were holed up. Thus, the Whartons and Gloria would be heavily guarded by professionals.

After the phone call, Al and Jimmy congratulated one another about finally corralling the microfilm. They then reached Hugh through an intermediary and made urgent plans with Hugh for him to use the phone to create a flow of disinformation knowing full well that Hudal was surely behind a phone tap and without any doubt had been and would continue to target Hugh's phone.

Al and Jimmy decided to fly from *Ciampino Airport*—another airport near Rome close to the *Greater Ring Road*. They landed in London and from there Jimmy and Al shook hands and said their goodbyes. Jimmy wished him luck, and Al immediately headed to *Heathrow* for a trip to *Idlewild*.

PART 3

BACK TO THE BRONX

· 11 ·

HUDAL'S PANIC

Gloria and Al knew everything there was to know about the Van Cortlandt Motel. Why? The answer is simple. Some years ago, when they first met, Gloria worked at a school near Poe Park, a small park in The Bronx celebrating the poet Edgar Allan Poe. They met because Al was investigating a case and was sitting on a park bench eating his sandwich. As Gloria was walking by and about to enter the park, she was passing by where Al was sitting. As Al was taking a bite out of his sandwich a slice of tomato squirted out from it and hit Gloria's light tan coat at about knee length.

Surprised with the suddenness of it, they both looked at the coat and then at one another. The coat was stained. It turned into a bright dark red spot. Al quickly handed her one of the napkins he was holding and Gloria quickly blotted the spot and scraped the portion of the tomato that was gently lingering on the coat, soaking as much of the tomato juice into the coat as possible.

Al profusely apologized and offered to pay for the cleaning bill or even to pay for the cost of a new coat. Yes, he did say that. But Gloria declined. Al was persistent and asked her if he could at least buy her some lunch. That she accepted. They later confessed that they were immediately attracted to the other. Obviously, both were happy about the incident and of course a relationship developed. It was a relationship that developed as though both were hit by lightening. They began a torrid love affair acting on it not far from Van Cortlandt Park itself. Their meeting place was the

Van Cortlandt Motel where they had their furtive assignations. Boy, were they in love, in sex, in a rhapsodic thrall, and, well, in everything.

Since the motel was where they met for their romantic encounters, it was a natural for Gloria to have it pop into her head in one of her quick decisions—to decide to get to this safe harbor. 'Hide at the motel,' a simple four-word sentence is what popped into her head.

*   *   *

Everyone was flying everywhere. The Whartons—father and son—were now on a flight to New York. Al was on a flight from London to New York. The 'uncles,' as it were, were on a plane from Idlewild to Rome and were whispering to one another conspiratorially.

About two hours into their flight one of the uncles, the one holding onto the package was eagerly anticipating what he would see if he opened the package. Then he could no longer restrain himself. He looked at his counterpart who returned the look with a knowing glance and they both looked at the package as the uncle holding it began to carefully nudge it open.

Inside was the other package which he also deftly opened. Nothing. The inner package was stuffed with strips of crumpled newspaper. All filler. Nothing else! They stared at the empty package, then looked at one another both feeling obviously taken. Their next reaction was to get worried and in their mother-tongue they began talking speedily—which in their broken English would be translated as:

"Karl, vee in dis trouble?"

"Yah, I tink so. Vee vill needing to explaining dis."

"But dis vas no vee fault. It must be dat dis teacher has dis real package or dat dis little girl fooling us. It ist possible dat little girl fooling us?"

"No, ist no possible because she knowing her father und brother could be danger if she doing someting like dat. No. No. It ist teacher. Vee must reaching Bishop. Vhen vee due to landing?"

"More hours."

*   *   *

"What?" Hudal shouted. "What?" He then held his stomach and slumped over in a crouched postion as though he was shot—hit with a shotgun dead-on. "God, Oh God. They have the microfilm. Oh God. What can we do? We need to know what to do? How could you let this happen," he shouted at them?

The 'uncles' were speechless but Karl regained his senses and reminded Hudal that they were instructed not to do anything with the package except deliver it. Karl confessed that he couldn't resist seeing what was in the package and opened it. It was then he told Hudal that he realized they'd been deceived.

"But given the circumstance, you could have had the sense to disregard the instruction and to open the package. It would have been the intelligent thing to do. You both are not novices. You've been through many adventures together. You should have known to open the package given the strange circumstances of the child, the school, the teacher, and so forth."

Hudal was out of his mind with blame and anger. He was barely listening to them. Then suddenly—he knew what he wanted to do.

"We must get the teacher. She has the microfilm. What do you think? Karl, what do you think?"

In a flood of realization Karl instantly said he thought it was complicated, because the Whartons and the teacher, undoubtedly were about to be, or were already in some safe-house. His reasoning was that such a strategic decision would be the only thing open to them—knowing full well that once he and Wenzel opened the package, that they would just as instantly understand what had happened. He also predicted that the teacher would no longer be in possession of the contents of the package because she would have necessarily handed it over to the police or to that private detective who himself must now be on his way, or even has already arrived at whatever secluded destination—possibly that same safe-house—in all likelihood agreed upon in advance. And as a conclusion, Karl stated that he didn't think he was giving them too much credit for possibly planning it that way.

Hudal then knew he must contact Monsignor Montini immediately and he set out to do just that. In their conversation Hudal was awkwardly trying not to convey his underlying panic. He was, as were most at the Vatican, aware of Montini's influence. However, Montini was not at all disturbed by the news. He knew it was simply an inconvenience. He also knew that the plan to retrieve the package was lost before it began. He had another idea.

"Hudal," he intoned. "Please realize we have two options: The first considers the fact that we have the means, the organization, and the ultimate patience for informing those we need to inform that we and they have been compromised. Because of that fact, we will suggest to them that for all concerned, both with respect to safety and potential incrimination—and that means us as well as them—should immediately seek shelter in their pre-planned secondary locations. This is true especially for I would guess about thirty of the most infamous of our clients. It is not possible even with our organization that ten-thousand individuals will move, with such short notice. Of great importance is that Eichmann, Mengele, Priebke, Stangl, and the others must move immediately because if they are caught they will without a doubt be tried in the courts or could easily be assassinated. I would think that Eichmann and Mengele are the two most sought.

"I know that Stangl, would leave Syria and relocate to Brazil, to Sao Paulo. Mengele will need to travel from Argentina to Brazil as well. We can't be concerned about the thousands here and there all over South America in Uruguay, Bolivia, Argentina, Chile, or even located in the Middle East like Beirut and Damascus, not to mention Cairo. Remember, Hudal, we are talking about perhaps nine or even ten-thousand who have already been sent to primary locations. Obviously, Eichmann must now immediately be alerted to this breach. The only question for Eichmann is his stubbornness. Will he move to his second location? That is the question. Mengele, of course would move in a second. I know we wanted his secondary place to be Paraguay but he also insisted on Brazil. Same for Brunner in Syria. Brunner will not want to move. His power there is immutable. Rauff in Chile, I don't know. But of course, whoever—it's up to them. We have done our part, except for this fiasco, in the best possible way. Now it is up to them.

"What I'm afraid of," Montini continued, "is that once people are settled, they may be reluctant to move again and will use any excuse about why they shouldn't move, thinking that it will all pass over—that with our power they would be unreachable.

"At the moment, I'm now also thinking of some others like for example, Roschmann in Buenos Aires. He must absolutely relocate to Paraguay. I seem to remember Paraguay as his second location. But I don't remember where in Paraguay. Most likely Asuncion. But I'm not sure where

Kutschmann's secondary is. I know he's now in Buenos Aires. Of course, it is of the utmost importance for Priebke to leave Buenos Aires and get to Bariloche. They are after him in a determined way. This we know. Stangl should leave Syria and relocate to Brazil. As I've already said, I know that Brazil is his secondary location. Again, the question is will he leave? Also, Kurger in Cuba must leave Batista and head for the United States. He'll be safe in the U.S. with a new name just blending into the country's middle southwest landscape.

"Let me think—a few more. Yes, Wagner, Sao Paulo to Paraguay—I don't remember where in Paraguay but we can be sure he will remember. Oh yes, Barbie. He's trouble shooting all over South America but we have him targeted with a secondary refuge in Bolivia. Whether he stays put or resettles there is going to be a dilemma for him. We shall see.

"We only need to inform perhaps twenty-five or thirty of the most wanted, and tell them to run! And, of course, for these twenty or thirty we need to emphasize the '*run*'! The only problem for us is that if any are apprehended, we and the entire enterprise we conduct would be revealed.

"There is a truth we need to face," continued Montini. "The truth is there's no doubt that no matter the commitment to it all, when offered a deal for freedom in exchange for certain information, the deal will be made. You understand? People will only want to save themselves even at the expense of spoiling everything we've done. Of that we can be certain!

"Therefore, as far as the package is concerned, it's an issue that may be out of our hands except for the second option. And the second option means that you don't call off your dogs. The point I'm making is that the question remains as to where the actual microfilm is? There still may be time to retrieve it so that we need not go to all the trouble of contacting all of our, shall we say, clients. I know you believe that our only chance of retrieving the package would most likely involve theft—theft that is supported by shooting, killing and intrigue. However, I believe, in contrast, that it can be done in a relatively peaceful way where our contacts in the United States simply tell us where the package is kept and only then do we need to confiscate it?"

Again, in his calm manner, Montini continued logically.

"In our terms, the package is probably located at what we would characterize as a convent—a place receded, concealed; a refuge impossible to breach. Yet, this presumed impossible place can quite possibly be found, provided we get in touch with our very informative mole. Therefore, I'm telling you to get the plan into motion immediately. Tell him to send us the information as to where the microfilm is hidden. He will be able to do it."

With that, Montini ended his dystopian disquisition.

"Yes, of course. That's good," Hudal answered. "Of course, that is the thing to do. That will put everything back on track. Yes. Anyway, Monisnor Montini, how would the Allies be able to round up ten-thousand men and put them on trial. They couldn't. And even if they could, they wouldn't. So, if the second option doesn't work, and we cannot contact them all, we must concentrate on securing those twenty-five most important—those who most likely would be put on trial, and certainly found guilty and then executed. Therefore, the first option you suggest solves the entire enterprise. The point is to just think about the twenty-five or thirty to rescue."

"Excellent," Montini declared. "And since it's these twenty-five or thirty that the Allies, as you rightly say, might actually be put on trial, then our job to protect such a small number becomes immeasurably more realistic. And to be blunt, even if one or two were assassinated, it would similarly subtract from our problem. It would mean, no rush, no extra urgent secretarial work, no phone messages to be sent. That means ultimately, fewer to worry about."

This conversation between Hudal and Montini raised the question as to who was really 'the ghost,' It had been believed by all that Hudal was the ghost. Now it was becoming gradually clearer that there possibly was a true King Ghost—Montini!

* * *

A phone call from Hugh O'Flaherty in Rome to Alex Kaye, who Hugh expected might still be in London, reached the desk of Loris McIver—Mac—who was in New York, in the Bronx. Before that, in London, Jimmy had advised Al to have his phone messages automatically transferred to any police authority Al felt he could trust. Al named Mac at the 48th precinct in the Bronx and obtained the 48th precinct number through an information operator in the U.S.

Of course, Al liked that idea so to set that all up, he first called Sgt.

Silverstein at the 48th, relayed the request about the transmission of his phone messages to Mac, was given an okay by Silverstein, and very soon after the call, Al boarded his flight. Thus, Hugh couldn't reach Al directly.

Simultaneous to this, on the other side of the world—meaning at the *Vatican*, and in broad daylight, and without a concern in the world, Alois Hudal asked to see Hugh O'Flaherty. After all, they were colleagues and since both Hudal and Hugh knew that neither of them could be tampered with or hurt in any way, they could be frank with one another each fully aware of the other's politics, theological understandings, sympathies, and so forth. And so, quite naturally, they addressed one another in a familiar way—by given names: Hugh and Alois.

"Hugh," Hudal said, "for the moment, let's not be repelled by one another's commitment to certain agendas. We both know what I mean. I want you to know that we've called off any need to recapture anyone who was involved in any aspect of the microfilm adventure. Yes, I know you know about it. There is no more adventure of that sort to be concerned about. Therefore, please, at your pleasure inform your friends that they need not fear anything or anyone. I'm telling you this because I assume such information will be important for you to have. But I'm a bit self-interested here because it occurs to me that at some later date, should I need a favor from you, provided it does not compromise others, that perhaps you would be amenable."

With that little exchange, Hudal bowed slightly and left Hugh's office.

Naturally, Hugh had listened to Hudal with interest but not only was he not convinced, rather, he was revolted to think that Hudal would consider some alliance. In fact, Hugh felt that this may have been Hudal's way of constructing a bit of disinformation. In all, and because of Hugh's doubt concerning what Hudal conveyed, Hugh was left, at the least, feeling uncomfortable.

Hugh then called Al but instead, of more directly reaching him, his phone call was transferred and it reached Mac at the 48th in the Bronx. Hugh told Mac that the 'ghost's' chase for the microfilm might have been called off but then again perhaps not. He didn't tell Mac why he was doubtful and Mac didn't ask. Even had he told Mac the why of it all, there might be a chance that it sounded so complicated that Mac wouldn't have believed him or just wouldn't want to deal with it.

On Hudal's side, however, there appeared to be a problem. Hudal was usually prideful of his command status with all who worked for him—with all of his operatives complying with his commands. He didn't ever count on personality features of individuals. What this meant was that Karl and Wenzel, Hudal's emissaries to London and the United States, the 'uncles', were terribly humiliated and desperately wanted to regain Hudal's respect and confidence.

Hudal had originally dismissed them with a touch of contempt, but in the moment, had informed them of the decision to again go ahead, and this time finally retrieve the microfilm. Hudal stated that this should be done with subtlety, and quietly, and with the help of the person they had in America who could get any kind of information needed, anytime, anywhere.

Without any hesitation or delay and before anyone knew it, both 'uncles' were now on their return trip to New York City, to The Bronx. They were determined to repair their reputations with Hudal and were going to overcome any obstacle that interfered with that goal, no matter how impossible it may all seem. Although Hudal said to do it quietly—meaning in the absence of any conspicuous fanfare—the uncles swore to one another that they were going to get the microfilm any which way because the basic issue was primarily to regain favor with Hudal.

Predicting what the uncles would ultimately do in order to achieve their stated goal could be seen in the mistaken sentiment expressed by Mrs. Wharton who had said that these 'uncles' were civil both in attitude and tone so that it appeared they would never do anything violent.

What Mrs. Wharton didn't know was that psychopaths in the service of a tyrannical leader will do anything necessary to achieve whatever the goal was. Anything! And to illustrate this point, the 'uncles' Karl and Wenzel although told to do the job with subtlety and quietly, nevertheless were overjoyed in getting the assignment. Thus, in their quest for respect and perhaps adulation, they were 'juiced' and ready to do *anything* necessary to get the microfilm. In this sense, and despite Hudal's warning, the uncles were ready and hopeful for a victory party—Nazi style!

* * *

Another kind of victory party was unfolding at the Van Cortlandt Motel. A large table was brought in that seated all of them in one room.

Ten altogether. Gloria, Al, Stevie, Stevie's brother Nate, Mr. William Wharton, his wife Mrs. Ruthie Wharton and Mac and Lyle and their little duo gang of Detectives Jack and Harry. When Al arrived, Gloria was visibly relieved to see him. They embraced very personally. Mr. Wharton, in an attempt at humor said:

"Hey, why are you so shy about everything?"

The point is they were all relieved, but before they ate—hamburgers, French fries, and cokes—Gloria took Al into the bathroom and finally showed him the microfilm. She showed him where she had stored the film, in the rear of the towel cabinet, hidden by stacks of towels. Al looked at her with a broad grin, took the package, and before they rejoined the others they embraced—tightly.

When they rejoined the others, Al asked Mac and Lyle to walk him to the door. He told them he was off to the police lab at Headquarters and was taking the package with him, and that he needed them to clear him both at Headquarters and at the 48th.

"I'm going to have them make an exact replica of the package and I'll drop the empty duplicate at the holding pen back at the 48th. When it's ready I'm getting on a plane and taking the real one to London. I'll meet with Jimmy and Imi. From there, the three of us will get the film to Simon. Tell Willy and Frankie I needed to go somewhere and I'll see them later."

But the 'uncles' had a different definition of going "somewhere" and they knew who their contact was in New York City and then *how* to make that contact. The F.B.I. was under the impression that it had fingers and ears plugged into just about all the Nazi sympathizers and spies that lived in the city. They were mistaken. They weren't even close.

Hudal had a large payroll for a few special ones in deep cover who, it was clear, could get practically any information that might be needed for one thing or another at one time or another.

The 'uncles' knew this and they were looking forward to greeting their special contact. They were going to utilize anything they could to unearth the invisible package. They were going to transform this invisible, and per-haps, intangible package into a quite visible and definitely tangible object.

They arrived and checked into the Waldorf. Obviously, money was no object. From their room at the Waldorf, they made the first call to their important contact. This contact was a man in the employ of no less than the State Department. It was not a secret that operatives in the State Department of the United States were never in favor of Israel becoming a nation-state and had always favored the Arab states, namely Egypt, Syria, Jordan, and especially Saudi Arabia.

One of these operatives was an aide to an undersecretary of the department. His name was Parker Martin and he had become 'in the money' way beyond what his salary could justify. The 'uncles' knew that Martin was given considerable payoffs at different times for various kinds of information that was always transmitted to the Vatican.

Hudal had Martin invited into this espionage-ring with an initial offer of twenty-five thousand dollars along with the promise of much more to come. Martin was interested. He was not an ideologue. In fact, he extolled wealth as a strong motivator, and as it turned out, apparently, he just didn't care where the money came from.

The phone call from the Waldorf was directed to Martin's phone at the State Department in Washington. It wasn't that Karl used code language in the phone conversation as much as it was more like some off-target implication-stuff. But Karl was also specific about the package.

Martin confirmed that he had been previously informed about such a package and that he had it traced.

"It was likely," he said, "the package is in the holding pen and stored at the 48th precinct in the Bronx; I was told it was under the supervision of Detectives Loris McIver, nickname of Mac—and Lyle Davis."

Karl and Martin then agreed on their respective descriptions of the package—what it looked like. This satisfied Karl who revealed they were carrying ten in exchange for the information, but that it was then up to them to retrieve the package from the 48th. Of course, Karl knew that Martin understood what "ten" meant. Thus, Karl and Wenzel were determined, and after the discussion with Martin, were encouraged about the possibility of success. They then reasoned that success would mean a regaining of standing in Hudal's favor, and for sure a regaining of favor in Montini's eyes.

They were certain all of this could be accomplished by doing whatever needed to be done to liberate that package from the American 48th police precinct in the Bronx.

· 12 ·

DECRYPTION AT BLETCHLEY

Everyone was focused on the 48th precinct in the Bronx, but hardly anyone was interested in a person apparently living in Jerusalem. That person was Shmuel Kishnov who was a known as a secretive type so that wherever he lived would be just about impossible to locate. When he was affiliated with Kovner's *Avengers*, he was consistently in deep cover and therefore not visible even as one of the more notable members of the group. Yet, he had the reputation within the group as a thinking, as well as a doing man. All the members of the *Avengers* admired him—especially as this *doing* man.

By the time the Kovner group for one reason or another began splintering, there was only one place for Shmuel Kishnov to go. It was to the Palestine territory and specifically to join the *Irgun* which was the Jewish violent offshoot of the *Haganah*. The Haganah was the Jewish Defense Force of the pre-Israel Palestine Mandate, and morphed as well into the overall Israeli Defense Forces post-1948 when Israel became a state.

From the early 1930's to the almost mid 1940's, the Irgun was less an organization of defense and more an organization of an attack force. Irgun became known as a violent Jabotinsky philosophical organization the motto of which could be defined as "with whatever means necessary" to create the Jewish state, Israel. This was of course, the nature of the Irgun that resonated well with the Kishnov *doing* mentality and because of it, in the mid to late 1940's he gravitated to this middle east region just as the birth of the new state Israel was then ratified by the *United Nations*.

Kishnov was drawn to Jabotinsky because Jabotinsky's inherent policy would need men like Kishnov to do what this militant Zionist revisionist wanted—to win at any cost and in any way. For Jabotinsky it was Israel or death, and Shmuel Kishnov was perfectly aligned with all of it.

Kishnov was Russian like Jabotinsky who was originally named Vladimir Yevgyevich Zhabotinsky, and who spent his early years in Berdychiv in Ukraine. Kishnov also came from Ukraine and this similarity of their origins appealed to Kishnov. His family lived in Yaruga, a little hamlet in Ukraine on the border of Romania divided by the Dniestr River.

After Kishnov had worked for a while for Irgun, it became obvious that he would be sanctioned to become an assassin. This role for Kishnov became known to insiders as well as to important others in and out of Israeli Secret Service.

As might be expected, Imi Lichtenfeld mentored Shmuel Kishnov during Kishnov's tenure and also as a Krav Maga fighter. From the mid to late 1940's to the present –1958—Imi again made another foray into the inner sanctum of Israeli Secret Service and Shmuel Kishnov was there to excavate for him.

They met in Jerusalem at the King David Hotel, and sat on the veranda sipping drinks. It was this year, 1958, twelve years since the Irgun blew up the Hotel to create continuing havoc for the British authorities who were ostensibly trying to manage the balance between British interests and anyone else's interests, of course in favor of British interests—broadly defined as continuing to have influence in this part of the world—oil!

It was suspected that Shmuel Kishnov was centrally involved in accomplishing the mission, but it was never proven. Be that as it may, Shumuel started the conversation.

"So, Imi, vhat we hav here?"

Imi had a lot to say over the course of more than two hours that the conversation lasted. Shmuel listened quite intently while Imi held forth as they sipped their drinks and nibbled on some Israeli dishes.

"You believe dis or no, Imi, I hearing about dis un when I did, dis interesting me. Still it do. Dis package un dis microfilm ist gold mine un you hitting as is day say, dis moder-vein. So vhat I can doing for you?"

"I'm not sure, Shmueli, but I do know it would be good if my group could meet with you and we could all talk it over. We've all agreed that you're the person we want. We know the situation might involve kidnappings or assassinations, or any number of other needs we could have including the non-violent one of assuring that the material gets to Simon. Are you anti-Simon or is he someone you could work with?"

"I loving Simon, Imi. Loving him. He ist dis vone who starting all dis Nazi hunting business. Vhen I vas mit Kovner, vee talking about Simon. Kovner liking him too. Of course, I understanding he no ever to be involved in dis physical violence. Ist clear un I sure you knowing, Simon ist only informational how you saying — yes, source — un excellent vone."

"Exactly. That's why we're all agreed that you're the one we need to get certain things done that Simon can't do. Do you need permission to go and join another force or are you free to take the assignment that interests you?"

"It is no deese two tings. I promising you I vill doing it only if certain dose of mine comrades saying no. But den I vould need to arguing it. But I sure it vill be alright. If day being stubborn, I also being stubborn. But I knowing day feeling to protect of me un day saying I being strong asset to dis vork dat vee doing."

"Yes, of course. And the work you do is not much different than the work you would be doing helping us. Understand?"

"Avadeh, understanding. Yah. So, vhen vee leaving un vhere vee going?"

*　*　*

"Jimmy, some good news," Al said on the trans-Atlantic phone call. "We've got the thing and I need to meet you at your place. I'll be there in a few days depending on how fast you can get Tim to arrange whatever he needs to arrange."

I'd also like our other friends to join us and if possible, you and I will get to see Maxie. That would be important. We'd need to go to Maxie's place so we could get the thing into English. Okay? I know you know what I mean."

Of course, Al's reference to their "other friends" was immediately understood by Jimmy to mean Imi, and Hugh. Then a few days later — especially with the help of Timothy Simmons — Al was on a TWA flight to London.

Tim was a forty-year old top pilot for TWA international flights. Tim had once helped Jimmy with some special arrangements to get into and out of Heathrow under and away from the throng of passengers that were always waiting on long lines for various flights. Thereafter, whenever Jimmy needed some special attention, Tim became his go-to person. They liked each other straight off and became friends who would see one another once or twice a year. And this was the second time Tim gave Al the special treatment—best seat, best food, best service, and uneventful flight—smooth landing ending at about fifty feet from Jimmy's waiting limo.

Jimmy told the driver to head out and the limo took them to M-16 headquarters, officially housed in London at number 54 Broadway with an annex at St. James Street. It was the unofficial address of *Ultra*—the overall *British Military Information Project*, the information for which was uncovered, gathered, and supplied by M-16.

However, with this sort of seriousness and business, most likely regarding crucial war-time information, Jimmy instructed the driver directly to St. Ermins Hotel. It was at St. Ermins that such crucial sessions were held.

At St. Ermins, floors three and four were entirely cordoned off and reserved only for use by *SIS* which stood for *Secret Intelligence Service*, the British Equivalent of the *American Office of Strategic Services (OSS)* that after the war became the *American Central Intelligence Agency (CIA)*. And that's where Jimmy and Al reached their destination—at St. Ermins.

They entered a wood-paneled office where Hugh and Maxie were sitting in comfortable club chairs. Each had a cocktail in hand. Al was excited to see the three of them—especially excited to see Maxie who he hadn't been in touch with for a few years. Max jumped out of his chair and gave Al a bear hug.

"Son of a gun," Max declared. "Look at you. You haven't changed a bit since you were twenty. No gut, got all your hair, and Jimmy tells me you still got Gloria. Lucky dog."

Al laughed out loud and Hugh joined the love-fest. Al tried to embrace them all as if they had all won some championship game and were piling on. But Hugh got right to it.

"Gentlemen, gentlemen, decorum please."

That did it and they all went to the conference room and where there was a small round table prepared for them that sat exactly six—for Hugh, Jimmy, Maxie, and Al and for Imi and a guest who had not yet arrived.

"Imi will be arriving, but with a guest," Hugh said. It's one of the main guys from Kovner's original group. His name, I'm sure you've all heard of, is Shmuel Kishnov."

"I know Kishnov," Jimmy said. "We've met before when he was consulted by M-16 about possibly getting some information from German intelligence regarding a Helmut Jenx who had been wanted for the molestation of young girls in Buchenwald. Kishnov knew all about it and told us that Jenx was a classic pedophile. He wouldn't even look at mature women. He was only interested in really little girls, children—probably about eight or nine-years old. According to Kishnov, Jenx couldn't care less about who knew what. He felt entirely invulnerable and would sometimes do his thing in public in front of everyone and anyone. He just didn't care."

At that precise moment, in walked Imi followed by Shmuel Kishnov.

They all stood up as though some revered figure had entered. And it wasn't in honor of Imi. It was as if they all had a unified admiration of Kishnov, since all were aware of who he was and his reputation—especially his history with Kovner and then later with Irgun.

Imi introduced all to Kishnov and announced for Kishnov's illumination briefly what each person was known for: Hugh, a priest at the Vatican, Imi, Kishnov knew, Al, a private detective from New York City, from the Bronx, Jimmy from M-16 who Kishnov remembered and nodded to, and Maxie, who Imi identified as an independent type, a Krav guy.

They all sat and filled Shmuel in on everything that was involved in this microfilm adventure from A to Z. As they were talking Jimmy summoned a wait person who appeared immediately. She was middle-aged, very attractive woman who seemed personable, dependable, and who had great gentility. However, she was also direct. Without waiting she said:

"May I suggest some champagne with strawberries followed by tea and crumpets. It's only 4 pm so this should be sufficient until dinner which will be served at 6 pm. I'm sure you will be quite satisfied. Is there anything else?"

No one said a word. Just nodded polite appreciation. This nice but presumptive lady thanked them and left. Hugh, in trying for humor said:

"Even if the Pope wanted me to say something, I don't think I could—except for that look she gave you as she was leaving, Max. Did everyone see that?"

With that, Al interrupted:

"I've seen it before. If you put Clark Gable, Gregory Peck, John Wayne, and let's say, Bogart or Mitchum in a room—even that heart throb, Sinatra, too, or that guy Brando—and Maxie's there as well, keep your eye on the women and let's see what happens."

That created gales of laughter from all the five others, including by their new companion, Shmuel Kishnov—laughter that was started by Max himself.

But then Al interrupted with something direct.

"Okay, guys, before she returns with the goodies lemmie give you the low-down. First, I've got the micro right here in my pocket. I always carry it on me. Imi, thanks to you, I hope no one messes with me because—well you know why."

Again, Jimmy, Al, and Maxie kind of tried to hold back their laughter but couldn't.

"An in-joke, Hugh," Imi said.

But Al didn't skip a beat and continued with his story.

"People have died over this microfilm. Some Nazi guys have tried to get it in all kinds of weird ways including pushing a kid off a third-floor ledge of an apartment building.

"Max, here's where you come in. The micro stuff is in code and we need Bletchley. We need it bad and we need it fast. We believe the film contains secret plans of the *Wannsee Conference* that has never seen the light of day. We know for sure, especially since Hugh has confirmed it that the head and brains of the operation to ferry wanted Nazis to other countries is directed by this Bishop Hudal whose location is the Vatican.

"The story of how we got the film is involved and I'll tell you the history later. Right now, we need you to arrange to get the deed done at Bletchley, pronto. And with your Texas background you know what pronto means. Jimmy and I talked about it and we both think all of us need to go to Bletchley and from there, once we have the micro stuff decoded, then contact Wiesenthal and get him the decoded material. We also think the decoded film will contain a full record of where these Nazi vermin were ferried as well as listing their secondary locations."

"Good, got it," Max said. "Got it. It's as good as done. We could leave in the morning unless you guys want to go right now before our lady brings all of us, as Al says: 'the goodies.'"

"I suggest we leave in the morning," Imi called out.

"That's a good idea," Jimmy added. "Talk about ferrying. The limo will ferry us the fifty or sixty miles to Bletchley in comfort. But right now, we should go to our rooms, take care of things, join again for dinner and then retire for an early night's sleep. But before we do that, I think we should wait to be served. Who here wants to disappoint our lady in-waiting? Any takers?"

It got quiet.

*   *   *

The following morning after a lavish breakfast and by the time they were half-way to Bletchley, Max had heard the entire saga, from Willy going off the ledge to the stories the captured terrorists were telling. Then Max shifted to what we should expect at Bletchley. He was excited and optimistic about what the geniuses at Bletchley could do. Part of what excited him was that he had the actual inside low-down on the whole Enigma story.

"As you know," Max opened it up, "Bletchley is England's advanced code-breaking center. They're the ones who broke the Enigma code that the Germans used to sink all our ships in the Atlantic. Those Nazi submarines got all the locations of ships with supplies we were sending to England. They did it through spotter planes who radioed our positions to their home base who, in turn then used the Enigma code to send the submarines all necessary information targeting the exact locations of the American ships. The American ships were carrying food supplies as well as other materials that England needed to survive. In fact, believe it or not, those ships carried one-hundred-thousand pounds of food each week! But those U-boats were torpedoing and sinking most of them. Imagine that waste, and American lives lost!

"It was Churchill who ordered British submarines to try at all cost to capture one of the Nazi subs and to glom an Enigma machine, along with manuals, and whatever else goes with it. The next thing you know one of the British subs did it. The Enigma went to Bletchley and they decoded it. Some people say it was the most important piece of action during the war that put us in a position of winning it."

Max then told this tight bunch, this diverse group of like-minded crime-fighters that he along with Shmuel Kishnov were happy that they were among the new cast of characters at Bletchley—though temporary their membership would be. Bletchley had changed from what it was during the Enigma saga about a dozen years earlier. He was sure that the level and creative energy they had now was equivalent to what they had at Bletchley back then. He especially mentioned how brilliant one woman was. He referred to her by his favorite nickname which he said he never mentioned to her. The nickname was Daisy as in: 'She loves me, she loves me not.'

He said her name is Dr. Janet Sirota and that they had been having a romance but that she seemed to have a problem with closeness. Apparently, she would run hot and cold and evidently for the first time in Maxie's life a woman had him on the run. Max confessed that he wanted to marry her and at the same time without skipping a beat Jimmy reminded him that when he, Maxie, and Al—all three of them—trained together with Imi, Max considered himself a sworn bachelor.

"After I met Janet, guys, it changed my mind—almost on the spot. But after we got together I started to notice that she could be very interested and at one moment into me and the very next time we were together, she could be indifferent. It was like that every time we met. She'd be not so much indifferent, but more distracted. It's tough because in the past if that had ever happened I would have blown whoever it was right off. But this one—I can't seem to shake this one."

"Max," Shmuel for the first time joined in. "She ist Jewish? Ayneh fun unzereh?"

"Yeah," Max answered. "But she's not religious and I'm not either. Does that matter to you, Shmuel?"

"No, not mattering to me. Every person do own vay. Dis is mine philosophy. I doing my vay so oder people doing day vay."

"On top of that," Max continued, "she's probably the real genius in the place and as beautiful to match. Al, trust me, like a Gloria beauty. In that league for sure. And as you know I've got the same eye disease as you, Al. Right Jimmy? Same eye diseases as Al? Hey Shmuel, you should see Al's beauty, Gloria. A real beauty."

By the time the banter got going, the limo was pulling into Bletchley Park. Max directed the driver to help find the building we needed, and the driver pulled in and parked. Max led the bunch into the building. As they entered and approached the switchboard operator, she and Max smiled at one another. Max made the introductions referring to all of them as the gang, not bothering to introduce each of them. Following Max, the gang walked further into the hall and Max whispered:

"Here she comes. It's Janet."

Dr. Janet Sirota came sauntering down the hall and when she saw Max she took him by the arm, pulled him aside not even acknowledging the rest of the gang, and began what seemed like scolding. No one could decipher what she said or what she did. Even, she, as the main code breaker at Bletchley wouldn't have been able to decipher what she just did. To assess what she did as rude, would not satisfy in any way anyone's sense of what it was that motivated her to do it. There seemed to be something unknowable about her.

The best that was said later was "strange, strange."

It was Imi who said it. It was the first thing he said since we started driving to Bletchley. Hugh, on the other hand, was careful about saying anything. He was concerned because he was an affiliate of the Vatican so he didn't want 'Vatican' to enter the discussion.

After Imi's comment of two 'stranges,' all eyes were on Janet. Of course, Maxie was right, she was stunning; a flavorful brunette with high cheekbones, full lips; posture was sexy without her really trying, and she was standing about five feet six or seven.

With the awkward pause that was taking place, and with Janet and Max in this ongoing 'strange' encounter, and as would probably be expected—Al couldn't take it.

"Max," he said, "we're going to the end of the hall and wait for you there."

They all walked to the end of the hall and stood at a window and talked. They tried to do it unobtrusively, and especially not audibly.

"Jimmy," Al said: "There's something wrong with her. Maxie's in trouble. We both understand his eye disease with this one, but she's mental. No doubt about it. It wasn't just rude, it was nuts. What the hell is wrong with Max. He doesn't have what some doctor might call diagnostic skill. I think his dick's getting in the way."

Looking at Hugh and Imi, Al said:

"Sorry guys there's no other way I could say it. That's how we talk."

"Right on all counts, Al," Jimmy answered. "Max mentioned possibly getting married to her, but I'm not going to that wedding. I can't support Max with this one. No sir."

"Me too," Al agreed. "And I'll bet anything that after his family tells him they're not going, his answer's going to be that he isn't either."

With that, Shmuel Kishnov, the new member of the gang asked: "Vhat ist mit Maxie? He having dis trouble mit hist eyes?"

"No, no, no," answered Al. "When Jimmy and I talk about eye-disease it means that someone like me or like Max is hopelessly vulnerable to a beautiful woman. I mean the accent is on 'beautiful.' You know like looking at anything stunning or gorgeous and you suddenly feel like the woman can take your life away. That's the way Jimmy and I talk about it. You know?"

"Ah, yah. Dat ist good vay to saying dis ting. I same. Having dis ting too—dis vhat you calling eye-disease. I understanding vhat you meaning mit dis."

Max came quickly walking to the gang and then without saying a word led them into a large conference room.

"Janet'll be here in a minute," is all he said.

"Max," Al started. "C'mon, you're not talking. It's because you know something strange happened there. What the hell happened?"

"Look," Max answered, "this is her. One minute ecstatic, another, gloomy. And she doesn't care if anyone sees it or not. I know there's some-thing wrong but like I told you I'm hopelessly hooked on her looks, num-ber one and her brains, number two. Entranced might even be a better word, or like I feel she has the ability to dispel my will. Al, Jimmy, I know you guys know what I mean."

Max then looked to Imi and Hugh, apparently in the hope of some support—obviously because he was a touch embarrassed—but they responded with blank expressions, not wanting to enter the fray or in any way say something negative. After all, Al and Jimmy were pals of Max's but Hugh and even Imi who knew Max felt it wasn't their place to be quite as personal the way Al and Jimmy naturally assumed they could be.

Janet entered the room and all eyes turned to her.

"It's my social disability," she suddenly and again perhaps inappropri-ately declared. "There's really no name for it but I sometimes can disre-gard social niceties and say or do something that's not only considered rude or crazy but is actually, I know, rude *and* crazy—not *or*. And I'll prove it to you now again. She turns to Max and out of the blue she looks at him and says:

"Poor Max. Poor Max Palace. Falls for me and I make it worse for him by falling for him."

Then she turns to the group, all of whom are staring at her with a kind of disbelief.

"I know you all need to freshen up after the trip but I'd like to spend some minutes here in order to hear what the precise problem is that I need to try to solve—that Max tells me I must, to the best of my ability try to solve—and also he says I need to place it in first position relative to any other work I have. Therefore, knowing about Al and Jimmy from Max, I would like to ask either of you, to please give me a capsule summary of the problem.

With that everyone turned to Al.

"Okay," Al started. "Here it is briefly. "We've obtained a microfilm that we believe contains the names of perhaps thousands of German and other Nazi criminals from other countries who are on the run from justice. We're fairly certain that a vast network of facilitators has already arranged primary residences and occupations for these thousands in other countries—mostly away from Europe—and then also arranged for secondary locations in the event that the primary one would be discovered. Therefore, we need the film decrypted. We all know that nowhere in the world would that be more possible than at Bletchley and then also knowing that Max works here, after we told him what I'm now telling you, he, with assurance told us that he had what he called 'juice' with the most scientific and artful person at Bletchley—and, of course he meant you, Dr. Sirota."

Al paused for a pregnant moment and then in a deliberate and almost confrontational manner continued:

"The term 'juice' is an American expression known as 'pull' or better, 'influence'."

Then in a supreme moment of confrontational satisfaction Al said something directly and frontally. Even considering that it might bother Max. He just didn't care.

"I defined 'juice' as an 'American expression' because it was important for me to remind everyone all over the world including everyone in Britain, including right here, right now, that if it weren't for America you all would be speaking German today. Not English. And that doesn't mean we don't like the British. We do. But we also know that even though you all are great fighters and don't give up, without America, the war was lost."

Then continuing to look directly at her—he asked the Bronx's Detective Mac's usual question: "Did I say something that wasn't clear?"

"Touche," Janet instantly answered. "I certainly see and even appreciate what you're doing. Okay, we're even. You can be crazy, too. But keep in mind that crazy only means angry so that both you, Alex Kaye—see, I'm familiar with your full name through Max—but you, Alex Kaye and I too, are a bit crazy. Me more."

With that exchange, Al and Janet kind of hit it off and Janet was actually better for the wear. For the moment, at least she became appropriate.

"So, I agree with Max, and I see that the decryption job is very important and I'll give it my 'best try' to quote Max. In the meantime, Max, I think we should have genteel introductions. So, everyone, my name is Dr. Janet Sirota at your service. And I mean it. Please call me Janet."

Max then made introductions for everyone including their occupations and Janet nodded whenever Max named the person to whom he was referring.

"Thank you, Max. I think I have all the names now. Max will show you to your quarters. I would like to have the film before you retire so please, someone let me know through the phone line in the room because I will need to have two of our security officers accompany me wherever I go with the film. At night before I retire, the tape will be locked in a maximum security vault deep within the bowels of Bletchley. Tomorrow will be the first day I and some others here will tackle the project. At the moment, I bid you all a peaceful night and look forward to speaking with you over breakfast or at the lab."

* * *

Janet received the phone call about twenty minutes after the group left the Administration Building. The microfilm was delivered to her as she waited in the lobby near her lab flanked by two security officers. She and the security men went directly to her lab. The Bletchley lab itself was a machine-filled encryption/decryption arena.

The next morning the group met with Janet in that two-room suite, and were asked to form a single line and then one-by-one they were patted down by the security officers, each waiting their turn. When they were all cleared, Janet explained all the security precautions at work at Bletchley and then introduced the group to two other decryption personnel in her department. Dr. Gerald Yagoda was a mathematician with a specialty in what Janet described as "number theory" as well as the fantastic mathematics of what became known as "hidden structures."

"How do you do," Dr. Yagoda greeted them. "Welcome to our modest abode here."

Janet then pointed to Dr. Adrian Applebaum. Dr. Applebaum seemed somewhat shy when she announced that he was an associate of Alan Turing, the man who broke the Enigma code, and that Turing's team was instrumental in developing what they termed the electromechanical machine, implicitly important in the development of what they named 'artificial-intelligence' as well as in the development of electronic computing, all within the general study and effectiveness of cryptography. She also said that Dr. Applebaum made some contributions to 'Boolean algebra" also ultimately contributing to cryptographic theory.

Dr. Applebaum nodded hello while Janet transitioned to the problem at hand.

"We've already looked at the code and have agreed it is of only moderate brilliance. Dr. Applebaum has ventured a guess that the algorithm is based on some alphabetized idea which is what the three of us have been discussing for an hour before you all arrived.

"That's all I can say at the moment. We'll be here most of the day but not into the night because we feel confident we can decipher the code before dinner. I know that sounds like childish fanfare or even egoistic flourish. Please excuse it. But we are serious and will do our best. Let me put it that way. Now, please get the hell out of here and let us work.

"I know you think I'm a bit blotto so I was trying to accommodate you and actually *sound* a bit blotto. I meant that facetiously and hope I was successful. What you're all trying to do is of course highly commendable and correspondingly, as I've said, we will put our best efforts to work.

"If it's alright with you, Adrian, Gerald and I could meet you at 1 pm for lunch at our dining hall. It's now 8 am so that means we'll meet in about five hours. In the meantime, Max, please make sure our guests have some crumpets and tea or whatever they need as an interlude before lunch. Till then my friends, we'll see you."

All at once the group said their thank-you's and were escorted out of the lab by the security officers.

At lunch, Dr.'s Yagoda, Applebaum, and Janet walked toward us and as they approached, we were acutely focused on their faces for what we all hoped would be a sign of success. Unfortunately, the deed had not yet been accomplished. However, with confidence, Janet announced that although the code was not yet breached, the good news was that they were onto it and they were agreed that they were getting still closer—hoping for the solution by dinner time.

Janet was wrong because later at dinner they again approached us but immediately confessed that as close as they were, it was still not close enough. That news disappointed everyone but the general response from the gang was an optimistic one. Speaking for them all, Al reassured Janet and her two scientific genius-colleagues that they had complete confidence in them.

That night, Janet slipped into Max's room, undressed, and slid into bed next to him. When he saw her he became aroused. They began making love. Once he entered her, suddenly out of nowhere, she admonished him.

"Listen, Max," Janet soberly said. "I don't want you to hold back because you think I need more time to orgasm. Understand? Just do it! I don't like it when you treat me as though I'm a little girl who needs help. It's you who needs the help, not I."

Max was obviously annoyed and didn't like her tone. Actually, he never liked it when she was like that. He only tolerated what he considered to be her nonsense because again, he had a very bad case of this terrible eye-disease and couldn't let her go. This time however, he seemed rather than over the moon, instead, quite out of patience—even possibly finally disgusted. He was not the type to tolerate any sort of injury to his pride as in even a little feeling of humiliation. So, at this point he began to feel no longer controlled by his hope that she would love him and ultimately be the one for him.

Second, again at this point he could feel that he was starting not to care about her, or even about how she felt—one way or the other. Third, again at this point he began, for the first time to notice that he was thinking about himself. He then knew he could not easily tolerate her with respect to what he understood as her on-again off-again moods.

And then for the first time, he said it to her:

"Janet, we're not doing this tonight. You can sleep here or leave. It's up to you."

With that, Janet felt him pulling away. It was his unmistakable anger that caused him to withdraw. That is, Max's libido had disappeared. He was angry and where there is anger there is no libido. And *that* is what's known as decryption!'

Janet slid out of bed, dressed and left the room.

Max lay there for some minutes thinking. He got out of bed, showered, dressed, and went to Al's room. Al was in bed reading. He told Al he wanted the three of them—meaning himself, Al, and Jimmy—to meet, right then. Al got out of bed, dressed, and off they went to Jimmy's room.

"Okay guys," Max began, "here it is. For the first time about a half hour ago, she did it again. The crazy came out and spilled all over the place. I'm pretty sure now that I've come to my senses. My feelings for her just disappeared. Just like that. It reminds me of when I was fifteen and had a girlfriend I was nuts about. Couldn't stop kissing her. Then one day out of the blue I woke up one morning and said to myself, actually out loud: 'I don't love her so what am I doing there?'

"I don't know what came over me, and maybe it was an adolescent phenomenon that one minute you love and the next it disappears. That's what's happened now with Janet. I think it's disappeared."

He snapped his fingers as he said it: "Just like that!

"The truth is that I was taking a lot of shit like you guys saw, but I couldn't do anything about it. Now I can. I'll never marry her. I must have been crazy to even contemplate it."

"I'm glad to hear it Max," Al immediately said. "I wouldn't have been able to attend the wedding."

"Me too," Jimmy piped in. I wasn't going to the wedding."

"Well, I'm not going either," Max laughed—and was joined in by both Al and Jimmy in an uproarious laugh session. Then, before they all decided to head to their rooms and off to sleep, Imi knocked and he and Shmueli entered.

"Gentlemen," Imi declared, "I have news. I've just heard from Simon. We've got a new wrinkle here. Simon wants the film altered. He wants the first fifty secondary locations changed and he gave me the changes. In other words, we need to get Janet to create an alternate, counterfeit micro that cannot be detected as anything that's been tampered with. I've got the changes here."

With that, Imi unfolded a sheet of paper that he had written by hand that listed fifty names along with new secondary locations. They all stared at the paper with no one uttering a word. They looked at one another and Imi broke the silence.

"Gentlemen, see you in the morning."

* * *

In the morning after breakfast the gang of Al, Jimmy, Max, Imi, Hugh, and Shmueli again convened at the lab. Janet, Applebaum, and Yagoda were there as well. Not at all responding to Max, Janet said they had been working since 5 am and they thought the code had finally been broken.

"We were right," Janet said. "Fundamentally the code is an alphabetical one but different than that used in the Enigma. This one used only one wheel. The Enigma used what was termed a 'polyalphabetic substitution cipher' which I won't explain except to say that repetitive sequences enabled the code to become almost decipherable. It had several wheels. It was originally designed in the early 1920's—I've forgotten the exact date—by both by a German engineer, Dr. Arthur Scherbius, as well as even earlier by a Dutch scientist, Hugh Koch.

"As I've suggested, in the code here, methodology was not as complex although an attempt at an alphabetical type was instituted, designed to imitate the polyalphabetical one used in the Enigma. And by the way, the British were not the first to break the Enigma, nor were the Americans. It was the Polish scientist, Henryk Zygalski who did it first before any of us even got to it. However, the one Zygalski unraveled was not as sophisticated a machine as Scharbius's, the one used in the 1940's during the War.

"In any event, this one that we've just decrypted is based on the use of all five vowels in addition to how consonants sound. Yes, for the first time that I know, this one also uses the variable of sound. For example, Syria could sound more or less the same if it were spelled Cireeah. It's similar to transliteration. It was Dr. Applebaum here who first hit upon the idea that this code has a single rotor cipher and then Dr. Yagoda picked up that it also could have a sound variable of consonants. At that point in seeing what Dr.'s Applebaum and Yagoda had discovered it was an easy step for me to synthesize both discoveries.

"You will be pleased to know that you were all absolutely correct. The deciphered code lists the names of exactly, the phenomenal number of four-thousand one-hundred eighty-six names along with primary and secondary drop-off spots, all outside of Europe—with the exception of one. The one exception goes by the name of Gustav Schell.

"We've looked up that name in the classified list of Nazis wanted criminals and there is no such name listed on any 'wanted' sheets. This Gustav Schell is the only one of the more than four-thousand whose directive was to remain in Europe. Schell has no listed secondary location. His only drop-off country is Monaco—actually near Monaco—but still in France adjacent to the microstate, Monaco. You know everything there is located on the French Riviera in Western Europe. Schell could likely be living on the lower edge of a mountain in that region. It's *Mont Tete de Chien*. It's the Alps-Maritimes, and it is overlooking Monaco. There are other micro towns in the area as well. I imagine you'll be sending some of your agents there in order to get a good diagnostic picture of the situation.

Of course, Dr.'s Applebaum, Yagoda and I recognize many of the names on the list. We can identify a dozen or so and it is frightening to think that these individuals are loose and are being protected. Who in the world is arranging all this protection for them? And again I must point out: smack dab in the middle of the list is this Gustav Schell who no one has ever heard of and who is the only one with no secondary drop-off destination.

"So that's it. Our secretarial staff is now transferring all the names and data to a folder that will be handed you. I've assumed that you might not want to possess too many copies, so I've directed the typing pool to provide you with only two. I'm sure you will need to send one of them to let's say 'someone,' and the other either to M-16, or perhaps instead to the CIA. In that case you might need a third copy. However, neither I, nor Dr.'s Yagoda or Applebaum need to know your plans."

"Speaking for all of us," Al answered, "I would like to extend our sincere appreciation for what you've done. Moreover, we've had a correspondence from someone to whom we're sending the decrypted micro. This person indicates that he and those he represents wants the information on secondary locations altered. He would like a new counterfeit film to be expertly fashioned so that no one will be able to detect that the information of the film was tampered with. To that extent, he has provided us with a list of fifty individuals whose secondary locations should be changed Could you create this new micro as what we might identify as our disinformation one?

"So," Al continued, "we would also like two copies of the altered film and two copies, as you've said of the original one. In fact, if you'd be able to provide three of each, that might even be more convenient for us."

"The answer," Janet said, "is — of course. That would not be difficult to do and if you give me the list we will do it. It should be done before the end of the day."

With that, Imi handed Janet the list, and led by Al, the gang of five burst into applause.

Later that evening, as promised, Janet, handed Al the package containing both the original and disinformation micros. They all said their goodbye's and Max saw them off as they were getting into the limo. But then Max had a last hurrah.

"I've decided," he said, "that I'm leaving the job here. Of course, that means no more Janet. I'm pretty sure that's finished. I think I'll return to Texas or maybe one of you might find me on your doorstep."

At that, the new gang-member, Shmuel Kishnov who hadn't intervened in any significant way since they all arrived, now volunteered his approval.

"Max," he said, "ist goot you making better problem mit eye. Ist goot. Congratulations. Yah, I can seeing ist very goot."

In the limo, Hugh also ended his own pent-up silence of several days by asking how Simon would get the new micro and who will deliver it? He turned to Al.

"Al, I think even Jimmy would agree that you're the one to do it. Imi, it's you of course who will need to contact Simon and set it up. I think you should ask Simon whether he wants us all to attend or is it sufficient for only Al to be the messenger?"

"Hugh," Al continued, "It's not a good idea for only one of us to deliver it. I agree I should be the point man on this but I'd be much more comfortable with Jimmy here backing me up. In fact, I think Jimmy should only shadow me. We shouldn't look like we're travelling together although Jimmy, you'll always need to have me in your sights. And Imi, at night when Jimmy and I are asleep, you have to be in an opposite room for night duty making sure no one's gotten wind of anything and is trying to break in.

"You know, the plan to get the material to Simon has got to be fool-proof. What we've been through to get it to this point is not enough. We need to redouble our scrutiny about who is around us at all times, night and day."

"Okay," Imi responded. "I'm on it the moment we get back to London. I'll be in touch with him through our channels. He'll tell me where he wants to meet and that'll be that. In the meantime, I think you and Jimmy need to do what you planned the minute we touch down in London. Let's not forget we're carrying a folder with papers in it and two microfilms—one original, one fake—and they can be snatched at a moment's notice. I'm always paranoid about that kind of stuff.

"Should someone try to snatch it," Imi continued, "keep in mind that it's not enough just to disarm that person and to reduce the threat to a minimum. With that kind of situation, you need to take the guy's windpipe out! Kill him! There's no other way. This is strictly a situation for maximum offense. Maximum—the Krav way!"

"Jesus would not like me saying this, Imi, but I agree," Hugh added: "I agree completely."

"Me too, of course," said Jimmy, with Al immediately nodding in agreement—'Yes.'

Now they were going to get the material to Simon Wiesenthal and it was strictly business—serious business. When they arrived in London, Imi went right to it. He made his contacts immediately, and sent out word that he wanted to speak to Wiesenthal. That message was relayed to his trusted people in various capitals of the world including of course, Tel Aviv, Vienna, Washington, D.C., and one or two other cities. The message was that Wiesenthal was to contact a Post-Office Box. Jimmy made sure to specifically alert his M-16, and of course, Shmuel Kishnov volunteered to alert Mossad, in Israel. It was the first time Kishnov had even hinted that he was in some way connected to Mossad, or at least knew how to enter their communication system.

It didn't take long. Wiesenthal got the message and sent word that he would like to meet with the entire core group: Al, Jimmy, Hugh, and Imi, including also Kishnov. Without having been told that Kishnov had entered the inner-circle, Wiesenthal already knew that Shmueli was with the gang.

Wiesenthal suggested they remain in London and he would come to them. He wanted to meet them at M-16 Headquarters at the St. Ermins Hotel, two days hence.

· 13 ·

BURN IT DOWN

Hudal called Montini the very next day and told him that if they couldn't retrieve it, he was sure the information on the film would eventually wind up with Simon Wiesenthal. Should that happen, he said, Wiesenthal would transmit the information to Mossad and then they could expect kidnappings at the minimum and assassinations at the other extreme. Or, he felt perhaps the least and most should be reversed; that is, that at most they should expect kidnappings and at least, assassinations.

His thinking about this possible reversal was that with kidnappings they were most vulnerable. It's the 'deal' business—meaning when you're captured the deal is usually made. If you give names you get a reduced sentence or get off entirely. With assassinations, there are no deals and no names are named so that Hudal and his entire organization would be safe from incrimination with assassinations and less so with kidnappings.

Monsignor Montini told Hudal he was worrying too much.

"The only thing to worry about is public opinion in the United States. The officials there are more interested in maintaining good relations with the Vatican so that incriminating news would probably be on a back burner. And furthermore, Hudal, no one except those Wiesenthal types are still interested in capturing Nazis. All they're doing now is concentrating on communists. This is especially true in the United States.

"In any event," Montini continued, "let's hope for a few assassinations. As you know some of our comrades are out of control, like Barbie doing police consulting regarding torture all over South America, or Stangl and Brunner, both in Syria doing the same kind of consulting. They're adding fuel to the fire and won't cease. There's nothing we can do about it. We've done what we can do."

With that, Hudal was left with an uncomfortable feeling. Hudal needed perfect closure. It wasn't enough that six million Jews were killed. The deed wasn't perfect. They all had to be killed. Then he would have closure. Also, they needed to protect all those Nazis on the run, not merely the ten-thousand. All of them, multiples of thousands and thousands. After all, Germany and their co-dependent axes were genocidal allies and multiples of millions upon millions were involved in the killings.

And Hudal needed his particular definition of closure, that is, perfect-closure—in order to sleep well. Otherwise he slept fitfully. A Freudian psychoanalyst would probably consider this kind of behavior as an excessive obsessive-compulsive need; that is planning and thinking the plan over and over as the obsession. Doing it perfectly would be the compulsion; the operative term being 'perfectly.'

So, if the person is not an extreme obsessive, imperfections work better because one in such a position can more easily rationalize that it didn't work out perfectly, but perhaps, just perhaps, good enough—so that good enough works. For the classic obsessive person, not good enough is almost equivalent to failure or at least the embarrassment of incompetence. Therefore, despite his intelligence and operational expertise, Hudal was a twisted person with virtuosity in 'twistedness.'

Hudal then, qualified as the classic obsessive: vigilant on top with the obsessive/repetitive thought, and rife with a compulsive energy to try to accomplish it all—perfectly! In psychoanalytic language, he was psychopathic as well as narcissistic—not really different from Hitler himself, as well as all of the others who were acting-out the Nazi criminal agenda. It was the Nazi ideology that gave them all the sense of superiority in the face of the inadequate underneath feeling. Because of the compensatory stance of superiority, it also gave them the feeling of always being in the ascendancy which for them was essential in sustaining their sense of adequacy or even superiority. And that's more or less the psychoanalytic take on it.

Now what does "psychopathic as well as narcissistic" mean? It's simple. What it means is that the psychopathic behavior involves crazy sadistic stuff such as for example killing someone because you don't like them or for whatever other number of reasons you give yourself, and along with it, you feel no guilt or remorse or any other responsible sense about it.

Along with this, the psychopathic person can't really stop seeking what we can call external stimulation; that is, they need things from the outside to occupy them and to animate their lives. However, practically speaking that sort of condition presumably results from not possessing any real tangible internal or interior thinking or introspective life. Thus, in the life of the psychopath exists a sense of an *impoverished inner life.*

The reason for not being able to feel responsible or to not even feel guilt or the like, also concerns the narcissistic part; that is, this kind of person's only concern is about the self. It can be considered a solipsistic-obsession meaning that anything is justified provided that it's based upon what you want to do simply because of the literal fact that you want to do it. In other words, nothing else counts except your personal agenda, your personal wish; what you want and when you want it—and here's the kicker—what you want to the fullest measure and not only to the measure of 'just good enough'.

Thus, to a person who we may identify as let's say someone equivalent to a theological Nazi, someone like Alois Hudal along with certain of his ideological Christian brothers at the Vatican, wanting something "to the fullest measure," becomes highly meaningful. To such psychologically deteriorated individuals, killing some Jews would not be sufficient. It had to be "to the fullest measure"! All the Jews! And then, even that might not suffice because others too, constitute unfinished business. Therefore, let's also kill Gypsies and then if still insufficient, get the disabled—even if we need to drag them out of hospitals and then kill them.

This sort of genocide also had its early evidence in the slaughter of the American Indian as well as the genocidal behavior over centuries with respect to slavery toward American Negroes. And this all started pre-20th century. Then in the early 20th century it started again with what could be considered another prodromal example. It was what the Germans did in Africa—the first genocide of the 20th century against the Africans in Namibia—to the Herero and Nama tribes. The Germans slaughtered a couple of hundred thousand of these people and took their land. They killed in order to steal. Plain and simple. Or how about what Turkey did to the Armenians starting at about 1915 when the Turks slaughtered a million or more Armenians.

Of course, "prodromal" is a perfect way to describe it all. It means something happening in the past that presages something similar that would be expected to happen in the future—only its eruption in the future would be with significantly greater severity. With respect to genocide, the genocide of the Herero and Nama tribes and then to the Armenians was a precedent to what the Nazis did some decades later mostly to Jews but also to others considered by these Nazis to be undesirable people.

But is a sweet innocent child undesirable? Or, how about a couple of million children? Are they undesirable? According to the Turks of 1915, and then to the official Wannsee Nazi Conference of 1942—regarding the so-called 'Final Solution' with respect to Jews—the answer is a resounding 'Yes,' they are assessed as undesirable.

Therefore, the answer is given as: 'So let's kill the children, too'!

*   *   *

Now, we belatedly come to Willy. In a way Willy was also twisted but his twistedness was strictly physical as a result of being pushed off a third story ledge of an apartment building and landing full force on the pavement below. At this point however, several weeks had elapsed and Willy was already walking with an aide's assistance through the corridor near his hospital room. He was walking ever so slowly and a bit bent, but he was walking. No longer was he hooked up to that contraption with his leg and arm hanging in slings from the top of the hospital bed—the kind of canopy bed with his limbs dangling by pulleys that were holding them elevated

As he was slowly walking, out of the elevator and just about meeting Willy and his aide at the far end of the hall, were Gloria, Frankie and Al—Willy's favorite people in the whole world. Following the greetings going both ways, Willy's first predictable question was about Stevie. Was she okay? He wanted to hear the entire story straight from Al.

He had already been told that Stevie who had been abducted along with her parents and brother, was soon thereafter, released. It was all about the package. Willy said he felt really bad about getting Stevie involved with it all. But Frankie piped in and said it was his—Frankie's own fault because Willy couldn't trust him with anything, so then Willy went to Stevie. Thus, it was Frankie's alcoholism that forced Willy to find a place to hide the package—but not at home. Then, rather reluctantly, Willy admitted to Frank directly, as hard as it was to say it out loud, for the first time in public:

"That's right, Frank, because of the drinking I couldn't—you know."

Willy, still being held by his aide, in a slow and direct way then followed what he said to Frankie with more narration of his condition. It was Willy's way of making short shrift of his confessional comment to Frank. It was also short in another way; that is, although Willy was uttering it all, hesitatingly and haltingly, his ability to convey it all was predictive of a reasonable if not full recovery of all of his cognitive faculties.

Then his aide Judy added some confirmation:

"See, Willy here is really getting better. The doctors say he's healing well. They're doing everything for him. Willy's mouth is getting fixed with some new teeth. His arm and leg are examples of how the healing process is succeeding. Look how he's already walking."

Willy picked up the narrative and declared with difficulty:

"You know, my talking is not good because my tongue and side of my mouth still hurt when I try to talk."

With that, both officers who were on duty at Willy's room congregated at this conclave.

"We've been told," one of them said to Frank and Al, "at the precinct they're talking over whether it's still necessary to have the twenty-four/seven routine here."

"Who said that?" Al asked.

"I'm not sure," the officer answered.

"Listen guys," Al continued, "no one should leave Willy unattended here without the okay from either Mac or Lyle from the 48th. The order, whatever it is, should only come from Detectives Loris McIver, Mac for short, or from Detective Lyle Davis."

"Yeah, we know Mac and Lyle."

"Good, so you know their voices, right?"

"Yeah, sure."

With that Willy's aide, Judy, suggested that Willy should get back into bed. Willy agreed and off the two of them went. The cops were about to follow but Al held them back.

"Listen guys, there's something going on that isn't clear yet. I've recently returned from Europe on a crazy wild goose chase and it was about things connected to Willy. The fact is we're not sure whether he still might be in danger. So, the order not to guard him must come from Mac or Lyle. In fact, I'd also like to know about that kind of order if you get it because then Gloria here, me and Frank could be replacements in the event you guys are ordered off the case. In my opinion, certain issues have not been put to bed. Not yet. We need more information."

At that moment who walks in but Mac and Lyle escorting the Whartons.

"Stevie insisted," said Mrs. Wharton. "She insisted."

It was in a sweet voice but not entirely shy that Stevie didn't just ask where Willy's room was — she proclaimed it:

"Which room is Willy's — please?!"

The officer in the hall heard her and pointed to Willy's room outside of which he was stationed. At that point, they walked to Willy's room and entered. Stevie was first one in.

Willy, in his whacky outfit of bandages through which he was barely talking spotted her instantly and shouted:

"Stevie!"

"Oh, Willy," she said, "you're talking. They told me you might not be ready to talk yet."

"I am," Willy said very slowly. "I am. Stevie, I'm sorry I got you into this. I don't really know what happened, but I'll bet it was bad. I'm really sorry."

"It's okay now, Willy. Now it's okay. We're all safe. And you know I was happy to help."

"Okay," Willy said, as he nodded. "But I still feel bad that I got you into trouble."

With that exchange, Willy motioned for Stevie to come closer to his bed, and she did so. Everyone could see how close they were and in the best sense, close — as though best friends, even like best siblings. Willy looked around at everyone, leaned a bit toward Stevie standing next to the bed and whispered:

"Do you still have it?"

Stevie shook her head, no.

"Who has it?"

Stevie leaned closer still, and said:

"Your police friends and Al, and your uncle, and Gloria know all about it too."

Willy nodded, looked up above at the canopy of the bed and thought for a few seconds. Then he asked everyone to come closer.

"Has anyone read the microfilm?"

It was then that Frankie knew Willy had opened the package and knew its contents.

"Willy," his uncle said, instantly figuring things out. "I think you opened the package even though you told me you had never done that. I'm right? Right?"

Speaking in a whisper and again slowly, Willy spilled the beans. He was talking, but as before, quite slowly.

"I lied, Frank. I did open it. And I did more." He stopped and took a breath. "I asked my science teacher, Mr. Yancey, what it was and he told me and said I should see the librarian at the big library in Manhattan. You know it was a little thing inside another wrapper inside the package. I took the El at Claremont all the way to Manhattan. That took me not too far from the library at 42nd Street and Fifth Avenue. I asked about microfilm and I got sent to a lady who knew about it.

"When I got there, I showed it to her and she told me what it was. She told me what microfilm was which was what Mr. Yancy had said. But this lady knew more about it than Mr. Yancey. She told me that this library in Manhattan was important in the country and that it had one of the first machines that other libraries didn't have. It was called the *Coddinger Magnifier*—I liked the way those words sounded. It could magnify whatever was on the microfilm.

"I told her I wanted to see what was on the microfilm. She took out from her drawer what she told me was a microcard. She did something with the card in the machine and then I could read what was—jibberish to me."

Al immediately asked: "Willy, did the librarian also read it?"

"No, I don't think so because she was standing behind me and my head was close to the machine. She wouldn't have known what it said either."

"Do you know her name."

"Yes, Mrs. Roth. I remember her name."

With that answer, Frank and Al looked at each other. They each could tell what the other was thinking. They both knew that the name Roth sounded Jewish and if so, she'd be aware it had something to do with Nazis so that she could report to someone what had transpired. And that could open the possibility that the story would wind up in the news.

They decided on the spot that the microfilm would indeed need to go to Simon Wiesenthal immediately. They also repeated what had been already decided—it would not be mailed. For sure, the microfilm needed to be delivered by hand. And, of course, as had been decided by their so-called *Justice Group,* it would be Al's job to deliver it personally—backed up by Jimmy and Imi. That meant he'd need to call Jimmy and to have Jimmy alert Wiesenthal of their plans. He knew he couldn't call Hugh and tell him about such an urgent plan because obviously, Hugh's phone was tapped. They had also figured that his mail was vulnerable. So, Hugh was out. But this time, Al thought that Maxie should be invited in. He decided that he would tell Jimmy to call Max and to tell him what was what and to tell him they needed him.

*   *   *

At that precise moment then, there were two plots simultaneously hatching. One with Al planning a European trip and the other with Karl and Wenzel planning to boost a microfilm from the property-office and evidence-section of a police precinct. It's actually a holding-pen for all sorts of items related to cases. In this case, stored at the 48th station-house in the Bronx. What they didn't know was that the microfilm stored there was not the real thing. It was a disinformation micro.

But at that moment Al was not finished with the Mrs. Roth deal.

"Willy, did Mrs. Roth ask you anything else, like your name or address or something?"

Willy answered immediately and thoroughly but slowly.

"I thought about that, because she didn't take any information from me. After I looked at what was on the microfilm—all those letters—and most of all there was a Nazi swastika on the top of the pages. I got some kind of idea of what it was about without even knowing what it was about. Know what I mean? But definitely something with Nazis.

"There were columns with jumbled letters like a code. Lists and lists of it. I remember that. The first line started with a capital E and the next line started with a capital M. Then there was a second column and a third and fourth one. That's about it. It wasn't clear. I had the hunch it was about names and places."

Gloria looked at Frankie, Willy's uncle, and said:

"Frank, that's why Willy's in the advanced program. He's very smart."

Addressing Willy, Gloria queried:

"Willy, the first column might be lists of people's names? Could that be?"

"Yeah, Gloria, that's what I thought. The first column could be names of people and the other three columns something about them. That's what I thought."

Willy looked at his uncle with a bit of evident remorse and just barely eked it out:

"Frank, I'm sorry I lied. I couldn't help myself. I had to see it for myself. Mom was always very careful about it. I remember how she looked when she talked about it. I couldn't give it to you because. . . ."

Frank interrupted him: "Gloria's right, Willy. Gloria's right—and so are you. Don't worry about it. Everything's alright now."

"I think I need to sleep now. Stevie come to see me again. Okay?"

*   *   *

The phone rang in their room at the Waldorf. Karl answered it.

"No names, please," the caller said. "I know you know who this is. Meet me right now down in the lobby. I'll be at the far end, opposite the main Park Avenue entrance. Go to the phone booths at that far end. I'll be on one phone, you lift the receiver of the other one as though each of us is talking to different people. Understood?"

"I leaving now," Karl answered.

Karl and Wenzel rushed to the elevators. One, two, three, they were on the main floor. To the back end they went. The mystery man, Parker Martin, was on one phone and Karl got on the other. They were standing right next to each other.

"They have the thing at the 48th Precinct in the Bronx. It's one block above Tremont Avenue, on I think Bathgate Avenue."

With that, Karl said "Yah, gotting it"—and as he turned to leave he furtively slid a briefcase on the floor with his foot, over to Martin, passing ten thousand dollars to him in the briefcase. Martin leaned down, didn't look at them, zipped opened the briefcase, Martin looked in, zipped it closed, turned toward the main entrance on Park Avenue and walked the length of the lobby out of the hotel

Back in the room, speaking German to one another, Wenzel asked Karl if he had any idea of how to execute the heist they sorely needed to achieve.

"Only one way to do it, Wenz. We burn it down. Everyone dies and the package dies too. We burn it all down."

"What about the two of our men they have captured?"

"What about them? I said everyone inside dies in a blaze. Didn't you hear me say 'everyone'?"

Wenzel looked at him and immediately felt more at ease. The ambiguity of it all evaporated for him. Burn it down meant just what it meant. Not wanting to squander any time they got right to it. They were going to get there in the wee small hours, at about two or three in the morning, pour whatever it was they were going to use around the circumference of the precinct along with tossing whatever it was they were going to toss into the precinct itself.

"We make it so the fire is too massive so no one can leave the building," Karl thoughtfully announced. Then he knew what they would use. "Chlorine triflouride. That's it. Heydrich used it once and said it was like the world was on fire. That should do it—chlorine triflouride. No one would have a chance no matter what kind of help they'd get. No one and nothing could survive chlorine triflouride.

Karl continued: "The Bishop told the story that some months before Heydrich was assassinated when he was ordered to liquidate a village in one of the eastern countries—I don't remember which it was—he herded more than one hundred Russians—oh yes, it was Russians, it was a Russian village—he herded them into the Town Hall, and used the chlorine triflouride to kill them all. The chemical was recommended by one of our scientists. The Bishop said that Heydrich swore the blaze was so overwhelming that it could get out of control and consume even those setting it. According to Heydrich, Hitler then ordered it only to be used when absolutely necessary.

"Wenz, for us, now, it is absolutely necessary. The Bishop's American chemist who lives in a section of New York City known as *Yorkville* has always been helpful when the Bishop called on him. There are so many

Germans in Yorkville, it should be named German-Town. This chemist will be able to acquire and deliver it."

The call to the chemist was made and the request was promised "as soon as possible."

When asked what "as soon as possible" meant, the chemist answered, "two or three days."

Karl didn't tell the chemist where he'd be staying but said he would call him every day for the next two or three days. And it happened. Karl and Wenzel called the chemist on the second day and sure enough everything was ready. They found the chemist's house in Yorkville at about midnight, and only then picked up the chemicals. There were no words exchanged. They had a car and Wenzel had also purchased several cans of kerosene. Earlier in the hotel, he had fashioned four torches—two small and two larger. Karl was oddly, and perhaps even amusingly observing him doing it so assiduously.

They exited the hotel but didn't check out. It was a touch before midnight. They located the chemist's address, and rang the doorbell. The somber chemist handed them the chemicals and as they were in the process of leaving the chemist shut the door. They had brought along several large towels liberated from their hotel towel rack. And, they had the Wenzel torches with them along with four cans of kerosene.

Wenzel had convinced Karl that the chlorine triflouride was much too dangerous and either or both of them could go up in flames. He persuaded Karl to think it over and then, Karl considered Wenzel's back-up plan, and agreed to it.

Now it was past midnight. They calculated that the police shift would be changing at about that time. They loaded everything into the car Wenzel had broken into a half hour earlier. Up to the Bronx they went. They found Tremont Avenue and after driving around for a few minutes they drove past the precinct on Bathgate Avenue.

Wenzel said, "There it is, speaking in German to Karl, who was driving. They cased the precinct as best they could from the front of the building. The rest of the street was blocked off by other structures. They realized there was no way to ring the place as in surrounding the circumference of the precinct with either the chemical or the kerosene. So, the plan instantly changed. Karl decided definitely to use the chemical but Wenzel insisted on the kerosene. A quick irritable discussion in rapid-fire German broke out between them.

"How are we going to get the kerosene into the precinct," Karl began, practically raving.

"Simple," Wenzel answered in an opposite Germasn rapid-fire way. "We walk up to the door, open it, each of us throws in two cans apiece and I shoot the cans and also any of the police in sight. I'll have the machine-gun. It is no contest! We keep the car running outside, we get out fast and drive away, leaving the station to burn down. That's how! Don't be foolish. We cannot use the chemical because it will suck us in before we know. It's obvious, Karl. Obvious. Remember what you told me Heydrich said."

"Okay, we do it your way. Make sure the machine-gun is loaded and don't get shot yourself. And make sure you shoot all the cans."

At that point, there was no suspense and neither seemed nervous. God knows how many other such nerve-racking, diabolic and genocidal adventures they'd already had. They seemed to know what to do.

They parked at the entrance to the precinct that was flanked by at least five or six police cars parked diagonally to the curb. They kept the engine running and the car in neutral. Wenzel carried his machine-gun strapped onto his shoulder and one kerosene can in each hand. Karl did the same also carrying two kerosene cans and all the torches strapped also on his shoulder.

As they approached the entrance to the station, there were no police standing outside of the precinct. Then as Wenzel directed, they walked in and both of them threw the cans into the precinct. Wenzel swung the machine-gun onto his hands, fired into all four cans while Karl threw in the torches all lit up. Wenzel was firing at will and at least six or seven in the precinct were down. All of those who were shot were badly wounded or dead. At the same time Karl was taking aim with his semi-automatic Mauser. He was not firing indiscriminately like Wenzel. He knew that other police would be entering from a different door. And so, they did. Two others came with another two following. They had their guns drawn and as soon as they saw it, all four started firing.

The truth was however, that the fire now ablaze was raging and any one who would be hit by any bullet going whichever way was hit by pure chance. That's how both Karl and Wenzel were hit — by pure chance. Wenzel was hit in the leg and arm. The leg injury was just a flesh wound and his leg bone wasn't touched. His arm was also a flesh wound and luckily no bone was touched. Nevertheless, Wenzel crumbled to his knees holding his arm and groaning in pain. But as things went, Wenzel was lucky. He could have easily been killed.

Karl was wounded in his left arm but managed to run out into the street. As he was about to jump into his idling car, Jack and Harry were pulling up in their police car, saw the commotion and blocked Karl's escape. Karl fired on them but bad luck for him—he was immediately killed by a fusillade of bullets raining down on him from both Jack and Harry.

By then, everyone was emptying out onto the street including the cops who were guarding Bishop Hudal's man, Ewald, as well as Peron's man, Eduardo, both who had been incarcerated—Ewald in the basement of the precinct and Eduardo in an upper-floor cell.

And there they both were, Ewald and Eduardo, standing in the street along with the police who, in all the confusion were putting out the fire both from inside the precinct and from the street itself. Before they knew it, fire engines arrived and firemen completed the deed. No more fire but plenty of smoke—a huge cloud of thick black smoke that seemed to be creating a dense atmosphere of gloom.

With the smoke and confusion, Ewald saw his chance and made a break for it. It was a dumb move because he was shot dead instantly. The police who were guarding him yelled: "Stop him. Stop him." That's when everyone started firing. Ewald wound up dead in a hail of bullets.

Three ambulances arrived from Montefiore Hospital. Six officers were dead, four others seriously wounded, and two others slightly wounded. A pall had come over the scene with some officers sitting with their heads in their hands—some crying over lost friends and partners.

Stretcher bearers started carrying the dead and wounded officers into the ambulances. It meant that three ambulances usually able to tend to two people each would each now be carrying three. Three of the wounded were transported in police cars.

· 14 ·

A HAIL OF BULLETS

Despite all the confusion, the fire didn't reach the basement. But the basement was filled with choking smoke that permeated everywhere — corridor, rooms, and the cell. It was the first time in New York City's history that a major assault was made on a police precinct.

Ewald's death generated a probe, but in no way could he be identified. He wasn't burned to a crisp from the fire as one might think. It was just that there was no way to know who he was. He was not noted in anyone's files — not even an American citizen.

When word went out to foreign governments, no government claimed him. In questioning, Eduardo stated that Ewald was German but he doubted whether the German government would bother with the case. Eduardo directly identified Ewald as an agent of Nazi organizations still operating in various countries, and he also stated that the current German government was officially anti-Nazi, but he was sure many officials were ideologically still loyal Nazis.

Eduardo readily conceded that he was in the employ of Juan Peron of Argentina and he and Ewald were connected in the same way that Bishop Alois Hudal of the Vatican and Juan Peron of Argentina were connected. Their objective was to ferry Nazis out of Europe entirely. Again, one could see that Eduardo was determined to invite consideration so that he could garner some possible leniency.

When Mac and Lyle tried to contact the precinct by intercom there was no answer. No answer at the precinct was alarming so they radioed other cars. They reached Jack and Harry. Jack filled them in.

"Mac, Lyle, I'm sitting here in the car with Harry. We're both okay. However, no more big guy, Ewald. Killed in a hail of bullets trying to escape. The precinct's in a mess. It was a major assault by two guys. They tried to burn it down. That's right, they tried to burn the whole precinct down. Like I said, one of the two, the big guy is dead, the other's in custody. They came in throwing kerosene cans, and torches and machine-gunned everything and everyone in sight. Sorry to say, Mike, Sy, and Teddy, dead. So are Jerry, Mikey, and Sonny. Awful. Chico's seriously wounded. Fremont, and Augusto sustained minor wounds. Others are wounded also but not seriously. They've been taken to Montefiore. Fire Department put it out.

"The good news is that Ewald is gone. With all that lead in him he probably weighs twice what he used to. Eduardo's still in custody and spilling his guts non-stop. He's a font of information and he's obviously bargaining for some leniency. And don't worry, he's very smart so even if there were no guards watching him and the cell door happened to be wide open, he still wouldn't have left. He swears he had nothing to do with Willy going off the ledge. He claims Ewald did it.

"The truth of it is that you can tell he's telling the truth. Like I said, he's the smart one. During all the commotion, he was holding his arms in the air in the position of complete surrender. Yeah, the big guy took off, but Eduardo didn't move a muscle."

"Yeah, we felt that way too," Mac answered. "Eduardo's the smart one. We're sure it was the other big guy who pushed Willy. But man, we're depressed that we didn't get a chance at that target practice. Lemme tell ya. Thinking of Mike, Sy, Teddy, and all the rest, especially Chico—unbelievable. Will Chico make it? How serious is he? Sounds to me they were trying to kill everybody!"

"Chico's situation is touch and go. He got it in the stomach. Was bleeding something awful. We didn't get to see him but we heard it from a few guys like in vivid detail—which to tell you the truth, we didn't need to hear and neither do you."

"Okay, Jack, here's the question. The package we had in the property pen—what about it?"

"The property room is untouched but the place is a mess. Wait a minute, you mean the package that you guys were hepped about?"

"Yeah, of course. That one. Why, is there something wrong?

"No, nothing's wrong but we sent a whole lotta material down to Police Headquarters. They recently sent all the precincts a notice saying that they've cleared out more than five-thousand square feet of storage space in their basement to give us all more room in our own pens. So, we sent whatever we had down. Day before the assault on the precinct, everything went. Our pen was stacked to the hilt. Now it's clear. Everything we sent was catalogued and the cataloguing was supervised by Silverstein."

"Okay, Lyle and me, we're going downtown to get the package. We'll keep you guys informed. There's no doubt in my mind that the package is what they wanted to destroy and no one's life mattered. It wouldn't have even mattered had there been children there because burning everything down only meant no more package. And that's all there was to it.

"It's obvious. There was no way they could get to the package so they figured burn it all down. It means that the brains behind pushing Willy off the ledge is somehow connected to the plan to burn the precinct down. The question is why and how they determined, or actually had hard information about the package ostensibly being stored in the precinct? How could they know?"

In the car, Mac and Lyle talked it over. They were certain there couldn't be a mole at the precinct. Not a chance. There must have been forty or more cops assigned to that precinct and they knew them all. So, they knew there was another explanation as much in deep cover and so hidden that it seemed equivalent to the secret of the Enigma code that the Nazis used for their U-boats during the war.

Even when it was determined that both of the attackers were foreigners, Mac and Lyle were desperately trying to figure it out; trying to unearth any information on how two foreigners who probably didn't even know that the Bronx was a borough or even where the Bronx was, could know that the package was stored at some precinct—and more specifically at their precinct in the Bronx.

In their discussion about how the precinct was targeted and who—a specific person—gave the information about where the precinct was located, that information must have come from either a mole at the precinct—a specific person—which they were sure was not the case, or, Lyle said, "from Ewald or Eduardo."

They puzzled about how that could be? Of course, they only had one lead—one informant. They had Eduardo. He would know. And if not him, they had Wenzel—he might know. But Lyle piped in again and made it even more specific.

"Mac," Lyle said slowly. "Yeah, Eduardo got it from someone but how did that someone get it? Could it be, like I said, that it actually came from our cooperative guest, Eduardo himself, and not from anyone else?"

"Okay," Mac answered. "We'll ask him about it.?

Eduardo and Wenzel were now both being held in Police Headquarters down near the courthouse close to Wall Street. They were separated so they couldn't communicate with one another. But, of course, they could—and probably would—talk to any of the officials who wanted to interview them. In that case, both Mac and Lyle wanted to interview each of those Nazi operatives separately. For no apparent reason, other than getting the chaff finished with, they decided to see Wenzel first. The three of them met in one of the interrogation rooms at central Police Headquarters.

"Okay Mr. Wenzel, last name please," Mac said.

"Last namen ist . . . no, I vanting lawyer."

"Well, that's okay, but you know you're in a lot of trouble and police personnel have been killed. You will definitely die in the electric chair, or you might consider talking to us and giving us some information and then let's see if we can erase the possibility of the electric chair.

"You understand that's the best we would be able to do for you. The truth is you and your partner killed some of our best friends, so this offer we're making is done with maximum regret in our hearts because both of us would love to see you burn. Vershtehen?"

"Ya, Ish vershtehen. Forgetting mit lawyer. I knowing vhat vee doing und I knowing in trial vill making me dead like you saying—in electri-cal chair. But how I trusting you vill keeping to true vhat you saying mit saving me?"

"You'll simply have to trust us—plain and simple. Take it or leave it. Vershtehen?"

"Ya. Ish vershtehen. Okay, I telling you important informatzi. Dere ist chemical man in New York City, he who ist on payroll of German Nazi organizatzi. Namen ist Dr. Hermann Strauss und he living in 87 Street, Yorkville, numer 345, ground floor apartment numer 1C. Dat is vot I knowing it. Chemicals vee hof from dis man. He calling chemical chlorine triflouride. Vee no using dis chemical. Vee knowing it making danger und vill taking us too into dis fire. So vee changing mind un did torch, kerosene und shooting.

"I sorry about dine frynds. Mine frynd Karl vant to use dis chemical but I saying no. Dere ist no reason dat I lieing."

"I understand you were the one with the machine-gun. Right?"

Wenzel nodded yes, and then there was a pause with Mac and Lyle just looking at him. Mac broke the silence.

"Okay, what else can you give us?"

"Dere is man at State Department. He getting money to doing dese tings for dee Nazi leaders in Germany und also from Vatican."

"What's his name?"

"I not sure. I hear Karl saying namen Park und oder namen. First namen ist Park but I no knowing famile namen. Dis ist all I knowing dis — tzvie tings: chemical man und namen Park."

"Yes," Mac said. "But you know other things too, like who sent you over here to do what you did? What was the mission? Why try to burn down the police station and specifically why that one in the Bronx?"

"Karl und me, vee no to getting package because dis voman in Bronx taking package. Vee getting package but inside ist empty. Karl und me, vee vher fail und putting out from leader's office."

"Which leader?"

"Hudal. Bishop Alois Hudal. He ist leader at Vatican. He hast office at dis Vatican. He hast vay to helping Nazi to escaping. Karl saying package hast namen und platz who ist dese Nazis und vhere ist it day going. Dis is vhat Karl telling me. Karl und me vee deciding to doing dis so to destroying package und den vee going back und being good in this organizati. No more to failing."

Mac and Lyle looked at each other and Mac said: "Thought so."

They ended the interview with Wenzel and told him they would look in on him at a later time. Then, before they went to interview Eduardo, they contacted the F.B.I. The chemist Dr. Hermann Strauss was now about to be out of business!

Eduardo was his usual cooperative self. But Mac and Lyle spoke to him in sober tones. It was not good cop, bad cop. It was bad cop, bad cop similar to what Mossad agents did with 'anonymous.' That's all it was. They told Eduardo he would wind up in a maximum security prison living with the most dangerous prisoners he could ever imagine.

"These are people who hate their lives, but when someone threatens America, that person doing the threatening is in big trouble with them. Keep in mind," Mac added, "these are all killers, but they are all loyal to America. Understand?"

"Si. I understand."

"I know you were searched when we brought you in," Mac continued. Then Mac stopped talking and thought for a while.

"Stand up," Mac told him.

Eduardo complied and Mac patted him down, checking his pants and shirt, around his waistline and his crotch. Nothing. Then, looking down at the floor and thinking, Mac realized he was looking at Eduardo's shoes.

"Take off your shoes," Mac instructed.

Eduardo did as he was told.

Mac handed the shoes to Lyle to examine. Lyle stuck his hand into each shoe all the way to the toe. Nothing. Mac retrieved the shoes and held them. He looked at the heels. Under the pressure of Mac's hand, the right heel moved a fraction. Sure enough, Mac put extra pressure on it and it slid it open There it was. A mini transmitter.

Lyle went: "Wow!" as Mac just looked at it minus any emotion. Then he looked directly at Eduardo.

"So, you've been entirely cooperative. Right? So, you want consideration. Right? So, Mister, before we finish with you the way we'd like to—who is it that you've been connecting with? Don't hesitate. Just say it!"

Eduardo didn't hesitate for a moment.

"There is State Department man. I think he is assistant. He work for Hudal in Vatican. It is known by Hudal that this man he is interested in getting money for this information. I tell him about package and he tell me he already know about package from man name Karl. This is all I know."

Eduardo looked down, then turned to Mac and said:

"I am sorry I did this thing. But after I did this only that time, I never talk to him again."

"C'mon, Eduardo, you're stalling and you know what I mean."

"Parker Martin. Parker Martin. That is his name."

That took care of that interview. Martin was immediately picked up after Mac and Lyle called it in to their contact at the FBI. Again, as they had done with respect to the chemist, Strauss, and on the FBI secure phone, they described the issue regarding Martin. The FBI agent, John Wilkins, was serious but he also laughed in a kind of weary, cynical tone:

"You guys are doing better than we are. Keep it up."

Mac also coughed up a laugh. And though his wasn't cynical he was surely weary. Later, at Precinct 53 in the Bronx which was now a staging place for all the cops at the 48th, Mac and Lyle met with Jack and Harry. Hesitatingly, Jack said:

"Mac, Lyle, bad news. Chico died. He died. We just got it over the radio. Chico's gone."

"Holy shit," Lyle said. Mac was quiet, and then a few seconds later he turned to Lyle:

"Chico died."

· 15 ·

PANIC

After the half day of quizzing both Wenzel and Eduardo in the conference room on the second floor of Police Headquarters, Mac and Lyle decided to check to confirm with their own eyes whether the package had arrived safely at the vast holding pen in the basement. Of course, they knew it was a counterfeit microfilm in the package, but still they wanted to see it sitting there.

After saying their hellos to some guys at Headquarters that they knew, they headed directly to the elevators and pressed B.

"Okay," Mac said, "first we went up and now we're going down."

"What does that mean?" Lyle asked.

The truth was that Lyle could hear the cynicism or pessimism or whatever the hell it was that was bothering Mac. They'd worked together so many years that each of them could almost read what the other was thinking.

"Look partner, we've been around the world with this one. One minute it's here, the next minute it's not. But now Jack said it's here. Okay, I believe it. But I'll believe it only when I see it. Jack said the package got here, but despite what he or me or you, or Harry or what anyone said, the final question is: Did the package in fact, get here? We'll see."

They exited the elevator and approached the fenced off pen. The pen officer, Dave Greening greeted them and asked whether they had a number or any identifying characteristics of what they wanted.

"No," Mac said. "It's a package, an oblong package that was sent by the 48ᵗʰ Bronx."

"Yeah, we got that," Greening said. "Wait a minute, let's see."

With that Greening rifled through his index file and pulled out the stack of cards listing numbers and items delivered from the 48ᵗʰ. He then started flipping the cards since Mac and Lyle didn't have the catalogue number for the package.

"We have exactly seventy-five items listed including a rifle, a box of clothing, even a diamond ring, and a lot of other junk. I don't see anything about an oblong package. Wait, let me go through it again."

"Do it by number this time," Mac said. "Let's see if there's a skip somewhere in the numbers."

Of course, as might be expected, the cards were not in sequence from one to seventy-five. So, with Greening sitting and Mac and Lyle leaning over him, they started to sequence the cards. At that point they were not reading any of the descriptions of the material typed on the cards. They were just looking at numbers. When they got to sixty-two, they couldn't find sixty-three, and by the time they finished the rest of the sequence it was clear that sixty-three was missing.

"I don't get it," Greening said. "Either they messed it up at the 48ᵗʰ or it got lost, or it's here somewhere."

"Dave," Mac said, "no use looking for it, because I can tell you for sure, it's not here. I don't even know if it ever got here, and I'm sure they didn't mess it up at the 48ᵗʰ. Thanks for trying. We'll see you. By the way, in case I'm wrong and you do find it, call me. Here's my card. And thanks again."

Back into the elevator, going up two flights to street level and driving back uptown, they both were trying to figure it out or at least trying to tease out something of importance about what may have happened. They knew it was no accident. Not with this particular package!

"It wasn't anyone at the precinct. That we can be sure of," Lyle said.

"Right."

"And it doesn't ring true to think it was someone at Headquarters."

"Right."

"It had to have happened on the way from the precinct to Headquarters."

"Right."

Mac snapped his fingers. "The driver or at least one of them, or the guy in the back, riding shotgun."

He looked at Lyle just as Lyle was looking back at him.

"That's what I'm thinking too," Lyle said. "We gotta get their names and we need to talk to them. It's gotta be one or maybe even both. But the guy in the back is my first choice. He's sitting there with all of the stuff while the other one is driving the truck. I think it's the guy in the back. I can smell it."

"You're right. That's it," Mac said. "That's it. The guy in the back is sitting with all of the stuff. Of course. That's it. The question is, how did he know what to look for. Someone got to him. You can bet either he or they didn't take hostages. That's a joke. It must be when he delivered it or someone came to pick it up, and he got paid." Mac then paused. "No, wait a minute," Mac continued. "He never got paid. They killed him. No doubt about it. That guy, whoever he is, is dead. D-E-D, dead!"

"Right," Lyle jumped. "Of course. That guy's gone."

"Lyle—headquarters. I want those names."

*   *   *

But they didn't call headquarters. They drove back to headquarters and practically ran in. They made a bee line to the Director's office. The Director, Steve Scribner, was sitting at his desk talking to another officer. His door was shut. They didn't wait. It was perfunctory.

It just so happened that Mac was a personal friend of Scribner's. It was Steve Scribner who had been Mac's orientation officer when Mac had just joined the force and right from the beginning they hit it off.

Steve wrote Mac up in his evaluation form as someone for the 'force to keep its eye on' because he felt Mac was an outstanding candidate as an almost certain future detective. So, Mac entered first with Lyle walking behind. They just barged in.

"Steve, sorry. Gotta talk immediately," Mac blurted out.

Without blinking, the Director excused the officer who was there and the officer left the room with alacrity and shot a friendly nod both to the Director and the new visitors.

"Director, Steven Scribner, this is Detective Lyle Davis. We're partners, Steve."

"Hi, Detective Davis. Okay, Mac, what's the rush?"

Mac then gave Scribner a quick review of the situation.

"Okay, let's get the names. I agree. It's gotta be the guy in the back."

Scribner then made an inter-office call, asked for the ledger with the names of drivers, and gave the date of transfer from Precinct 48 in the Bronx down to Headquarters. He said he wanted to be called back immediately—he wouldn't be doing anything but waiting for the call.

It took all of about ten minutes during which time Mac and Scribner were talking, when Scribner got the return inter-com call and wrote the information on a pad on his desk.

"Mac, the driver's name is Jeffrey Stoller. He's been with us since 1950. I can vouch for him. He's definitely clean. The other guy is new. He came on exactly eight months ago. He was the one in the back. His name is Raymond Tokoly. Address is 711 Miller Avenue in the East New York section of Brooklyn. I know it. The El-train there stops at Van Siclen Avenue and Miller is a few blocks from the El.

"According to what I was just told, Tokoly is married. No children. Except for his job and address and phone, that's all they had on him. But I know the neighborhood. It's a peculiar mixture of Jewish, Irish, and Polish. Tokoly sounds maybe Polish. I know it because I grew up around there. Miller is a street with two-story houses. They're not quite garden apartments but still it's a quiet street. Strictly families. No elevators in the buildings. A friend of mine lived on that block, probably a few doors down. It's probably on that same block. We went to Jefferson High School together—Thomas Jefferson High School. Oh yeah, Tokoly is married, no children. Oh, I said that."

The next thing you know, Mac and Lyle are careening toward the Brooklyn Bridge and zipping all the way. With traffic, it took them about forty minutes to get to Miller. They parked and walked from where Miller Avenue began, a few blocks from the El, until they hit 711 Miller. It was on the first block after Miller began. Scribner was on the money. Miller was a quiet street. A few people were sitting on chairs in front of their houses.

From this little sample of people, the overall population living on this quiet family street who were sitting and talking, gave the entire neighborhood a feel of middle-aged family people, maybe in their fifties.

Mac and Lyle climbed a few steps, opened the door to the little alcove lobby of 711 Miller, and Mac traced down the ledger of listed names and apartment numbers with his finger, stopping at Tokoly, apartment 2B.

That meant one flight up. They both un-holstered their weapons from their shoulder holsters as they climbed on their toes. They reached 2B. It was one of two apartments on the floor. The door was slightly ajar and they quietly entered, guns drawn.

Sure enough they were faced with a man sitting on a chair in the kitchen. He was severely wounded, obviously in the stomach, and was hunched over. They could tell he was dying. But his eyes were open and he was un-mistakenly looking directly at them.

"We're police." Mac showed his badge.

The man began breathlessly mouthing words He was obviously in pain. Mac and Lyle both leaned into him, very close, so they could hear him.

"My wife . . . She knows . . . They got her . . . Sister's house Carol...It's the package . . . Carol was keeping the package for us. I think my wife took them there. I wanted . . . more dough . . . Carol at Saratoga Ave . . . 345. 3A . . . Go . . . quick."

With that, Tokoly, the guy in the back of the police van charged with guarding the stuff, died sitting in a chair.

Mac and Lyle dashed out of the apartment, closing the door behind them. In the car, Lyle radioed Headquarters. Mac took the radio-phone and spoke to his buddy the Director. He told Scribner that they're onto it and are following the lead but that Raymond Tokoly was dead and Tokoly's next stop would be the coroner's lab. He told Scribner that Tokoly had been shot in the stomach and that he and Lyle we're heading for the address they had on Saratoga Avenue. Scribner quickly told them it was only two or three stops from the Van Siclen station.

Scribner stayed on the line directing Mac and Lyle driving helter-skelter through the streets of East New York mostly under the El, directly to Saratoga.

Now Mac and Lyle were in a panic. Would they get there soon enough to get the shooters? Of course, they didn't know what the elapsed time was from when Tokoly was shot to the time they themselves had reached him. That time difference could be the difference between getting the guys or not.

As they pulled up to 345 Saratoga, they instantly spotted a middle-aged woman running toward them as they were approaching. She was running as fast as her age would take her. Her arms were flailing. She was shouting: "Police, police."

Mac and Lyle both jumped out of the car and grabbed her. She started to scream again, "Police, Police." Mac flashed his badge and said emphatically: "We are policemen." He said it twice. The lady calmed down but then became hysterical again. They moved her to the car and sat her in back. She was sobbing. Mac sat next to her. Lyle sat shotgun in the front seat but kept looking at them both even as he continued to watch the street.

In what seemed like a long minute the lady again calmed down.

"Are you Mrs. Tokoly?" Mac gently asked.

"Yes," she answered. "They shot my husband. Oh, I hope they didn't kill him. He's all I have. We have no children. Oh, my sister. Carol. Oh Carol."

Mrs. Tokoly began sobbing again and again Mac tried to comfort her. It took some moments before Mrs. Tokoly calmed down. She told them she had escaped when her sister jumped out of the window onto the fire-escape and climbed up onto the roof. I know where she was going but one of them went after her and that's when I had the chance to run because I dropped the package they wanted and the other one bent down to pick it up. That was my chance.

"I had no choice. I had to take them to get the package or they would have killed me. That's what they said. Oh God, I think they killed my husband. I'm so nervous. My sister would have climbed over a short barrier onto the next adjoining roof and down one flight to her friend Joyce's house who lives on the top floor of the other building. That's the floor below the roof. I'm sure Carol's there—I hope. Carol and Joyce always visit each other that way. Up to the roof, over and down to either's apartment.

"You know, I think that if they followed her they wouldn't know which apartment she went into or if she quietly ran down the stairs into the street. So now I'm thinking that maybe one of them ran down into the street to see if he could see her but the other one might be trying to break into apartments searching for her. Oh God, they both had guns. Oh God, I hope they didn't get her. Oh God. My husband. Oh Raymond."

Suddenly, Mrs. Tokoly spotted one of them coming out of the building into the street. She was about to scream but Mac put his hand over her mouth until she understood not to make a sound.

"Mac, I got him."

With that, Lyle calmly got out of the car and walked in the opposite direction to where the assailant was standing who was then looking with an alarmed expression in all directions. Lyle lifted his foot onto the fire hydrant so it looked like he was tying his shoelaces. Instead, he furtively looked to see whether the suspect was aware of him. He could instantly tell that the guy was not suspicious of him in any way.

With that in mind, and in a split second, Lyle reversed his direction and walked toward the assailant. Lyle pulled out his gun only when he was about fifteen feet away and shouted:

"Don't move or so help me I'll kill you. I'll blow your mother-fuckn' head right off. Don't move a muscle. Not a muscle. Don't even breathe. You wanna try it, gohead, try it!"

The guy didn't move. He believed what Lyle promised. Lyle then approached and disarmed him, and brought him over to the car. Mac handed Lyle a pair of handcuffs. Lyle handcuffed the guy and threw him into the front seat of the car. Meanwhile Mac called-in for backup. The guy in handcuffs in the front seat didn't turn around to look in the back. He just sat there not saying a word.

And that's the way it remained for no more than six or seven minutes when two other police cars with the new Chevy two-way radios and revolving red Beacon Ray lights answering Mac's call for back-up, pulled up—two cops in each car. Immediately, the prisoner was efficiently transferred to one of the other police cars and sat in the back. It was fully wired with that chain-link cyclone fence material encasing the back as a temporary jail cell—without giving the prisoner any chance of escaping.

Lyle quickly briefed the four cops from both cars as to what was what.

"The only unfinished business then," Lyle said, "is to flush out the other one.

Lyle took two of them and pulled them to the other side of the car and quietly said:

"Look, if the other guy has a package we need to let him escape. We've got this one over here. It's enough. I'm giving this to you on orders of Headquarters. Call up the Director. He's the Commissioner's right hand man. He's the one who approves it this way. But after he confirms it all, nothing of this can be written. We simply agree that the guy escaped. Period! The Director's name at Headquarters is…"

The cop cut him off. "I know. Scribner. Okay, I believe it. We'll let him go."

As the cop spoke, Mrs. Tokoly's sister, Carol, walks out of the building with her friend, Joyce. They both instantly spot Mrs. Tokoly, and the police, and walk calmly over. The women hugged each other and they all started crying.

"I was going to give him the package no matter what," Mrs. Tokoly suddenly continued. "But after the one jumped onto the fire escape, that's when I dropped it. The other one was distracted by it and in that split second I ran out of the apartment."

At that moment Mrs. Tokoly hesitated.

"Oh God. Did they kill him? Tell me. Did they kill him? The other one must have the package. He's probably on the roof and is hopping over three or four other rooftops. Right Carol, right? They're all connected you know. Then he could get to the corner one and that's the one that leads to the first house around the corner. He'd probably be exiting the building there. You should all run and get him. He has a gun. Oh God, look, I'm shaking."

With their prisoner in tow, Mac and Lyle assured her that the armed guy must already be far away but that they would get him another time. At the same moment Carol and Mrs. Tokoly didn't know what to do or where to go. But Mrs. Tokoly certainly knew what to ask.

"Please tell me my husband is alive. Please tell me. Please. Is he alive?

She was looking at Mac and Mac hesitated.

"Oh no," she whispered. "Oh no."

Yes, they let him get the package, but of course the film had already been altered. Now when Al, Jimmy, Kishnov and Imi got to Simon they would be able to tell him that the counterfeit microfilm is pretty clearly on its way to the Vatican into the hands of Alois Hudal.

Mac and Lyle were relieved. But they talked about Mrs. Tokoly. They felt bad for her.

*   *   *

Mac and Lyle were off to Montefiore Hospital where they would see Frankie and Willy and beautiful Gloria. They bantered with Willy and told him he was improving and doing it at record speed. Willy really appreciated their visit and how they responded to him—like he was their buddy. Yes, he was kind of proud that he had buddies who were real police detectives. Willy felt protected. It was a definite contrast he was feeling, from being below the zone-of-death when he was pushed, to now being in the center of the zone-of-safety. He was surrounded by pure protection: two officers 24/7, uncle Frank, and Gloria, and now Mac and Lyle too—not to mention Al, who Willy felt was never far away no matter where Al was. And now he was there with them all.

Mac, Lyle, and Frank stepped out into the hall while Al stayed with Willy. Frank got right to it.

"I'm really sorry about the guys. I knew Chico well. He would stop in to see me at the bar sometimes, maybe once every two or three weeks. He'd always say to me that a drink is okay but getting smashed is not. That was how he always put it. 'Don't get smashed.' I'm feeling very bad about Chico. Very bad! I'm going to send the family something. I'll do whatever I can."

At that point, Willy's inner circle, his own gang, was splintering. Gloria was headed back to the motel escorted by Mac and Lyle, but Frank and the two officers on duty remained.

Willy said his goodbyes. Al was then on his way to meet with Jimmy and Imi to deliver the package to Simon and then meet with the entire gang.

PART 4

HOME BASE

· 16 ·

INFORMATION TO WIESENTHAL

"Aye, aye, aye. Look at this. Unbelievable. You did it. You did it. We've been looking for this list for years. I'm not going to ask how you did it but you did it."

That was Wiesenthal's first comment when Al, Jimmy, Imi, Hugh, Max and Shmuel had all arrived. It felt like a miracle occurred. Al handed Simon the authentic microfilm along with the one that was a facsimile, but entirely misinformationed.

Weisenthal had arrived at their meeting place with two very strong looking Israeli Secret Service men right out of Imi's Krav Maga class that was required for all Mossad agents. Of course, they were carrying weapons but that was for distance shooting. Up close there would be no need for weapons. This was Wiesenthal's personal body-guard squad.

Wiesenthal was a modest looking gentleman of about fifty. He was about six-feet tall which was on the tall side for a Jewish man who was born in a Ukrainian hamlet — a shtetl — and he was of moderate build. He actually looked like a French resistance fighter, especially because he was wearing a beret a bit tilted. But of course, he was not in the least interested in how he looked because upon seeing the material at hand he almost howled:

"Look at this: Eichmann, Mengele, Priebke, Brunner, Katrink, Sommer, Kopkow, Danz, Abel. Look at this list. And the countries: Argentina,

Brazil, Chile, Egypt, Syria, Canada, even the United States. How many did you say," Wiesenthal asked Imi?

"Exactly four-thousand one-hundred eighty-six," Imi answered. "But here's the thing Simon. Right in the middle of it all is listed—you can see at number two-thousand forty-two—exactly halfway into the entire list, the name of Gustav Schell. But nowhere on anyone's list in any country is the name Gustav Schell known as an escaped Nazi criminal.

"Another interesting thing is that of all the names each have two destinations—one primary and one secondary. The second one is a just-in-case. Schell only has one destination and it's in a place different from where the others go—just in case. Schell, apparently is supposed to be living at the bottom of a mountain near Monaco, you know, the French Riviera. It's either these mini towns near to *Mont Tete de Chien* like *La Condamine*, or *Mentone*—all on the French Riviera. *Mont Tete de Chien*; that one we can't figure out unless *you* might have some inkling about it. Could it possibly be what I'm thinking?"

"I don't know—but on second thought," Simon said, "maybe I do know. Well, let me put it this way: Is it possible that we're both thinking the same thing? But, in any case, Imi, why would you guess those particular towns?"

"Well, they're all in some way related to Monaco. As a matter of fact, one of them, I think it's *Tete de Chien*, looks directly down over the entire principality of Monaco. In addition, *La Condamine* and *Mentone* have all sorts of relationships with Monaco. Importantly however, is that they have access to waterways. In fact, in our preliminary investigation, we've found that in the harbor of *Mentone* a large yacht is anchored that we also found out doubles as a speed boat. And—it boasts a radar detection-system. So, of course, this Gustav Schell increasingly becomes more interesting. Is it his yacht, is the question? Who the hell is he? He certainly must either be very high on the list or else could be some outside source who's important to their cause and perhaps must, at all cost, be protected, or disguised."

"I also wish I knew who Schell is," Hugh said. That comment was seconded by Al, Jimmy, and Max together.

"For the first time, we're not unanimous in our vote,"

Then Al caught himself, looked at Jimmy, who got it also and they both looked at Max, and then at Hugh and Imi, and then finally at Shmuel. It almost stopped there except for the unmitigated fact that they then all together finally looked at Wiesenthal.

"I guess," Hugh jumped in, "it might be a wild guess, though am I right to think it's unanimous?"

"Wild guess is right," Wiesenthal said. "I and others will consider this Schell thing very carefully. But if we're right, well, we'll see. Gentlemen," he ended, "my escorts and I will now leave with our heartfelt thanks for what you've done. I say that in the most coveted and revered way. From this point, we'll do what we need to do. Of course, Eichmann and Mengele are top priorities. As I'm sure Shmuel will tell you, they will be captured one way or another and if it needs to be—although it's not my way of doing things—legally or not.

"I'm sure Kovner's spirit is with us, certainly with Shmuel here, and I assure you that the days are numbered for these murderers."

Then Shmueli took it upon himself to add to Wiesenthal's declaration. He said:

"If you reading in dese papers dat day, Eichmann un Mengele both, or only vone of dem he die of accident, or of even natural cause I telling you now no believing dis because if it looking like accident or natural cause it vould be because I un some oders making it looking dat vay. Vould be because legal vay could be escape routing for dem. Mit uns ist no escape routing. Mit bullet, mit car accident, mit falling, mit drowning; also, mit execution like mit assassination—all dese tings could it being."

Then Shmueli additionally swept himself into some kind of reverie.

"Like I saying, Eichmann, who vee chasing many years vill be mine first target. Vee not debating 'ifn.' Vee only interest 'Vhen.' Simon here vould vant to putting both deese murderers on trial un making big news vit dis. Leaders in Tel Aviv tinking over this all time. Day vant also ist to putting deese murderers on trial un in Israel. Only qvuestion is to getting dem out like from example of dis Argentina. It ist problem dat Argentina no giving extradition. Dis ist meaning vee needing to taking tings in own hands just like day tooking tings into dair own hands.

"Iz trut vhen vee getting him un bringing him to Israel for dis trial, he vould definite be convicted un vee vould make dis exception to capital punishment law, un maybe too, to hang dis Nazi svine for all world to seeing dis—but only after Jews all over vorld see vhat vee do to Nazi.

"Some like me vould say dat dis ting is no revenge. No. But it is message to vorld dat vee Jews, vee no forgetting. Never!"

Then Al said it the way Dr. Janet Sirota would: "Sorry Mr. Wiesenthal

I have to say it my American way. It's like saying to the world: 'just don't fuck with Jews. Plain and simple. That shit is over with.'"

Almost surprisingly, Weisenthal answered: "Yes, you are right. But first let's *all* be on a first name basis. Please call me Simon. Second, as I've said you're right about the specific message. But I believe there's a larger more global message. That more global message could be this: 'Don't be involved in genocides toward any people!' As the Italian saying goes: 'Genocide would be an infamnia.' In Yiddish, the word might be 'shanda' meaning 'shame' or 'tragedia' or a 'zind' meaning plainly, a sin. Yet, I think such a word as 'infamnia,' suffices and is suitable to what the Nazis did. But like I said, it is exactly the same for all people involved in genocidal acts toward targeted groups. They are involved in an infamnia and a zind.

Looking to Hugh, Wiesenthal then says: "Hugh, as a Christian honorific, I'm sure you agree that the world is still in a primitive state."

"Yes, of course I do."

To that, Simon said: "Thank you all for that. And gentlemen, in contrast to all such sentiments wrapped in the term 'infamnia,' I need to add that deeply embedded in Jewish culture is something special. And this something else, this something special is not only the need to achieve things. What needs to be known is that buried within the Jewish cultural tradition regarding achievement is the idea of 'contribution.' Implicitly, with respect to Jewish culture, Jews must make contributions to society and in any numbers of ways. But it is definitely not achievement for achievement's sake.

"You know, in this world we're about two-hundred-fifty thousand years away from Neanderthal sensibility. Therefore, what is patently clear is that with respect to the pace of evolutionary development, like now in the mid 20th century, civilization as well as the human condition is really in a rather primitive state. In other words, the world is in a state of existence where genocides are still occurring as typical sociological phenomena. Therefore, it's a situation in society where good deeds need to be rewarded while bad ones need to be punished. At this stage of evolution, it is how and what the world understands.

"In the end however, I must say that I live with contradictions as I'm sure is the case with every living person. What I mean is that I'm absolutely against 'killing' — both mass killing as well as individual murder. Yet, I definitely would vote for hanging Eichmann, Mengele, and all of the others. Yes, I mean *all*."

"Un ifn government no doing it, den yah," Shmuel suddenly intervened," I believing in dis aggression, un how you saying in America, 'justified manslaughter or even dis justified homicide.' Saying any vay you vanting. So, if Israeli government no doing, den I doing. Un dis I meaning ist definite assassination!"

And that's how Simon Wiesenthal left them with Shmueli's pointed reference to 'assassination' ringing in everyone's ears.

* * *

Further, with respect to this entire unfolding drama, there were blueprints being drawn at just about everyone's home-base. Al was again going home to Gloria. Frankie and Willy were planning on seeking a kind of hopeful closure with the Whartons—even though in his heart-of-hearts Frankie wasn't sure if danger to the Wharton family was, in fact, at an end. Similarly, what if it wasn't over was always the question that both Al and Gloria were concerned with—not to mention how such a possibility also hung over Mac and Lyle.

Jimmy was exhaling and reconnoitering within the safety of M-16. Hugh was returning to Rome and to his polar opposite cohabiting neighbor, Hudal, and Imi was off to training Mossad agents in Krav wherever that might be—this time, probably Haifa.

But Max was in a quandary. He knew he no longer had a home base since he split from Janet and departed Bletchley. Yet, Max wasn't sure where he would ultimately land; maybe Texas where he knew people and had some family members, or maybe the Bronx with Al—or even maybe somewhere else.

However, Maxie's new friend, Shmuel Kishnov, had a different idea. He suggested that Max hook up with him because: a) he needed a partner in the things he had to do, and, b) after meeting Max and discovering to his delight that Max was a Krav expert, he thought they'd be good together—again, in the things he knew he had to do.

Max looked at Shmuel, thought for a few seconds, and then with only the subtlest nod, accepted the invitation. It seemed that perhaps now at least Max had an interim destination—one invited by that Kovner acolyte, Shmuel Kishnov. When they talked it over later, in serious unemotional terms, Shmuel told Max that they needed to depart for certain places in order to arrange for certain people to disappear. Max didn't blink. He just gestured okay, again with that subtle nod.

And Simon? Well, Simon was leaving for parts unknown in order, one could be sure, to seek justice, to fight oppression and to make sure the world will begin to understand—albeit in a series of successive approximations—that there is no statute of limitations for evil!

Before he bid us farewell, he reminded us that since the end of the war and the beginning of the trials for some of these murderers, each and every one of them claimed that they didn't know a thing about it all—especially that they didn't know what was happening to the Jews. At some point earlier, Simon had noted that in contrast, these Nazi perpetrators all certainly did know what was happening because they were the one's carrying out the genocide. Even when eye-witnesses pointed to them and swore that they remembered each one, they still denied knowing what had been happening. Then Simon said it eloquently:

"Their lying was like a yawning abyss where echoes were screaming the lie: 'I didn't know anything about it.'"

* * *

And of course, what about Alois Hudal? They were all certain that Hudal was now at the drawing-board in some God-forsaken room at the Vatican, both knowing and validating all that Nazi guilt and then also knowing full well that in the other's possession of the microfilm, his Nazi overall cover could be blown. Therefore, he was sure that notice needed to be sent to thousands in many countries to alert them to the certain danger that now existed about where they were living or where they were hidden. Hudal needed to make sure they all knew that their so-called concealment game was over and that all secondary locations needed to be, if possible, changed immediately. He knew it would be the Israelis collectively and even Simon Wiesenthal and his gang separately, that they all needed to be worried about.

What he didn't know was that his microfilm was a fake but on the other hand he really had no worries about Simon because Simon was not a wartime 'consigliari' and wouldn't have anyone assassinated. However, what he more importantly really didn't know, but desperately needed to know was that Shmuel Kishnov was now on the case.

Hudal had other desperately pressing issues at hand. Despite the work it would take to notify them all, Hudal took it on as a task that was in all respects worthy of his efforts. To this end he called a meeting a week hence of his Executive Board. This included Montini himself, Dragonovic, Ruffinengo, Tisserant, Caggiano, Siri, Filiberto, Nix, Heinemann, Bayer and Kaltenbrunner. They represented: the *Vatican*; *DAIE*—meaning *The Delegation of Argentine Immigration in Europe*; the *Undersecretary in the Vatican Secretary of State office*; his supply source; and, the *Security Office SS*.

Hudal was successful in getting almost full attendance with the exception of Kaltenbrunner and Nix who couldn't make it. Otherwise the room was almost to capacity and in total included ten out of the twelve.

Hudal apprised them of the situation in soft but concise tones.

"We've got the microfilm. And we're fairly certain we're safe. We do know however that if they don't have it, it was nevertheless a close call. Therefore, again, we're just about in a position to relax, except that it's not one-hundred percent certain. Thus, this bit of uncertainty does, in fact, creates an urgency."

They all understood that 'urgency' therefore, was the utmost agenda item. It all hit home and so Hudal had begun making arrangements for his administrative assistants—three of them—to have everything that was on the microfilm printed. Then he had the lists parsed so that each of the three would need to have their office secretarial services responsible for the contact of about four-hundred or so individuals in any number of countries. He felt that bringing the total of over four-thousand to about only four-hundred for each of the three—about thirty percent or so of the total—would make the task more workable and certainly more efficient. He saved his fourth assistant to only handle the case of Gustav Schell which meant to get word to Schell about some possible invasion of information.

It was a bad decision that Hudal made because he hadn't even looked at the detail of the film. If he had, he possibly might have spotted some evidence of tampering. The only sure thing he did do was to keep on a separate list those top names he felt needed at all cost to be protected by immediately leaving for their secondary locations where they would be provided safe houses as well as potential work places. He had also decided to tell these top-priority individuals that even the second locations might be dangerous so that they themselves would now be able to change even those destinations.

When Hudal's assistant completed the urgent message to Schell, she delivered it to the stack of all outgoing priority messages. It so happened that Hugh had been spying on all the ongoing activity of Hudal's assistants and followed this personal assistant of Hudal's to where she delivered her note. From his distance Hugh knew he needed at all cost to liberate that note. He immediately contacted his ally nun, Sister Agnus Furillo, and told her what needed to be done. Sister Agnus followed Hugh's instruction and casually picked up the note, took it to Hugh, who read it, instructing then Sister Agnus to rewrite the note simply sending Schell greetings from his friends and wishing him well. Sister Agnus did just that and returned the changed note in record time to the stack of urgent messages that were slated to be sent immediately.

On Hudal's list were an even fifty that he handed to his chief assistant Joseph Prader with the instruction to address these fifty, first. It was because at least that these particular fifty would be those most sought. Of course, in a stream of consciousness he could recite the first ten or twelve or so who would certainly be prize catches. He reeled them off in his mind: Eichmann, first in line because of his management and direction of the 'Jewish issue'; Mengele for sure, obviously because of his evil sadistic practice at Auschwitz especially against children; Priebke because of his ordering the massacre at the 'Adreatine Caves'; Stangl, the head of 'Treblinka Concentration Camp'; Kutschmann, known as 'the killer' of twenty-thousand in Poland; Roschmann, the 'Butcher of Riga'; Guth, the mass killer in France; Barbie, the Gestapo 'Butcher of Lyon'; and, he also rattled off in his mind, Kurger, Wagner, Sommer, Brunner, Katrink, Knochen, Kopkow, Danz, Schafer, Abel, Sandberger, and, of course the others. These he knew would be at the top of anyone's seek-and-destroy list.

He knew that Eichmann must at least move to his second destination immediately; in other words, from the point of view of the unaltered film, the remote province of Tucuman to Olivos at the outskirts of Buenos Aires.

Believe it or not, the truth is that Hudal had been so overwhelmed with all of his transport details and with reference to so many of these Nazi criminals, he never had time to be current with information regarding even top-level Nazis who had already been situated in their primary locations. This was true of Eichmann, who in 1953 had shifted from Tucuman to Olivos. Eichmann attributed his shift to job considerations and personal contacts but it was obvious that he possibly had been spooked in Tucuman.

Therefore, in 1958 when Hudal was having these urgent missives sent to his own prescribed list of over four-hundred escapees– especially his top fifty—Eichmann was already in his secondary location for about three years.

Mengele was another story. He was typically always at high alert and was prepared with more than two locations. He had Sao Paulo, Brazil as his secondary location which he initially insisted he wanted. But at first this 'Angel of Death' arrived in Argentina in 1949 and settled in Buenos Aires as his first location. However, instead of only a second destination planned for him, he insisted on a third as well. And if needed, he planned to use all three.

When the plan for Mengele was hatched, Hudal needed to do some extra work to persuade Mengele to leave Buenos Aires, his first location, and to travel to Paraguay, his proposed second one, to see if Paraguay suited him. To this, Mengele actually communicated with Hudal and conveyed that so far he felt safe in Buenos Aires but that even if he utilized the escape route to Paraguay, he was sure he would one day eventually want to be in Brazil, especially in Sao Paulo where many Nazis were firmly entrenched and particularly in positions of power. What Hudal of course didn't know and wouldn't know was that in the counterfeit film, Mengele's ultimate destination-plan would be Bertioga, Brazil.

Mengele was as shrewd as they come. His subterfuge even eluded Hudal. Mengele must have figured that if Hudal's microfilm was ever revealed, he could be dead in the water. But Hudal and his unholy alliance of these poor excuses for true Christians located at the Vatican and elsewhere, were too busy to worry about such details. They never expected that any of their clients would even dream of deceiving them. They were all busy sending massive numbers of messages to their contacts, these criminal escapees who were holed up in countries such as Argentina, Brazil, Chile, Ecuador, Egypt, Libya, Syria, Jordan, Canada, and, unfortunately, in the United States as well—but interestingly, *none* in the Soviet Union.

All this urgency was in response to the information on the counterfeit microfilm that Simon Wiesenthal figured would ultimately create havoc in the stampede of Nazi criminals seeking safe havens all over the world. They would end up in this situation of havoc and uncertainty, and thereby threatened with being uncovered and seen.

Hudal was not the only busy one. Others were also back to the drawing board and working at their home base. For example, after Al's group would be dispersed to each one's home base, they had all agreed to do whatever was necessary to counteract whatever Hudal was doing. And they knew exactly what Hudal would be doing. It was Hugh O'Flaherty's job to try to monitor whatever he could regarding Hudal's activity at the Vatican.

Jimmy McKay's job was to keep his ears open at M-16 Secret-Service regarding anything related to unusual movement of suspected Nazis in various South American countries—especially with a focus on Argentina.

Imi Lichtenfeld's job was to be the switchboard operator between Simon, Jimmy, and Hugh. Al Kaye's job was to keep in touch with Detectives Loris Mac McIver, and Lyle Davis, in order to continue the debriefing of their captives, the operatives—the Juan Peron operative, Eduardo Velaro, and the Alois Hudal one, Wenzel Wagner.

Maxie had already headed for points unknown under the expert tutelage of Shmuel Kishnov. In addition, Imi told Al that after he'd heard about what had happened to the kid, Willy Travali, that he'd like to keep abreast of Willy's progress. They then all said their farewells and departed for points that would ultimately take them to destinations all around the globe.

· 17 ·

BACK TO THE DRAWING BOARD

The moment the plane touched down at Idlewild, Al looked for a phone to call Gloria. The good news was that Willy was recovering nicely. She told Al it was slow but Willy was walking carefully and slowly and was looking better and better. She also added that Willy had become more talkative without it being too painful for the effort.

"All the nurses have fallen in love with him. They say they've never seen anyone so cooperative and nice. It's true, Al," she said, "Willy is such a nice kid."

"You're the nice one, Gloria. They need to write a song about you."

"Al," Gloria responded, come right home."

And that's exactly what he did. Al made a bee-line for the Bronx and for Gloria.

Hugh O'Flaherty landed at Fiumicino International Airport in Rome, better known as Leonardo da Vinci International Airport as one of the first landings at the newly constructed part of the airport. He was met by a Vatican service-vehicle and driven to his apartment just outside the Vatican walls. After bathing and resting, he walked to his office within the Vatican, all the while wondering how he was going to access the kind of information that would be valuable for Wiesenthal.

As he passed through the threshold of the Vatican entry point, the Swiss Guards greeted him. As he was walking to his office located at the

Apostolic Palace, here and there he exchanged greetings with people he knew. At his office, he immediately began to go through a stack of mail on his desk. He selected several letters, he had received, put them in a folder, left the office and walked directly down a corridor to Sister Agnus Furillo's office. Sister Agnus was one of Hugh's trusted lieutenants and worked with him on his so-called transport project whereby hidden allied soldiers and Jewish people in hiding were escorted to safe houses and then out of the country. It was sort of what Hudal was doing but, of course, somewhat different.

Hugh went right to it: "What's he doing?"

"I don't exactly know," Sister Agnus responded. "But the interesting thing is that he has several new secretaries feverishly working on something. Typing, typing, typing is all you hear from their offices. I personally witnessed the handyman, Mr. Stellini making two or three trips into Alois's offices with typewriters under his arms. Do you have any idea of what could be happening?"

"Yes, I do. I do," Hugh said. "I think everything is good."

Imi Lichtenfeld landed at Lod Airport, outside of Tel Aviv. From there, a non-descript auto took him to a destination in the town of Haifa. There he disappeared and then reappeared at a secret Mossad training camp. He immediately reported to Mossad Captain, Ariel Lash. Imi briefed her and together they decided that Imi would set up shop in Lash's adjacent office. Imi would have access to all communication and any other necessary services whatever they might turn out to be. Imi felt that in Israel women, have as much opportunity as men and further, he was sure they would eventually or in fact very soon, have a woman Prime Minister. He was betting it would probably be Golda.

Jimmy didn't need to land anywhere. He was already home in London. No wife, no current girlfriend, only M-16, of military intelligence of the *British Intelligence Agency*. Jimmy reported in as Imi had, and like Imi he was given an assistant, an office, and free reign to do whatever he needed done.

So, in quick order, they were all set to see whether the flurry of activity coming out of Hudal's Vatican would enable them to understand where certain of their targets were in fact living and where their escape routes would possibly take them—their pre-arranged secondary destinations—those now and newly-arranged through the counterfeit micro, or wandering untethered here and there seeking safety but actually being conspicuous.

Except for Wiesenthal, now a first-name friend, Simon, the others didn't really know how it would all work. Would they be capturing Nazi escapees or not? Of course, Simon knew. He knew that to corral hundreds of these vermin would not be possible. He also knew, as did his cohorts that it would serve important objectives to put only a few on trial. That meant Eichmann, Mengele, and three or four others. Only a few.

He wasn't privy to Shmueli and Max's plans, both who were sharp-shooting Krav Maga magicians—and both not at all squeamish about killing. This, at least would comprise a two-man private assassination squad.

Shmueli held forth for Maxie. "Vee no veapons had, no Jewish State, no money, un vee live most in Ghettos, und poor. Un stupid vorld say vee all rich un secret group. Day use vord 'passive' un say vee be meek un valk inside dis gas chamber. Vell, now vee having Jewish state. Now vee be having some of dis money, un vee having guns! So, because now unzer planning, un how vee hoping, un how vee knowing to do tings, vee go definite to make assassination. Un deese vill be no-passive assassination. Be active assassination. No far away behind dis tree. No. Dis assassination vill be close in face. Direct! No meek. If I deciding den I vant more should be hand-to-hand combat mit deer best fighters. Den vee see who say dis passive un meek—especially vhen vee destroy dem! Un I vant to see dis destroy vone by vone!"

So, there it was for all of the *Justice Brigade*, each of whom was proceeding to do things in different ways but with one common goal. It all boiled down to 'just desserts.'

Oh yes, with respect to Simon's philosophy he had it down—at least in his mind this way: 'Morality is relative' he believed. In other words, first, in this primitive world and in an absolute sense, absolute morality becomes an abstraction. Second: 'One must stand against oppression of any people and for fairness, otherwise one permanently loses integrity, loses oneself. And finally, third, he had the answer to how evil should be treated with respect to any statute of limitations; 'Evil has no statute of limitations'! That was Simon's unequivocal answer. Of that he was sure!

Simon Wiesenthal, the Nazi hunter, was going to see to it. He was going to prove in no uncertain terms that evil has no statute of limitations—none at all.

*　*　*

Information reached Shmuel Kishnov about Albrecht Schmidt. Schmidt was Heinrich Muller's right-hand man. Muller was head of the Gestapo in Berlin and responsible for many murders as well as horrible tortures. Shmuel also knew that Schmidt, even though he was an aide to Muller, was instrumental in these abominable acts as well. And, as far as Shmuel knew, Schmidt had disappeared immediately after Muller's body was found, when the war was essentially over, in 1945. Muller's body was discovered in a mass grave. Either he and the others in that mass grave were caught in a bombing raid and were all killed, or some Jewish assassination squad took care of it. In this latter case, they must have machine-gunned a dozen Nazi escapees or even more.

Certain people weren't satisfied just with Muller's death. They also desperately wanted Muller's main aide, Albrecht Schmidt. Schmidt, like Mengele was very smart and like Mengele didn't solely rely on Hudal's pre-arranged locations. In 1950, he disappeared from the scrutiny of Hudal and from Hudal's blameworthy cohorts. However, there were what Shmuel Kishnov considered to be reliable reports of Schmidt's where-abouts, most likely in central Buenos Aires. One report was of a Jewish former prisoner of the Gestapo who was held in Muller's charge in Berlin. This man, this former captive of Muller's, swore he saw Schmidt in a place called Plazoleta Cortazar, roughly translated meaning Plaza Serrano in the Palermo area of Buenos Aires. And he swore he would know him anywhere.

This man promptly contacted the Jewish Agency in Buenos Aires who in turn gave the information to government sources in Israel. That's how Shmuel Kishnov eventually got wind of it. This was early in his not yet full career as a Kovner Nazi-hunter or as an Irgunist, and he did not have a full enough budget to go after Schmidt.

However, now, in 1958, more than a half dozen years after Schmidt was first sighted, Shmuel, Maxie, and two others personally went look-ing for the eye-witness. The man's name was Arthur Libman. He was an American former paratrooper whose plane was shot down. He parachuted out with others doing the same but they were all caught and sent to Stalag III in the town, Sagan, in Silesia, Germany. He and scores of other allied prisoners decided not to spend the rest of the war in this German Stalag camp. At one point in 1944 many escaped but most were caught and returned to the camp. Libman was one of the returnees.

Shmuel and Maxie tracked down Libman who, had not returned to America. Rather, at that point in his life he was a cab-driver in Tel Aviv, but in reality, was an operative of one of the Israeli secret services—that of Shin Bet. Roughly translated Shin Bet means 'invisible ones.' Shmuel and Maxie knew this because they got his name through Shmueli's contacts at Mossad—another of Israel's secret services—where they were directed to Libman.

During their interview with Libman his story was that he was on assignment that took him to the main shopping area of downtown Palermo, Buenos Aires, called *Palermo Norte*, when he first spotted none other than Evita Peron, accompanied by an escort. When he glanced at her escort, Libman said he was instantly electrified. He actually felt he was in shock and almost couldn't move. He kept staring at the escort. He knew who it was. It was Schmidt, Albrecht Schmidt, himself. Clear as day. It was Albrecht Schmidt, Chief Aide to Heinrich Muller, the former Chief of the Gestapo in Berlin. He hadn't seen Schmidt in more than a dozen years but recognized him immediately.

Apparently, Schmidt, the Gestapo guy was the one assigned to interrogate the recaptured prisoners at Stalag III, and Arty, as he was known to the other prisoners, was interviewed by Schmidt himself. Thus, Arty Libman told Shmueli and Maxie that Schmidt behaved in a calm manner during the interrogation but claimed there were unusual ways to get people to talk which he further claimed he was not going to use. Arty Libman, from Brownsville, Brooklyn knew very well that Schmidt was playing the good guy, bad guy game, but was only expressing the good guy part.

So, this time Maxie took the lead probably because he spoke English without the broken Shmueli Kishnov accent.

"I know you're called Arty, right?

"Yeah, right."

"Where'd ya go to high school—probably Brooklyn, right?"

Libman confirmed it was Brooklyn. He said he knew that they were getting the entire Schmidt story and that he'd been told they were going to reach out to him. With that, Libman related everything he had also told Shin Bet personnel.

Later, when Shmueli and Max were sitting with their two other so-called assassinational associates, Sam Silver and Shimen Pargament, they similarly reviewed the story that the Shin Bet cab driver, Arty Libman had told them. Then Shmueli pulled out the necessary ID photos.

"I having pictures of dem un I knowing dis one of Schmidt. Eskenazy he in Buenos Aires un he vill getting Schmidt's trail. Vee knowing dat no vone hast here also no seeing Schmidt, excepting maybe dis Shin Bet secret service man, Libman. So, Schmidt he carefulness un smart un hiding. Vee need to figure vhere to starting dis. Dee Peron lady she die few years back so vee no more can getting her. Peron, too, he deposed vone year or two back so also catching him ist vaisting of time. So qvuestion ist: Who can vee knowing could leading Eskenazy to finding Schmidt?"

Shmuel then made a phone call to his Eskenazy contact in Buenos Aires. As far as Eskenazy's history was concerned, he was a Jew of Turkish nationality whose family had settled in Spain and then emigrated to Buenos Aires not realizing that the future Argentine leader, Juan Peron, was a Jew-hating fascist, who along with his wife Evita, were Nazi lovers who were adored by an under-educated and unsophisticated Argentine populace. The best that can be said is that apparently Peron had a vacuous nationalistic and chauvinistic appeal to Argentineans in general. However, it became clear to those dealing with Peron that his main interest was money. And he became known as someone who was insatiable about increasing his money supply—increasing his wealth endlessly, in avaricious redundancy, with no end in sight.

In any event, Eskenazy, who Shmuel was banking on, would possibly be helpful and provide some lead. When Shmuel mentioned Schmidt to him, Eskenazy, who had made an avocation of learning about escaped Nazis, knew all about Schmidt, his connection to the Gestapo and his role as assistant to Muller and earlier, as assistant to Eichmann himself.

"I know about him," Eskenazy said. "He very well could be an anonymous person in the German neighborhood of Belgrano within Buenos Aires. There he might be recognized, even though he would surely be in disguise, with perhaps a beard or beard and mustache and maybe have a weight difference from what he weighed before. But my hunch is he'd be in Belgrano because it's loaded with Germans, all or most who were little Hitlerites, so he'd feel safer surrounded by like-minded people. That kind of population, in a crisis, would help him in any number of ways but mostly, with facilitating an escape to who knows where. "First," Eskanazy went on, "I'll investigate the neighborhood. I'll drive through."

"Joseph," Shmuel answered, "I being dere mit friend Max un mit Sam un Shimen. Vee vill helping you."

* * *

Meanwhile, back in New York City, Mac and Lyle were again interviewing Wenzel Wagner at Police Headquarters near City Hall and Wall Street. They had been at it for about three hours.

"I don't knowing vat of dis I can saying," Wenzel pleaded.

"Okay, we thought if you told us something that you know would be helpful to us, be sure you also know we then might be able to make it easier on you. It might be instead of the electric-chair. See? Because shooting down police is considered very serious in America. And I'm sure Detective Lyle here wouldn't be able to name a single case where someone killed a police officer and lived. And you killed more than one in an act of malice. 'Malice' means having a premeditated idea of doing something very bad. And 'premeditated' means planning it in advance. And 'advance' means before you do it, you plan it out before. Get it?"

"You can promising no electrical chair?"

"Well, we know people and we can talk to them and it could be they would listen to us. You understand?"

"Okay, I knowing tings. Pliss, you asking me dese tings you vanting."

"Good," Mac answered. "I need some names of Nazis who escaped and are hiding somewhere like maybe in other countries that you know about."

"Yah, I knowing. Vone year back I hearing dat Kurt Blome, he ist scientist. He discovering biologic germ dat ist for the killing. He pay money to escaping from prison. In Paris. Mit money he pay so all record of Kurt Blome namen no more to finding. Nobody knowing vhere he ist in dis hiding place. But I knowing. He paying me und Karl—Karl ist now tote you knowing dis.

"To helping Blome vee bringing him to Buenos Aires in Argentina. He vant to going Buenos Aires. You verstehen me? Blome, he vant to going Argentina. Dis vhat ist I meaning it. Dis happening two years back. Now I tink no person knowing vhere he live. So, dis I not knowing. But I knowing vhere he chief aide living. Namen of Freundel Dunst. It ist Dunst who ist killing many people, und many children too. Und he living in

Belgrano in Buenos Aires in street namen Belgrado. Ist this good for you informatzie?"

"Yes, it's very good—if it's true. We'll be back to talk to you more. I think you have more such information. Yes?"

"Okay, I vaiting for you. You pliss coming. I vaiting for you."

"I say again, you have more information. Yes?"

"Yah, I giving you."

On the way out of Police Headquarters, Mac and Lyle agreed that Imi must get Wenzel's information immediately. To that end, they had an intermediary's contact number in Rome that Hugh had previously provided. When this intermediary received the news provided by Mac and Lyle, he walked over to Hugh's apartment knowing full well he wouldn't be able to telephone him. When he got there, he motioned to Hugh for them to take a walk. As they walked, this intermediary conveyed the information about Dunst's address.

Hugh made a call from a public phone and, in no time, was in touch with Simon's office. Hugh asked them to get in touch with Shmuel Kishnov immediately and to have Simon call the number Hugh was calling from. Hugh said he would wait by the phone.

In less than twenty minutes the public phone where Hugh was standing, rang. It startled him but he lifted the receiver and heard a stranger's voice.

"Hugh, I'm calling for Simon—I'm Eskenazy calling from Buenos Aires on Simon's orders. If you want to check this, call him to confirm. We're after two who could possibly be living in the German quarter called Belgrano. It's about two of them: Albrecht Schmidt and Freundel Dunst. And I know both. I know who they are and pretty sure where they are. They're probably living an anonymous life style. I'll bet no one, not even Hudal would know where they are.

"I've been told," Eskenazy continued, "that one of the terrorists, a Wenzel Wagner who incidentally is in custody, tried to burn down a police station and killed some police. Also, Simon specifically told me Freundel Dunst is living in the Belgrano area probably on Belgrado Street. Simon mentioned his name and Schmidt's name specifically. Many Germans live in that street in that neighborhood".

"What's interesting here, Hugh, is that at this moment, as we're talking, I'm standing right in the middle of the Belgrano neighborhood looking for them both. I'll keep you informed through Simon. And, by the way, you'll be interested to know that I'm with Shmuel Kishnov and Max Palace. Looks to me like they will undoubtedly be invaluable in the search for whatever else is needed."

Eskenazy hung up, turned to his associates, and with a sober tone said: "Who is not armed?" Each of them looked at him and pulled open their jackets, showing their weapons.

* * *

Back in Haifa, Simon pulled out a photo of Schmidt for his associates to see. "I've sent this photo to Eskenazy," Simon said. "You'll find Eskenazy at the phone number I gave you. And keep in mind, Belgrado Street. We've got a chance that it might be staring right at us."

In Buenos Aires, Eskenazy looked at Shmuel and Max and said:

"If we come across either one or both, there is no rule as to whether we capture them alive or otherwise decide what to do. But we will need to get rid of the bodies. We'll need to pile them on the floor-boards in the back of the car and drive to the country maybe twenty miles out of Buenos Aires. Then bury them.

Eskenazy looked at them and said: "Let's go!"

· 18 ·

BELGRANO

In Buenos Aires, Eskenazy greeted Sam Silver and Shimen Pargament. Now Joseph Eskenazy had Shmuel, Maxie, plus these two—including him, five altogether. He had sent his other two associates on another mission. He thought that with him, the five he now had should, without a shadow of a doubt, surely be sufficient. This, he felt was even more certain especially since they were armed with photos of both Schmidt and Dunst. In addition, Eskenazy was also confident because he knew that this personal group of his were all Krav Maga trained personnel.

Eskenazy drove around a bit and, of course, circled Belgrado Street. Belgrado was about four blocks long, beginning to end. The street was bound by cul de sacs at either end with two cross streets in-between. Although the entire neighborhood of Belgrano was rather blighted, Belgrado Street seemed opulent by comparison—an oasis in the desert.

"No doubt," Eskenazy said, "they escaped with plenty of money. Look where they might be living. They paid that Ghost good money for protection. But no matter how anonymous they wanted to be and still want to be, they would probably never resist good living and would only want the best jobs.

"I think we're on the right street. Let's park it and wait. Look, there's a café on the corner—there diagonal to us. Sam, you go and sit at the café. Get something to eat or order coffee."

Sam did as Eskenazy suggested. They all waited and waited and watched and watched but no dice. They carefully scrutinized the faces of every man who passed by, but no luck. After about an hour, Sam paid and walked away. He didn't return to the car. He walked around the block and approached the car from the rear. As he was walking up to the car, a door opened onto the street from one of the building hallways and out stepped Albrecht Schmidt! Sam could see instantly that it was him, and didn't hesitate. He took out his pistol. It had a silencer over the muzzle in position — the gun ready to be fired.

Schmidt looked up. Sam said: "Albrecht, hello." Schmidt stopped in his tracks, and with no hesitation Sam said:

"In the car."

As though the car door had a mind of its own, it opened. Sam pushed Schmidt into the car as Shimen pulled Schmidt in from inside. Schmidt did everything he was told without the slightest attempt to put up a fight. Sam thought:

'That's kind of like walking into a gas chamber when told to do it especially when the other person telling you to do it is armed and you're not. Isn't it?'

Eskenazy was sitting in the front, also revolver in hand, with Shmuel next to him. Sam joined them. Shmuel started the dialogue.

"Telling me story for Freundel Dunst or I killing you here, now. Right now!"

"No, no shoot. I telling you. He living in mine building. In dis street in dis building."

"Vhat floor?"

"Mine floor. Tsvei door down in hallvay. Numer Zex. No shoot."

At that point, not hesitating, Eskenazy nodded and Kovner's boy, Shmuel Kishnov, put two bullets directly into Schmidt; one into his chest, the other into his stomach. At the same time Sam's compatriot-shadow, Shimen, along with Sam, pushed and pulled and finally Schmidt was laid out on the floor-board of the car as they had previously planned. Sam then slammed the door shut. As the door closed, Eskenazy drove away. As he was driving, he looked at Shmuel and said:

"One down, one to go."

* * *

Simon contemplated the news and without skipping a beat said: "You see gentlemen, yet, we are not gentlemen. We are feral. We are animals. That is the truth. Because when you treat someone like they treated us, forcing us to be helpless animals—and they did without any human concern—and continued to torture us without any hesitation or let-up, then you turn that tortured and murdered man into a rabid animal. And he will do to you what he learned from you.

"It's as Eskenazy, Shmuel and Maxie, Shimen and Sam have just done, and what they apparently are now planning to do to Dunst. There is nothing I can do to stop it. If I could I would stop it, but the truth is that in my heart there is a feeling of 'good'—it was deserved! In a way, I hate myself for feeling it, but I do feel it even though I would never do it that way—and then again I wonder if I'm really happy that they got what was coming."

The next evening they were there again—Eskenazy with Sam and Shimen, on Belgrado Street hunting for Dunst—with Shmuel and Maxie doing the walking in the neighborhood. But now they had the address. Eskenazy remembered Dunst from Buchenwald where Dunst would assist Blome who experimented with euthanasia projects, anthrax, and nerve agents like Sarin that they actually sprayed on people.

"I'd recognize him anywhere," Eskenazy proclaimed to Sam and Shimen sitting in the parked car. "When he answers his door, I'll know if it's him immediately. But this time we don't kill him immediately. We should have gotten more information from Schmidt. We will need to get as much information as we can from Dunst about any others before we do him."

"Joseph," Sam said, "we shouldn't go into the building. We got Schmidt directly in front of the building. And it worked very well. Let's do the same with Dunst. We wait for him in the Street and wait to see if he is coming out of the building or walking toward the building to enter. It's then that we'll get him."

Eskenazy saw the logic and agreed. As fate would have it, suddenly Eskenazy could swear it was Dunst in the flesh walking down the street.

"Oh God, yes, that's him coming down the street. Hasn't changed in more than a decade. Hasn't changed a bit. Same way he walks. He walks like an emperor—proud, superior. See it? Sam, get out of the car now. He's a half block from us. Walk toward him, pass him by then turn quickly and get him from the back. Force him to the car. Shimen, do the same as before. When he's at the car, push the door open and this time Sam will pull him in."

"No, no," Shimen said. "Look, Shmueli's on it. He's got him."

Shmuel, like a predator had instantly recognized Dunst and deftly moved toward him. Shmuel whirled around, forced his revolver into Dunst's back and pushed him toward the car.

Again, the door opened as though by itself as if the door knew what to do. In went Dunst with help from Sam who was pulling him in.

"Don't say a word or you're dead," Eskenazy ordered.

"Okay, vat you vant? Here, you taking money. I having money. I giving you."

"You are Freundel Dunst," Eskanazy said. "I know you. I saw you for many days when you visited Buchenwald. You with that Sarin experiment, helping Blome. All the prisoners were scared to death. I was there. Oh yes, I saw you."

"You going to killing me."

"Probably."

"Vat you meaning? You meaning maybe you no killing me?"

"You've got to tell us names. Where are the others? If we kill five others maybe you live. Where can we find them? We know you know."

"I no knowing five. But I knowing two. Ist two good to having me going?"

"It depends which two."

"I believing dis two vill be interest to you. Deese ist Werner Kruger. Kruger, he vas Alois Brunner's assisting man. Brunner vas too assisting to Adolph Eichmann und den he vas Commandant of Drancy Camp ver vas Jews das people. He ist vone to gassing tousands Jews in 1943. Kruger he helping Brunner und goot helping mit Eichmann too."

"I know Drancy," said Max, who, for the first time, uttered a sound. "It was an internment camp for Jews who were waiting for transport to Auschwitz. The camp was located outside of Paris. They had more than fifty-thousand Jews there including thousands of children — more than five or six-thousand children. Only a fraction survived."

They all were silent after Max's description. But Dunst continued:

"I never meeting him but I knowing from him. I knowing he ist vone who he disappear but I knowing dat tzvay year back he use dis help by people in dis Vatican, in Rome, to going to Syria. I hearing he, Alois Brunner, hast changing hist namen—vas changing to Georg Fischer—Dr. Georg Fischer. At Vatican day laughing. Day knowing Syria vill protect—no extradition. But I having namen of man for bribe. You giving money und he helping. I knowing hist namen. Mit him you getting Brunner.

"So far, you're doing good," Eskenazy said. "Who else? You said you know about two. Who's the other one?"

"Dis man, hist namen ist Hermann Streicher. Streicher main assist to Ludolph von Alvensleben. I knowing Streicher he doing much execution in Poland. He vone who helping Alvensleben make "Valley of Death" mit zex, zeben tousand Polish killed. I hearing he too mit new namen. New namen ist Franz Engel und he go to Buenos Aires. Tzvay, two years back, in yahr 1956 he moving to Santa Rosa de Calamuchita in Platz Cordoba, Argentina, un Ish hearing he be now in Buenos Aires. I no knowing vhere. I not knowing address exact. Dis ist everything I knowing. Ist good? No?"

"Are you sure there's nothing else, Eskenazy prodded?"

"Dis ist only two I knowing. No more. If you no killing me, I vork for you und finding more namens."

Eskenazy contemplated the offer. He thought that Dunst, in fact, might be able to do just what he said he could do. However, Eskenazy also thought that Dunst would have to be watched every second and that would be an impossible task. In any event, the Nazi's had killed Eskenazy's brother who was caught in a net during his stay in Berlin and then perished in one of the concentration camps. No, Eskenazy felt it was also personal and that Freundel Dunst would need to be erased in order for the planet to be a little bit rid of its poison. And it didn't matter whatever implicit agreement Dunst felt had been struck.

"We will talk more," Eskenazy said. "But not here. We will drive some distance and talk more when we get there. Sit here quietly and there will be no trouble."

So, Dunst sat between Sam and Shimen while Eskenazy drove the car with Maxi and Shmuel in the jump seats. Eskenazy then nodded to Shmueli as Shmueli blithely shot Dunst and killed him right there and then, where he sat between Sam and Shimen.

* * *

With Simon, it was all about on to the next project; that is, Sam and Shimen had returned from their mission in Belgrano, Buenos Aires, and had just given Simon a blow by blow with respect to how it was all accomplished — that is, the Schmidt and Dunst episodes.

"There are two things I regret so far," Simon said. "First is that we can't seem to get a fix on where Blome himself is. Muller we know was killed in 1945. But Blome, He's the smart one, like Mengele. Neither of them trusted Hudal's so-called safe escape-plans with all of the secondary sites. Mengele and Blome and some others obviously discarded Hudal's secondary sites and developed their own plans. So, with Mengele and Blome as well as with these others, we have problems. We have trouble tracking them. My second regret is that I now know about assassinations that will perhaps be attributed to me. Henceforth, if there are any more shall we say erasures, I'm not to know about it. Please.

"One thing I do know and that is that these Nazis were particularly psychotic sadists which was their typical mode of operation. Even when they weren't in the throes of this kind of craziness and perhaps more tranquil, their typical mood and attitude which for them was so-called being normal, comprised a tenacious perniciousness with solely intrusive thoughts about killing."

Finally, Simon, rather than showing his agreement and admiration of Shmuel, began considering other issues.

Then to Sam and Shimen he declared:

"Okay, enough. My friends, look how much effort went into finding Schmidt and Dunst. Something is wrong with the correspondence of our wishes and goals as they relate to implementation. At this rate, even though there are really no limitations to the statute-of-limitations when it comes to evil and evil-doers, nevertheless, I say we need something equivalent to Truman's bomb. Something equivalent so that rather than putting in maximum effort with minimum results, instead we need to create a paradigm that allows us to gain maximum results with whatever is the degree of effort we put in. We can call this paradigm the *minimax-solution*. So, Sam, Shimen, how do you see it? Am I right?"

"Simon," Shimen answered, "Sam and I along with Joseph, Maxie, and Shmueli, have been talking about this since we did the deed in Belgrano. Yes, it required tremendous effort and the reality of it all, is that all we got was — two. Now, since you've brought it up, it gives us a chance to pro-

claim that to work like that is practically working against ourselves. With
the amount of energy we put into this, it should have been a hundred and
two, not just two.

"So, Simon, of course you are right," Shimen added. "We've all been
contemplating it. The only thing that comes to mind is a saying: 'Cut off
the head of the snake!' And I'm not even sure what I mean by it. Who is
the snake? I guess we could say it is Hudal. Alois Hudal."

"Or," Wiesenthal picked it up: "Perhaps Hudal is the snake but it might
be another if not him."

At that, Wiesenthal impulsively said: "I'm going to New York. I want
to be with all of those who got us the microfilm and who also provided
the counterfeit one. This means I want us all to convene: Imi Lichtenfeld,
Jimmy McKay, Shmel Kishnov and Max Palace—all from the continent.
Maybe Hugh, maybe not. We may need him to be at the Vatican. I will
depart from Tel Aviv. We will all convene along with Alex Kaye and his
group in the Bronx. Then we will all together discuss the snake and the
head of the snake.

"In the meantime, Sammy, Shimen you both will come with me and
I'll call for Joseph to arrive from Buenos Aires on his own. I want Alex and
all the rest to hear what has happened, what we've already accomplished,
and what we are now thinking."

*   *   *

Simon had Alex Kaye informed of the plan and Al set out to prepare
lodging and so forth, where else but at the motel—the Van Courtlandt
Motel.

What Simon didn't yet know was that they would also be joined by the
Wharton family and by Gloria, Gloria Messer that is, and probably also
by Detective Loris 'Mac' McIver, and Detective Lyle Davis, not to mention some other police such as Mac and Lyle's detective soul-mates, their
sidekicks, Detectives Jack Lehrman and Harry Harrison.

Obviously, this was going to be quite a group—even if you don't count
Willy and Stevie. But then Alex had second thoughts. He realized that
the motel would not be suitable for such a large group and so he decided
instead to convene at the *Concourse Plaza Hotel* located a stone's throw
from Yankee Stadium on the Grand Concourse and 161st Street in the

Bronx. He was familiar with the *Concourse Plaza* because he had attended a New York Police Department conference in the ballroom of the hotel.

At the same time on the other side of the world, Alois Hudal was about to receive visitors from Buenos Aires. They were Albecht Schmidt's mistress who was accompanied by Freundel Dunst's wife. They were arriving from Buenos Aires more or less directly to Rome, and then immediately to the Vatican.

· 19 ·

MENTONE

"I am Marlena Jollenbeck, she announced to Alois Hudal. I am the friend of Albrecht Schmidt."

"And I, Herr Hudal, I am Frieda Dunst, the wife of Freundel Dunst, of whom I'm sure you are aware. We are here because both Albrecht and Freundel are missing. They each disappeared within a day or two of the other. We are frantic because we know they both were in deep hiding and we were trying to be certain that they were actually in protected seclusion.

Marlena and I have also known for some time that each of them was always on the lookout for anyone of who may have been hunting them. I say 'hunting' because I know what I am talking about. I know what I'm saying. And we believe that you, too, know with what we are concerned. We'd like to know whether you have any information for us. Do you? Please be frank."

Hudal paused and looked at them seeming to be considering something serious. Frau Dunst, obviously an educated woman, had relayed information that made him certain that they had both been assassinated. But he didn't tell them that. What he did was attempt to pose as a calm interlocutor while actually he shuddered within. And his interest in Frau Dunst's intelligence was evidently focused because she was talking to him in Italian and German and he answered in both languages.

"No, I haven't heard about it except for what you have just told me. I cannot venture even a guess. I can understand that you both might think no good has come of it, but about this we cannot be certain. Of course, I share both your concern and imaginings but the truth is, I have absolutely nothing to report. However, I promise you the moment I do hear something I will contact you both. You have my word."

With that, the ladies had no choice but to depart. They bade farewell to Hudal, who again assured them that the moment he heard anything he would let them know.

As soon as they departed for Buenos Aires, they lamented the trip to Hudal and in German complained to one another all the way on their flight home.

"Marlena, the trip has been a waste of time. They are gone and gone for good. Marlena, stop weeping. I know you are hurt. But keep in mind, each of them did horrible things during the war and there are people out to get them. To our misfortune, well perhaps to yours, we know they got them both. For me, Marlena, Freundel was an impossible man to be with. We were married for twenty miserable years. I confess this to you. Twenty terrible years. Freundel was an overly sensitive man, especially with regard to feeling humiliated in response to the slightest, what he would label as an 'offense.' He would take umbrage to the slightest affront to his so-called superiority — to his masculinity. I again confess to you that this superiority of all the Nazi higher-ups makes me sick and has always made me sick. They are all, all of them, disturbed people!"

"Then why did you marry him? Why?"

"He was handsome, he had wealth, he appeared to have confidence, and it seemed to be a good choice. However, my impression about him literally disintegrated, shattered within a month of our marriage. He was nothing but an insecure, insensitive, narcissist who used his so-called superiority to compensate for a definite inferiority complex. Believe me. I lived it. And I only joined you on this trip because we are friends and I wanted to support you. I did not come because of Fruendel"

For most of the rest of the trip, Marlena and Freida were quiet and staring blankly, as though in some deep reverie — but not a quiet reverie.

On the other hand, Hudal did not feel calm or quiet. He decided to call Montini and talk it over. Montini apparently had an instinct for what he considered the difference between random events versus pre-planned events. In this sense, he needed to reassure Hudal that whatever happened to Dunst and Schmidt did not have the earmarks of some precise assassination event as might be carried out by Mossad, for example. Nor did it have the ring of truth that the discovery of both men was based upon their whereabouts derived from possession of information that they, in turn, would have gotten from the microfilm.

Montini explained it to Hudal by simply saying that 'yes, they were probably assassinated but not as a result of information gotten from the microfilm.' Hudal was reassured, especially because it was Montini who was reassuring him, and so with greater confidence, Hudal quickly went on to other things. He didn't spend another moment worrying or even thinking about the visit from Marlena Jollenbeck and Freida Dunst.

*　*　*

In contrast, from Simon's new perch somewhere now in Europe, plans were being made for him along with Sam and Shimen to travel to New York City headed directly to the Bronx. When he and his men were finally in transit, he couldn't stop thinking about the region around Monaco and the little village, *Mentone*. He was also focused on the information he had received regarding the large yacht with the radar detection-system visible for all to see above the deck of the yacht directly on the roof of the helm. The yacht was moored at *Menton Harbor* near to the outskirts of *Menton* not far from the base of *Mont Tete de Chien*.

The name of the yacht was: *Salvation*. Also, Simon was told by some of his other contacts that it was a sixty-foot Bertram that was purchased and then sailed across the Atlantic from Newport Beach, Rhode Island, eventually landing near Monaco and then was moored at *Menton Harbor*.

Simon, of course had begun to acquire information concerning this entire business of deciding whether the name Gustav Schell was authentic or whether it was some kind of ruse to perhaps throw code breakers off the track—and further whether there might be other similar deliberate errors on the microfilm that were inserted to do the same. In addition, initial information reaching Simon traced how the *Salvation* was decked out with speed altering mechanisms. Obviously, Simon's 'handlers' had ways of ascertaining the information they needed.

The information he obtained was quite interesting and specific. He learned that a Jack Plate was installed to reduce drag on the yacht, the propeller was fine-tuned even after it was replaced to an upgraded level, and the electronic control module was reflashed. This meant, he was told, that the rocker of the boat was blueprinted—meaning that the boat now was able to ride on its lines with the subtraction of the rocker, making the boat more stable. The yacht also had a supercharger installed. It was bolted to the engine, Finally, a system of packing more air and fuel into the cylinders before the pistons could compress the mixture resulted in the yacht gaining more power.

As Simon was reading over his notes and sharing the information with Sammy and Shimen, he mused: 'Whoever owns that boat figured that some day they might need to head out fast—very fast.'

Immediately before Simon left for New York, he very excitedly contacted Jimmy in London, relayed all this information about the yacht, gave him the particulars, and told Jimmy that M-16 needed to send some agents to the area and identify who owned the yacht and to pin-point where in or near *Monaco* that person who owned it, lived. Simon told Jimmy it could be important, even essential, so that speed was the issue. He then wished Jimmy a safe trip to New York and said he looked forward to seeing him there.

Simon was awakened by the Stewardess who instructed him and his two-man crew to buckle their seatbelts as they were about to land at Idlewild International Airport.

There was no need for Simon or Sam and Shimen to hassle with anything because as they deplaned, Mac and Lyle were waiting for them. The detectives introduced themselves and Simon expressed his pleasure in meeting them. When they went to pick up Simon's luggage, along with the other luggage belonging to Sam and Shimen, the luggage was already waiting for them. It was Al who had the foresight to set it up with Mac and Lyle and therefore to streamline Simon's arrival.

Simon told Mac and Lyle that he had heard all about them from Al but it was great to meet them in person. All the way back to the Bronx and to the *Concourse Plaza Hotel*, they talked non-stop. Mac and Lyle filled Simon, Sam, and Shimen in on the so-called 'Holocaust' at the precinct, the detainees they'd gotten, and the entire story about this captured duo including information they had gotten from the Peron/Argentina connection.

From Simon's side of it, he asked Mac and Lyle whether Al had mentioned *Monaco* and the clues they had about a Gustav Schell, but Mac answered that they hadn't heard about that. Simon then told them all about their suspicions and about the yacht moored in *Menton Harbor*.

"Detectives, tell me," Simon queried, "don't you think it's strange that in that sort of very affluent and gambling region of the world, for such a ship to be moored? Why such a concentration on speed?"

Mac quickly answered that any detective worth his weight would, of course, perhaps see it that way too, except for the idea that some of these hot-shot trillionaires might like it fast—actually want to be the fastest.

"I have to admit," Mac said, wanting to confirm Simon's feelings, "it is definitely suspicious." Of what was it suspicious, Mac couldn't, be sure. But it was definitely suspicious regarding something—and something important. Of that he was sure.

The reason Mac wasn't sure about its importance was that Simon had not really explained the entire Gustav Schell thing. What Simon had omitted in his story regarding the Schell name listed in the middle of the microfilm was who in the world Gustav Schell might be.

"So," Simon continued, "the value and element of 'importance' does in fact enter the picture—yes?"

"Oh sure," Mac answered. "Oh yeah. I can feel it. Looking to Lyle, Mac said: "Lyle?"

"No doubt Mr. Wiesenthal. No doubt," Lyle answered. "There's something important there. No doubt."

The trip from the airport took less than an hour when they pulled up to the *Concourse Plaza Hotel*.

* * *

Waiting for them at the entrance of the Hotel on the traffic-busy Grand Concourse, was Alex Kaye, who had become the nucleus of the entire adventure, soup to nuts, involving all of the participants representing those on four continents, as well as connected to his own gang of Frankie, Gloria, Mac and Lyle, and Harry and Jack, along with a few others. This didn't include the Whartons and of course, Willy and Stevie—not to mention Simon, and the European/Middle Eastern contingent of Imi, Hugh, and Maxie, along with their newest member—the irrepressible Shmuel Kishnov.

Al escorted Simon and his crew consisting of Sam Silver, and Shimen Pargament to their rooms. He had already checked them in so that they and all luggage were escorted directly to their rooms. The others that were to arrive within the next twenty-four hours were also all already checked in. The Whartons, Frankie, Willy, and Gloria were likewise checked in and in their rooms. Due to arrive were Jimmy, Imi, and it had been finally decided that Hugh should be there as well.

So, Hugh, from Europe, and Eskenazy from South America, namely Buenos Aires, and Shmueli—from who knows where? But Al knew Shmueli and Max were informed and promised to attend this all important meeting.

Coming in on the midnight flight at Idlewild were Jimmy, Imi, and Hugh. They cabbed it directly to the *Concourse Plaza Hotel* and were in their rooms, and asleep, by 2 am. Over the next several hours, Eskenazy arrived and hit the hotel at about 10 am, and finally, Shmuel Kishnov and Max Palace walked in on them having brunch in the dining hall at about noon.

Hellos were permeating the dining hall and lots of laughter and introductions were being made. Now the Bronx gang was introduced to the Europeans and Middle Easterners as well as to Eskanzy the Argentinean. Then within a minute or so, Al was quick to quiet them down and to take the floor.

He introduced Simon and asked Simon to say a few words. As it was, the dining hall was quite crowded so Simon simply suggested that after brunch they should all take care of whatever they needed to do and meet in the large conference room on the second floor which had been scheduled for them at 2:30 pm.

At about 2:20 pm, people began trickling into the conference room. Shmueli was the first one in followed by Max. They weren't timid. They walked in energetically, and immediately began rearranging the chairs so that instead of rows of chairs and the frontal position of the dais lectern, they moved the lectern to the side of the room and separated all the chairs by setting them in a large circle that would, with their count, accommodate sixteen people around the circle. They were sure Simon wouldn't want the Wharton children to attend nor would he want Willy, who he knew started the entire shebang, to attend. As it turned out, Willy couldn't attend because of obvious reasons, and Al had Gloria's best friend, Joclyn to come and baby-sit Stevie Wharton and her little brother down in the lounge. He also arranged for Mac to see to it that Joclyn had her own baby sitters with her — two Bronx cops. Mac stationed one in the corridor of the lounge and one inside with Joclyn and the children.

By the time the room was rearranged, Simon and the rest were trying all to be punctual so the room filled up quite quickly. Al took the floor and asked each person to rise and stand while he gave a thumb-nail sketch of who they were and what they did. The others were so taken with each introduction that at the end of each, they all applauded. Al introduced Simon, last. But of course, last was not least. Even Bill and Ruthie Wharton had heard of him.

The first thing Simon did was to apologize to the Whartons for their terrible ordeal. He said he was speaking for all of them in feeling enormously thankful that they all came through it with flying colors. Then, without any drama, he surprised Bill and Ruthie Wharton by telling them that the meeting had some crucial classified secret material that needed to be discussed and he thought it would be to their advantage not to be privy to it. He apologized and he hoped that, despite missing this meeting, they would indeed attend the dinner, that was planned for them all at a little Jewish restaurant/luncheonette in the southeast Bronx run by Mrs. Esther Pellis and her husband Mr. Sol Pellis, an immigrant Jewish couple from Ukraine. He also reported that all the food is homemade and that Al had it all arranged for transportation to and from the luncheonette.

Al then told them that the store was located just about across the street and a block away from where Mac, Lyle, Frankie, Jack and Harry corralled a couple of wanted criminals who where the ones responsible for Willy's unfortunate misadventure off the ledge. But Al assured them that Claremont Parkway was now as safe as ever. As a matter of fact, in trying for levity, he also mentioned that the two of Stevie and Willy's friends, Richard Grillo and Henry Namrellek, would probably be playing ball in the lower schoolyard of P.S. 42 even though it might be getting a bit dark later in the meal. He said no matter when it was, there they were, those two, throwing and catching.

The Whartons graciously thanked everyone and declared that without a doubt they would attend the dinner. Then they left.

Al immediately gave the floor back to Simon who instantly launched right into how they came to know something about the name Gustav Schell.

"And this is the foremost theme of this get-together. We're really all here, of course, to pay our respects to Mr. and Mrs. Wharton, but the overriding issue is what we all would guess as to who is Gustav Schell? Is the name a deliberate way to throw decryption experts off the track and along with this, perhaps on the microfilm are other such tricks? Or, is it a misprint—which I strongly doubt? If it is a reference to an actual person, who might that be?

"The issue is that this person, Gustav Schell is the only one of more than four-thousand names without a secondary location. The microfilm listed names of Nazis who were or would be indicted for war crimes. Alois Hudal of the Vatican was in charge of getting this multitude of thousands furtively out of Germany or Austria and then dispersed in many different places, but mostly in South America, with a strong emphasis on Buenos Aires, Argentina. But certainly not solely, since quite a number went to the Middle East, mostly Egypt, Syria, and Saudi Arabia.

"The point here, however, is that each of these thousands had second-ary places pre-arranged just in case the primary location was in some way breached—except....except for Gustav Schell. With Schell there was no secondary location and he was not ferried out of Europe proper. We know he lives somewhere in the south of France on the Riviera near *Monaco*, probably in a little town named *Mentone*.

"We've also uncovered the fact that a boat, a yacht is registered in his name. The interesting thing about the yacht is that it's outfitted with spe-cial mechanics so that the average speed of this sixty-foot American made yacht is equipped to increase its speed by a rather large factor. So, why such speed? Is the situation and speed of the yacht somehow equivalent in the compensatory sense to a second location? Does Hudal decide whether Schell gets a secondary location or does Schell decide where he would like to spend the rest of his life in a place of Nirvana such as the French Riviera equipped with all the possible conveniences money can buy.

"Some of us here, like Sammy, Shimen, Imi, Hugh, Joseph, Jimmy, Maxie, and Shmuel have a common hunch as to who Gustav Schell might be. Of course, there is no hard evidence to support it and therefore, I firmly think we need to break wide open what this is all about. Now, one of the things that is supposed to throw decryption experts off the track is by tricking them with fraudulent names and locations. However, this doesn't wash here. Why? Because we had, with the valuable assistance of an inside man named Max—our own esteemed Max Palace here who set up with genius decryption scientists the ability to have the code of the microfilm decoded and in record time. In other words there were no tricks that derailed the decryption experts in breaking the code.

"Thus, lady and gentlemen, whoever Gustav Schell is, is something we are now planning to uncover. I believe my good friend Jimmy McKay here from M-16 will enter the fray on the French Riviera along with the help of Maxie and Shmuel. They'll have further support and assistance from Imi and Joe Eskenazy. My squad of Sammy Silver along with Shimen Pargament will also be involved. In this case, we need Hugh to be at the Vatican and *not* in *Monte Carlo*. And that's it.

"I'm not including Alex Kaye here or detectives Mac McIver and Lyle Davis. They, including their support detectives, Jack Lehrman and Harry Harrison, are our New York City or Bronx contingent who will probably still be working on their captives held at police headquarters in lower New York City.

"Tomorrow, me, Sammy, Shimen, Hugh, Imi, and Jimmy, leave for London. From there at Jimmy's office we will plan how to gain entry, how to arrange an infiltration into the arena of *Monaco* and from there how to blend in to *Mentone* and its surroundings. We will also need to find out who it was that contacted the engineers who subsequently signed on to increase the speed on the *Salvation*. We know the hyped-up yacht is in Schell's name. Knowing who in Schell's command contacted these suppliers could provide essential information. Further, we need to identify where Schell lives. After that, it's a crap-shoot which as I think about it is not a bad metaphor for the area surrounding Monaco, and especially *Monte Carlo*.

"I'm sure each of us might have different ideas as to what to do once we put our hands on Gustav Schell. In the meantime, I believe it will take us at least a week to plan it all including who to contact in order to set up smooth transit points including, of course, escape plans."

At that moment, who else but Shmuel Kishnov piped in. He said:

"Yes, I too tink dere vill be oder ideas to tink un now I have also idea. Max un me, vee not meet mit you all at Jimmy's in London dis veek. Dis reason ist because now vee going to oder place."

With that, Shmuel Kishnov excused himself and he and Maxie walked out. They went to their rooms, packed their bags, and checked out.

At the airport Shmuel asked Max to head for *Monaco* and to set up a post-office box in the name of *Clearwater Company* at the address of *18 Square Victoria Mews, Mentone, France*, in care of S.K. He also told Max to get some rooms in *Monte Carlo* at the *Hotel Columbus*. He said the *Hotel Columbus* was an inexpensive place, not a high-end hotel, so people there are generally rather inconspicuous. He also suggested that Max take a guided tour to *Mentone* to survey the place in order to see what he could as related to the yacht, *Salvation*—like for example, did it have a crew, and if so what did their behavior reveal about them? Then Shmuel further suggested that Max keep his ears open about anything regarding a Gustav Schell.

Max agreed to everything and told Shmuel he would simply wait for further instructions or just wait for him to show up. Max had undying respect and confidence in Shmuel and Shmuel also knew that his partnership with Max was perfect. Max, he knew, was fearless.

· 20 ·

THE HOLLOW CYLINDER

Well, Shmuel Kishnov was gone and wasn't gone. Of course, he knew where he was going. He travelled cross-country three-thousand miles to Palo Alto, California to visit a dear friend who he befriended when he was in the Treblinka concentration camp. This friend was Yasha Greiner. They both survived by the skin of their teeth.

Treblinka was run by the Commandant, Franz Stangl, and Shmuel had always promised himself that he would himself kill Stangl. He would do it slowly and very painfully and if at all possible he wanted to film it and distribute the film to all media outlets. The film would be subtitled with all the atrocities Stangl committed as an example to what could happen to any individual who does the things that Stangl did.

The firm *CPE* was located In Palo Alto. The initials stood for *Chemistry, Physics, Engineering. CPE* did work for companies all over the world and especially for companies in the U.S. including the U.S. government. And lo and behold, Dr. Yasha Greiner was *CPE*'s chief scientist. And that was his official title as well—Chief Scientist.

Dr. Greiner spent his childhood in England and spoke English without a trace of an accent, while Shmueli grew up in a shtetl in Ukraine and learned English after the war when he was liberated from a Nazi work-camp that was part of the Triblinka extermination camp located in Poland outside of Warsaw. There, both Shmuel Kishnov and Yasha

Greiner were assigned to work in the gravel pits. They became fast friends although they couldn't really communicate very rapidly. Greiner, whose family were German Jews spoke German, and Shmuel spoke Russian, Ukrainian, and Yiddish which was typical for Jews who lived in these little hamlets called shtetls—especially in Ukraine. So, the friends talked to one another mostly in a combination of German and Yiddish.

Coincidentally, Dr. Greiner's family then went from London to Germany because Yasha came there to study scientific subject-matter in chemistry as well as in industrial design. However, in the process he got caught up in the Nazi juggernaut ultimately winding up in the same concentration camp as Shmueli.

Yasha's parents and two siblings, older than he, were killed, and Shmueli lost his mother, sister, and sister's family. After the war, both of them spent a year working in a kitchen washing dishes and cleaning everything in sight at an allied field-hospital where Shmueli learned a rudimentary albeit broken English. At that point, they spoke to one another mostly in English. When they separated it was the end of 1946 and they had both now discovered what had happened to their families. In parting, they promised to surely keep in touch. Yasha made plans to return to England but Shmueli disappeared into the Jewish underground and their promises to one another about being in touch faded. Yet Shmueli, surreptitiously, always kept tabs on Greiner's whereabouts but knew that because of his newly acquired underground Kovner Avenger work—and later his work with the Irgun, the Jewish terrorist group that was now attacking British installations in the Palestine Mandate—it was impossible for him to even reveal a hint of his ongoing and varying locations, no less reveal his home-base address.

Shmueli arrived unannounced and without an appointment. The receptionist at *CPE* told Mr. Kishnov that it would be impossible to arrange an audience with Dr. Greiner without a pre-arranged appointment. However, Shmuel insisted that Dr. Greiner would see him and continued to insist until the receptionist used the intercom to page Dr. Greiner. The receptionist said that Dr. Greiner is usually at the company at all hours since he is the company's trouble shooter and consultant to various departments. Nevertheless, even though she was impressed with his importance, Shmueli didn't blink.

The receptionist asked Mr. Kishnov to take a seat because it could take some time before Dr. Greiner answered the page. After about ten minutes, the receptionist paged again.

"Dr. Greiner, Dr. Greiner, please call the desk. Dr. Greiner, Dr. Greiner, please call the desk."

This time it took all of about two minutes and Yasha Greiner returned the page. The receptionist relayed the name, Mr. Shmuel Kishnov, and she gasped at how quickly Dr. Greiner hung up the phone without even any verbal response.

In another few minutes in burst Dr. Yasha Greiner and practically jumped all over Shmuel. They both cried. Greiner wept while Shmuel handed him some tissues from the tissue box on the waiting area table. Shmuel also took a couple for himself. They hadn't seen one another since they separated from that allied field-hospital and therefore had not been in touch for the past dozen years.

"Come, come to my office. We'll talk there," Greiner said urgently.

In Yasha Greiner's office, the walls were lined with book shelves fat with overflowing books and the desk was filled with stacks of folders and papers. African masks and all sorts of cultural artifacts accented the office and these, without a doubt would make a powerful impression on visitors. The office was quite large with an adjoining conference room.

"Now, Shmuelikle what's going on that you give me such a surprise?"

"Vell dis reception lady no feel dis vay, I assuring you."

"Ha, that's really funny because I don't usually accept unscheduled appointments. I'm so busy consulting with various scientists here that I can't always keep up with it myself. So okay, Shmuelikl if you're here like this, I know I should be on my toes because whether you know it or not, I know what you do. I'm so proud of you.

"Let me ask you first: Did you ever get a line on Stangl? I'll answer it myself: probably not because I would have heard by now that he got dead one way or the other. That would have been the best news from you whether or not you personally informed me. You can imagine I've kept a file on every article or news story about him but nothing about where he might be nor if in fact he's still living. Of course, you and I know him and how determined he is, so we both can feel it—we know he's still living. That skunk."

"Yah, I do knowing dis for sure he ist alive, but vhere ist anoder story. I hearing he ist doing killings somevhere in dis Middle-East, maybe could be ist in Syria, un dat dis Syrian government ist giving to him complete protect. But you right, Yashie, I having him alvays in mine mind un some day ifn he ever leaving Syria, I promising you, Yashie, for you un for me un for dis millions, I kill him."

"By the way Shmulik, I know about you and Kovner. Those Nazis and Christians deserved to die. All of them."

"Vie Christians, Yash? Vie you say Christians?"

"I've thought about it for a long time, Shmueli. Who killed the Jews? Men from Mars? No, it was the Christians who killed us because that's what they learned in church about what to do with Jews and at the same time what they learned at home about what to do with Jews. That's why I say Nazis and Christians. Shmueli, I am not wrong!

"Do you knowing," Yash, "dere vast a group visitor from United States two years back un day no knowing of such tings like this — like who vas Jewish and who no Jewish. Vone of dis men saying dat he never meet Jew un dat in dis place, Oklahoma, people in dis man's church who say Jews day having horns — un day believing dis. Dis vhat deese priest day teaching, dat Jews having dis horns. Un day saying dat dis horns from head ist liking to horns mit dis Devil. You seeing vhat I meaning, Yash?"

"Yes I do. And these people," Yash answered, "are so stupid. You kill six million Jews, you idiots. Don't you know you killed the cure for cancer, heart disease, diabetes and all other kinds of dreadful killing diseases. Don't you realize that? This is what I'd like to say to them. These moronicos!"

"Ya, you no wrong, Yash. You no wrong. It is church un priests un den it go to deese families. Vee knowing dis. But now vee talking on Nazis. I needing to concentration on Nazis as vee knowing dem. Und I meaning 'vee,' you und me. Vee leaving dis talking of Christian un church un priests. Now only vee talking Nazis."

"Okay, Shmueli, shoot."

"I needing informatzie on two tings un I tink you getting vone of deese making for me un in platz like dis I tink you make oder vone too."

"So, what are these two things?"

"I needing hollow metal cylinder dis to being two feet vide un seventy inches long. Dis no able to be corrode by acid if acid ist poured into dis cylinder. Should no be corrode by any form of dis acid vhen dis acid be pouring into dis cylinder. You could doing dat? It vould taking long time?

"Okay, oder ting ist dis acid. Vhat ist most strong acid dat can dissolving dis bone un no leaving anyting—no bone, no teet?"

"Wow, Shmueli, no wonder you traveled all this way even though I don't know from where you came. Don't tell me anything else but let me think. Okay, here it is. I think hydrochloric acid, lye, or sodium hydroxide, are possibilities but it doesn't seem to me that any of those could fit the criteria you set. Therefore, I think the best acid would be hydrofluoric acid but which does react with metal so that we would need to use a glass container within the metal cylinder that in turn would be coated with wax. That would satisfy the chemical interactions you set, so that the metal will never corrode.

"This distillation, this little cocktail is something I can have made for you here and bottle it so that you don't have to do the mixology yourself. Anyway, you certainly don't want to handle the hydrofluoric acid by carrying it in an unprotected package. Trust me.

"Also, we can fashion that cylinder in no time and include a glass insulation within, necessarily coated with wax. All you would need to do is to position the body in a way that all the acid thoroughly bathes the body. Get it?"

"Ya, I understanding. Okay, if you getting starting now how longing to vait?"

"You wait here for me and I'll get it started immediately, and then we go for dinner and talk. By the time we get back from dinner, it will be all ready. I still don't want to know details but believe me Shmueli, I know it's for a reason, for a cause that's good, and one that I would surely agree with."

"Vait, Yash. I almost forgetting dis. I needing dis cylinder to being closed so to being never again open at end of dis cylinder. At dis oder end should being open but mit latch so to being later to being locking un goot closed.

"Yash, I paying for dis. How much dis company charge for dis? I having dis money."

"C'mon, Shmueli, you know—with you and me, there's no such thing as money."

Later on that evening when Shmuel was getting ready to leave, Dr. Greiner had the entire package ready for him. It was three pounds of hydrofluoric acid in a non-corrosive container—tightly bound. One end was closed and the other open but with a latch just the way Shmuel asked. Yasha told Shmuel it would take approximately a day and a half for all live tissue, bone and teeth to disappear, to dissolve without any trace such as a tooth or even some stray piece of bone remaining.

In addition, this genius, Dr. Yasha Greiner wanted to know what Shmuel was going to do with the three or four pound package that included the weight of the outer package itself.

"I vanting to mailing dis package. Yash, could be in dis mail, yah?"

"The answer is yes but it's required to register any chemical that could be dangerous."

"Maybe I sending dis chemical un mail but no saying vhat ist dis?"

"But Shmueli, if it gets damaged someone could get hurt or worse."

"Okay, so I carrying dis vit me ven I going. Yash, how much dis package it veigh?"

"Let's say four pounds."

"Okay den vee send cylinder in dis mail—un I carrying package. Yash, cylinder? How longing dis ist?"

"Five-foot ten-inches."

"Okay, you sending. I giving you address."

With that, Shmuel Kishnov dictates to Greiner: "*The Clearwater Company*, care of S. K. Address ist: 18 Square Victoria Mews, Mentone, France."

After another couple of minutes of conversation, Shmuel Kishnov said his goodbyes to his forever friend, Yasha Greiner. They embraced and kissed, Again the promise to keep in touch was agreed upon even though they both knew that Yasha couldn't be in touch but that Shmueli would if he could.

Shmuel got into the cab carrying his four-pound friend. His destination was Palo Alto Airport. Shmuel Kishnov was on his way to visit with Max Palace who was waiting for him in their pre-arranged destination—*Monte Carlo*.

*   *   *

Meanwhile at Jimmy's office in London, Simon and the gang were planning an invasion of *Mentone*, France. They had no idea that Max and Shmuel had already 'parachuted' in and had their lodging confirmed at the *Hotel Columbus*. When Shmuel arrived at the Hotel, he checked in under the name, Selwyn Kalin — (initials, S. K.). Then he contacted Max, and they met in Max's room.

"Vee calling Jimmy," Shmuel said, "but no from dis Hotel. Vee finding public phone un vee could using dis public phone in lobby from dis hotel."

In a few minutes they were in the lobby and made the call to Jimmy's office in London. Jimmy picked up on the first ring.

"Jimmy, ist Shmueli. I here in Monaco mit Max. Vee living at dis *Columbus* in dis *Monte Carlo*. Vhen you guys getting here? Vee already having interesting informatzie. Vhen you coming here?"

"Good to hear from you Shmuel. We'll be there in two or three days. I'll contact you immediately after arriving. We're coming in at *Monte Carlo Airport*. Just me and Imi. We decided only Krav guys."

"Goot. Goot decision. I having more surprise vhen you being here."

"Okay, Shmuel, tell Maxie hello. We'll see you shortly."

Shmuel and Max then went out for dinner. After dinner, they walked around and got acquainted with the surrounding scene. They decided, if possible to pick up a couple of women, but in this case, it wasn't for the usual reason.

It wasn't long before they saw two young women probably in their late twenties or early thirties, who seemed interested in talking and then in turn were immediately willing. One was attracted to Shmuel and the other to Max. Shmuel later said he understood why Max's girl flipped out over him, but he was surprised that the other one wanted him.

Once they got acquainted and talked, Max suggested that they go over to *Mentone Harbor* and see the sights. He said it was very romantic and quieter over there. The women seemed interested and when Shmuel seconded the motion, off they went.

It wasn't that far to *Mentone Harbor* but nevertheless they taxied over. At *Mentone Harbor* the women were smitten with the scene. By this time, it was early evening and the Harbor was beautiful and lined with yachts. The gulls were swooping all around singing their gull songs — arrrr, arrrr. Maxie gave Shmuel a look and motioned over to his side. Then reality set in. They were both looking at the yacht named *Salvation*.

They both found it interesting that there was only one sailor on board and he was visibly lounging on deck. They assumed there were others in the interior of the yacht, in cabins, but that was only a guess. The women were continuing their rhapsodic take on it all and wanted to sit at a beach café right at the shore to watch the sunset and to see the night begin to conquer the dusk. They were obviously in a romantic swoon. It was obvious to them why so many people flock to the south of France, to the Riviera.

So, the four of them sat at a little table at the outdoor café that was tailormade for them, while others were sitting at the bar some yards away.

In contrast, to the romantic ambiance, although Shmuel and Max were smiling with them and engaging in conversation, at all times they kept checking out the scene for purposes other than having any plans brewing with respect to the women.

Suddenly, both Shmuel and Max noticed another sailor emerging from the interior of the yacht. This one was an officious type. Both Shmuel and Max could tell. He was formal as though he had some command position. When the sailor who was there saw him, he immediately stood straight up.

Even with the women sitting with them, Max looked at Shmuel and said:

"You see that? That's military stuff."

Shmuel nodded, looked at the women who seemed curious about what Max had said, and Shmuel casually responded:

"It all depending vheder you liking dis tequila mit zaltz oder mit no zaltz. Mit dis zaltz, I meaning ist no strong. Mit no zalts, you taking dis like mit military vay un dat ist vhat mine frient here saying vhen he seeing deese two guys at dis bar drinking vhat looking like it being tequila but mit no zaltz. You seeing vhat I meaning?"

That did it and the women laughed. Then, Max ordered another round. They were only drinking daiquiris but after three or four, the women were a bit blotto. It was then that Shmuel spotted the formal military man telling the other one something and pointing away from the yacht and harbor toward the mainland. The sailor immediately got off the boat onto the dock, and then walked swiftly along the wide path leading past the café.

In a moment's glance, Max picked up Shmuel's intent and without hesitating, disregarded what the women were saying, excused himself by mumbling a few words, and in a split second he was off trying to tail the swift-footed sailor. The sailor was significantly ahead of Max and no matter how fast Max tried to walk, he simply couldn't keep up.

After about five minutes, he finally spotted the sailor who, by this time was way ahead of him, turning onto another path. When Max reached that point in the road and made the same turn as did the sailor, he no longer could see anyone. What he did see were many little cottages along the road with other cottages atop them on stratified tiers of a hill with a large house at the top tier; that large house sitting recessed from the ledge of this top tier in a way that the house was not quite, but just about, out of sight from ground level where Max was standing and looking up.

Max tried to see what that house was all about but even climbing further up the hill didn't help. He knew in his gut that this house was something important and that Shmuel needed to know about this hunch even sooner than now. To say that Max was excited would be a monumental understatement!

Max slowly, but with his destination in mind sauntered back to where the four of them had been sitting. He moved in what could be described as a three-beat horse-canter all the way back to Shmuel. The horse-canter was Maxie's version of sauntering. He didn't want to call any attention to himself.

When he reached Shmuel and the women, he motioned to Shmuel that they should get the women back to the main drag. Shmuel picked up the cue and announced that they all really should get back. The women seemed a bit perplexed but nevertheless, complied.

Shmuel and Max tried walking with them all the way back to the hotel but the women couldn't make the walk so they all cabbed it back. By the time they reached the hotel it became evident that Shmuel and Max would need to walk the women to where they were staying. At the hotel, they all said their goodnights and goodbyes.

Now, Max couldn't get the news out fast enough. Yes, he lost the sailor but in following him he hit upon where the sailor may have gone. And of course, he then he told Shmuel about the big house perched, but recessed on the ledge of the top tier of the hill.

Shmuel was overjoyed because he also could sense they were onto something important; possibly, hopefully, nothing less than probably or perhaps, Gustav Schell's location. It was precisely then that Shmuel and Max were overeager to meet with Jimmy and Imi whose arrival was imminent. Max needed to ask Shmueli a final question. He asked whether anyone would believe this because what everyone had been told with newsworthy finality didn't jibe with what he and Shmueli and the others now strongly believed they knew—and therefore what they were about to do.

"Max," Shmueli instantly answered, "it no mattering. Vhat vee know un vhat vee did—dis vhat it counts. Dis vorld ist how you saying—stupid, un how you say—brain ist dead! So, no mattering vhat day knowing or vhat day no knowing! World no learning from dis experience. Holocausts happening before dis vone—you knowing like Armenians un vhat Turks did dis to dem—un I knowing deese tings like in Africa mit dis tribal varfare, mit lot hunger for dis vealth un conqvesting of dis Africans. Oders—also like dis Spanish Inqvuisition. So, history dis ist show den vill happening more times, un vherever. Un again un again un again."

"Of course, Shumueli," Max answered. "In our case, it was the church that did it. These atavistic, primitive Christian priests who only had religion but no culture, just religion. And they swallowed whole the hatred of Jews based on the lie about killing Jesus and then infusing the world with anti-Jewish hatred—and this along with the counterfeit *Protocols of the Elders of Zion* written by Russian Orthodox Christian priests claiming world-wide conspiracy nonsense. It was they who did it. Even now, in 1958, they continue to fulminate, to rage and lie and as they've done in the past like during the Inquisition, to plunder all possessions of Jews that they've murdered and then to conveniently confiscate the homes and businesses of these murdered Jews and then more-so, even to the vicious, avaricious extent, of digging out gold or silver teeth or even teeth fillings.

"The only solution," Max continued, "is to get the top guy. When you get the chance, just take him out. And if you don't get the chance then make the chance. Just do it. Plain and simple. You don't mess around with a rabid dog. You stop it in its tracks. You kill it!"

PART 5

CODA

·21·

GUSTAV SCHELL

Late the next morning the gang showed up and checked into the *Hotel Columbus* keeping their distance from one another by checking in within about twenty-minute intervals. Along with Jimmy in the group that arrived were Sam Silver, Shimen Pargament, and Joseph Eskenazy. Imi Lichtenfeld was absent but Jimmy said he was on a specific mission and would join them later.

Now, altogether, and not yet counting Imi, they were six. They all also arrived in a staggered fashion to Shmueli's room and after the excitement of seeing one another, laid out tentative primary plans as well as backup plans. They all knew who they were after.

But it was Shmueli who launched into some kind of idiosyncratic speech. But what he was saying was intensely felt. It boiled down to a disquisition of a dystopian view of the world; simply said, stuff that was horrible about the world. What he essentially laid out was that with counting only those of our action-group in the physical pursuit of these Nazis, we are seven: Jimmy, Imi, Max, Sam, Shimen, Joseph, and himself. He then started by noting that seven is the number of shiva-sitting days—days of mourning. In addition, he actually recounted that there is an Eastern mythology about 'seven' that he'd apparently read about. He said it is called the *seven blunders of the world* and is reputed to be the iron-clad cause of violence.

He called it a very interesting list. He reported that these so-called blunders will, in the long run, lead inexorably to violence: stolen wealth; pleasure without conscience as for example in sadism; knowledge but no character—like the person knows things but has no integrity; money dealings but no honesty; also another one is like being scientific but disregarding humanity; and another is making political decisions for self-interest but not having any principle—meaning not standing up for what's right; and he thought the last one is practicing religion minus considering the troubles of others which then makes the religious thing being venerated, as not meaningful—even perhaps, evil.

He continued to say that other than the hard-core of the 'why' we were here, that in addition, the so-called soft-core reason was because this 'seven' business gave him the feeling that this evil character who they were after—assuming their guess was correct, was surely doomed. And this, Shmueli also noted was not because of any Shiva call. Rather, he further felt that the call to the 'seven,'—labeled as 'blunders'—is a function of a Devil's work and as far as violence is concerned is profoundly more serious than any random blunders.

Shmueli felt that all of it, especially the main part, meaning our suspicions, along with all of the hard and soft-core mythology combined, makes this, our mission, sacred. Whoever he is, this evil one, if he truly is who we think he is, then he's guilty. We the jury declare him guilty.

"Shmueli," Jimmy said, "I like the way you express yourself. Of course, we all agree. But, we need anything we can get to justify this mission and then to get some data that would verify our guess. Now, let's stop the philosophizing and get down to business."

"Okay," Shmuel answered, "but I vont to knowing vott Max tinks. Max, he von who fin informatzie. Max, please, you telling."

"Okay, here it is. Shmueli and I were out last night and spotted the yacht. We saw two sailors—one obviously low rank, the other more of a commanding rank. The low rank one was given an order and then jumped off the boat and headed very quickly out into the interior of *Mentone*. I followed him but lost him. But in following him I stumbled upon a hill with cottages set in tiers on the hill with a large house on the very top that was recessed and was mostly hidden from the road. That spot was on the road from where I think the sailor disappeared.

"Of course, I was considering that maybe that sailor made it up to that house before I got there. If our guy is who we think he is, then having that conspicuous yacht named *Salvation*, in a way corresponds to having the biggest yacht and the biggest but most difficult house to see with the naked eye.

"Early this morning, at nine o'clock, when the Post-Office opened, I asked about that big house on top of the hill that looks onto the harbor. I was told that Jean Cocteau, the novelist, artist, film-maker and poet, once lived there. The woman behind the counter also said that Cocteau was an apologist for Hitler, no less. You hear that? She also said she never liked Cocteau and hated Hitler. Can you imagine that? It's the house where Cocteau lived! I then asked her who now lived there and without blinking she said the magic words: Mr. Gustav Schell. She said she knew he was either Austrian or German because mail he received was sometimes addressed as Herr G. Schell. Then she added: "I never met him. He never comes for his mail. We have his signed letter that was notarized stating that a Mr. Thomas Aquilo is authorized to collect all mail for Mr. Schell."

"Okay," Jimmy said, "I guess we need to get a closer look at that house. I'd like to see what this Schell looks like. Yes, I know, we all want to see what he looks like.

"By dis vay," Shmueli piped up. "I too, having mail coming. If he ist dis who vee tink he ist, den dis mail vill be zeher vikhtik—dis meaning much important to taking care of body when vee killing him."

It became silent.

Shmueli's mail did arrive the very next day and now he had both cylinder and acid. Jimmy then shared what the first plan was as well as describing the back-up plan and still another little thing that had to be done. As a matter of fact, it was essential that this other little thing, get done.

"Okay, this is it," Jimmy started. "We can't waste any time. It could take us who knows how long to gain access to the house or in some other way find things out. So that leaves us in a position of no control. What we at M-16 decided, along with advice from some others was this: We do a house break-in, if necessary, even in broad daylight. We approach from both sides of the house and just break the door in. We'll come in first with two of us leading and then another two after us. That leaves three standing watch outside. Only if he puts up armed resistance do we shoot. It's good that Max got to that house and knows where it is. That was luck but it was luck with preparation.

"When we get him we'll inject him with a Nazi favorite. It's the truth serum called Scopolamine. Then we take him into the woods. Max, since you've seen the terrain, at least some of it, you need to lead us to a place in the woods that's secluded. Okay?"

Max nodded.

"I have another surprise for you, Max," Jimmy continued. "I need to announce that you're a trained frogman and not all of us know that. True?"

Max nodded.

"So, look at this."

With that Jimmy pulls an oxygen tank out of the hotel's closet along with an attached breathing tube, and he didn't forget frogman flippers.

"This is the essential tack we need to take. Max, you need to somehow swim under the *Salvation* and in whatever way you can, to de-salvation it without those aboard seeing or hearing it! We can't chance it that Schell might be on the boat and not at home. Therefore, if he gets wind that we've broken into his life, there's no doubt he'd take off in that speed-demon yacht."

"I'll reconnoiter it tonight after dark," Max said. "I'll take a swim with the equipment and of course, carry my trustworthy underwater single-beam flashlight. My hunch is that the propeller is the soft spot of the boat. Deactivate or neutralize it, and there *is* no boat."

At that moment, Imi entered.

"Okay," Imi said. "I've got the information on who ordered the upgrades on Schell's boat. It was the same company that built U-boats during the war in the North of Germany in a town called Bremen. Bremen had several shipyards and was the largest shipbuilding arena in all of Germany. A Herr Kupperblatt was very cooperative and told me that his records show all orders for the upgrades were signed by a Herr Gustav Schell and materials were sent to *Monte Carlo, Monaco* to be picked up for delivery to the address in *Mentone Harbor* for the yacht named *Salvation*. The company that sent the material that was ordered was the Atlas Werke Shipbuilding Co. And, by the way, it was the Atlas's shipyards that were bombed during the war. But now they manufacture and supply all sorts of advanced equipment for large yachts as well as for ocean liners. And that's that."

"See," Jimmy said, "our guy's familiar with it all—with all the ins and outs of inside stuff that only the high command in Germany was privy to. At this point we have to wait and see if Max can do the job and neutralize the yacht. So, I think we do it tomorrow. All of you, get some rest, have lunch and dinner but not together. Then get a good night's sleep. We'll meet in Max's room tomorrow morning after breakfast at about 9 am. Keep in mind we have a watch on all night. I'll take the first shift from ten to midnight. I'll be sitting in the lobby reading—but watching. Then Jimmy, you go from midnight to two, followed by Sam, from two to four, and then by Shimen from four to six. Joseph, you do the last lap from six to eight.

"Max, I agree," Imi finally said. "If we're doing it tomorrow, then tonight is your night like you said, for reconnoitering. Alright?"

Max nodded.

*   *   *

Max got everything he needed ready. He had his oxygen tank, the breathing tube, flippers, and a roll of wire—and his trustworthy flashlight with the single-beam. He thanked Imi for mentoring him not only in Krav but also in frogman tactics and use of necessary frogman materials. Then he carried everything to a taxi and took it directly to *Mentone Harbor.*

It was still evening but getting late. Max waited some distance away from the main road leading to the dock where many boats, including *Salvation,* were moored. He looked at his waterproof watch which read 11 pm. Luck was with him because the moon was obscured by cloud cover.

He hooked up his paraphernalia and slid into the Mediterranean. He swam directly toward where the *Salvation* was moored and every so often, would surface and gauge where he was in relation to the yacht. When he was no more than fifty yards from the yacht he submerged and swam for it. He reached it and swam under it. As far as he could tell, he heard no voices.

He reached the propeller shaft, looked around, and with his single-beamed flashlight held in his mouth and pointed directly at the propeller shaft, he tied a wad of wire around the housing unit and then squeezed the wire around the rim forcing the wire into the housing unit. It was the kind of job that could be done silently and even if the propeller was later examined, it would be difficult to see the wire inserted into the housing unit thus interfering with the function of the propeller itself.

Before swimming away, Max decided to surface once more to see if he could spot anyone on board from about ten or so yards away. The darkness shielded him but any light on board would reveal who they were—man or woman, tall or short, and so forth. What Max saw startled him. There he was! In a flash, the face in detail but in the next second, escorted off the yacht by two men flanking him who then accompanied him off the dock and onto the path which in all likelihood was leading as best that Max could tell, in the direction of the path that in turn led to the house on the hill.

Max then swam back to his take-off spot and furtively as possible crawled out of the water. He changed his clothes dressing in those that were stored in a plastic bag covered by foliage. He then carried all this paraphernalia to a cab which brought him back to *Hotel Columbus*. He entered through a side entrance to avoid any conspicuous glances, and headed directly to the elevator and to his room.

"Jimmy," Max said into the phone. "I did it. I did it and I saw something you need to hear. Come over."

Jimmy arrived in less than a minute.

"I saw him. I saw him. It's him. He was on board and then was escorted off the yacht by two men. They walked him toward the path leading to where those cottages are and where the big house on the hill is located. I swear to you. I saw him."

The next morning, after breakfast, they all met in Max's room and Max told them all what he had told Jimmy. They were all stunned. Over-stimulated and hyper-tense would probably be more accurate.

"Okay, we got him," Jimmy said. "We got him. Now all we have to do is get him. So, today, the house break-in is on just as we planned. Everyone's got to be armed. Let's face it, he's not going to be unguarded and the place is not going to be an unarmed refuge. On the contrary. We need to expect that it will be very well armed and even ready for just about all possible occurrences—like ours, for example. Max, tell them."

"Well, I've got the spot," Max declared. "Last night before I swam to the yacht, I located a spot more to the interior of the land and away from the cottages and from the house. I think it would be the perfect place. My feeling is that me, you Sammy, and you Shimen, are the ones to dig the hole and I think we should do it now before any more time passes. I've got shovels and spades to dig. It's going to be tough because we need to dig twelve feet down and two feet across."

It was agreed that Max, Sam and Shimen should do it and they immediately took off. They arrived at the spot that was actually a distance away from where Schell's house was located, and, from that spot the house and all of the other cottages couldn't be seen. It took them three hours to dig out what needed to be done. By the time they got back to the hotel it was late afternoon and the original plan to do the deed that day was postponed for the next day. Then Max, Sam and Shimen, exhausted as they were, were all asleep even before it was time for dinner.

The next day they all met after breakfast, and one by one they left the hotel—each fully armed. They headed for *Mentone* sharing three different taxis. They reached *Mentone*, and regrouped. Max took Shmueli, Sam, and Shimen and narrated to them the scenic route which was going to take the four of them extra time because they needed to reach the house from the far side. Jimmy, Imi, and Joseph walked straight up the same path Max took when he first followed the sailor.

Jimmy led his team of Imi and Joseph but they waited to make sure Max could see them from the far side of the house. When each group saw one another Max, Shmuel, Sam, and Shimen approached the front door from the blind side—away from the main road and away from the path that Jimmy's group had taken.

The situation was additionally tense because along with their general tension they were surprised to see no guards anywhere around or near to the house. They inched themselves toward the front door and then, suddenly, in one muscular thrust, Max kicked the door open. Two by two, as planned, first Max and Shmueli, and then Sam and Shimen rushed into the house.

And just standing there with no one apparently around, was their target person who looked at them as though frozen in place.

He spoke in German: "You're going to kill me."

"Dis ist absolut correct," Shmuel Kishnov firmly but unapologetically answered.

"But why? I did the necessary things," said this man who was no longer the mystery man."

"Dis ist vie vee killing you now. Dis ist because vee too doing necessary ting. No feel goot. Yah? No feel goot to be dis person who getting killed for dis necessary ting? You vould agree it not feeling goot?' Yah?"

Even though Shmueli got his chance to express outright his righteous indignation—the rest didn't wait for any answer. So, with this part of the plan at hand, it was Joseph Eskenazy's assignment, the man from Buenos Aires, who lost relatives in the Holocaust, to inject the Scopolamine. As he walked over to do it, another door suddenly opened and a thin blonde woman appeared. Before she could see Eskenazy, who was about to do the injection she said:

"Liebste . . ." and then she saw it all. In her panic, she froze. In contrast, Eskenazy was not in the slightest unnerved. He just went ahead and did the injection disregarding who she was—although he did of course recognize her. In the end, there was no resistance from either of them. Yet, although he just stood there agape and aghast, in a few minutes he was drowsily slurring words, but only for a few seconds and then—without fanfare silently dropped to the carpet in a seemingly unconscious state. Shmueli then calmly walked over to the woman who uttered the word "Liebste" and without a moment's hesitation or any sign of regret, put a bullet in her head. She collapsed on the carpet in a pool of blood with brain tissue strewn near her liebste.

Max, Sam, and Shimen then immediately carried their Scopolamine captive out of the house, exiting from the back door that led from the kitchen. They all walked that way with two others flanking the pall-bearers making it virtually impossible for anyone to see what was happening. Back at the house, Shmuel and Imi wrapped the lady in a sheet and Shmuel carried her fireman style out of the house through the kitchen back door.

They had no interest in cleaning up the place and within a few seconds Shmuel and Imi and their unfortunate female guest caught up to the others.

Within less than ten minutes they arrived at the burial site. The first body was in a comatose state but alive. The question was how to kill him. Jimmy turned to Shmueli.

"What do you think?

Shmueli started talking and at the same time, with Maxie's help, removed the cylinder from its package. Then he removed the impervious container of acid, and explained:

"Dis special make metal cylinder. Ist two-feet vide. Dis ist twenty-four inch vide, un five-foot ten-inch in dis long. Dis mean ist 70 inch dis long. Inside ist lining mit glass coating un den mit vax. Now I having dis container mit tree pound hydrofluoric acid. Ven ist pour in dis cylinder vill den eat all dis living tissue—mean bone un teet un no leaving no evidence. Deere ist much coatings in dis cylinder so to preventing no damaging to metal cylinder. It dissolve calling degrading-protcess vill take maybe tzvie day. Den no tracing deere ist left.

"You can see, yesterday, Sammy un Shimen, mit Maxie help digging for dis straight down hole. He vill be alive but not knowing vhere he ist. Vee must push cylinder in dis hole. Vee making him naked un putting him in dis cylinder—head ist go first so den he ist upside down. In dis vay, vee burying him alive upside down un he dying from dis asphyxiation, also dyhydration, also starving, un also vhat called decompose because of dis acid.

"I knowing dis book mit Lilliputians peoples ist namen, *Gulliver's Travels.* Dis Lilliputians peoples in *Gulliver's Travels* day too doing dis upside-down ting. Vee must keeping dis in mind please—dat dis grave vill no have marker for memorial. So, in dis case such person be subtract from dis civilization. Maybe dis can meaning dat everything day doing ist now no more real so dat dis protcess maybe reverse all bad day doing. You see vhat I meaning?

"I saying dis because it make me feeling better. Vhat vee are here doing," Shmueli continued, "den eh, how vee say, oh yah, vee desecration dis person for history—un dis ist vat ist."

It became quiet after Shmueli's sincere but torturous syntax in his considerable broken language. Then Max broke the silence.

"Shmueli also has told me what a Rabbi had told him—that the soul that would ordinarily lift to Heaven for its one-year journey, will not have a chance to lift because the acid will do the job before the lifting process even begins. Thus, the acid destroys the soul-lifting process. Is that right Shmuel?"

"Ya, ist is. I vould suggesting vee getting on mit it."

"Wait," Imi interrupted. "I think it's clear that in all of it we've found a *Hydra*. This is Greek mythology I'm talking about. The Hydra had many heads. Therefore, in our case we've been dealing with more than one head, more than one ghost. Get it? Yes, Hudal was the ghost, and a big one, and as far as I'm concerned, he too needs the upside-down treatment. And so does that other ghost, Montini. That sort of Hydra doesn't have its head grow back. So that means he's conquered. Montini, now there's a definite Hydra's head and I repeat, that one needs to go as well, because that one too, will not have its head grow back. But now, here we have what in Greek mythology was considered the immortal head, the one that couldn't be erased by cutting it off because I believe it *would* then grow back.

"I'm not sure I have it down exactly as it is in Greek mythology, but I believe its close enough. What we've done here is answer the Greeks. Shmueli here has provided the answer. Yes, Shmueli has solved the problem with this upside-down process and to finally end this so-called immortality head by the decomposition based upon use of Shmueli's hydrofluoric acid. In other words, with this process, with all of it, the vertical upside-down position is reserved for Devils. The process of the acid means the head can no longer be an immortal head."

Imi had finished what they all agreed was his interesting interruption and they all got on with the process at hand. Shovels and spades were not necessary because Sam, Shimen, and Max had the hole prepared by previously digging it out then concealing it by covering it with branches and leaves. But there was no grave for the lady..

So, Max looked at Sammy and Shimen and said:

"Boys, she goes first. Let's dig it as usual, horizontally. For her we'll only dig one that's seven feet deep — one foot extra for good measure — and don't get fancy; we'll bury her like I say, horizontally."

Max, dead-panned it all. It was clear that Max was a cool guy. It would be hard to rattle him. Then as he, Sam and Shimen got to it and started digging, Jimmy himself stripped the main body and in less than three or four minutes or so, it was all done. No one said anything. They waited for more than an hour and the seven-foot grave was dug. They quickly buried the lady and filled up the grave. Then they turned to this funerary-ground, inserted the cylinder with the sealed bottom and fit it perfectly into the twelve-foot hole with two feet of space on top for earth to be shoveled in after the body would also be inserted into the cylinder and also after the three pounds of hydrofluoric acid was poured in.

After it was done, the top of the cylinder also would be hatched closed and sealed. Only then would the two feet of earth be shoveled in on top of the cylinder, now sealed at both ends. With these precautions and preparations, the likelihood of anyone detecting and/or uncovering that spot was highly unlikely.

At that point, Max and Shmuel were given the honor of lifting the unconscious body and head first, slid it into the cylinder. They had tied cord to the feet so that they actually lowered the body slowly, straight down the cylinder, yes, head first. They then tied the cord around the top of the cylinder. In that way, the body would be hanging head-down and feet-up entirely straight so the body, all of the body, would decompose that way until the cord disintegrated. Jimmy volunteered to pour the hydrofluoric acid into the cylinder. He was wearing gloves that Max gave him.

In went the three pounds of acid filling up part of the cylinder also showering and washing over the naked body. Then, as planned, they closed, hatched, and sealed the cylinder. Immediately afterwards that they began shoveling earth into the remaining upper part of the hole on top of the sealed cylinder. They patted the earth down and then spread some leaves and branches over it.

Then, the deed was done. Was it ever!

Jimmy asked Shmueli to say some words over this once in a lifetime grave site.

"I needing to saying dat if any peoples from outside see dis vhat vee doing here, day vould feeling sorry for dis man. But ifn day knowing vhat he do un how he doing it, maybe den day even vant to join mit uns, un den no more feeling sorry for dis dog dat ist evil. But now I saying real ting; for dis six-million. Dat ist vhat ist first," Shmueli said. "Den in unser namen un also mit Simon, un Hugh, un dis child, Villy, un all villy's groupa—Alex un hist detective groupa un also mit remember mine own familia un also in dis namen of mine frient Dr. Yasha Greiner un hist familia, un in namen of all dis Jews who losting familia un frients, I now ending dis ceremonia—but maybe vee call dis vhat vee doing here—celebratzia."

After the so-called send-off funeral and without any post-event events, they all departed to various points. Eskenazy was the first to say his good-byes. He was flying back to Buenos Aires. Sam and Shimen were planning to arrange their meeting with Simon, this time in Haifa where they also would be accompanied by Imi. Jimmy would be landing at Heathrow and heading straight to his office at M-16. Maxie wasn't sure where he would be going, and Shmueli wouldn't *say* where he was going. But Shmueli had one last conversation with Jimmy before Jimmy took off.

In the end, they all reached their respective destinations. The first thing Sam and Shimen did was to sit with Simon and describe the entire fantastic story. The first thing Eskenazy did when he hit Buenos Aires was to call Simon in Haifa as well, and told him the same story that Simon had heard from Sam and Shimen.

With that, Simon sat with two of his aides and in kind of an amazed way ruminated on his quest for justice and his hope for universal punishment for each and every of these inhuman Nazi vermin. His eyes told the story of an exquisite sense of righteous indignation—to this point at least, where this indignation was almost gratified with the news he heard.

Simon was in a thrall with what Shmueli had accomplished even though he realized that Shmueli, like him, was already corrupted with hatred and seeking in some way, some as yet undiscovered way, to deal with it all. Of course, Shmueli's way was a decision to kill them. It was a *Kovner* resolution. In contrast, Simon's way was to get them all and put as many on trial as possible.

On the other hand, Shmueli found some strange way of expressing it with the particular funeral he imagined and actually implemented. How Shmueli ever had the patience and foresight to be able to accumulate the materials for that unimagined funeral was a mystery to Simon—a fantastical reflection of a transformed mind—Shmueli's mind—from what it probably originally was: normal, to what it became, anormal, and perhaps even abnormal. Yet, Simon was not going to attribute anything 'abnormal' to Shmueli. He would simply call it 'anormal.'

"It's going to take me a long time to integrate this information," Simon said. "Just thinking about it makes me jittery and I guess I could say, like nervous. But as I think about it, I get the feeling that underneath it all, I'm really angry when I imagine who it was. But it's not Shmueli that makes me angry. It's him! It's the one they buried. No, I'm not angry at Shmueli. Shmueli is a hero of the Jewish people, whether the world knows it or not. And of course, the world doesn't know it because of what the ignorant world was initially told about Jews, and what the world still believes to this day!"

Then Simon excused himself and told his aides he needed to rest, perchance to sleep. But as he was leaving, he turned to his aides and was about to say his farewell when Shimen said:

"Simon, what about these other Hydras like Hudal? Head or no head growing back, he still lives."

"We're already doing a lot, gentlemen," Simon answered. "Shmueli and Maxie and all the others will now continue to do what they do best and so assassinations will sound throughout the world with bells ringing. Hudal? We can't touch anyone at the Vatican. However, I believe that in the future there's a very good chance that some Pope who is more human than some of these other execrable, heinous Popes will, because of his own reasons, choose to release all sealed Vatican archival files related to specific Vatican agencies that were directly implicated in their assistance to Nazi atrocities and who were facilitators to the entire program of Vatican escape routes for thousands of these Nazi vermin. It will be at that time that the world will see an example of it all in the display of a naked, vile Hudal. And, gentlemen, with that I bid you both farewell."

Shimen wouldn't let it go.

"Simon," Shimen again intoned, "not yet. Before you go, I don't think you know what happened to Shmueli's family. In 1941 his mother and a sister with the sister's husband and their two children, ages ten and twelve, escaped from Yaruga, their shtetl in Ukraine, to the Crimea to a place called Yevpateria. But the Nazis, the infamous Einsatzgruppen, with the help of the vaunted so-called Nazi-neutral Whermacht surrounded Yevpateria. Yevpateria was not far from Simferopel. There, the Nazis rounded up twelve-thousand Jews including Shmueli's people.

"After the war, Shmueli received a letter from an eye witness who reported that all of the twelve-thousand were shot execution-style after which they fell into what was later called the Yevpateria Ditch. It was a gully then covered over with earth which took a series of dump-trucks all day to fill. In that letter was also indicated that infants held by their mothers were first shot in the head and then after the mothers witnessed it, the mothers were also killed. Those of Shmueli's family were among the murdered. The letter also stated that people, Christian peasants of these little towns, these shtetles, would angle for the best viewing of the carnage. Then for a couple of days the earth kept moving. Apparently, some of the people were buried though still alive.

Then these wonderful Christian peasants who never spent a day in any school — not one day — began digging it all up to see if they could scavenge anything that looked valuable. The only learning these uneducated people had was at church where they were told that the Jew was the Devil.

"For Shmueli, that did it and it was then that Shmueli began gestating the idea of assassination. He eventually joined Kovner and took it from there."

Simon listened. Then, as was his M. O., he nodded and departed—to who knows where?

On the other hand, from London, Jimmy called Alex Kaye in the Bronx. He told Al that Shmueli said Maxie had decided to hang with Shmueli but that Max was also planning to eventually head to the Bronx. Jimmy then said his goodbye and told Al to definitely send Willy, his best wishes. As for Shmueli, Jimmy said Shmueli also sent Al best wishes. Al asked where Shmueli was going and Jimmy answered he didn't know.

· 22 ·

HOMECOMING

For the first time since Willy was pushed off the ledge, Al's life was now more stable. For one thing, he was no longer traveling every five minutes to various places in Europe and back, or to the Middle East and back, or especially and particularly and specifically to London and back. No more goodbyes to Gloria. Now it was always 'hello," and for all intents and purposes it seemed that it was always going to be 'hello,' largely because Jimmy's news was kind of putting an exclamation point on the larger picture.

Not only that, but Al and Frankie always had a game of catch going on using a Spaldeen — that is, a pink bouncing ball. Wherever they were, they were tossing a ball around. It was typical of Bronx boys to do that. When it was pointed out to them, Frankie started laughing and said it was the happiest time of his life to have a catching and throwing friend. Al agreed. They loved doing it. Al said you could even see it in the new generation with Willy and Stevie's friends in the P.S. 42 schoolyard; those nine or ten year old boys, Henry and Richie doing it also.

It was Sunday and Mac and Lyle had the day off. When they walked into Willy's room, Al was happy to see them but he was focused in wanting to know whether the 24/7 watch on Willy was still in effect. Gloria told him it was but that it was becoming a struggle to sustain it. She told him that the compromise they made at that stage was that instead of two cops stationed there with one in the room and one outside of the room, there would only be one on duty on each of the eight-hour shifts.

"What we arranged," Mac continued, "was that an attendant would take the cop's place when he went to lunch or to the bathroom. That was the best we could do."

The truth was that Gloria was there every spare moment she had so that Willy was hardly ever alone. Willy, of course, was first and foremost overjoyed to see Al. He loved Al.

"He's tired of me, Al," Gloria said. "He's just happy to see you."

"That's right," Willy said and laughed.

Everyone there knew that Willy loved Gloria so they all joined in on Willy's joke—and that included the cop on duty.

Before you knew it, they were talking in the corridor of the hospital outside of Willy's room. Frankie actually took out a Spaldeen from his pocket and tossed it to Al. Al caught it and laughed. However, they went back into Willy's room and Al told Willy how well Willy looked and that he would see him later. Willy said he'd hold him to the promise and Al replied, telling Willy how well he was speaking and that he could see that Willy was getting much better. He then leaned into Gloria, and kissed her also promising to see her later. Then he and Frankie, and Mac and Lyle all left the hospital.

When they were walking to Mac and Lyle's police car, Al began to give them the briefing he got from Jimmy. They all got in the car. Al and Frankie in the back and Lyle in the companion seat with Mac driving. Al started relaying in a general way what Jimmy had told him. He deliberately omitted certain of the sub-rosa stuff. He talked to them about the ghost and mentioned the stuff about the Hydra but never mentioned names nor did he mention anything about what Jimmy had told him regarding the cylinder stuff. He told them how the guys, including Max, Jimmy, and Shmueli, took care of what needed to be taken care of on the French Riviera. He also added names of the others: Sammy, Shimen, Eskenazy, and Hugh, but then again didn't identify who the 'who' was. He finally said that Maxie was thought of as indispensible, and that Shmueli emerged as the key guy especially at the end when things got gruesome.

After that discussion Al said it was Mac's and Lyle's turn, because he was very curious about the data generated from their captives—the one from Buenos Aires and the other from Germany. So, on the spot, they decided to see what else they could get from these captives. Al was really hoping to see if whatever they said was at all necessary because, from what Jimmy told him it looked like the counterfeit microfilm was doing its job and that Shmueli, Max, Eskenazy, Sammy, and Shimen, as well as others had already jumped in and picked off a few. In other words, Jimmy told them the hunt was still an effective ongoing project.

But that was the least of it. Apparently Shmueli and Max along with Imi, Jimmy Eskenazy, Sam, and Shimen, actually cut off the head of the snake who perhaps, despite the fact that he was no ghost, made the other ghosts like Hudal and Montini seem rather irrelevant. But, in truth they were not irrelevant. And Al, with Mac and Lyle as his audience, drove down to Police Headquarters in downtown Manhattan where they were joined by Harry and Jack.

"You see guys," Al declared, "this is how I get the situation. It's true that Shmueli, Maxie, and the others got the snake's head and severed it. There were all kinds of people responsible for the genocide against the Jews and others, but especially against the Jews. And many of these so-called innocents were just as responsible as those Nazi swine. What I mean is that many of the Generals and other high ranking military men who claimed not to be political, knew what was happening but still fought on the Nazi/German side with all the expertise and power at their disposal. In that sense, they were as guilty as all the ghosts who were behind the scenes fomenting as many atrocities as possible, and on the other hand creating processes which made sure that these Nazi bastards escaped justice — and by the thousands."

"You know," Al continued, "not even one-tenth of one-percent of all the Nazis that were indicted for criminal acts, even murder, were tried, and of the ninety-nine percent of that small number that were tried and given jail time, practically all of them eventually were freed. You believe that? So, in that case, it makes me sad and then mad that I wasn't part of the Shmueli/Maxie/Jimmy/Imi team along with the few others, who all were involved in doing some numbers.

"The truth is that my feeling is that Shmueli and Maxie along with Sammy, Shimen and Eskenazy should keep it up. They should keep doing it. I know that Simon wanted a mini-max procedure instituted, but getting that done would necessarily involve Kovner-like activity and nowadays it doesn't exist. You can't knock off thousands with one sling-shot like

Kovner planned with those thousands and thousands of SS prisoners we had lumped together in that concentration encampment after the war and with Kovner wanting to poison their bread, or with wanting to poison the water system of five German cities and kill off those entire populations.

"So, Mac, Lyle, whatdya think? Is it justified to unearth the locations of these scumbags and do it to them even probably only one by one — or not?"

"Al, I say yes," said Lyle, "but I know Mac likes to do everything legally. So, since Mac and I are long-standing partners in the professional sense but also best pals personally, I'll need to have my vote match his. Right, Mac?"

"Al, it's hard for me to say this but Lyle's right, even though I also think you're right. That's the contradiction in life I live with. My head says legal, legal, legal, while at the same exact time, my heart, my stomach, my guts say do it, do it, do it. So, you see, in contrast to what physics tells us, I've just proven to you that two different things can absolutely and in fact, without exception, occupy the same space at the same time. Ha."

Al wasn't finished. "You know guys I've been thinking this for a long time now and Jimmy and I once had a talk about it when I was in London. Jimmy had a great idea about the sons actually being responsible for the sins of the father insofar as he said the sons shouldn't repeat the sins of the father; that they had a responsibility not to repeat it. That got me thinking about the Nazis being the biggest gang of crooks that ever lived. They took everything the Jews owned and kept it. So, I would like to ask every German son and daughter whose parents were old enough to do this or that during the war, to talk up. In other words, I'd like to know how many of these sons and daughters actually asked their parents what they did during the war.

"Like say something like: 'Father, what was your job during the war? Father, how did you get this nice house we've been living in? Father, were you a soldier in the war, or a guard in a concentration camp, or did you kill anyone — any children? Father, we have lots of cultural artifacts like paintings and sculpture. Where or how did you acquire these? Father, you own the factory. When did you buy it? Did you buy it? How did you get to own it? How? Father, did you turn any Jews in? If so, were they neighbors or friends of ours? Father, are you a Nazi? Father, do you think Hitler was wrong about it all or not?! Father, am I the son of a murderer? Am I the son of an idiot? And also, Father, isn't it true that thousands and thousands of Germans enriched themselves because of and in spite of the war? And, Father, do you think Dresden was justifiably carpet bombed and entirely destroyed, or not? And, Father, if you feel it was not justified because innocent people were killed, then why did the innocent Jewish people who were killed not, in contrast, invite your sympathy as well?

"Father, Father, you are not talking. And if that's the case I'm going to scream!

"You see, guys, if you're Jewish like me, these are the things Jews think about. Especially red-blooded Jewish men. Even people like you guys who understand everything I've said and agree with me, probably are never really occupied with such thoughts. But I know that that's natural. People are obsessed with things that personally happened to them or to their own sub-group. I get it. I'm not blaming people for only concentrating solely on their own lives. I'm guilty of it too. But it makes me feel that we are really at a primitive stage of evolution where we are still not our brother's keepers. People are entirely absorbed in their own issues, and empathy kind of evaporates in the wake of this self-absorption, this ego stuff.

"It's that this whole thing starting with Willy off the ledge and with what Shmueli and the guys finally accomplished in Europe. The whole thing got my blood boiling. It renewed my political consciousness. I know you know what I mean. But, and it's a big 'but'—I've become a big fan of Shmueli's. The problem is that I know he's a killer and an expert at it at that. Nevertheless, I'm a fan. And what does that say about me? I haven't the slightest idea.

"Ah, on second thought, forget it. Call it the ramblings of a deranged American—an American Jew."

*　*　*

Mac and Lyle told Al he couldn't accompany them to Police Head-quarters and be privy to the interviews they were planning with Wenzel Wagner and Eduardo Velaro, so Al said goodbye. Al understood it. He wasn't a police officer and so did not have the privilege of being witness to official police work. So, Al then added to his goodbyes, the ones to Mac and Lyle, and they arranged to have breakfast the next morning.

At this point it was the meeting and interview with Wenzel Wagner that interested them. They were curious about whether Wenzel knew anything about the Gustav Schell who was living in the south of France. If Wenzel did know about it then it would be clear that he had information on a whole lot of highly secretive documents and occurrences.

They waited for the police escort to bring Wenzel into the interrogation room. The room was sort of out of a movie with a table in the center and two chairs at the table on opposite sides of it. In addition, lighting was dim except for a swinging lamp over the table. Before they knew it, Wenzel was brought in. Of course, he knew Mac and Lyle having met with them several times.

"How I can helping you," Wenzel said.

"What do you know about a person, a Nazi person who could possibly be living in the South of France on the French Riviera? Does that ring a bell? I mean do you know of this?"

That one affected Wenzel and he was for a moment or two, speechless—which was not like him. At all other times he was more than willing to strike a deal for his life and would hold forth without let-up because it was obvious that his familiarity with these Nazi backdoor channels seemed to actually impress Mac and Lyle and he felt, gave them a favorable sense with regard to his cooperation.

Of course, Wenzel knew that his life was at stake because of killing the cops stationed at the 48th precinct. Therefore, what Mac and Lyle felt was that any opportunity Wenzel had to blame his willingness to be involved in that crime on his partner, Karl, he took. His consistent refrain was that he was always intimidated by Karl and even felt that Karl could kill him if he didn't obey.

That was Wenzel's out. He blamed it all on Karl. Mac and Lyle didn't really care about Wenzel's stage craft. They just wanted to see how much he really knew and whether he may have known about Schell and all about the stuff surrounding where Schell lived, and with whom. And sure enough Wenzel surprised them with what he actually knew.

"Yes, I knowing of dis person he go to Riviera. I do not know namen of dis person. Ven Karl, he meet vit me, vit Cardinal Caggiano who bringing Karl to meet vit me in Buenos Aires. Dis ist first time ven I see Caggiano. He from church in Argentine. He telling of, oh, how you say, ah, yes, he say in German und he make translate, und he use dee vord he say in Spanish vord for living for Herr Schell, 'elaborar' und den he make dis translating ind German und first say 'laborate', und den you know vord ist erarbeiten heiligtum. So, dis I know in English it mean—how you say—'elaborate sanctuary'. Dis I understanding. I am know dis vord 'sanctuary.'

"Caggiano, he speak mit Dr. Villy Nix und vat I hear, dis person Herr Schell is true leader, more leader dan even Hudal und Montini, und rest of dese people. Ist dis goot informatsie?

"Yes, it's good," Mac answered. "It is good. What else? Anything else?"

"I vill tink of uder tings und den I vill tell. Ist dis goot?"

"Yes, okay, we'll see you again."

Of course, the truth is they were not going to see him again in any interrogation. They knew that the next time they would see him would be in court where the prosecutor would ask for the death penalty. Mac and Lyle were sure that Wenzel would be electrocuted. It was clear that no matter what kind of information he gave to authorities, wantonly killing cops would not hold up, no matter the reason.

When they finished the interview with Wenzel, Mac and Lyle decided to pay Eduardo Velaro a final visit. And as usual Velaro was happy to see them. Velaro was from the beginning very cooperative except of course when Mac and Lyle found the transmitter in the heel of his shoe. Eduardo was hoping they would forgive him because despite the transmitter, he was easily forthcoming with a torrent of information. The problem, of course, was that he was an accomplice with Ewald of pushing Willy off the ledge on the third floor of an apartment house. And even though Eduardo claimed that Ewald did it, and that Frankie even in his drunk state verified Eduardo's description of it all, the prosecutor would also go after the death penalty. However, Mac and Lyle felt that Eduardo's cooperative spirit and his refusal to make any gesture of protest or escape might be enough to get him a life sentence. The problem was that Mac and Lyle also felt it was highly likely that even if Eduardo got off with life imprisonment, he would, sooner or later, be murdered in prison by one of the inmates. It's true these inmates were in prison but it was an American prison and most of them hated the enemy.

Eduardo had nothing really to add to what he had already professed. He claimed not to know the Germans especially since he was from Argentina and had never been to Germany.

With that, Mac and Lyle said they would see him again, but they didn't say what the venue would be. Then, like with Wenzel Wagner, where the German government did not request extradition, the Argentine government followed in line regarding Eduardo Velaro.

As far as the entire case was concerned — the one that began with a boy being pushed off a ledge of the third story of an apartment building in *The Bronx*, New York, and then ending with shall we say an unheard of one-of-a-kind funeral in the French Riviera in a little village called *Mentone*, and with an ending to boot insofar as the boy who was pushed, was now in a splendid recovery — Mac and Lyle as well as Al, calmed down.

They were all going to visit with Willy at the hospital.

WHO'S WHO

Forces for Justice

Civilians
Willy Travali — Frankie's nephew
Frankie Carbone — Willy's uncle
Alex Kaye — Al, Private detective. Member, Justice Brigade
Gloria Messer — Teacher, Al's girlfriend
The Wharton family:
Mr. & Mrs. Wharton
Sheila (Stevie) Wharton (Willy's friend), and Nate Wharton, Stevie's brother

Police Personnel
Detective Loris McIver — Mac
Detective Lyle Davis
Detective Harry Harrison
Detective Jack Lehrman
Steve Scribner — Police Headquarters Chief

Justice Brigade
Alex Kaye, (Al) Private Detective
Jimmy McKay — M-16, U.K.

Father Hugh O'Flaherty, Vatican rescuer of Jews and American pilots
Emerich Lichtenfeld (Imi) — Krav Maga chief teacher
Max Palace — Krav Maga expert
Simon Wiesenthal — Nazi hunter
Sam Silver — Wiesenthal aide
Shimen Pargament — Wiesenthal aide
Joseph Eskenazy — Buenos Aires Wiesenthal contact
Shmuel Kishnov — Assassin
Dr. Yasha Greiner — Scientist extraordinaire
Tatiana Gerhardt — Translator, Mossad agent
Dr. Janet Sirota — Bletchley decryption scientist
Dr. Gerald Yagoda — Bletchley decryption scientist
Dr. Adrian Applebaum — Bletchley decryption scientist
Arthur (Arty) Libman, Shin Bet, Israeli Secret Service
Morgan and Tommy — Police officers guarding Willy at hospital
Sister Agnus Furillo — Assistant to Father Hugh O'Flaherty

Forces Facilitating Escape from Justice, and List of Assassinated Nazi Escapees

Assassins and Spy Personnel
Ewald Krauss
Eduardo Velaro
Karl
Wenzel Wagner
Parker Martin of the American State Department
Hermann Strauss, chemist

Vatican Personnel
Bishop Alois Hudal
Monsignor Giovanni Montini
Joseph Prader
Anton Weber

Others

Raymond Tokoly — dying thief who stole package
Mrs. Tokoly — Raymond's wife
Carol — Mrs. Tokoly's sister
Joyce — Mrs. Tokoly's friend
Two cops in police car at the Tokoly scene
Dave Greening — Holding-pen officer at police headquarters
Marlena Jollenbeck — Mistress of Albrecht Schmidt
Frieda Dunst — Wife of Freundel Dunst
Joclyn — Gloria's friend
Judy — Willy's aide

Assassinated Nazi Escapees

Albrecht Schmidt
Freundel Dunst
Gustav Schell's lady
Gustav Schell

Also by Henry Kellerman

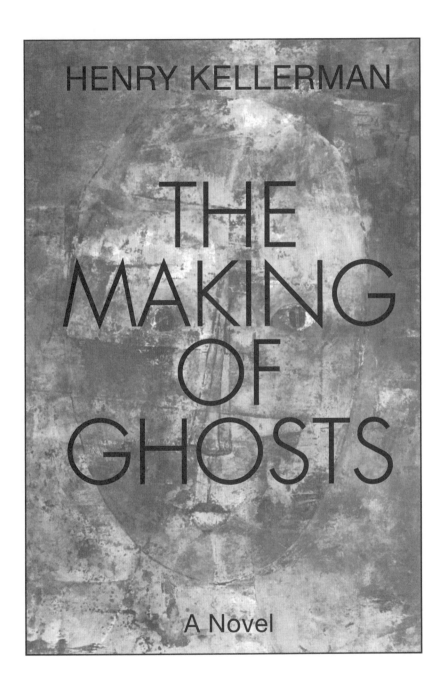

HENRY KELLERMAN

THE MAKING OF GHOSTS

A Novel

Book I

Also by Henry Kellerman

Book II